The Mirror of Christ

Dorsey Edmundson, Ph.D.

Wayne,
Hope you enjoy
reading this.
God bless,

Bedside Books
An imprint of American Book Publishing
5442 So. 900 East, #146
Salt Lake City, UT 84117-7204
www.american-book.com
Printed in the United States of America on acid-free paper.

The Mirror of Christ

Designed by Jana Rade, design@american-book.com

Publisher's Note: *This is a work of fiction. Names, characters, places, and incidents either are the product of the author's imagination, or are used fictitiously, and any resemblance to actual persons, living or dead, events, or locales is entirely coincidental.*

ISBN-13: 978-1-58982-440-9
ISBN-10: 1-58982-440-7

Edmundson, Dorsey, The Mirror of Christ

Special Sales

The Mirror of Christ

Dorsey Edmundson, Ph.D.

Acknowledgments

First and foremost, I want to thank God for giving me a story to tell. Thanks to my editor for her patience and guidance. And a special thank you to Sydney, who helps remind me of how great God truly is every time I see her smile.

MATTHEW 23:34 "I will send you prophets and wise men and teachers of religious law. You will kill some by crucifixion and whip others in your synagogues, chasing them from city to city."
(NLT)

Prologue

Marc Jones walked up the weathered marble steps and through the oversized white doors of the Mount Olive Chapel of God. People dressed in expensive suits and designer dresses fell silent as he passed. His sweat-stained, threadbare T-shirt hung loosely on his small, wiry frame, as did his worn-out jeans. His long, brownish-blonde hair was pulled into a ponytail, and his graying beard was untrimmed. The deep creases around his brown eyes spoke of a lifetime of hurt.

As he headed toward the middle section of pews, several people muttered unpleasant comments. Others shook their heads and pointed at him as if he had a contagious disease. Marc didn't stare at the Christians passing judgment on him. Instead, he smiled warmly at those who would meet his gaze. He sat down, closed his eyes, and began to pray.

The chimes rang promptly at eleven o'clock, and the service started with the choir singing a beautiful hymn. The assistant minister spoke about the Christian duty to give, and after a prayer, the ushers came forward to take up the offering. As people passed the shiny golden plates, several made a show of reaching into their wallets and giving large amounts of money. When the usher approached Marc's pew, Marc hesitated and shook his head. The usher moved on. A few people noticed the nonverbal exchange and whispered about Marc's refusal.

He probably doesn't have any money since he spent it on cheap wine or drugs.

The minister took the pulpit and solemnly told the congregation that they were going to burn in hell if they didn't change their ways. He told them society was filled with sin. He explained it was wrong to listen to rock-and-roll music and to let children watch Harry Potter movies. True Christians, he said, don't drink alcohol or go to nightclubs. He slammed his hand down on the pulpit and pronounced thunderously that all of these things were from the bowels of hell. He finished by telling the congregation it was their duty as Christians to root out the evil that existed in society, and only by doing this could they hope to see The Glory Land.

With this challenge set before them, they rose and sang "Amazing Grace."

Wiping beads of sweat from his brow, the minister stepped down from the pulpit and told the congregation about upcoming church events. He asked if anyone had anything to add.

Marc quietly stood and began to speak.

"I've been sent to save you from yourselves and to plead with you to ask for forgiveness for *your* sins because the Kingdom of Heaven is near. You need to start *doing* things instead of worrying about telling other people what to *stop* doing. The kind of music you listen to or whether you drink beer or dance doesn't make you a Christian. How often you go to church or how much money you give doesn't make you a Christian, either. These things don't determine if you will be saved or not. Only the grace of God and the *quality* of your relationship with Him through His Son decides that."

People were grumbling. *The unmitigated gall of this bum. He's just another homeless addict that's out of his mind. All you have to do is look at him and you can tell he doesn't know anything about being a Christian. Probably the only thing he knows about is how to survive on the streets. We're* much *better than that.*

The minister attempted to interrupt, but Marc wasn't easily deterred.

"An owner of a team pays a great deal for two talented athletes," he went on. "After several games, the coach reviews their progress. The first says he's happy to be on the team and talks about how valuable he is to the organization, since he doesn't make mistakes like other players. The second says he too is happy to be on the team, but feels he makes many mistakes. He asks the coach to help him improve so the team can be stronger. At the end of the season, the owner discusses the team with the coach, who suggests cutting the first athlete. The player's attitude causes dissension and keeps the team from winning. The coach explains how the second athlete recognizes his weaknesses and asks for help. This athlete is far more valuable and should remain on the team."

Marc paused, then finished. "The season will soon be ending. Anyone that hears what I'm saying will listen and understand."

A large, muscular man named James Highsmith was the first to stand up and tell Marc to leave. When Marc didn't move, an usher approached. He and Highsmith tried to force Marc out, but he resisted them without any apparent effort. A woman screamed as the two church members fell to the floor.

Several men went to their aid. An elderly woman sitting across the aisle shouted, "He's got a gun! He's got a gun!" People screamed and ran for safety. Pews were overturned in the stampede. A few older members were pushed down.

Someone called the police, and three cars rushed to the scene with lights flashing and sirens blaring. When the officers approached Marc, he was still standing quietly in the middle of the sanctuary with Highsmith and the usher lying dazed on the floor at his feet.

The officers drew pistols. "Put your hands in the air and turn around."

Marc complied, but the closest officer to him grabbed him around the wrist, pulling his arm down and bending it behind his back. The officer forced Marc to the floor and handcuffed him.

Some of the men who had run out of the church came back in to gawk at the scene.

"Stupid bum," someone said. "He came in here and tried to cause a riot."

The officers frisked Marc, then grabbed him by the arms and hauled him up off the floor. They escorted him from the sanctuary through the throng of church members gathered along the sidewalk to watch.

One woman spit at him and muttered, "You deserve to burn in hell."

The officers shoved Marc into the back seat of the nearest police car and left the scene.

MATTHEW 24:3 "What events will signal your return,
and the end of the world?"
(NLT)

Chapter 1
Monday

When his mother committed suicide, Donnie Thompson had figured it all out. He had become a doctor and decided God was a concept he just didn't need.

Now, as the acres of wide-open farmland passed by, he turned right at the fork in the road north of Enfield and recalled the series of events that had brought him back to North Carolina. He smiled at how foolish he'd been.

After his residency, Donnie had moved across the Mississippi River from his downtown New Orleans apartment to Gretna, Louisiana. Along the way, he had noticed a faded sign with an arrow on it. Above the arrow was written "Gretna United Methodist Church, Sunday Service at 11:00 a.m."

When Donnie had seen the sign, he had heard a small voice. He didn't know what it was or what it was saying. He ignored it and finished moving.

As he settled in his new place, he had found himself reminiscing about the Christian influences that had been a part of his life. He remembered his grandparents' tremendous faith. He thought about his sixth-grade Sunday school teacher and her loving encouragement as he prepared to speak to the church on confirmation Sunday. He thought about vacation Bible school and church youth meetings on Sunday afternoons. He remembered his first Bible, a gift on his fifteenth birthday from his best friend.

The memories had surprised him. He hadn't been to church since his mother's funeral. It had been so long since he'd prayed that he wasn't sure he remembered how. In Donnie's mind, God had left him when He let his mother kill herself. Donnie had been so angry. He felt he couldn't trust God to take care of him.

So he had been quite surprised that first Sunday morning in Gretna when he woke up without setting his alarm clock.

He attended church that morning and several more. The voice grew louder and more frequent.

One Sunday afternoon, Donnie told Pastor Brunell, the church's minister, about the voice he had been hearing. The pastor told Marc about Jesus. Then he spoke a verse of scripture.

"I stand at the door and knock," he said. "If anyone hears my voice and opens the door, I will come in and eat with him and him with me."

Pastor Brunell and others at the church had helped Donnie learn about the man who knocked. They showed Donnie how to open the door to his heart and invite Him in.

Donnie had made the decision to give his life to Christ.

Now, as he crossed Highway 125 and passed Crowell Baptist Church, Donnie smiled. How quickly things had changed once he made the decision. He remembered noticing things he'd never seen before. And instead of viewing people's problems in a detached, clinical manner, he felt empathy for them. He spent hours studying the Bible and gave a tenth of his income to the church. He donated his time to working with the church's youth program and reached out and witnessed to anyone who would listen. He even found a Christian radio station and listened to nothing else.

Then he had started having feelings that he was supposed to leave Gretna and return home. He researched job possibilities and found an announcement in the *APA Monitor* that the North Carolina Department of Correction was looking for a psychologist.

When he'd called, he was told that the advertised position had been filled, but an unadvertised position at Caledonia was open.

Donnie was driving there now. He slowed his old, dented pickup truck as he passed the one-room, white-cinderblock post office in Tillery. He went left at the intersection, then turned off Highway 561 onto the three-mile road that dead-ended at the gravel parking lot in front of the prison.

He had no idea of the *real* reason he was sent.

red color, had been painted many times. These units were not air conditioned. They were made up of five dormitory-style cell blocks that contained about twenty bunk beds each, depending on whether a broken bed had been replaced or not. Relative to inmates in Units 1 and 4, these prisoners were well behaved, but they were still housed at Caledonia because they were too much of a problem to live anywhere else. They were allowed outside their cell blocks in groups to recreate on a large, fenced-in field behind the complex. They could attend classes or religious services. They ate in a dining hall, and they could work. They were permitted to buy items from the canteen, to make collect phone calls twice per month, and perhaps best of all, to have contact visits.

Most of these inmates were older, experienced cons who had spent time in Units 1 and 4, and although they hadn't learned to stay out of trouble, they had figured out how to keep from getting caught.

Over the twenty years Tony Jackson had been in prison, he had become an expert at not getting caught. Tony grew up outside of Benson, North Carolina. His criminal career got an early start when he was caught stealing cigarettes at the age of nine. He remained in and out of trouble for mostly minor things until 1972, when he shot a man while robbing a convenience store. Twenty-four years old at the time, Tony was convicted of first-degree murder and given the death penalty by an all-white, Johnston County jury after only forty-five minutes of deliberation. He was sent to death row at Central Prison in Raleigh to await his execution.

There he met Ramone Williams, who was, by inmate standards, a very wise and powerful man.

Ramone had grown up on the streets of New York City. During the late 1960s, he became a member of the Five Percent Nation of Islam, a loose-knit religious organization founded by Clarence Smith, a former student minister under Malcolm X. Smith's movement was heavily influenced by the Islamic faith. Five Percenters were classified by the North Carolina Department of Corrections as members of a security-threat group and were considered a gang by the FBI.

A main principle of the Five Percenters was Supreme Mathematics, which held that eighty-five percent of the population was ignorant and only fifteen percent knew the truth. Of that fifteen percent, ten percent used it for evil purposes and to keep the masses in the dark. These people were considered devils and included most religious leaders such as the Pope.

The other five percent tried to enlighten those who were ignorant.

As one of the five percent who knew the truth, Ramone Williams was always on the lookout for young black men who didn't. Sensing Tony Jackson was one of these people, he had decided it was his duty to enlighten him.

Ramone began by having Tony read portions of the *Qur'an* and Elijah Muhammad's *Message to the Black Man*. He taught Tony that the black man was god and explained that the black man was the first human creation. The white man was made from the black man and tricked him into slavery. Ramone taught Tony that there was not a God in heaven, and that instead, *he* was a god and should pray to himself, not anyone else.

Tony was attracted to this black supremacist ideology and the Five Percent movement. Not only did it provide a way to protest the racism he had experienced all of his life, it gave him a way to use his intelligence to earn the respect and power he had always felt he deserved.

Tony's education continued until the U.S. Supreme Court overturned North Carolina's mandatory death penalty and the inmates awaiting execution had their sentences vacated. Tony and Ramone received new trials and were re-sentenced to life in prison. Ramone was reassigned to Central Prison, where he was murdered by another inmate over control of the drug trade at the facility. Tony was transferred to Odom Correctional Institution and changed his name to Lord Abdullah.

While at Odom, Lord Abdullah was labeled a problem inmate. After several disciplinary infractions, he was transferred to Caledonia. He was housed in Unit 1 on the farm for almost five years until he figured out that one of the benefits of knowing the truth was getting the eighty-five percent who didn't to do his dirty work.

LUKE 10:3 "Go now, and remember that I am sending you out as lambs among wolves."
(NLT)

Chapter 2
Friday Morning

Donnie spent his first four days at Caledonia learning about the institution and getting to know his secretary.

Amber Parker was an attractive blonde-haired woman who had grown up in Roanoke Rapids. She began working at Caledonia after finishing her associate's degree in medical transcription at Halifax Community College.

Amber was an extremely organized, capable woman, unafraid of anything or anyone. She told Donnie she liked her job and explained she'd practically run the department by herself for quite some time. She said that since she started working at Caledonia, five psychologists had come and gone, and there hadn't been one in over a year. In her opinion, which she was more than happy to share, she thought the job wasn't right for everyone and required a special person who wasn't afraid of inmates.

On Friday morning of his first week at Caledonia, Donnie pulled into the dusty parking lot and was surprised to see Amber's dark blue Ford Explorer. She didn't usually arrive until after eight because she had to take her children to school.

"Good morning, Mrs. Parker," he teased as he opened the door and made a show of looking at the clock. "You're here mighty early. Is school closed today?"

Smiling, Amber shot back, "Well, I thought I'd try and find you something to do so you'd stop bothering me with all your questions. It's keeping me from staying up to date on the Roanoke Rapids gossip."

Donnie laughed and went to his office to put his things down. Amber followed him in.

"Seriously," she said, "I thought you should start seeing patients today. There's a large number on the waiting list. I came in early so I could schedule a clinic in Unit 1 this morning. I've already called the sergeant and told him you were coming." She handed him a sheet of paper. "This is the list of patients. I'm going to the clinic to pull charts. They'll be waiting for you when you're ready."

The most important function of a prison gang is controlling drug traffic. Through this control, gangs generate income to pay for other activities, including financing future drug purchases, bribing officers, paying for protection, and hiring visitors to bring drugs into the facility during visitation. Since the prison drug business is so profitable, money is also sent to gang members outside to finance activities on the street.

At Caledonia, controlling the drug trade also provided a way to recruit members and increase a gang's power. This came about by selling drugs on credit and charging interest rates as high as one hundred percent. Borrowers were given only five days to repay, and since inmate jobs paid between forty cents and a dollar per day, debts frequently were not paid on time. When this occurred, the debtor got caught in a vicious cycle and was eventually forced to work to pay off his debt. Depending on the amount owed, this work included any number of illegal jobs such as "muling," or transporting drugs, hiding contraband, or serving as a lookout. Debtors who refused the offer of employment paid an even higher interest rate.

One year, a gang member and drug dealer named Willie Harrison had tried to collect a forty-dollar payment for a twenty-dollar drug debt. The debtor, Jamal, was about to get out of prison. He couldn't pay, and he refused to work. Several inmates decided to take up a collection to pay the debt. Willie informed Lord Abdullah, who was furious. He explained to Willie, who was in the ignorant eighty-five percent, how the disrespect made him look weak. He told Willie to make an example out of Jamal so other inmates wouldn't dis' him in the future.

That night, with Lord Abdullah's words of enlightenment fresh in his mind, Willie had visited Jamal in the shower. He had a five-inch shank hidden beneath his T-shirt. Jamal never saw what was coming. Willie stabbed him more than forty times. The veteran officer who had been the first to respond to Jamal's screams described it in court as being bloodier than any hog killing he had ever seen.

Willie was convicted of first-degree murder and sent to death row. Lord Abdullah made his point and escaped criminal charges, since no one dared mention his part in the murder.

Donnie's first patient, Derrick Lancaster, was in prison for the second time and had spent the last three years at Caledonia. He was twenty-eight years old and was serving time for brutally murdering an elderly couple with a shovel after breaking into their home. He had been high at the time and was looking for something to steal so he could buy more crack. Following a short trial, he received two life sentences. He had no remorse, and like most maximum custody inmates, he had quite a reputation for causing problems.

Derrick was initially assigned to Central Prison before being transferred to Nash Correctional Institution. Soon after he arrived there, an officer ordered him to mop a cell block, and he refused. When the officer approached him, Derrick made comments about the officer's family and then spit on her. He was immediately placed on intensive control status and sent to the farm. Two days later, he got into an argument with another inmate over a pack of cigarettes and cut him with a shank made from a piece of scrap metal. For this, he received additional prison time and was placed in maximum custody.

Derrick's medical referral indicated he was having trouble sleeping and eating and was having thoughts, but no intentions, of hurting himself. Donnie was expecting to see someone who was quite depressed. Sleep and appetite disturbances, along with the suicidal ideation, were classic symptoms that even first-year psych students knew. But when Derrick entered the conference room, he was joking with other inmates and laughing.

Derrick stared intently at Donnie and sat down across the conference table. Neither of them said anything. Derrick was dressed in the maximum custody uniform consisting of an orange jumpsuit, a white T-shirt, orange flip-flops, and a solid green baseball hat. He had a large, three-dimensional cross drawn with a magic marker on the bill of his hat, which he wore at an angle, high on his head. He had a large, protruding forehead and big eyes set above bulging cheekbones. The thumb and index finger on his right hand were yellowish-brown, indicating he had spent quite a bit of time violating prison policy and smoking hand-rolled prison-house cigarettes down to the last drag.

"Look, Doc," Derrick said condescendingly, "you're new around here and I know you're busy. I'm just depressed and need some meds."

Somewhat surprised by the inconsistency between Derrick's behavior and what he had been expecting to see, Donnie hesitated before trying to explain his role. "I'm not a psychiatrist, Mr. Lancaster, I'm a psychologist. I don't prescribe medicine, but if I think that's what you need, I'll refer you to someone who does. What makes you think you need meds?"

Derrick's demeanor changed dramatically. He slumped in the chair.

"Man, I can't sleep," he moaned. "I can't eat, and you know, I just feel depressed all the time. Doc, you gotta give me somethin'. I can't take it." He stared intently into Donnie's eyes as if he was trying to look through him. "If you don't do somethin,' I'm gonna blank on somebody and then, you know, it ain't gonna be my fault when I hurt somebody."

Donnie raised an eyebrow. "How long have you been depressed?"

"Doc, it seems like I been feelin' this way all my life." Derrick's eyes teared up. He took a few exaggerated, deep breaths. "I grew up real poor and never had nothin'. My momma did drugs and my dad was messed up too. He was in and out of jail and left a few years after I was born. I dropped outta school in the tenth grade and started hangin' with the wrong people. They made me do all kinda things and I just ended up in trouble."

Donnie tried to move the conversation to where Derrick would begin to accept responsibility for his behavior. "Sounds like you've had a hard life. Is that why you're in prison?"

"Look, Doc, why you wanna ask all these questions?" Derrick crossed his arms, defensive. "All I want is somethin' to help me do my time and stay outta trouble. The other docs I seen just gave me medicine. So why don't you just chill out and give it to me?" He paused, looking directly at Donnie. "I really need it, man." He wiped the tears from his eyes.

Donnie decided to change tactics. "I like that cross on your hat. Are you a Christian?"

Derrick sat up in his seat. He smiled for the first time since his act began. "I sure am," he said confidently. "I been lovin' the Lord since I was saved a few years ago. Are you?"

Donnie told him he was. They talked about their faith for several minutes, and Donnie wondered if witnessing to inmates was why God had brought him to Caledonia.

After a few minutes, Derrick looked at Donnie sheepishly. "Look, as a brother in the Lord, you gotta help me, Doc," he pleaded. "I need medicine so I can stay outta trouble." With manufactured pain in his eyes, he added, "Please, Doc, you gotta help me."

Donnie had expected this. He responded as gently and as respectfully as possible. "Mr. Lancaster, I have to be honest with you. I don't think you need medication right now. But I would . . . "

Before he could finish, Derrick, in handcuffs and shackles, jumped out of his chair and started around the table. With eyes wide and nostrils flared, he began shouting profanities. Seconds later, the officers who had witnessed the abrupt change through the Plexiglas windows at the front of the room rushed in and forced Derrick to the concrete floor. Donnie stood there, semi-paralyzed, while Derrick screamed, "I'm gonna kill you, man, when I get outta here!"

Steve Johnson, the unit manager, came out of his office to see what the yelling was about and observed the officers escorting Derrick back to his cell. He smiled when he saw Donnie and shook his head.

"I don't think you have to worry, Doc," he said. "Derrick's going to be about five hundred years old when he gets out of here. And I don't think he'll be too tough to handle then."

2 PETER 2:1 "But there were also false prophets in Israel,
just as there will be false teachers among you. They will cleverly teach
their destructive heresies about God and even turn against
their Master who bought them . . . "
(NLT)

Chapter 3
Friday Afternoon

Steve Johnson looked like he had stepped out of the pages of *GQ*. He wore a white, crisply-starched shirt with the sleeves folded under to just below his elbows. His silk tie was expertly knotted, and hand-tailored cotton pants hung perfectly above his tasseled loafers. He had piercing dark eyes accentuated by small, wire-framed glasses. He looked like a serious, no-nonsense type of man in complete control of himself and the job he was assigned to perform.

Steve had worked at Caledonia for twelve years. He started as a correctional officer after being honorably discharged from the Navy, but he had always dreamed of advancing within the prison system and becoming a prison superintendent. At thirty-eight years old, he became the youngest person ever promoted to a unit manager level at the farm.

Donnie followed Steve to his cramped office. Numerous awards and plaques hung on the hideously colored wall behind a beat-up but well-organized desk.

"Is this the first time you've worked in a prison?" Steve asked.

"Not really," Donnie replied, sitting down in a cushionless chair in front of the desk. "I did some forensic work when I was in school. Back then, though, I always had supervisors to help me. Here, my supervisor's in Raleigh and I'll only see him occasionally."

"Well, I'm not a psychologist, but I've worked here for a long time," Steve said. "If you'd ever like to talk, I'll be happy to listen."

Donnie immediately liked Steve and sensed the offer was genuine. "Honestly," he said, "I'm not sure what happened with Derrick. We got off to a rough start, but I thought things had settled down. Then all of a sudden, he got upset when I wouldn't give him meds. Has he always caused problems when he doesn't get his way?"

Steve laughed and began punching keys on the discolored computer keyboard in front of him. "Seems every inmate I've known gets upset when they don't get what they want."

Donnie grinned. "I'm glad to know it's not just me."

Steve studied the black-and-white monitor and followed his finger across the screen until he found what he wanted. "Looks like our friend has received one hundred and twenty-four infractions since he's been incarcerated. Most of them were minor, but a few were very serious. He was caught plotting an escape and he's assaulted an officer." He continued to read to himself. "It also says Derrick was one of the inmates that started an uprising at Eastern Correctional Institution a few years ago during his first sentence."

"This is unbelievable," Donnie said, thinking about the conversation they'd had about faith and God.

Without looking up, Steve shook his head. "I'd say it's very believable. Derrick's pretty much the type of inmate we have here." He tapped the screen. "Ah, here it is. This is what I was looking for."

"What's that?"

"A few years ago, Derrick met a married female chaplain and got her to start seeing him for pastoral counseling. Over several weeks, he got her to do favors for him—give him change for drinks, bring him food, mail letters, and let him make phone calls. After a while, the favors became bigger, and they started having an affair. They were caught in her office one night and she was forced to resign in disgrace."

"No way."

Steve pointed to the screen. "It's right here. You can read it for yourself." He continued. "According to investigators, Derrick used the chaplain's religious beliefs to gain her trust and then exploited her. He told investigators he set the trap for her and just sat back and watched while she walked right into it." Steve looked up. "Did you notice the cross on Derrick's hat?"

"Yeah." Donnie's stomach sank. "We even talked about each other's Christian beliefs."

"Well, just so you know, Derrick once told me he uses that cross as a test to find out if staff members are, in his words, religious suckers. He told me that if they say they love the Lord, he'll tell them he loves the Lord, too. He just won't let Him interfere with what he's doing."

A chill moved down Donnie's spine. He had trouble concentrating on the rest of the conversation. When the meeting was over, he headed back to his office and shut the door. He sat down hard behind his desk. He realized he'd had his first encounter with evil in its purest form.

His hands trembled. For the first time in his life, Donnie thought about how vulnerable he was and how much he needed God's protection.

Friday is the most important day of worship for Muslims and is the time set aside by Allah to express collective devotion. At Caledonia, these religiously mandated prayers occurred in the Unit 2 visitation area and were led by an inmate prayer leader, since there was no Islamic chaplain.

To fill this role, Chris Ratliff had gone through several steps. He was voted on by the Muslim inmates and was presented to the prison chaplain for consideration. The staff went over his record to determine if he had a history of committing infractions and might cause problems. After he passed the check, he assumed the position of acting prayer leader. He was closely observed to assess his ability to carry out his duties appropriately.

Unlike many young black men who became Muslims after being incarcerated, Chris sincerely wanted to become more conscious of Allah. The rituals that were a crucial part of the faith initially drew him to the religion, and through them, he learned to focus on Allah not just in thought, but also in action. He legally changed his name to Abdurahman Abdul-Ahmad and believed that he was in a better position, despite being in prison, to receive Allah's endless bounties.

Three weeks earlier, the prison chaplain had contacted the Office of Islamic Affairs in Raleigh to inform them that Abdurahman was being considered for the position. The program coordinator, Ima'am Mohammed, came to Caledonia and interviewed Abdurahman, who had studied hard to prepare. On Monday, Abdurahman received word that his recommendation had been forwarded to the Caledonia superintendent, Lee Powell, who approved it.

Since then, Abdurahman spent a great deal of time preparing for today's Jumah and writing his khutbah. For Abdurahman, it was not only an opportunity to lead men to become more conscious of Allah, but it also validated his dedication to Islam, for which Allah would surely reward him in the future.

Donnie was exhausted when he left Caledonia. He looked forward to getting home to his one-bedroom apartment in Rocky Mount, which claimed to be "the City on the Rise." He'd been to Rocky Mount many times as a kid, and he wasn't quite sure what the city was rising from, but he liked the motto anyway. The people he'd met while moving in were very friendly, and the location was perfect. He was close to Raleigh and to the Research Triangle Park, which offered plenty of cultural activities. And he was only thirty-five minutes from work.

On the way home, he used the time to plan what he wanted to do over the weekend. He had enough furniture, but he thought he would look around Rocky Mount and pick up some items to decorate with. The most important thing he wanted to do was find a church. He'd looked in the phone book and was pleased to see there were quite a few, which presented him with his biggest problem—choosing which one to try first.

On the way home, Donnie stopped at Food Lion to get something to make for dinner. At the meat counter, an older woman came up beside him. She looked very distinguished in a neatly pressed, navy blue designer pantsuit. Her makeup was flawless and her jewelry looked expensive and tasteful. Her white hair was carefully styled. She looked as if she had just come from the salon next door.

The woman looked several steaks over and then put one in her cart. Donnie smiled at her as she turned to leave. "It must be nice to come in and find exactly what you want," he said. "Some of us spend all afternoon trying to figure it out."

The woman laughed. "I guess it just comes from years of practice and being able to cook lots of things."

"So that's the secret. I just need to learn how to cook."

"Either that or spend more time in the frozen foods section."

Donnie grinned.

"Good luck trying to find something," the woman said and walked away.

After choosing a steak, Donnie went to the produce section for a potato and a package of pre-made salad. He got in line to check out. The woman came up behind him.

"I suppose you want my recipe for steak," he teased. Then he introduced himself. "I'm Donnie Thompson."

"Patricia Wilson," she responded. "It's nice to meet you. I don't think I've seen you here before. Are you from around here?"

"No, ma'am. I grew up in Garner, but I've been out of state for several years."

They moved forward in the line.

"What brings you to Rocky Mount?" she asked.

"I just started working at the prison. Caledonia. Have you heard of it?"

"Oh yes," she replied. "Some men from my church used to go there and lead a Bible study group. They stopped going after a terrible experience with an inmate. I hear it's an awful place."

Donnie set his groceries on the checkout counter. "I just started working there this week, and from what I can tell, you're right."

"What type of work do you do?" she asked. "You don't look like an officer." She looked at Donnie's long, sandy-blonde hair and the diamond-stud earring in his left ear. He wasn't wearing a tie or uniform.

"I'm a psychologist," he answered. "I just finished doing my residency in New Orleans."

Mrs. Wilson peered at his face as if she was trying to figure out how old he was.

"I know I don't look much like a doctor," he said. "But I assure you, all of the student loans I'm repaying say that I am."

Mrs. Wilson smiled. "You should be happy you look so young."

"I'll take that as a compliment."

"Well, you should. I'm sure a nice-looking young man like you gets lots of compliments."

Donnie knew what was coming next.

"Do you have a girlfriend?" Mrs. Wilson asked.

Every woman Mrs. Wilson's age seemed to know someone he should meet.

"No, ma'am. I'm very happily single." Donnie emphasized *happily* so she wouldn't go any further. It didn't work. She proceeded to tell him about a wonderful woman in Rocky Mount who was single, too.

Donnie pulled out his wallet and paid for his groceries. He politely changed the subject as Mrs. Wilson began putting her items on the counter.

"Where do you attend church?"

Her face lit up. "I've been attending Hillside since I was a little girl. It's a wonderful church with about three hundred members. You should come visit. I think you'd like it a lot."

Donnie waited as she paid the clerk. They walked together to the parking lot.

"So, is it easy to find Hillside?" Donnie asked as he helped put groceries in the trunk of her car. "I don't know my way around Rocky Mount very well yet."

"It's easy to get there," Mrs. Wilson said. She gave him directions. "I look forward to seeing you again. I really want to introduce you to someone. She hasn't been in Rocky Mount very long either. I think the two of you will have a lot in common."

Donnie ignored her comment and helped her into her car. "Thanks again," he said as she shut her door. "See you Sunday."

Mrs. Wilson drove off. Donnie picked up his bag of groceries and thought about how God worked in his life.

Maybe He's pointing me in the direction He wants me to go yet again. Funny how many ways He does that . . .

As he got in his truck, Donnie heard the little voice. His eyes filled with tears.

While at Odom, Lord Abdullah had met Abdurahman and talked with him as a potential Five Percent prospect. The worlds they came from were very similar. Both had grown up poor in the projects, where everyone knew the war on drugs just meant keeping them out of the good parts of town. Both were from undisciplined homes run by young, single mothers and went to schools where they pledged allegiance to a flag and country that neglected them. They were taught about Martin Luther King, since he wanted blacks to turn the other cheek when whitey smacked them in the face, but they never learned about Malcolm X, because he wanted to educate and liberate blacks everywhere to fight back.

Yes, in Lord Abdullah's mind, the worlds they had grown up in were very similar. And now they were being unjustly punished for trying to deal with it.

The difference between them, in Lord Abdullah's opinion, was that he used his intelligence to gain importance and the envy of other men, while Abdurahman used his intelligence to learn about a spook god that no one could see and remained ignorant in the ways of the world. Abdurahman's intelligence was wasted, and he was reduced to praying for what he wanted. Lord Abdullah went out and took the fruits of the earth that he so rightly deserved.

Lord Abdullah hadn't been able to change Abdurahman's mind at Odom, but he hadn't given up. He'd known they would meet again in prison. Now, he considered it his duty to educate the man properly. A man with Abdurahman's intelligence could be a valuable asset to his organization.

Lord Abdullah looked forward to shaping him into the prayer leader *he* knew Abdurahman could be.

1 CORINTHIANS 1:25 "For the foolishness of God is wiser than man's wisdom, and the weakness of God is stronger than man's strength." (NIV)

Chapter 4
Saturday

Donnie spent Saturday shopping at Golden East Mall and the downtown shops along the railroad tracks. He purchased a copy of the *Evening Telegram* at the convenience store across from City Lake and sat on a park bench to read. People held hands and walked around the asphalt track circling the water. In the distance, teenagers leaned against tricked-out vehicles and listened to music coming from stereos that cost more than Donnie's truck.

Saturday afternoon was visiting time for inmates lucky enough to have family or friends willing to travel to the farm. Those not so fortunate spent their time on the recreation field, watching visitors come and go, wishing someone would come see them.

Lord Abdullah and the Five Percenters used the time to cipher and conduct business.

Five men had already gathered when Lord Abdullah approached and started ciphering. "The diameter of the sun is 853,000 miles wide."

One of Lord Abdullah's lieutenants, Pete Holloway, who preferred to be called Al-Shirazi Khomeini, stood on Lord Abdullah's right and immediately joined in. "The sun is seventy-eight trillion years old."

The man to Pete's right spoke up without missing a beat. "Sunlight must travel through three spheres before reaching Earth."

"The diameter of Earth is 7,926 miles wide," said the next man.

Malique Mohammed, whose real name was Terrance Worthy, had been with Lord Abdullah the longest and didn't want to be outdone. "The land on Earth is 57,255,000 square miles."

The fifth man, Dashon Hartman, was the newest member, and this was his first cipher since Lord Abdullah had loaned him a handwritten copy of the *99 Actual Facts Sheet* he had gotten from Ramone Williams when they were on death row. Dashon, like the others, had copied and then studied the sheet so he, one of the soon-to-be-enlightened Five Percent, could teach others.

Dashon stared at the ground and spoke hesitantly when his turn came around. "The Earth travels around the sun at fifty-six, I mean sixty-six thousand miles per hour."

Lord Abdullah smiled but didn't comment. He quickly began another round. "The Nile River is 4,690 miles long."

Al-Shirazi immediately chimed in with another fact. The ciphering continued for twenty-five minutes until Lord Abdullah decided to end it.

"Why did we run Yacub, and the devil he created, from the root of civilization over the Arabian Desert to live in the caves of West Asia?"

This was the clue that Lord Abdullah was taking over. Everyone knew better than to answer.

"The reason," Lord Abdullah began, "is that they started makin' trouble among righteous people by accusin' them of things and causin' them to kill each other. Yacub was an original black man and was the father of the devil. He taught the devils to do *devilishment*.

"The root of civilization is in Arabia and the Holy City Mecca. Mecca means where wisdom and knowledge of the original man first started when the planet began. We ran the devils over the Arabian Desert and took from 'em everything 'cept their language."

"How long ago was that?" Dashon asked.

"It occurred six thousand and nineteen years ago. Two thousand years later, Mossa came and taught 'em how to live respectful lives and how to build homes. He also taught 'em some of the *tricknology* that Yacub had taught him which was *devilishment*: things like tellin' lies, stealin', and how to master the original man."

Dashon looked confused. "But, sir, how can anyone master the original man? We're descendents of the original man and 'cause of that, we're gods. Since no one can master us, how did they master them?"

"You're right, Dashon," Lord Abdullah replied, pleased to have such an eager man in the group. "The devils can't master us, but I ain't talkin' about us. I'm talkin' about people who were part of the eighty-five percent that was ignorant of the truth. It was, and still is, those people that are easily played by the devils that know the truth. You see, Dashon, the devils use knowledge to keep people ignorant so they'll work for 'em without questionin' 'em."

Lord Abdullah sensed an opportunity to further shape Dashon. He brought up the new prayer leader. "It's kinda like what's goin' on here. We just got a new Muslim prayer leader that's bein' misled by the devils in the prison administration to keep our black brothers from knowin' the truth. The way they use him is by makin' him feel important and givin' him a title. I met him at another camp and have always thought that if he were properly enlightened, he could be a strong and powerful warrior for the cause."

"I want you to know that I'll do anything I'm told in order to save one of my black brothers and guide them to see the truth that you have so graciously shown me," Dashon said.

Lord Abdullah smiled. It was exactly what he wanted to hear.

LUKE 11:35 "Make sure that the light you think you have is not really darkness."
(NLT)

Chapter 5
Sunday

Donnie felt like a kid on Christmas morning. He arrived at Hillside early, parked beside Mrs. Wilson's silver Cadillac Seville, and went inside.

Mrs. Wilson sat toward the front of the sanctuary. He joined her on the wine-colored wooden pew.

She patted his hand. "I'm so glad you came. I prayed that you would."

"I thought you might need a few cooking lessons after the service," Donnie said.

Mrs. Wilson laughed. "What did you do on your first Saturday in Rocky Mount?"

Donnie hardly heard the question. A beautiful woman had just walked in. She wore a red, knee-length skirt, black heels, and a long-sleeved white blouse. She had dark brown eyes that matched her silky, shoulder-length hair. She greeted several people. Donnie noticed how happy she looked.

"That's Karla," Mrs. Wilson whispered, following Donnie's gaze. "She's the girl I wanted you to meet. Beautiful isn't she?"

"Yes, ma'am." Donnie couldn't take his eyes off of her.

Karla came over to their pew and hugged Mrs. Wilson, who, without hesitation, introduced Donnie.

"Dr. Karla Lynch, I'd like for you to meet Dr. Donnie Thompson. Dr. Thompson, this is Dr. Karla Lynch."

Donnie stood as Karla put out her hand. He felt like a teenager who'd just been introduced to the most popular girl at school. He was unable to hold her gaze as they shook hands. "It's really nice to meet you," he said.

"Mrs. Wilson told me about you." Karla smiled. "I'm glad you came."

"Me too." Donnie realized he was still holding her hand.

"What brings you to Rocky Mount?"

"The short version of the story is simple," Donnie said. "It was God. I was doing my child psychology post-doc in New Orleans and started to feel I should come back to North Carolina. I prayed about it, and here I am."

Karla nodded and smiled. "God brought me to Rocky Mount three months ago. I'm a pediatrician."

Donnie's nervousness evaporated as they talked.

As only a skilled matchmaker could do, Mrs. Wilson shifted her place on the pew. Karla sat down next to Donnie. Neither noticed Mrs. Wilson's satisfied smile. They were much too engrossed in each other.

Abdurahman Abdul-Ahmad entered the visitation area, recently transformed into a sanctuary of sorts by rearranging furniture and placing prayer mats on the concrete floor. Eager to begin teaching, the new prayer leader was pleased to see that the number of men in attendance had increased since Jumah on Friday. He knew a lot of inmates had converted to Islam by signing a Shahadah, but only a few were serious about the faith and attended services. The rest, he supposed, signed the declaration of faith to get special treatment or had become disillusioned by the lack of proper Muslim leadership. Abdurahman believed he had been chosen to lead the misguided back to Allah, glory be to him.

"I want to begin with a quote from an unknown source," Abdurahman said. " 'God created man in His image. Then the Christians recreated God in man's image.' I'm going to prove to you that Jesus was a prophet and not, as the Christians want you to believe, God. Because of this, the most important man in history isn't Jesus Christ, peace be upon him. No, the most important man is Mohammad, peace be upon him."

The men shifted and settled in. Abdurahman continued.

"Mohammad's the final prophet, and his ancestry goes back to Ishmael, who was the son of the Prophet Abraham, peace be upon him. He was born in Arabia in 570 A.D. and meditated in the Cave of Hira near

Mecca. At age forty, the angel Gabriel appeared to him and he had revelations for twenty-three years that were compiled in the *Qur'an*. The *Qur'an*, along with the *Sunnah*, which are the traditions of the Prophet Mohammad, make up the comprehensive Muslim law called *Sharia*."

Abdurahman consulted his notes. "In First Corinthians, chapter fifteen, verse fourteen, Paul says, 'If Christ was not raised, then our preaching is useless, and your trust in God is useless.' According to him, if Jesus didn't die, and wasn't resurrected, there can't be no salvation in Christianity. Well, brothers, in the *Holy Qur'an*, chapter four, verse 157, Allah tells us, 'And they said (in boast), "We killed Christ Jesus the son of Mary, the apostle of God": but they killed him not, nor crucified him but it was made to appear to them so, and those who differ therein are full of doubts with no (certain) knowledge. But they follow only conjecture for of a surety they killed him not.' "

The room was quiet. Abdurahman's voice gained strength.

"Like all Qur'anic statements, we believe this is from Allah, glory be to him, the all-knowing, omnipotent lord of the Universe, and as a result, we seek no proof and need to ask no further questions." He looked at his audience. "The Christian, who says the only way to be saved is to believe that Jesus died on a cross for your sins and then rose from the grave, disbelieves Qur'anic teaching and attacks everything that's Islamic. Since Allah commands us to demand proof of their claim, I did, and I found that what they say is a lie."

Abdurahman held up his hands.

"When Jesus was placed on the cross, his legs were not broken like the men that hung beside him. The Christian will say this was to fulfill prophecy, but I think it's something else. You see, a way to make death by crucifixion faster was to break the individual's legs so their arms would support their full weight and they'd suffocate quicker. With that being true, why do you suppose the men that hung beside Jesus were still alive when he was already dead?"

Abdurahman paused and rubbed his chin. "The answer is, he wasn't. And this is why he was taken down from the cross so fast. You see, he had to be removed quickly so his wounds could be treated. This is what happened when Joseph of Arimathea and Nicodemus supposedly placed his body in the tomb while Mary Magdalene and the other Mary watched."

He lowered his voice, building up to his point.

"Another thing is that the tomb wasn't sealed until the next day, which gave them plenty of time to move him. Why do you think Mary Magdalene returned to the tomb on the third day to anoint a man who'd been dead for three days?" Abdurahman looked around. Some of the men were nodding. "We know a body that's been dead that long would fall apart if it was rubbed with anything, right? Had she gone there to take care of a body? Or is it more likely she went to see a living person?"

Abdurahman frowned. "So you see, the crucifixion is a hoax. Christianity is based on a lie." He raised his voice again. "We can't give in to Christians and Jews who want to save us. We've got to be strong because we're told by Allah, glory be to him, in chapter two, verse 120 of the *Holy Qur'an*, 'And they—the Jews and the Christians—will never, never be satisfied with you until you follow their religion.' "

After the service, Mrs. Wilson introduced Donnie to Reverend Charles Hurley, a distinguished-looking man in his late fifties. His hair was turning gray, and he had broad shoulders and an athletic build. His handshake was firm but not overpowering.

"You must be the young man Mrs. Wilson told me she'd invited to worship with us." The minister's voice was deep, and his eyes were filled with a warmth that put Donnie at ease. "I'm glad you came."

"Thank you," Donnie replied. "It's great to be here."

"Where are you from?"

"I grew up outside of Garner, but I just moved here from New Orleans a week ago."

"Mrs. Wilson tells me you're a doctor," the reverend said. "I see she wasted no time introducing you to Dr. Lynch." His eyes twinkled.

Mrs. Wilson piped up. "I'm hungry. Let's all go out for a bite to eat." The reverend started to decline, but Mrs. Wilson cut him off. "Now, I know you all don't have plans for lunch, and I'm just not going to eat by myself."

Donnie looked at Karla, then at Reverend Hurley. He raised his hands in mock resignation. "Well, I guess that settles that. Can I follow one of you?"

"Hold on a second," the reverend said under his breath. "I'm sure she'll let us know the transportation arrangements, too."

"Karla, you ride with Donnie," Mrs. Wilson said. "Reverend, you can take me."

Reverend Hurley winked at Donnie. "See?"

Donnie laughed as he followed Karla to her car. "How long do you think it'll be before she wants us to get married?"

"Hopefully after lunch," Karla said. "I'm hungry."

Karla told the hostess two more people were coming and requested a table in the back of the dimly lit, crowded restaurant.

"Mrs. Wilson likes to sit back there because she says the air vents don't blow on her," she told Donnie. "Between you and me, I think it's because back there, she gets to see who's here."

The hostess seated them, and Mrs. Wilson and Reverend Hurley soon joined them. After the waitress took their orders, the reverend turned to Donnie. "What was your church like in New Orleans?"

"It was very special with incredible people. That's where I made the decision to give my life to Christ, after the people there showed me how." He paused. "I'm truly grateful for that experience and also for being led to Rocky Mount. It kind of feels like I'm supposed to be here, although I'm not sure why."

"Well, we're glad you came to Hillside," the reverend said. "The members there are also very special people. Take Mrs. Wilson. There's no telling how many people you saw at church today who go there because she invited them."

Nodding, Karla reached across the table and gave Mrs. Wilson's hand a squeeze. "You're sitting here with one of them."

"How did you decide to become a minister, Reverend Hurley?" Donnie asked.

"Please, call me Charles," he said. "When I was in college, I had a terrible wreck. I was a freshman and had been out drinking. I tried to drive home and ran off the road and into a tree. I spent two weeks in a coma. Before then, I didn't know what I wanted to do with my life. I had gone to college because my high school friends went. Following a full recovery, I felt like God was telling me He wanted me to minister to others. After that, I totally gave my life to Christ and entered the seminary."

Charles didn't come across as someone who thought he was special because of his title. Donnie felt an unexplainable connection with the man. He realized there was a great deal he could learn from him.

"While I was in seminary," Charles went on, "I was blessed to meet an extremely loving and beautiful lady. We got engaged while I was in school and got married after I graduated. We moved to Rocky Mount, and I began preaching at Hillside about thirty-three years ago."

"How long were you married?" Donnie asked, noticing the absence of a wedding band.

"Thirty-two years," Charles answered with pride. "Nancy was an extremely wonderful, caring woman, even during her battle with cancer." He briefly closed his eyes. Then he smiled. "In my heart I know she's no longer in pain because she's in heaven."

The waitress brought the sandwiches and Reverend Hurley said the blessing. As everyone started to eat, Donnie looked at Karla. "How about you?" he asked. "Any stories to tell?"

Karla paused and swirled a French fry in her ketchup. After a long moment, she said, "I learned about Christ from my parents. They took me to church every Sunday. They died in a boating accident when I was nine. I grew up with my grandparents and became very rebellious. I was always in trouble. I quit going to church. I was so angry with God for letting my parents die." She set down the French fry without eating it. "Thankfully, my grandparents refused to give up on me. Because of their love and perseverance, I finally learned that God didn't take my parents away to punish me."

After pausing to fight back her emotions, she apologized. "I'm sorry. It's been a long time since I've talked about this. Please excuse me." She dabbed her napkin at the tears in her eyes.

Donnie reached over and touched her arm. She looked up at him and they made eye contact for a long moment until they realized Charles and Mrs. Wilson were watching. Karla quickly looked away.

"I lost my mother when I was nineteen," Donnie said. "She battled mental illness most of her life and finally gave up the first week of my freshman year in college. She took a bottle of Thorazine. My dad found her lying in bed when he got home from work. He thought she was asleep. He didn't bother her for a few hours. Then he went to the bathroom and found the empty bottle of pills sitting on the counter. He called my school, and a counselor came and told me what happened."

Karla stared at her hands while she listened.

"For a long time I was numb," Donnie said. "I didn't like to talk about it and got upset when people asked me about it. I got really angry, and I quit going to church. I questioned if God existed and doubted if He cared about me. I was so bitter with life. I was unable to have much more than superficial relationships with anyone. To avoid dealing with it, I spent my time by myself studying. I think it helped me be a successful student, but it made me an extremely lonely and depressed person. It wasn't until I went to Gretna United Methodist Church that I began to heal."

When Donnie finished, everyone at the table sat in silence, not knowing what to say. They had revealed a great deal about themselves, but no one felt embarrassed. In a way, it seemed like they had been initiated into a special club with perhaps a special purpose.

ROMANS 6:6,7 "For we know that our old self was crucified with him so that the body of sin might be done away with, that we should no longer be slaves to sin—because anyone who has died has been freed from sin."
(NIV)

Chapter 6
Monday

On the way to work Monday morning, Donnie thought about Karla. They had spent the previous afternoon together and made plans to stay in touch during the week. But his excitement was tempered by the thought of the patients he was scheduled to see. Remembering his encounter with Derrick, he began to feel uneasy. He turned off the radio to talk with God.

As he listened for His voice, Donnie thought about the scripture he had recently been studying. In First Thessalonians, Paul tried to encourage people so they would strengthen and mature in their faith. He told them to always be joyful, pray constantly, and be thankful in everything.

Pulling into the prison parking lot, Donnie recalled Paul's letter to the church in Philippi. Despite being in jail, Paul spoke of the joy he had through his relationship with Jesus. It was something Donnie decided he should keep in mind.

On his way to see his patients, Donnie went by Steve's office. Steve laughed when he walked in. "I wasn't sure if you'd be back after Friday." He stood and shook Donnie's hand. "You know, quite a few psychologists have come and gone through here, although, I have to admit, I didn't lose much sleep over it."

"Honestly, I only came back so I could get you to help me learn how to dress."

"Well, Doc," Steve said with a grin, "I'm not sure I can help. You take the business-casual thing to the limit. I wasn't aware that J. Crew pants and shirts could even be paired with Timberland hiking boots. Except maybe for lumberjacks."

"Hey now."

"By the way, do you own a tie?"

"Sure. I just don't know where it is."

Steve laughed again. "Seriously Doc," he said, "I'm glad you came back. But you need to know, it probably won't get much better today. In fact, it might be worse."

"Worse?"

"Well, when we hire someone new, regardless of their position, the inmates usually test them like kids, trying to find out what they can get away with."

Donnie sighed. "Thanks for letting me know." He handed Steve a list of inmates to be seen.

Steve picked up the phone to call a sergeant.

Donnie stood to leave, but couldn't resist one more jab. "I think I know what the problem is."

"What's that?" Steve asked.

"The real reason you don't want to help me change the way I dress. You want to see how I do it so you can change your stuffy image."

"Doc, you better get out of here before I have one of my sergeants lock you up."

Donnie smiled and headed for the door. "I'll talk to you later."

Across the hall, Donnie's first patient and his two escorts were waiting.

Lorenzo Walls was twenty-eight years old and no stranger to the criminal justice system. He had been incarcerated previously for breaking and entering. This time, he was in for assault. He had also attacked a correctional officer who told him to go to the back of the canteen line after he had jumped to the front. Lorenzo hit the officer in the face several times, breaking his nose and knocking out two teeth. He was convicted as a habitual felon and sentenced to at least forty years. Lorenzo was requesting mental health treatment because he couldn't sleep and wanted medication.

The evaluation room contained a deeply scratched, dark wood table. Several gray plastic chairs in various states of disrepair were stacked in the corner. The officers escorting Lorenzo pulled two chairs over to the table and instructed Lorenzo to sit in the one furthest from the door.

Lorenzo was a few inches over six feet tall. His thick body appeared firm, and Donnie guessed he weighed over three hundred pounds. The sleeves of his jumpsuit were rolled up. His biceps stretched the orange material to the limits. He had huge forearms and hands, and both were covered with scars that attested to numerous fights.

Donnie prayed for protection, because the department of corrections didn't authorize using medication to treat insomnia.

The officers stepped outside, and Lorenzo began. "Look, Doc, if you don't give me some Navane, I'm gonna hurt you real bad."

Lorenzo's voice was soft, and his threat was calm, but there was no mistaking the deadly serious intensity in his cold, dark eyes. Donnie moved away from the table and again asked God for help.

Then, with Lorenzo glaring, he surprised himself and began to speak.

"Mr. Walls, Navane isn't in the Department of Corrections' drug formulary, which means it's no longer available."

A long silence followed. Lorenzo stared without blinking, and Donnie prepared himself for the worst.

Then, unexpectedly, Lorenzo's demeanor and posture changed. "I guess I don't need it anyway," he said reasonably.

Donnie was completely at a loss for words.

Lorenzo admitted in a roundabout way that he had difficulty controlling his temper. He told Donnie he was sorry for the things he had done and said he wanted to change, but he didn't know how.

Donnie was having a hard time processing what was happening. *Something's not right . . . This man assaults people when he doesn't get his way . . . He doesn't talk about feelings . . . Is this an act? What do I do? What do I say?*

He sat down on the edge of his chair and searched his mind for answers. And then he heard it. Faintly at first, and then louder. He didn't have to think about what it was. But he wasn't sure what to do.

During his training, Donnie, like many psychologists, learned that God was a concept that couldn't be quantified and had little place in therapy. What mattered was a person's behavior and tangible things that could be measured and counted. Donnie had been taught that people used God to keep from taking responsibility for their behavior and to put a Band-Aid on emotional problems.

So he was quite surprised to hear himself ask, "Have you tried to give your anger to God?"

Lorenzo shook his head. "I don't know how, Doc. I've never even thought about bein' angry. I guess I've always blamed it on other people." He leaned his forearms on the table. "Can you show me how?"

With an unexplained warmth spreading over his body, Donnie folded up the chart in front of him and began telling Lorenzo about the Son of God that died on a cross for his sins. He explained how Jesus, who was without sin, suffered for Lorenzo so that he would be forgiven for all of the things he'd ever done or would do.

"Lorenzo, are you sorry for your sins?" Donnie asked. "Do you want Jesus Christ as your Savior? Do you want to give Him your anger and let Him control it?"

"Yeah," Lorenzo said softly. He looked down with tear-filled eyes.

"Then bow your head and pray with me." Donnie closed his eyes. "Lord, forgive me for my sins. I believe in Jesus and know He's Your only Son that You sent to die on a cross for me. I want to have a relationship with Him and I want Him to be my Savior. I know that only through Him will I be saved and that with Him, all things are possible."

They sat there until Lorenzo, with tears running down his face, quietly stood and shuffled around the table. "Doc," he said, "for the first time in my life, I feel like I'm free. Thanks."

He reached out and shook Donnie's hand.

The officers came in to escort a new man back to his old cell.

Donnie saw eight more patients before calling it a day.

As he was packing up, Steve knocked on the door. "Doc, do you have a minute? I've got an inmate I'd like for you to see. He's been here for two weeks and seems very quiet. Too quiet. Maybe that's just the way he is, but something about him seems odd."

"How do you mean?"

"Well, when I talked with him, he just looked at me and didn't say much. It seemed strange, but I didn't think too much of it until a few officers on his block told me he was acting weird."

"Like how?"

"Officer Franks told me he didn't take his dinner tray. Instead, he gave it to the inmate in the cell next door. Franks said he didn't owe the guy money or anything like that."

Donnie nodded. "That does seem a little odd."

"When inmates behave this way, it usually means something bad is about to happen. A few years ago, an inmate who was in prison for seventeen years started giving things away. He got really quiet, and a few days later, he hung himself from a rope he'd been making from a shredded sheet."

Donnie agreed to stay late and see the inmate. "Of course, you know you're going to owe me one, though," he joked.

"Well, I'm sure I'll end up owing you quite a bit," Steve said. "Maybe even enough for me to take you shopping so you can get some clothes like grown-ups wear."

The officers stayed outside when Marc Jones entered the conference room. Donnie nodded for him to sit.

"I'm Dr. Thompson, the psychologist here. Mr. Johnson's concerned something's wrong. Are you alright?"

"Yes, sir. I'm fine."

He's polite . . . appropriately groomed . . . long hair pulled back into a ponytail, gray beard . . . hygiene is fine . . .

"How long have you been here?" Donnie asked.

"I was in jail for fifteen weeks and came to Caledonia two weeks ago. I was arrested seventeen Sundays from yesterday."

Normal rate, tone, and volume of speech . . . Memory' s intact . . . He knows where he is and what day it is . . . A little strange how he uses Sunday as a benchmark day . . .

"Have you been hearing voices or seeing things?"

"No, sir, I feel fine," Marc answered easily. "The only problem I have is that I'm in prison. Other than that, I'm great." He flashed a genuine, natural smile.

Doesn't endorse having perceptual disturbances . . . Recognizes being in prison is a problem . . . Unlike most of the men I've seen today, he isn't trying to convince me of his innocence . . . He doesn't seem to be depressed but kind of seems happy . . . Too happy? Maybe too happy to be in prison, but not remarkably so . . .

"I understand you gave your dinner away this afternoon," Donnie said. "Why'd you do that?"

"I didn't want it," Marc answered plainly. "I thought instead of wasting it, I'd give it to someone who was hungry."

A socially appropriate response . . . Didn't evade the question . . . Not argumentative . . . Didn't attempt to deny it . . . Didn't really try to make an excuse, either, he just told me why . . . Something about the way he's still looking at me is uncomfortable . . . What's bothering me about that?

"Have you thought about hurting yourself or anyone else?"

"No, sir."

Denies suicidal and homicidal ideation . . .

Donnie tapped his pen on the table. "What do you think the saying 'still waters run deep' means?"

"I believe it means that while things may look okay on the surface, they can be made up of many underlying dimensions or facets."

Abstract thinking . . . Relatively high intelligence compared to his peers . . . Able to express an abstract thought coherently . . . Able to focus without becoming distracted . . . Thought processes seem goal oriented . . .

"Do you, or does anyone in your family, have a history of mental illness?"

"No, sir."

"Why are you in prison?"

"I went to a church, and people got upset when I told them they should try to be more aware of what they do instead of concerning themselves so much with what everyone else does."

Ah . . . Here's something . . . Surely he's minimizing . . . People aren't arrested and sent to prison, especially Caledonia, for that . . . There has to be more to it . . . Push him and see how he responds . . .

"Are you sure that's all?"

"Yes, sir," he replied without hesitation or emotion.

"That's hard to believe, Mr. Jones."

"That's why I am here," he said respectfully and without sarcasm.

He knows I don't believe him and yet, he's still respectful . . . He's either hiding something or doesn't understand what happened . . . He seems to be of relatively high intelligence so I guess it's the former . . . I'll have to find out what really happened . . . Make sure to ask Amber to get the information . . .

"Mr. Jones, thanks for coming to talk with me," Donnie said. "Good luck to you."

Marc's smile never drooped, and he never broke eye contact. "You're right thinking God's power and might *is* above all understanding. He was the beginning and will be the end. Nothing that has been created or happened has occurred without Him. It's because of His grace that we're here and it'll be because of His grace that we're saved. Only when we turn our lives over to Him, through His Son, can we truly live and begin to prosper." Marc stood to leave, and the officers came to escort him back to his cell.

He stopped at the door and looked over his shoulder. "Thanks for coming to Caledonia to see me. I look forward to talking with you in the days to come."

Before Donnie could respond, Marc was gone. Donnie knew he could call him back, but since he wasn't sure what to say, he let him go.

He still didn't think the man was dangerous to himself. But he was sure that something was going on.

Why did he start saying those religious things? It sounded like the first chapter in the book of John . . . what did he mean, "I was right to think?" I wonder if he believes he has the ability to read people's thoughts . . . He doesn't seem psychotic, though . . . Why did he thank me for coming to see him? *He made it seem like the only reason I came to Caledonia was to see him . . . Maybe this man's just a narcissist, thinks the world revolves around him . . . That's got to be it . . .*

Pleased that another inmate hadn't tricked him, Donnie went home.

As he drove toward Rocky Mount, Donnie thought about Marc Jones. He didn't meet the diagnostic criteria for narcissistic personality disorder. Except for his last statement, he wasn't grandiose, and he wasn't hypersensitive to what others thought about him. He hadn't presented himself as special. He even showed concern for others by giving someone his unwanted food.

A person with a narcissistic personality disorder usually has trouble relating to others. He tends to speak in a degrading, condescending manner and acts in ways that make others feel inferior. Since he believes he is unique and better than everyone else, he usually demands special treatment and can become enraged when he doesn't receive it.

Marc had demonstrated none of these characteristics. According to Steve, he got along well with everyone. He had asked for no special treatment. He stayed to himself. Come to think of it, Donnie had to admit that when they talked, Marc's tone of speech was calm and respectful instead of emotional and degrading. True, when he'd talked about God, he'd spoken with an air of authority, but it had come across as loving and caring instead of spiteful and demeaning.

It had been like he was teaching and connecting with Donnie, rather than showing off or tearing him apart.

Hmmm . . . I've got to think about this some more. Something isn't right . . .

Lord Abdullah hadn't been able to meet with Abdurahman on Sunday because of business meetings, and he'd spent most of Monday distributing the goods and services bought during those meetings. Now finished, he walked over to D block for the visit. It was against prison policy. But rules didn't really apply to him. It was another perk that went along with his lofty position.

Besides, I pay these officers a lot to open doors for me.

Abdurahman was awake when Lord Abdullah entered. He got up and followed him to the bathroom area in the back of the block.

"What's up?"

"Hey, man," Lord Abdullah greeted him. "I wanted to tell you how impressed I was with your teachin' Sunday. I been meanin' to come by, but I ain't been able to get away."

Taking the compliment as another sign Allah was pleased, Abdurahman puffed up with pride. "Thanks, I appreciate that. I studied hard to get my position."

Lord Abdullah looked at him. "I know you did, which brings me to the other reason I wanted to talk. I got this question I thought you could help me with."

"As the Muslim prayer leader, that's one of my functions," Abdurahman replied, for a moment feeling the respect and importance he'd always wanted to have. "What is it?"

"Have you ever wondered why the color black has a negative meaning?" Lord Abdullah rocked back on his heels, setting Abdurahman up for his graduate education.

"Sure."

"It seems to me we've been programmed to think of black as bein' bad and white as bein' good. I mean, it's like we been taught that bein' black is somethin' to be ashamed of."

"Yeah, I know what you mean," Abdurahman replied, but he was wondering why Lord Abdullah wanted to talk about racism at this time of night. *Something's up . . .*

"It ain't always been that way," Lord Abdullah said. "I mean, black used to be the most powerful color in existence. Our ancestors put black capstones on their pyramids. Some of the world's most sacred icons are black. The Black Madonna and the large block of stone in Mecca, called the Ka'bah, are black."

Abdurahman stroked his neatly trimmed beard, trying to look like he was contemplating what he was hearing.

Lord Abdullah's ego soared. *Not everyone can make an educated man stop to consider what they say . . .*

"I've also been thinkin' about the color white," Lord Abdullah continued, gaining momentum. "And how it used to represent bad things. When a fire goes out, all that remains is white colored ash. Mourners used to cover themselves with it to represent the end of life. The Bible describes death as ridin' on a white-colored horse. I guess what I'm tryin' to say is that white used to represent the absence of life."

"I see what you mean." Abdurahman nodded, still not sure where the conversation was going.

"I guess my question for you is this: Why do you suppose black was good and white was bad, and now it's the opposite?"

Abdurahman had guessed the question would be about racism, but this wasn't what he expected. Fortunately, he remembered what Ima'am Mohammed had taught him about racism, and he thought it applied to the situation.

"You've asked an important question," he said. "I'm impressed with how much you've thought about it."

Lord Abdullah lit up.

"I think your question has to do with racial inequalities, and that is something well addressed by the Islamic faith. In the opening chapter of the *Holy Qur'an*, Allah is referred to as the *Rabb ul-AlamIn* or as *Rabb of the Worlds*. *Rabb*, according to Ima'am Raghib, means the Cherisher, Sustainer, and Fosterer of a thing in such a manner as to make it attain one condition after another until it reaches its goal of completion and perfection. For this reason, Allah, as the Rabb of the Worlds, deals with all of us alike, no matter if we're white or black."

Lord Abdullah tilted his head and listened.

"The *Holy Qur'an,* chapter forty-nine, verse thirteen, tells us that Allah created all of humanity from a single male and female and then made them into nations and tribes so they could get along instead of hate each other," Abdurahman said. "It then goes on to tell us that the most honored people in Allah's sight will be the most righteous ones. Because of this, I believe true Muslims aren't affected by racism."

Lord Abdullah smiled. *You didn't answer my question, but I guess that's 'cause it was too hard. At least you recognized my intelligence.*

"Well, I'm not nearly the authority you are on the subject," Lord Abdullah said. *It never hurts to build people up.* "But I think what you're sayin' is that Allah, glory be to him, made all of us alike."

"Yes."

"With that bein' true, do you think the devil has caused us to change how we think about the colors by trickin' people into goin' against the wishes of Allah, glory be to him?"

The two things weren't connected, but Abdurahman didn't want to push Lord Abdullah away. "I can see you're a very wise man and have given this much thought," he said. "I agree with you that racism is a problem, but I think there are many causes. Perhaps you could give me an opportunity to study more about this and we could talk at a later time."

Having gotten what he was seeking, Lord Abdullah was willing to leave it at that for now.

"Abdurahman Abdul-Ahmad, I want to thank you for sharin' your knowledge with me. Allah has truly blessed us by makin' you our leader, and I look forward to havin' many more conversations in the future."

HEBREWS 11:35 "But others trusted God and were tortured, preferring to die rather than turn from God and be free." (NLT)

Chapter 7
Tuesday

I've never seen an inmate act so calm . . . it was like . . . like what? What was he hiding? What did he mean about being glad I came to see him?

Donnie rolled over and saw three thirty-seven in bright red numbers on the alarm clock. He decided to go to the prison to find some answers. He got out of bed, made coffee, and took a shower.

Driving to Caledonia at night seemed quite different. With the exception of a few streetlights and the orange and black Hardee's sign in Enfield, no other lights could be seen. The shapeless black landscape merged with the dark, cloud-covered sky so that there was no contrast between where land stopped and space began. It wasn't until Donnie passed Tillery and saw the yellow glow of light from the prison on the horizon that the perception changed.

I didn't end up in space, I went right past it and found the other side . . .

In his office, Donnie made more coffee and logged on to the Department of Corrections mainframe to look up Marc Jones' prison record. He discovered Marc was thirty-three years old and didn't have a middle name. He had no previous arrests and no next of kin listed. No one was registered on his visitors list, and neither his place of birth nor his hometown were given. He didn't have a social security number or a driver's license.

He hadn't received an infraction in the two weeks and two days he had been at Caledonia.

Why's most of this blank? . . . Is it because he hasn't been in the system that long? Ask Amber when she gets here . . .

Sipping his coffee, Donnie entered commands on his keyboard and looked at Marc's mental health and medical records. He discovered Marc hadn't received treatment, except for standard intake screenings upon admission. He had obtained a BETA IQ test score of one hundred thirty-seven, placing him in the very superior range of intelligence.

Maybe this guy is different . . . He didn't act that way, though . . .

Donnie studied Marc's official crime report and found he was convicted of one count of inciting a riot, two counts of assault with intent to kill inflicting serious injury, twenty counts of destruction of property, one count of criminal trespassing, and two counts of resisting arrest. His sentences were to be served consecutively and meant he would be incarcerated for at least forty years.

I thought he was minimizing, but this is ridiculous . . . He conveniently forgot to tell me about the assault and a few other minor details . . . Surely, he knew I'd find out . . . He didn't act very assaultive . . . Hmmm . . .

Donnie continued to read and took notes.

Marc had arrived at church on the day of his arrest dressed in worn-out jeans, a white T-shirt, and hiking boots. He was homeless and had gone there either to panhandle or get out of the weather. After going inside, he'd sat in the middle of the sanctuary, and at the end of the service, he started making inflammatory and offensive comments.

I wonder why he waited and what he said . . . I'd love to see the transcript . . .

Marc had gotten upset when politely asked to leave by two ushers, and he assaulted them, causing unspecified injuries. Witnesses testified that he pulled a gun, which caused people to flee, fearing for their lives. Several people in the congregation were injured, and when the police arrived, Marc resisted arrest. The gun was never recovered.

Donnie went online to search for newspaper articles that had been published about the crime and the trial that followed. He found several stories from the *Mount Olive Times* and the *Goldsboro Observer*. It seemed the incident had been the talk of the town. After two hours of reading and making notes, several things became apparent. There was no doubt Marc was guilty. The minister of the church where the incident happened was quoted as saying he thought Marc was Satan. Several people who were interviewed said they thought no punishment was too severe for him.

Guess that's why he's at Caledonia in maximum custody . . .

Marc was not represented by an attorney.

Pretty dumb move for a man with an IQ of a hundred and thirty-seven . . .

One writer reported that Marc had asked for nothing to assist in the preparation of his defense. He didn't call witnesses or cross-examine the prosecution's, and he didn't take the stand to testify on his own behalf. Instead, he sat quietly at the defense table and listened to what was said about him.

That sure isn't the behavior I'd expect from an assaultive man . . .

One story indicated that both the judge and the district attorney were members of the church where the incident occurred, but weren't present when it happened.

Sounds like the reporter had already convicted him . . . I wonder where he *goes to church . . .*

Following the seemingly one-sided trial, a guilty verdict on all counts had come back quickly. Everyone was pleased with the extremely harsh sentence that was handed down. The judge was quoted as telling Marc during sentencing, "I hope you'll learn from this and change your evil ways so that you'll never again harass and accuse God-fearing Christians of being sinners."

What's up with that?

The article ended by saying that Marc was led away from court in leg irons and handcuffs while people cheered and clapped.

Donnie had read nothing that indicated Marc might have been innocent, or, for that matter, that he was anything less than pure evil, but somehow, he wasn't convinced. Instead, he had even more questions without answers.

Like Donnie, Lord Abdullah wasn't able to sleep well, but it wasn't because he was concerned about someone else. He'd never really cared about anyone but himself, and last night's meeting with Abdurahman was no exception. Instead of listening, he had paid more attention to how he was being treated. For the first time in years, someone respected him for his intelligence, not just his power or position.

Lord Abdullah sincerely believed he was intelligent. The only reason he hadn't become a successful lawyer or doctor was because of the racism he'd grown up in. It kept him from getting the opportunities others received and using his knowledge to its potential. All that had changed, though, when he met Ramone Williams. He was motivated to study hard and learn the truth, as Ramone defined it, so he could prove he belonged in the intelligent five percent.

After meeting with Abdurahman, he started thinking about how comfortable he felt accepting praise and compliments. But although he deserved them, they weren't being offered for the right reasons. No, he realized for the first time that most things people said and did for him were out of fear. It was good for business, but it did little to assure him that people recognized his superior intellect.

He decided to attend Islamic services.

I'll take care of two things at once. . . . I can recruit new members for the Five Percenters, and I'll be able to share my intelligence with people like Abdurahman who recognize and appreciate it . . . Man, I'm smart . . .

Donnie had started running in graduate school and was addicted to it. He enjoyed getting away from everything so he could think. He spent the rest of the morning completing progress notes and developing treatment plans, and at lunchtime, he went to the staff training house to change his clothes. Running on the rarely used dirt roads that snaked across the farm enhanced the experience at Caledonia, and Donnie was looking forward to his thinking time today. He laced up his Nike Air running shoes and headed out.

Where did Marc Jones come from? he thought as his feet pounded out a rhythm on the dirt trails. *Where had he been before going to the Chapel of God? Why'd a man with such a high IQ choose to represent himself in court and then not call a single witness or take the stand in his own defense? If he was all the things the news articles said, then why hadn't he been in trouble before? What type of work did he do? Is he a Christian? What made him decide to talk to the people at the Chapel of God? I wonder what he said . . . Why is there so little information on his prison record demographics page? Why do I feel such a strong need to pursue this?*

After cooling down and showering, Donnie decided to meet with Marc and ask him the questions he had come up with. He called Steve to let him know he was coming, but no one answered. Not suspecting anything, Donnie grabbed two protein bars from his desk and left for Unit 1.

He drove to the end of Caledonia Road, past the Unit 1 yard, and saw twenty-five inmates in orange jumpsuits standing in the cages. More inmates were being supervised by more officers in what used to be a basketball court in the middle of the yard. Sensing something was wrong, Donnie parked underneath the main guard tower and went to the front lobby. Lieutenant Robbins breezed past, and Donnie followed him out.

"What happened?" Donnie asked.

"Well, Doc," Robbins answered without stopping, "one of your bugs set a fire a few minutes ago. I think his name's Danny something or other."

"Danny Jerguson?" Donnie offered, remembering from his files that Jerguson had a history of setting fires.

"Yeah, that's it," Robbins said as the gate opened and they went toward Unit 1. "Look, I'd like to chat, but I've got to help out on the yard. Your boy's still in the clinic bein' checked out by medical."

"Thanks," Donnie said as the lieutenant disappeared around the corner. He went to the clinic. Two men from the Halifax County EMS were in with Danny and about to transport him to Halifax Regional Medical Center in Roanoke Rapids. Steve was also there. He motioned for Donnie to meet him in the exam room.

"Looks like you've had some excitement," Donnie observed, shutting the door.

"*I* wouldn't really call it exciting," Steve said, "but an inmate might."

"Doesn't look like he's having much fun." Donnie nodded in Danny's direction.

"He probably isn't. He does this a lot, but we usually get to him before it gets this bad. Today he lit some paper, a pile of clothes, and his mattress on fire. By the time we got to him, he'd already inhaled so much smoke that every time he opened his mouth, a puff came out."

"Really?"

"I imagine that if he lives, his nickname's going to be Puff, like the dragon, from now on."

Donnie smiled uneasily, unsure how to respond. "You don't seem very upset about this."

"Hey," Steve said, "inmates do this kind of thing all the time. This is the fifth time Danny's set a fire. Every time, we tell him what could happen. It's not like we don't care, it's just that we know things like this are going to happen no matter how hard we try to prevent them. That's why we laugh at the funny stuff, so the job won't break us down."

"I guess I haven't thought about it like that."

"Well, I'm sure there's plenty about this place that most normal people haven't thought about." Steve smiled. "But remember, just because you're normal doesn't mean you know how to dress."

Donnie laughed. Then he remembered why he'd come to Unit 1. "I need to ask Marc Jones some questions. Can we do it tomorrow?"

"That shouldn't be too much of a problem. That is, assuming the place isn't burned to the ground by then."

"Yeah, I guess that would make it tough," Donnie said. "I'll call you tomorrow after lunch."

"Sounds good." Steve went back outside.

Donnie headed back to his office, wondering if he would ever understand the world that existed inside the fences.

A benefit of being the Islamic prayer leader was also getting to work as the Unit 2 dorm janitor. This highly sought position didn't involve a great deal of work, and it permitted movement among five dormitories. The job allowed plenty of time to study the *Qur'an* and preside over the five daily prayer services prescribed by the Islamic faith.

The early afternoon prayer, called Zuhur, had ended, and everyone was heading back to their work assignments when Lord Abdullah caught up with Abdurahman.

"Hey man," he said, "I enjoyed our discussion last night. It really got me thinkin', and I'd like to get more involved in Islam."

"That's great," Abdurahman said. *Thank you, Allah, for showing me how to help this man find you.* "I look forward to having you. I'm sure your wisdom will help many."

Lord Abdullah grinned.

Donnie saw the flashing red light and crossed his office to play back his messages. The first voice he heard was Reverend Hurley saying he'd enjoyed having lunch and would like to get together. He left a number where he could be reached.

The second voice made Donnie's heart beat faster. It was Karla. She said she hoped they could talk again soon. She left her pager number and asked him to call.

Donnie phoned Charles first. The reverend answered on the second ring. They talked for a few minutes before agreeing to meet for breakfast.

Then Donnie paged Karla and waited.

When the phone rang, he instinctively reached for it, then pulled back, not wanting to seem too anxious. But when the second ring started, he lost his cool and grabbed it. "Hello?"

"Hey, Donnie. This is Karla."

"Hi. Thanks for calling me back so fast."

"How have you been?"

"Things have been pretty hectic at work. There hasn't been a psychologist there for a long time. I've thought about you a lot, though."

"Yeah," she said sarcastically, "I guess that's why you waited for *me* to call *you*."

"No, really. I haven't been able to *stop* thinking about you. You are so . . . " He stopped abruptly as it dawned on him she had been kidding.

Not missing her chance, Karla said, "I'm so what?"

Donnie could hear the smile in her voice now. "Okay, so now you know that I can't stop thinking about you. Is that so bad?"

"It's not bad at all for me."

"Really?"

"Really." She laughed. "I just hope I don't always have to trick you into telling me how you feel."

"I think the price for tricking me is breakfast tomorrow morning," he said. "Think you can go?"

"Well, since you think I'm so wonderful and all, how could I say no?"

"You can't. Besides, I'd love to get your opinion on a patient I'm seeing. If it's okay, I'm meeting Reverend Hurley at the IHOP, but I'd love for you to come along. I can pick you up around seven thirty."

"Well," Karla said, as if she were considering, "I guess that'll be safe, since the minister is going to be there."

"Then it's a date. I'll see you bright and early."

After hanging up, Karla sat back in the leather swivel chair in her office. Part of her was excited about her feelings for Donnie. He was a great guy, and most importantly, a man of God. She liked that he was shy around her, yet confident in himself. Sure, it had only been a few days, but there was something there. That was very obvious, and also very scary.

It had been a long time since she'd been on a date, and even that had been more of a friendship. Her last serious boyfriend had been in her anatomy class in medical school. Two years after they began dating, he proposed marriage and she said yes.

After they moved in together and began planning their wedding, Karla realized something was missing from her life. She started feeling a pull to return to church. Her fiancé quietly went along at first. But after a while, he made it clear he didn't believe in church. When Karla tried to talk with him about God, he dismissed her feelings as unscientific. He told her God was just an idea men had invented to represent an ideal state of being. He said it wasn't possible for humans to be Christ-like, and to try was just a waste of time and a setup for failure.

It wasn't until she took off her engagement ring and gave it back that he understood the depth of her convictions and beliefs.

Karla had shut down emotionally after the break-up and began living in a world of her own. She'd taken a chance by letting her guard down, and someone had crushed her feelings and hurt her deeply. To cope, she spent her time building her career and became totally involved in her church. She remained sociable and always seemed friendly and happy, but she kept people at a distance and refused to talk about her feelings. She became quite skilled at deflecting questions and using her keen sense of humor to laugh intrusions away.

Her strategy of building a wall around her feelings was one of the reasons she'd become such a successful physician in such a short time, although it was also the reason she was a very lonely and isolated person whom no one truly knew.

Now, here she was calling a man she'd just met and joking with him like she'd known him all her life.

This is serious business . . .

Donnie was falling for Karla, which was about as scary a thing as he could imagine. He'd learned a long time ago that when you let people get close, something bad always happened.

It first became apparent when his mother committed suicide. For years, they hadn't had a relationship because of her mental illness and his selfish nature. But the summer after his senior year of high school, he'd spent time talking with his high school psychology teacher and learning about his mother's illness. He began to accept her for who she was and was starting to emotionally reach out to her when he went to college. And then she died.

After that, Donnie decided he couldn't trust people. He had learned that making himself vulnerable by caring for another person resulted in being hurt in the worst way possible. The one person in the entire world who was supposed to love him no matter what had killed herself and walked away forever. No matter how much he loved someone, Donnie learned, it wasn't enough to keep them from hurting him.

Donnie had gotten very good at talking with people, sometimes for hours, without divulging personal information. He lost his interest in dating. He not only stopped asking women out, he became an expert at turning down those who asked him.

So Donnie was surprised at the feelings he was having for Karla.

This is serious business . . .

ACTS 2:17 "In the last days, God said I will pour out my Spirit upon all people. Your sons and daughters will prophesy, your young men will see visions, and your old men will dream dreams." (NLT)

Chapter 8
Wednesday Morning

Officers escorted the inmates who had attended Fajr to the dining hall for breakfast, which usually consisted of a scoop of scrambled eggs, fresh from the farm, mystery meat that no one knew where it came from, and burnt, unbuttered toast. An extra scoop of eggs or a bowl of oatmeal was provided to Muslims and others who didn't eat pork.

Abdurahman sat on the stainless steel seat welded to the immovable stainless steel table. As he prayed over his food, Lord Abdullah sat down beside him.

"Mornin'," Lord Abdullah interrupted in a tired voice. "Sorry about missin' Fajr. I fell back asleep after 'dey woke me up."

Abdurahman restrained himself from chastising the undisciplined man in front of his peers, choosing to focus on the fact that at least Lord Abdullah had told the truth about his absence.

"Well, there's several prayer opportunities each day," he said. "Hopefully, I'll see you at one of them."

Lord Abdullah could sense Abdurahman's disappointment, and he was pleased.

He values my intelligence and wants me to be a part of the group . . .

"The other reason I came by," Lord Abdullah said with his eyes downcast, faking respect, "is that I plan on bein' at Ta'alim this evenin', and I wanna know what you're plannin' on teachin'. I wanna be, you know, prepared."

Sure that he wasn't being told everything about why Lord Abdullah missed Fajr but afraid to interrogate him, Abdurahman carefully considered his response.

"I'm not sure yet what I'll be teaching, although I've got some ideas I'm praying about." He looked closely at Lord Abdullah. "You know, sometimes I believe it's better to listen with your heart and let Allah, peace and glory be upon him, place upon it what he desires for you to say out of your mouth."

Lord Abdullah pressed on. "I guess I've found I'm in a better position to hear Allah's voice when I'm prepared." *That sounded pretty good . . . Hard to argue with that . . .*

"Maybe it is how one prepares that's important," Abdurahman countered. "Prayer and submission to the perfect will of Allah are what matter most. Only when a person does that and gives up his games can he hope to be called upon by him."

Abdurahman wasn't going to tell him what he was going to discuss, and Lord Abdullah let it go. It didn't matter anyway. He'd been well trained by Ramone to speak on a variety of subjects.

No need to push too far . . . for now . . .

"I understand, Abdurahman, and I appreciate your wise counsel," Lord Abdullah said. "I'll try to remember that in the future."

Donnie's thoughts raced on the way to Karla's house. He felt like a teenager going on his first date. When he got to her place, he sat in the truck to collect himself before going to the door.

When he finally got up his nerve to ring the bell, Karla answered quickly. She opened the door and gave him a hug. He was caught off guard and pulled back slightly. Then he gave in to how natural it felt and tightly squeezed her back.

"You know," he said as he walked her to the truck, "I'll be happy to help you anytime you'd like."

Karla froze. "Excuse me?"

"I think your hugs need some work. You could use some practice."

She punched him on the shoulder as he opened the door for her. "You're a goober."

"Is that a good thing?"

"Well," she said, smiling, "in your case, I guess it's okay."

"Maybe *you* can help me work on *that.* Deal?"

"Deal," she said as Donnie started the truck and pulled out of the driveway.

Charles was already seated when Donnie and Karla arrived at the restaurant. He was drinking black coffee as he stared out the window. He jumped slightly when they sat down across from him.

"I was just thinking about a dream I've been having," the reverend said. "Want to hear about it?"

"Sure," Donnie answered, "but I should warn you, it's been a while since I've done dream interpretation."

The waitress came to take their orders. When she left, Charles told them what he remembered.

"It starts with a man standing in front of a church. He seems to be preaching, but I can't hear what he's saying." The usual glow in Charles' eyes was replaced with a distant, detached look. There was a hint of concern in his voice.

"Then what?" Donnie asked.

"A man dressed in faded jeans, brown hiking boots, and a stained white T-shirt appears in the back of the church. He has a ponytail and a long gray beard. The preacher stops talking when he sees him."

Donnie's pulse quickened. He thought of Marc Jones.

Charles took a sip of coffee. "Sometimes the man in the back of the church stands there for a few seconds and then starts speaking. Other times, he walks up the aisle before he speaks. In both versions, he always says the same thing over and over until I wake up. 'You will find me when you seek me, if you look for me with all of your heart.' I thought I remembered those words coming from scripture, so I looked it up. Sure enough, it comes from chapter twenty-nine, verse thirteen in the book of Jeremiah."

Donnie chewed on his lip. He wondered whether he should tell the reverend what he knew about Marc Jones.

The waitress brought a pitcher of warm syrup to the table. Donnie was glad for the distraction. When she returned with their food, Donnie asked the reverend to say a blessing and pray for guidance and wisdom.

When the prayer was over, Karla reached for the syrup. A few moments into the meal, Donnie put down his fork and took a deep breath.

"I have something you need to hear." He told them about Marc and how Steve was concerned. He described why Marc was in prison and how he was dressed when he was arrested. He told them what his research had turned up and the questions that resulted from it.

When he finished, Charles and Karla sat back.

Charles finally broke the silence. "Now I understand why you asked me to pray for guidance and wisdom. I think we need it."

Karla reached across the table to hold Donnie's hand.

"You know, since the first time I had the dream, I thought it was special," Charles said. "It seems like more than just a coincidence that I'd dream about a man who looks like someone who's in prison for something that happened at a church."

"Maybe it is more than a coincidence," Karla observed, "but I think we need more information before we can make any conclusions."

"I agree," Donnie said.

"Are you planning on speaking with him today?" Karla asked.

"Yeah, this afternoon."

She frowned. "I sure would like to know what happened at the church that day."

"That's why I had my secretary contact the Wayne County court clerk to have the trial transcript sent to my office," Donnie explained. "I should receive it today."

"I'll tell you what," Charles interjected. "I'll do some research on my dream, and you find out about Marc Jones. Let's meet tonight at the church and talk about what we find. Can you be there around seven?"

Donnie and Karla realized he meant both of them. Smiling at each other, they both said, "Yes."

Why does Lord Abdullah want to get involved with Islam? What's his motivation? How do I handle this?

Finishing his breakfast, Abdurahman thought about how odd it was that Lord Abdullah had come by so late the night before. Their conversation had started with a question, but Lord Abdullah didn't seem to listen to the answer. Instead, he'd wanted to argue.

Perhaps he didn't want an answer, Abdurahman thought. *He wanted to debate something he thought he already knew*. This would also explain why he wanted to know what was going to be presented at Ta'alim. He wanted to prepare so he could sound intelligent and impress the men at the meeting.

Abdurahman sat for a while longer and thought about the best way to handle Lord Abdullah. He decided he would attempt to educate him in the ways of Allah without making it seem like he was being taught. The challenge, he knew, would be knowing how far to push and when to back off. For this, he would definitely need the guidance of Allah.

After taking Karla home, Donnie went to Caledonia and began reviewing mental health records. He worked for almost two hours until he was having difficulty concentrating. He decided to take an early lunch so he could go running and clear his mind.

His pager went off as he finished his fifth mile. He ran back to the training house to return the call.

"Hello," a voice answered.

"Hey, Amber, this is Donnie. What's up?"

"Steve just called. I told him you were out running, and he wanted me to tell you to come and see him. He said it wasn't an emergency, but I could tell he was excited about something. He was talking really fast, which isn't like him."

"What do you think is going on?"

"I don't know. Steve just said to go and see him when you get back."

"Hmmm." Donnie sighed. "Call him back and tell him I'll be there as soon as I shower and change clothes."

Donnie got ready and drove the short distance to the prison. Entering through the main gate and turning left, he followed the sidewalk along the fifteen-foot-high perimeter fence topped with razor wire. Large signs posted on the fence informed anyone approaching it that they may be shot if they attempted to pass underneath, over, or through it. These signs usually served as a reality check, but today, Donnie was too preoccupied to notice.

He headed to the downstairs Unit 1 lobby area. The officer in the control booth recognized him and pressed buttons on his control panel to let Donnie through the back door of the medical clinic.

Inside, the mood was tense. The usually loud, frantic clinic was extremely quiet. No one seemed to notice Donnie as he passed through. He wondered if it had anything to do with why Steve wanted to talk.

He went to the front door and got the officer to let him through so he could go upstairs.

An officer in the central control booth at the top of the stairs electronically opened the door.

Steve was on the phone in his office, staring into space. He shook his head as he hung up.

Donnie sat down hesitantly. "What's going on?"

"I've worked here for a long time and seen a lot of things, but I've never seen anything like this." Steve rubbed his tired eyes. He picked up a stack of papers. "This morning, at approximately ten o'clock, inmate Jake Tomkins was found lying in a pool of blood in the upstairs back hallway of Unit 2. He'd been stabbed and cut multiple times and didn't have a pulse. The medical clinic was immediately contacted, and the officers that found him began performing CPR until the nurses arrived and took over. Jake was put on a stretcher and taken to the clinic. After several minutes, the doctor said he'd lost too much blood and pronounced him dead."

Donnie was shocked by the violent news, but he was having a hard time understanding why it bothered Steve. He knew Steve had dealt with many stabbings and inmate deaths over the years.

"Hold on a second—it gets better," Steve said. "The medical examiner's office was contacted, along with the Halifax County Sheriff's Department. While the nurses and officers in the clinic were making calls, an inmate saw another patient come out of the room Jake's body was in. A minute after that, Jake walked out and asked for some water."

Donnie stared in disbelief.

"Two nurses fainted, one hyperventilated, and two others took Jake back to the exam room and checked his vital signs. All were normal. Except for the massive cuts and stab wounds requiring sutures, Jake appeared to be fine."

"Who was seen leaving the room?"

"Are you ready for this?" Steve said. "They think it was Marc Jones. The inmate you talked to Friday."

Donnie felt like his heart was going to leap out of his chest. Steve looked at him expectantly, but Donnie was too numb to speak. The only thing running through his mind was that he had to go somewhere to be alone. But it was almost impossible to be alone in the prison. This was usually a good thing for safety reasons, but at the moment he felt trapped.

As if on autopilot, Donnie crossed the room and shut the door. He took a deep breath and slowly let it out before speaking.

"Steve, are you a Christian?"

The question caught Steve off guard, but he paused only briefly before answering. "Yeah, I'm a Christian. I was saved when I was twelve. Why?"

Donnie told him about his conversation with Marc. He shared the reverend's dream and the information he had collected from the newspapers. He then told Steve what he found in Marc's prison file and why he was at Caledonia.

"This is strange," Steve said. "Who is he?"

"I'm not sure," Donnie answered. "But *something* is going on."

Steve leaned back in his chair. "I know what you mean, Doc."

"I'm meeting with the reverend this evening," Donnie said. "Why don't you come and help us try to figure it out?"

MALACHI 3:1 "Look! I am sending my messenger, and he will prepare the way before me . . . "
(NLT)

Chapter 9
Wednesday Evening

After asking Allah to open the men's eyes and to give him words of wisdom, Abdurahman began teaching.

"I want to talk this evening about fasting and why it's important. When we fast, we're not only learning discipline, we're also learning to appreciate things we don't have. You see, it takes self-control to resist eating when you're hungry, and then, when you get some food, you'll be more thankful."

Lord Abdullah joined in. "I wanna give you another example. All my life I've wanted nice things, a big home in a good 'hood and a nice ride. The problem, though, was that white society prevented me from havin' 'em. You see, they forced me to fast and forced me to accept it."

"I understand how you feel," Abdurahman said. "The way society has treated blacks can certainly be thought of as a form of forced fasting. We weren't given chances while they had them all. We weren't allow to attend the good schools they attended and on and on. But if we've been forced to fast, why don't we appreciate the things we weren't allowed to have, now that we can have them?"

The debate was on.

"I can answer that," Lord Abdullah said confidently. "I think all of us appreciate 'dem things you said. Who wouldn't? I mean, for most of us, that's why we're in prison. We wanted the things we were prevented from havin' and were forced to commit crimes to get 'em." He looked around the room for support. "No, I don't think us appreciatin' things is the problem. I think the problem is that we're still bein' prevented from havin' 'em. Sure, society says that we're all equal, but if you believe that, you're crazy. I mean, if we're so equal, how come there wasn't a single white family livin' in my 'hood?"

"Yeah, man, why's that?" asked a member.

"Go ahead on, man."

"Tell it like it is," someone said in a voice just below a shout.

Lord Abdullah felt more intelligent than usual while educating the men in the eighty-five-percent group. It felt natural, and hearing their support only made him want to teach them more.

He stood.

"My brothers, we, the descendants of the original man, have been forced to fast for many, many years 'cause the white devils tricked some of 'em into believin' what they taught many years ago. 'Cause of this, we're still payin' the price. And I believe with all of my soul that we need to declare a jihad on racism and the people that have forced us to fast all of our lives!"

Donnie spent the afternoon in a daze. He tried reading Marc's trial transcript, but was only able to concentrate for short periods of time. He knew Jesus had brought people back from death, had been crucified and buried, and on the third day rose from the grave. There was no doubt those things happened, and he believed them without question.

The problem was that those things involved God's Son, who was, and is, without sin, not two inmates at a run-down maximum custody prison in the middle of nowhere.

He left the prison, tired and emotionally drained.

After a quick stop at his apartment to change clothes, he headed to Karla's to pick her up for the meeting with Charles. He still felt like he was in another world until he started up the steps and she greeted him at the door.

As if by magic, his worries disappeared and everything seemed to be okay. It was the first time since his meeting with Steve that he smiled.

He waited in the living room for a few minutes while Karla finished getting ready. When they arrived at the church, Steve was waiting for them in the parking lot. He got out of his car as they drove up.

Donnie introduced Karla, and they headed in.

Charles invited them into his office. Donnie and Karla sat beside each other, and Steve sat at the other end of the conference table. Charles decided to stand.

After they prayed, Donnie asked Steve to describe what had happened at the clinic. Donnie then pulled papers from his book bag and gave everyone a copy of the information he had gathered about Marc, along with a copy of the trial transcript.

Steve flipped through the papers. "Donnie, when we talked earlier, you said you were unsure about the charges. Why is that? I thought everyone agreed he was guilty."

"I'm not a lawyer, but I guess I'm having a hard time understanding that Marc actually committed a crime," Donnie said. "I mean, with the exception of possibly trespassing, the rest of the charges seem to be trumped up. Do any of you know an attorney that could look into this? Maybe someone from the church?"

"Kenny Wilson is a very successful local defense attorney," Steve said without taking his eyes off the papers he was reading. "He's a good friend and a deacon at my church. I'll call him first thing tomorrow morning." He looked up at Donnie. "What does the asterisk mean beside the description of Marc's clothes and his appearance?"

Charles spoke up. "It's a very close description of the man in the dream I've been having." He opened the Bible in his hand and read Jeremiah 29:13.

Karla propped her elbows on the table. "What do you think it means in the context of the information we have so far?"

"I'm not sure," the reverend said. "I guess it could mean a lot of things. I think the obvious thing is that we have to be confident and believe that when we truly look for the Lord, we'll find Him. He made us that promise."

Abdurahman had been waiting for Lord Abdullah to declare a jihad. He'd seen many young black inmates become Muslims out of anger and try to use that part of Islam to achieve revenge. Christians did the same thing, he thought, when they misquoted the Bible or used a passage of Scripture out of context.

Lord Abdullah was misusing Islam to fulfill a selfish purpose, and Abdurahman had to stop it. But it had to be done tactfully, or he knew he would end up dead.

"Racism *has* been a terrible injustice for years," Abdurahman said. "I don't think anyone doubts that."

"They'd be lyin' if they did, man," a member of the group spoke out. "Lord Abdullah's right about us needin' to declare a jihad."

There were shouts of approval, and the supervising officers exchanged nervous glances as the tension in the room escalated.

Things were getting out of control. Abdurahman quickly spoke up. "Let's make sure we're all talking about the same thing. For true Muslims, a jihad means a struggle or a determination to do the right thing. A jihad ain't a war, it means doing justice even when it's against your own interests. In a way, a jihad is an individual struggle. We have to look inward and decide who we are before it's possible to promote outward causes like social justice."

"So you're sayin' it's okay to declare a jihad if we have a clear understandin' 'bout who were are and what we stand for?" asked Alan Anderson, who was in the process of legally changing his name.

"Well, Alan, I think that's the first part of it, but there's more," Abdurahman said. "We have to meet those things, but we've also got to have a morally accepted and righteous position to stand up for."

Alan fired back, much to Lord Abdullah's delight. "Well, man, I'd say hundreds of years of repression is a moral enough reason. I mean, come on man, how much more of a righteous cause is there?"

Lord Abdullah was letting Alan fight the battle for him. Abdurahman went on the offensive. "I agree that racism is a righteous cause, but my questions for you are these: what is it that you want, and how's what you're planning on doing going to get it for you?"

Alan had no answer. The others, who had been so ready to fight, avoided eye contact.

"You see Alan, a jihad isn't just something that men declare and then go fight," Abdurahman said. "No, a jihad is used to describe a moral battle that you're fighting within yourself—not on a battlefield, or in an alley, or anywhere else, for that matter."

He paused. When no one spoke, he tried to summarize the important principle. "Yes, I do believe we've experienced years of racism, and yes, it's possible it has played a part in why we're in prison. I'm not doubting that. What I'm saying is that if a true Muslim is going to declare a jihad on racism, then he has to battle it within himself and try to treat others fairly without concern for their race . . . even if they're racist."

"My secretary went through and pulled out what witnesses testified Marc said at church the day he was arrested," Donnie told the group. "I think you'll find the story he told especially interesting."

Everyone read in silence. Charles finally spoke up. "This seems like a parable."

"That's what I was thinking," Steve said.

"Me too, and I think it brings us to the big question," Donnie said. "Who is Marc Jones, and why is he telling this in a church?"

"Not to mention possibly bringing Jake Tomkins back to life," Steve added.

Charles broke in. "I don't know who Marc is, but we need to talk about something else that may add to what we've already discussed."

"What's that?" Karla asked.

"The man in my dream keeps repeating a verse of scripture from the book of Jeremiah. One of the general themes of that book is how the people of Israel had not only forsaken the Lord but had also stopped fearing Him. In essence, Jeremiah talks about how people had taken God's forgiveness for granted and stopped having any shame for the sins they were committing."

Steve looked up. "Are you saying you think Jones might be the prophet Jeremiah?"

"Maybe he's a modern, Jeremiah-like prophet," Donnie said.

Karla shook her head. "It's also possible that all of this is just a coincidence and means nothing. I still think we need to slow down before we start drawing any conclusions."

"I thought that, too," Charles said, "until I heard about what happened at the prison this morning. I think we need to at least consider the possibility that God used Marc to perform a miracle." He looked around the room. "I'm not sure who Marc is. And I really don't know if that matters as much as the fact that he's a special person in God's eyes."

LUKE 8:54,55 "Then Jesus took her by the hand and said in a loud voice, "Get up my child!" And at that moment her life returned, and she immediately stood up . . . "
(NLT)

Chapter 10

Thursday

Steve went to Caledonia earlier than usual to check on his unit. Then he called Kenny Wilson. Since Kenny wasn't scheduled in court, he suggested they meet for lunch. Steve finished responding to grievances before driving to Rocky Mount. When he arrived at Kenny's office, a secretary showed him back.

Kenny was fifty years old and overweight. He'd grown up in Rocky Mount, and had returned to start his practice after attending law school at Campbell University. He hadn't been adversely affected by his success. He took pride in his southern heritage and still referred to himself as a good-ole boy. When Steve entered, he stood and walked around his mahogany desk to shake hands.

After asking about Kenny's children and hearing about their sporting accomplishments, Steve presented Marc's case. He'd been thinking about what to say since he left church the night before. When he began, he was surprised at how easily the words came out and how succinctly he was able to summarize the information. He gave Kenny a copy of the trial transcript.

Kenny stopped taking notes and scanned the information.

"A friend I went to Campbell with told me about this a few months ago," he said. "He's from Mount Olive and practices in Goldsboro. I remember him saying something seemed strange with the case, but he never said what it was. Looking at this and hearing what you've said, I think I'm beginning to understand what he meant."

"So you don't think we're totally off base?"

"Not unless we're missing something," Kenny said. "Let's go eat and talk about it some more."

At Chico's on the upstairs balcony overlooking the muddy Tar River, Kenny asked questions. He seemed fascinated with what had happened and offered to ask around to see what he could find out.

"To pay me for my help, you can teach my son the jump shot that made you the talk of Rocky Mount," Kenny said. Steve laughed. Kenny promised to call him to let him know what he found out.

Donnie woke up early thinking about Marc. Unsure what he was going to say to him, he spent the drive to work praying and listening for God's guidance.

When he got to his office, he realized the meeting with Marc would have to wait. Amber had scheduled him to see patients in Units 2 and 3.

His first patient, Brad Saunders, looked like he was seventy years old, but he had only been fifty for two weeks. This was his third stint in prison, and the years of hard time were etched upon his face. His dark eyes had lost their glow many years ago when he realized he would never leave prison and gave up hope. Brad merely went through the motions of existing behind bars, waiting around to die.

Like many inmates, Brad was bored and lonely, but because he hadn't exaggerated his distress in an attempt to get medication, Donnie felt sorry for him and his situation. He told him he wanted to see him, not for therapy, but just to talk. He explained that since he was the only psychologist at the prison, it would have to be whenever he got a chance. Brad said he understood and politely thanked Donnie for his time, softly shaking his hand before leaving.

Donnie saw several more patients in Units 2 and 3 before going to Unit 1. He knew that Steve was in Rocky Mount, so he decided to see Marc in Steve's office. He asked the officers to get him.

Marc entered the room and smiled warmly. There was an intangible quality about Marc that instilled a sense of trust. Donnie wondered if he'd been smiling when he was arrested.

Then, before he knew it, Donnie blurted the question out.

Marc sat for a long time, seemingly contemplating his answer. Finally, he responded. "Yes, I was. I was trying to teach people how to change so they wouldn't spend eternity in hell."

Donnie's palms became sweaty. His thoughts raced. "Who are you, Mr. Jones?"

"Who do you think I am?"

"I'm not sure," Donnie said. He told Marc about Reverend Hurley's dream. "I don't think it's just a coincidence that the man in the reverend's dream is dressed like you were at the time of your arrest." He told Marc that the scripture the man in the dream kept repeating was from the book of Jeremiah. He explained that while he didn't think Marc was Jeremiah, he wondered if God had sent him.

He paused, assessing Marc's reaction. "I think maybe your purpose is to warn people or teach them about God. I mean, the story you told at the chapel sounded like a parable. When you were arrested, no one had seen you before and no one knew where you came from. Besides that, you don't have a driver's license, social security number, or any visible means of supporting yourself."

Donnie looked for confirmation in Marc's eyes but received only a smile.

"After we met," Donnie said, "I sensed there was something supernatural about you. I found out later that several people at the church made similar comments when the ushers tried unsuccessfully to make you leave. That supernatural quality comes across when you speak. You sound authoritative, but aren't condescending. It's almost like you have firsthand knowledge of the things you're talking about."

Donnie took a swallow of his protein drink. "The last thing is what happened to Jake Tomkins yesterday. The man was dead, and after you were seen leaving his room, he got up and walked to the nurse's station."

Marc sat for a long time. Then he quietly stood. "Later on you'll see for yourself who I am and why I'm here." Reaching out his handcuffed hands, he touched Donnie's shoulder on his way to the door. "Pray for wisdom and ask God to guide you in what He wants you to do." He left without saying another word.

Reverend Hurley knew there was something special about Marc and spent most of the morning studying the book of Jeremiah. He learned that Jeremiah served as God's prophet to Judah from 627 B.C. to 586 B.C. The first part of the book described the numerous ways people turned from God and rejected His way. Jeremiah pleaded with them to stop and prophesied about what would happen if they didn't, but no one listened and he was thrown in jail for no reason. His family and friends rejected him, and his country was destroyed as he predicted. Nevertheless, he never disobeyed God and continued delivering His message that repentance was one of the greatest needs of an immoral world.

Reverend Hurley wrote in the margin of his notepad, " . . . they have worked hard, but it has done them no good. They will harvest a crop of shame, for the fierce anger of the Lord is upon them."

He wondered if this referred not only to the way people ignored God's teaching but also to how they unsuccessfully tried to earn His favor. He thought how similar this was to the way the Pharisees, during Jesus' time, had made laws and then judged people on the basis of whether they obeyed them.

Doesn't this continue today? . . .

Abdurahman awoke at his usual time before sunrise. He was thankful to be seeing another day after what had happened at the previous night's Ta'alim. Although Lord Abdullah hadn't said anything, Abdurahman knew he had to be angry at not being able to have his way. Like everyone at Caledonia, Abdurahman knew that Lord Abdullah always got his way. He thanked Allah for giving him the words to say. He asked for continued protection and then begged Allah to open his brothers' hearts and minds so that they could learn more about him.

Jake Tomkins was assigned to Tom Harrell's unit after the "accident" because doctors felt it would be easier to care for his wounds if he were in a single cell, rather than a dormitory.

Harrell had been the Unit 4 manager for fifteen years and was only two years away from retirement. He was a tall, slender man who commanded respect without ever raising his voice. He was extremely fair and had learned many years ago to manage by using common sense.

Donnie had heard Harrell was a caring man. When he got to the unit manager's office, Harrell was counseling an inmate on the proper way to request medical treatment.

The inmate left, and Harrell stood to shake Donnie's hand. "I'll sure be glad when today's over," he sighed, pointing Donnie to a chair against the wall. "My day began with an inmate trying to pull a female officer into his cell. Only God knows what would've happened if he'd been successful."

Donnie shook his head.

"She's only been here for two weeks and probably would've been a good officer, but I think this scared her pretty bad, and she'll probably resign. It seems like this kinda thing is happening more frequently these days. We have a good officer come in, and before we can teach them enough to handle the job, something happens and they leave."

"It must be rather hard being a female officer in a male prison," Donnie commented. "Are assaults on females common?"

"Believe it or not, Doc, inmates are more likely to assault a male officer than a female. In fact, they'll often take up for a female officer and usually do what they tell 'em to do."

"That's interesting," Donnie said. "Why do you think that is?"

"I think sometimes when a male officer is involved, it turns into a power struggle and inmates don't know how to back down. Instead, they handle the situation like they do on the street, by using their fists."

Donnie grinned. "Ever thought about becoming a shrink?"

"Yeah, right," Harrell laughed. "Hey, I know you didn't come here to listen to my insights on inmate-officer behavior. What can I do for you?"

"Well, I guess you've heard about Jake Tomkins and what happened yesterday."

"Sure. I've heard lots of stuff. But like most things around here, I just thought it was probably gossip. I mean come on, the word is that he died and came back to life."

Not sure how to respond, Donnie hesitated. "I don't know what happened, but I'd like to talk with Jake, if that's okay."

Harrell shook his head, as if he was surprised Donnie believed the rumor. "You can use my office if you'd like. I'm going home for the day. I'll have Sergeant Holloway get Jake for you on my way out."

"Thanks, Tom," Donnie said. "I appreciate your help."

While he waited, Donnie logged on to Harrell's computer and scanned Jake's record. Jake was forty-nine years old and in prison for second-degree murder. This was his second incarceration. He'd been sent to Caledonia eight years earlier after assaulting another inmate. He hadn't had an infraction in two years and worked as a canteen operator, which meant he was considered to be a relatively trustworthy inmate.

Donnie looked up from the screen when Jake and the officer escorting him arrived outside the door. He motioned for them to come in. Jake took a seat in front of the desk. The officer remained in the hall.

"Mr. Tomkins, I'm Dr. Thompson, the head of mental health. Looks like you've had a pretty tough time," Donnie said, noticing the sutures covering Jake's face and arms. "How are you doing?"

"Look man, I ain't no bug," Jake responded defensively. "I ain't never seen the bug doctor before. Why'd you call me out?"

"Well, I was hoping you could tell me what happened."

"Look, I done told the po-lice. Why don't you just ask them?"

"Well, I guess I was just hoping you could tell me what it was like being dead." This caught Jake off guard, and when he hesitated, Donnie knew he almost had him. "I bet the police didn't care to hear about that, did they?"

Taking the bait, Jake launched into his story as if the pressure to talk had been building since it happened. "I was the last man in line gettin' a change of clothes. After I got 'em, I headed back toward the stairs to go to my bunk in Unit 2 A block. Two men was hidin' 'round the corner and attacked me. They threw a coat over my head and pulled me off balance, then started stabbin' me. I yelled for help, but with the coat over my head, nobody heard me."

"Then what?"

"After they cut me, they stole fifteen dollars and walked away. I couldn't see 'em 'cause I still had the coat over my head, but I could hear 'em walkin'. I was layin' on the floor and remember thinkin' how cold it felt. I tried to stand up, but when I got to my knees, I collapsed. I knew I'd been hurt real bad 'cause I could feel all the blood around me. I felt like I was gonna die but I wasn't scared."

Jake looked out the window. "I don't know why, but for some reason, the last thing I remember is prayin' that God would forgive me for all of the bad things I'd done."

"Why's that hard to believe?"

"Doc, before *The Rock of Ages* program, the last time I went to church was twenty years ago. I mean, I just ain't the Christian type. The only reason I went to the program was 'cause I was bored. Shoot, if you knew what kinda person I been, you'd know why it was so strange that I started prayin' when I thought I was dyin'."

Conflicted between trying to tell Jake he was no worse than anyone else and trying to get more information, Donnie searched desperately for what to say. Before he could respond, Jake continued. "After prayin', the next thing I remember is openin' my eyes and not knowin' where I was. It kinda felt like I was dreamin'. Everything was fuzzy but I could tell I was layin' on a stretcher and a man was standin' over me. The man touched my shoulder and my whole body got real warm. He said, 'Go and sin no more,' and then told me not to tell anyone that he had healed me. I musta closed my eyes 'cause when I opened 'em, he was gone.

"I stayed on the stretcher for a minute before I went to get some water. When the nurses in the next room looked up and saw me standin' there, they freaked out, like they'd seen a ghost. Finally, two of them, the ones that didn't faint, took me back to the room."

Sitting in awe of the miracle he was hearing about, Donnie was jilted back to reality when Jake asked, "Do you think I'm a bug, Doc?"

"Tell me about *The Rock of Ages* program," Donnie said, ignoring Jake's question.

"I didn't really do anything 'cept talk with this man."

"What did you talk about?"

"He told me about Jesus and how He was God's Son. He said that Jesus died on a cross for my sins and all I had to do was ask God to forgive me and believe that stuff about Jesus. He told me if I did those things, I would be forgiven and have eternal life."

"What did you do?"

"I told him I'd think about it."

"Did you?"

"That night I kept wakin' up and thinkin' about what that man said. When he came back the next day, I told him I wanted to do it. He told me to repeat a prayer after him, and that was it."

"How did you feel afterwards?"

"Kinda weird. I mean, I was still sittin' in my cell and all, but I felt like a weight had been lifted off me. It was kinda like for the first time since

I'd been down that I wasn't so angry. Let me ask you somethin', Doc. Are you a Christian?"

"Yeah, Jake, I sure am."

"Then you know what happened was a miracle and God's the reason I'm still breathin'. I don't know why. But I know He does."

Steve arrived at Hillside first, with Donnie and Karla not far behind. They were hardly inside the rear door of the church when Reverend Hurley met them and began telling them what he learned about Jeremiah. No one seemed very surprised when he mentioned the similarities with Marc Jones and suggested Marc might be a prophet.

Steve spoke next, summarizing his meeting with Kenny Wilson. "Kenny told me he didn't know how Marc had been convicted. He talked with a lawyer friend who lives in Goldsboro, where the trial was held. His friend told him Marc was convicted not so much because he violated the law, but because he offended some important people. The district attorney and the judge who presided over the trial were both members of the church where it happened. Kenny said based on that alone, he thought he could probably get Marc a new trial."

Donnie was clicking the button of his ballpoint pen. He stopped when Karla placed her hand on top of his.

"I met with Marc today and asked him who he was," Donnie said. "He turned the question around on me. I told him I didn't know who he was, but I explained to him why I thought he might be a prophet. He didn't say I was right, but on his way out of the room, he told me to pray for wisdom and guidance."

"That's pretty interesting considering my dream," Charles said.

"It gets better," Donnie said. "Before I left, I met with Jake Tomkins, the man who was brought back to life."

"Did he say it was Marc?" Steve asked.

"He said he didn't know the man. I'd say it's a very good possibility, though, considering the reports that say it was."

"I'll find out the name of the inmate that made the report," Steve said. "I'll talk with him tomorrow."

"You also could find out from the clinic if Marc was there when this happened," Karla said. "They should have a list of patients that were seen that day, and if not, you could always ask them to check his medical chart. If he was seen, there'll be a progress note for the visit."

Steve nodded. "I'll do that."

"Something else Jake told me, which you'll find interesting, is that he said he knew what happened was a miracle," Donnie explained. "He also said that whatever was going on was being led by God."

The room fell silent. After a few moments of reflection, Steve asked the question they all had been wondering. "Now what do we do?"

The previous night had been an informative evening for Lord Abdullah. He'd learned much about Abdurahman and was impressed that the man hadn't gotten flustered when the group got agitated. He liked how Abdurahman tried to use the situation to make a point. He also thought it was especially interesting how the prayer leader tried so hard to keep from disrespecting him in front of the others.

It's a shame that I won't think twice about disrespectin' you . . .

COLOSSIANS 1:13 "For he has rescued us from the one who rules in the kingdom of darkness, and he has brought us into the Kingdom of his dear Son."
(NLT)

Chapter 11
Friday

Donnie and Karla went out after the meeting at church. Over doughnuts and coffee, they generated more questions that needed answers. Things were becoming more difficult for Donnie to understand, and he was beginning to feel out of control.

Since his mother's death, Donnie had unknowingly built a lifestyle based on self-sufficiency. He learned not to trust people or to put himself in positions where he'd have to depend on them. He became obsessed with being in control, not just of his emotions but also over the outcome of situations, and he became very successful at assessing people and helping them solve their problems.

Until Donnie met Marc, his Christian walk was straightforward; he believed Jesus died on a cross for his sins and then rose from the grave. It didn't involve issues of control. Instead, it seemed logical. Now, however, the events that were transpiring were testing this logic, and he was having a hard time imagining how they would lead him to the promised ending.

That night, with these thoughts racing through his mind, Donnie finally fell asleep, only to be awakened by his pager. He called the prison and was informed an inmate had told officers he swallowed a razor blade and a handful of Remeron tablets. The nurse said the inmate had been sent to

Halifax Regional Medical Center in Roanoke Rapids for an evaluation. Donnie told her to place the inmate on self-harm precautions when he returned from the ER.

Unable to go back to sleep, Donnie finally got up and drove to Caledonia, arriving before shift change. He used the opportunity to talk with Captain Waters, the officer in charge.

Captain Waters had worked at Caledonia for twenty-four years, ever since graduating from Roanoke Rapids High School. He started as a correctional officer and obtained his current rank nine years later. A physically unimposing man, his respect came from his dedication to the job and his skill in reading inmates' behavior.

" 'Morning, Captain," Donnie said. "Seems like you've had a busy night." He sat down in front of the captain's well-organized desk.

"Ain't it a little early for you to be here? I didn't think you docs got outta bed 'til eight o'clock," Waters joked in a raspy voice, the byproduct of chain-smoking unfiltered Camel cigarettes for years.

"Yeah, yeah. I wish I had it as good as everybody thought I did. Maybe then I wouldn't have to carry this pager and could get some sleep every now and then. Speaking of a lack of sleep, you know anything about Jeff Charles, the inmate they woke me up about?"

"Yeah, I know Jeff real well," Waters answered between drags. "He's been here off and on for fifteen years or so. He's a pretty bad gambler and loses a lot. When he can't pay, he borrows and then tries to get transferred before he has to come up with money. This so-called suicide attempt probably just means his other methods haven't worked." He paused to light another cigarette off the one he was finishing. "When I heard he was on self-harm, I asked around and found out he owes Billy Ricks a hundred dollars, which means he'll probably end up having to pay back a couple hundred bucks."

"Sounds like trouble," Donnie said. "No wonder he wants to get away from here so bad."

"I guess the bad part is that he knows better and keeps on doing it. One day he's not gonna be able to get out in time and he's gonna end up dead."

"I hope you're wrong, Captain, but I imagine you're not. Thanks for the info. I'm going on over to the clinic. I have patients to see."

Donnie stopped by the clinic to pick up charts and check in with the nurses. Then he headed upstairs to the Unit 1 conference room to review his first patient's file. Ricardo Benson was twenty-eight years old and in prison for life plus ten years for first-degree murder. He'd been incarcerated for nine years, the last six of which had been spent in maximum custody at Caledonia. The referral form he completed indicated he'd been having bad dreams and wanted something to help him sleep.

When Ricardo entered the room, he didn't look up or speak. He hadn't shaved in days and had dark circles under his puffy eyes. His long hair was oily, and the spider-web tattoo on his left elbow let everyone know he'd killed someone.

"Mr. Benson, I'm Dr. Thompson. I received your request to be seen by mental health. What's going on?"

"I'm depressed and havin' trouble sleepin'," Ricardo said in an unsteady, barely audible voice. "When I finally fall asleep, I have a terrible nightmare."

"How long's this been going on?"

"I ain't ever had bad dreams like this," Ricardo explained. "I guess they started 'bout a week ago. You gotta help me, Doc. It's all I think about, whether I'm awake or asleep."

"Tell me about the dream."

"I'm in a woman's house in Wilmington, and I'm stabbin' her," Ricardo began softly, looking at the floor. "She's screamin' for help and a man appears outta nowhere, dressed in a white robe, holdin' a double-edged sword. Lightnin' is flashin' all around, and he's starin' at me with these scary eyes. His voice booms like thunder and he says, 'Woe to you for the evil you have done. Repent or endure the fires of hell for all eternity.' He waves his sword and the scene changes." He looked up. Donnie saw genuine fear in the man's eyes.

Ricardo quickly looked away, and his bottom lip began trembling. "There are people layin' everywhere and they're in terrible pain. They're bein' tortured and are beggin' to be allowed to die, but whatever has 'em refuses. That's when the red hot flames shoot up and start burnin' 'em." Ricardo closed his eyes. "I always wake up after that, soakin' wet."

He seems genuinely distressed . . . Is this a message or a warning? . . . Does the man in the dream represent anything? . . . What do I do now? . . .

Donnie considered how to respond and went with his instinct. "Ricardo, do you believe in God?"

Ricardo didn't respond for a long time. When he answered, he seemed hesitant. "I've been to church a few times but I didn't ever get into it. I mean, I've heard about God but I don't know. It seems like the only people that believe in Him are the weak ones. Seems they can't take care of themselves so they convince themselves that this God person will do it for 'em. I guess it makes 'em feel better."

"Do you think those people are afraid of their dreams?"

Ricardo fell silent and struggled against his handcuffs.

Donnie prepared for the worst and leaned back from the table. Then, gradually and with obvious effort, Ricardo relaxed. "No, I guess they ain't," he answered softly, avoiding eye contact. "Can you tell me about Him?"

Donnie spent an hour teaching Ricardo about Jesus and why God sent Him. He explained how Jesus gave his life on the cross and how God would forgive his sins, no matter how bad Ricardo thought they were. He explained that all Ricardo needed to do was repent and ask Him to come into his life.

"Will you help me? You know, show me how to do it?"

"Just talk to Him like you've been talking to me," Donnie said. "Tell Him what you're sorry for and ask Him for forgiveness. I'll be here to help if you get stuck."

Ricardo closed his eyes. There was a tremor in his voice. "God," he began, "I ain't sure about what I'm supposed to say. I've been really bad all of my life. I can't even remember all of the bad things I've done but I'm sorry, and if I could change 'em I would. You've gotta believe me." He stopped, not knowing what else to say.

"You're doing great Ricardo," Donnie encouraged. "Keep going."

"I guess the worst thing was murderin' Mrs. Williams. I wish I could take it back," he said, struggling to fight back the emotion that had been eating away at his heart for years. "I wish I'd never done it, that I'd never decided to break into her house and had just walked away. I know I can't change it now and I'm truly sorry for what I've done. I'm not sure how you can forgive somebody as bad as me, but this man here told me You could. I want to believe that more than anything. Please God . . . please."

Several moments passed. Donnie asked, "Ricardo, do you believe Jesus is God's Son and that He was sent to die for your sins?"

"Yes," he answered between sniffles.

Donnie fought back the tears forming in his eyes. After another moment, he said, "Amen." He looked across the table. Ricardo's eyes were still closed tightly, but he was smiling. When he looked up, he simply said thank you and asked what else he needed to do.

Donnie told him there was nothing else he could do. He explained that forgiveness and being saved were the result of God's grace.

"I know that God forgives sins, because He tells us in the Bible," Donnie said. He offered to get a Bible for Ricardo.

Ricardo stood up, thanked Donnie, and shook his hand. When he left, he was no longer afraid of his past or his future.

During his dorm-janitor duties, Abdurahman thought about what to say at Jumah. He doubted Lord Abdullah would attend. It wasn't the right forum for him to impress people with his secular intelligence. Abdurahman thought it would be a good time to begin preparing the men who would be there, the true Muslims, to face the assault on their faith that men like Lord Abdullah posed.

With this in mind, he spent the morning studying the *Qur'an* so he could remind his brothers what Allah had told his final prophet in regard to handling those who do not truly believe.

While Donnie waited for officers to get Billy Drake for a follow-up appointment, Donnie thought about the men he'd talked to about God. He felt very good about what had happened with Ricardo and patted himself on the back.

Sure, pride can be a terrible thing, but come on, who talked to those men? . . . Who led them to accept Christ? . . . Dr. Donnie Thompson . . . That's got to be the reason God wanted me here . . . He knows I have a talent for saving people . . .

Donnie was still stroking his ego when Billy shuffled in, slumped over and looking at the floor. His long, greasy hair looked as if it hadn't been combed in a month. His hollow, tired eyes gave him the appearance of a defeated man.

"Billy," Donnie said hesitantly, "what's going on? You don't look very good. Are you alright?"

"I ain't been sleepin' too good. I keep havin' this dream over and over."

Donnie set his pen down slowly.

Billy glanced up, but only briefly, and then looked away. "In my dream there's a man wearin' a white robe." He wore the same look of terror Donnie had seen on Ricardo's face earlier. "He's holdin' a sword and lightnin' is strikin' all around him. Everything he touches catches on fire, then turns brown and dies. I'm on the ground and he's standin' over me yellin' that I'm gonna suffer forever if I don't repent. He waves his sword and everything changes. I think I'm in hell, 'cause there's thousands of people layin' around with terrible sores all over their bodies. They're moanin' in pain and the man keeps sendin' red-hot flames to burn 'em."

"What are you doing in this part of the dream?"

"I'm just layin' there thinkin' 'bout all the terrible things I've done. Then I wake up in a cold sweat." Billy paused. "I ain't told no one but you about this. You gotta help me."

Donnie was stunned.

Two inmates having a similar dream . . . What're the chances of that? . . . Maybe they're trying to fool me . . . They seem too scared to be faking, though . . . Besides, what's the secondary gain if they are? . . . They both know they won't get sleep medication, and neither of them asked . . . Hold on a second . . . they said their dreams started about a week ago . . .

That was when Reverend Hurley had begun experiencing his dream.

Donnie quickly recovered and spent the rest of the session talking about God. He told Billy about God's grace and how to ask Him for forgiveness. He guided him through it like he'd done with Ricardo. When they finished, Billy, who took pride in being an extremely tough man, was reduced to tears. He apologized for his unmanly emotions. Then he thanked Donnie and shuffled toward the door.

"By the way Billy, what cell block are you in?"

"F block," he said, looking over his shoulder like he was suspicious of the question.

"Thanks." Donnie wondered if it was just a coincidence that this was the same block where Marc was housed.

He got up and told the officers who were getting patients for him that he had to take care of something. He left the prison to go back to his office. He suddenly felt he needed to get away from everything so he could think.

Sitting at his desk, he recalled what Ricardo had said about Christians being too weak to take care of themselves. Although Donnie knew it wasn't true, it did seem like all he was doing lately was running away from situations and praying for guidance about what to say or do.

This thought bothered him greatly because for the first time in many years, he realized that he was helpless.

Still think you're so big now, Dr. Thompson?

Friday was inmate payday, which also made it the day drug loans were due. But not even the thought of collecting a few thousand dollars elevated Lord Abdullah's mood. At breakfast, his most trusted lieutenant, Malique Mohammed, informed him that an officer had told him about a sting operation that was planned. She said she'd heard Lord Abdullah's name being mentioned.

If the information were true, it wouldn't be the first time he had been a target of the prison administration, and he was sure it wouldn't be the last. For some reason, though, he was more upset than usual about this one. He wasn't sure if it was because he'd been struggling with not being respected for his intelligence or whether it was just because he was tired of the hassle. Nevertheless, he decided to spend the day finding out what was being planned so he could take the necessary precautions and teach a few lessons.

Somebody's goin' to get schooled . . .

Donnie sat in his office for a few minutes to regain his composure before calling the clinic to let them know he was on the way back. The nurse on the phone told him his next two patients had refused treatment. She asked if he wanted to see Jeff Charles. He told her that would be great. He grabbed a protein drink before heading over.

When Donnie arrived at Unit 1, Jeff was leaning back in a gray plastic chair in the multipurpose room. The officers went to sit in the hall when Donnie entered.

"I can't believe you put me on cold steel," Jeff growled as Donnie sat down. "All the other Docs always sent me to CP mental health. You know, if you don't send me pretty soon, I'm really gonna hurt myself. I've done it before."

"Why are you trying so hard to leave here, Mr. Charles?"

"I'm just depressed," Jeff answered with a smirk. "Why won't you send me?"

"I don't think you're mentally ill. I think you *are* trying to manipulate the system to get a transfer."

Jeff cussed. When that didn't work, he tried insults. "You think you're so much smarter than everybody else. Well, you ain't nothin' man!"

"Who do you owe money to, Mr. Charles?" Donnie asked, catching him off guard.

Jeff feigned surprise. "I ain't got no idea what you're talking about."

"Hmm . . . I see. So, you're telling me you're still having thoughts about hurting yourself?"

"Look, I said if you don't send me outta here, I'm gonna do something to somebody."

"Okay, then, I guess I don't have any choice but to keep you on cold steel." Donnie motioned to the officers to come get Jeff.

"I'm gonna kill you when I get outta here!" Jeff screamed as the officers led him out the door.

Unfazed, Donnie never looked up while signing the self-harm order.

"I believe we gotta pay attention to what people say, because sometimes they try to tempt us to do the wrong thing. In the *Holy Qur'an*, chapter nine, verse seventy-three, Allah, all praise and glory be upon him, tells us: 'O Prophet! Strive hard against the unbelievers and the hypocrites, and be firm against them. Their abode is Hell—an evil refuge indeed.'

"I think what this means is that the unbelievers will come against us and we're supposed to resist them," Abdurahman said. "The way we do that is to stand firm, and as it says in chapter twenty-five, verse fifty-two, '. . . strive against them with the utmost strenuousness.' In my opinion, this means we gotta stick to the things we know come from Allah, peace and glory be upon him.

"I also believe Allah, peace and all glory be upon him forever, wants us to show patience and restraint in these situations. In chapter sixteen, verses one hundred twenty-six and one hundred twenty-eight, it tells us that Allah is with those who restrain themselves and that it's better to be patient in a conflict. With these things in mind, I don't think it's too hard for us to think of how our enemies come against us in prison.

"Well, the same thing happens when unbelievers attack our faith, only it ain't so direct. Usually it happens when someone disagrees with us about somethin' we believe. They debate with us and tell us lots of reasons why they're correct. When we don't stand firm against them or lose our cool, we become corrupted. In a way, we become vulnerable, and then that person comes back and attacks our faith even more directly until finally, we're left with nothin'. For these reasons, brothers, pay attention to what people say and think about the meanin' of their words. By doin' this, standin' firm, and showin' restraint, Allah, all peace and praise and glory be upon him, will bless us tremendously."

Donnie finished Jeff's progress note while the officers went to get Marc Jones. Marc entered with the same inviting smile he always seemed to have, but to Donnie's surprise, he spoke before he sat down.

"How are you, Dr. Thompson?"

"I've had better days," Donnie answered without much thought.

Marc didn't respond. He looked at Donnie as if he were deciding for himself.

"Tell me," Donnie said. "What do you know about the dreams the men in F block are having?"

Not seeming surprised by the question, Marc answered without blinking. "You're correct. God is working on those men. But before this is over, you'll see many more miraculous things than that."

Donnie's thoughts raced, but before he could respond, Marc asked, "Tell me, why are you feeling so helpless?"

"How'd you know what I was thinking?" Donnie waited for an answer, but didn't get one. "I'm tired of this. You've gotta tell me what you want." He was speaking loudly enough that the officers seated in the hallway heard and leaned their heads in.

"You shouldn't be surprised," Marc responded. "If you believe God can give someone the power to move a mountain through faith the size of a mustard seed, then certainly you can believe that He can give me the ability to know your thoughts. So, I ask again, why are you feeling helpless?"

Donnie stared at Marc. His frustration dissipated, and he sorted through his confusion.

This man is telling me God has given him special powers . . . I know he's not psychotic . . . Why's he doing this?

Sighing, Donnie answered, "I'm not sure."

"Dr. Thompson, dependence on God is necessary for doing His work. It's a sign of being broken and characteristic of the only one that's served Him perfectly. Because of this, you should constantly strive for dependence on Him and know that His perfect will is always going to take you to where He wants you to be, when He wants you to be there."

The notion of giving up control was the scariest thing anyone could have told Donnie to do.

"I'm aware you love God, Dr. Thompson," Marc said matter-of-factly. "The problem is, you've only given Him part of your life, not all of it. You've been holding back."

This was too much to handle. Donnie defensively began adding up the things he'd done for God.

I've done everything God has wanted me to do for the last several months . . . I haven't missed a Sunday service . . . I've given more than ten percent of my income to the church . . . I've volunteered my time to help others . . . I've witnessed to people and brought them to Christ . . . I came here to the middle of nowhere 'cause I thought that's what He wanted . . . Now, this inmate is saying it still isn't enough . . .

"No, it's not enough," Marc responded, as if reading Donnie's thoughts. "For all of those things, you'll do ten things wrong. You aren't perfect. No one is, except Jesus, and even He didn't earn His way in to heaven. Instead, He became dependent on His Father, God."

"So what do you want from me?" Donnie asked.

"You have to give Him your life," Marc answered patiently. "All of it. Not just part of it."

There's no way I can do that . . . What am I supposed to do, pray twenty-four hours a day? . . . What's wrong with how I've been doing things? . . .

"Okay, Mr. Jones, what am I supposed to do?" Donnie asked flatly.

Marc smiled. "You already know the answer." He stood to leave.

Donnie knew Marc was right. The problem wasn't what to do; the problem was how to do it.

Officer Sarah Hunter was twenty-two years old and had been at Caledonia for five months. Prior to that she had been unemployed and had never worked at the same job for more than a few weeks before quitting for one reason or another. Until recently, she and her two-year-old daughter lived with her mother in a trailer park outside of Weldon. She had supported herself with welfare checks and food stamps. A few months ago, Sarah's mother became engaged for the fourth time, and her future husband wanted Sarah to be with him also, or she and her daughter had to leave. Sarah left and went to find a job. Since Caledonia always had openings, she applied and was given a job a few days later. The twenty-one-thousand-dollar-a-year salary she was offered was more money than she had thought she'd ever be paid.

Sarah was assigned to Unit 3, where Malique Mohammed approached her and offered her twenty dollars to let him make an unscheduled, not to mention unauthorized, phone call. Thinking the extra money would be nice to have and that it wouldn't hurt to let an inmate who was so respectful and polite call his dying grandmother, she agreed.

That was three months ago. Since then, Sarah had gotten to know Malique very well. He seemed like a nice man who was in prison for something he didn't do. She liked the way he paid attention to how she looked, and how he cared if she had enough money. When she didn't, he found ways to help her out. So Sarah had no problem telling Malique what she'd overheard Captain Burnette and Lieutenant Alexander discussing.

Donnie went home after seeing several more patients experiencing bad dreams. Two men wanted help asking for forgiveness and accepting Christ, one said he would think about it, and the others threatened to kill Donnie if he didn't get them medication.

It seemed odd that while so many inmates said they were having a nightmare, they didn't seem to know that other inmates were experiencing something similar. Donnie wondered if this was because the men were frightened and didn't want to discuss it, since fear was seen as a sign of weakness, or if God was preventing them from talking. At first, this seemed ludicrous.

Then he remembered what Marc had said.

If God can make a mountain move through faith as small as a mustard seed . . .

"Mr. Jackson," Sarah said respectfully, "it's good to see you."

Lord Abdullah wasn't particularly upset that she didn't use his Five Percent name. Most officers didn't. Besides, she'd shown him respect by referring to him as mister. He decided to overlook it. "My good friend Malique was definitely right about you. You really are a beautiful lady."

"Did he really say that?" Sarah asked. She was not used to hearing compliments about her looks.

Sure he did . . . NOT . . .

"Yes, ma'am. He also said you're the kind of person that helps a brother out if he's bein' treated wrong."

If given enough money . . .

Feeling better than she had in ten years, Sarah blushed and was at a loss for words.

Lord Abdullah read his prey perfectly and pressed on. "Malique also told me you got the 411 'bout us 'dis mornin'."

"Yes, sir. I heard the captain and lieutenant saying how they was gonna get you once and for all. I didn't hear everything, but from what I could tell, I think they're gonna try to set y'all up. It sounded like it had somethin' to do with drugs, but I couldn't swear to it."

"Did you hear 'em say who they was gonna use?"

"No, sir, I didn't. Want me to find out?"

"Won't you get in trouble?" Lord Abdullah asked, as if he cared.

"I don't mind," Sarah answered, desperately wanting to demonstrate how willing she was to help. Not only did Lord Abdullah have money, he was also able to see the beauty hidden inside her almost two-hundred-and-fifty-pound body. "I'd be happy to help."

"I sure would appreciate it," he said, reaching into his pocket and watching Sarah's eyes light up as he discretely slid a twenty into her hand. "It's a shame the po-lice have to do stuff like this to innocent men."

ROMANS 16:17,18 "I urge you, brothers, to watch out for those who cause divisions and put obstacles in your way that are contrary to the teaching you have learned. Keep away from them. For such people are not serving our Lord Christ, but their own appetites. By smooth talk and flattery they deceive the minds of naïve people."
(NIV)

Chapter 12
Saturday Morning

When Officer Hunter got home, she was too excited to sleep. She and several officers had met at Dillon's for a drink after work, and Lieutenant Alexander had been there. He seemed intoxicated and started bragging to his date about a sting operation he was involved in. It was obvious he was trying to impress the woman, so Sarah inserted herself into the conversation by boosting his ego. He told her everything she wanted to know. Later, at her newly rented trailer, she made notes about everything Alexander said so she wouldn't forget.

Donnie went to bed thinking about the times in his life when he'd tried to do things his way instead of God's way. Looking back, he realized he hadn't recognized there was another way to do things, since he didn't know God then or care about anything except himself. With this in mind, Cassidy LaClare's face flashed across his mind.

Cassidy was nine years old when Donnie saw her for the first time in the child psychology clinic at Charity Hospital. He'd been an intern doing his child rotation when Cassidy's mother, a crack addict, brought her in to be seen. Cassidy was having behavioral problems and had recently been suspended from school for the fifth time in three years. Donnie saw her weekly for four months, and her grades and behavior improved, which made him look good to his supervisors.

After that, his confidence grew too big too fast, and he no longer listened to his professors. He thought he knew all the answers, and much against the advice of his clinical supervisor, he discontinued seeing Cassidy because he believed she no longer had a problem.

Five weeks later, she took her mother's gun and shot a boy after arguing over a bicycle.

Donnie thought about Cassidy as he drove to Karla's. *Would things have been different if I'd only been willing to listen? Was that a time in my life when God was using people in my world to talk to me and I refused to hear?* His eyes filled with tears, and he knew the answer. As he turned into Karla's driveway, he prayed for help to realize when he was making that mistake again.

Still sitting in his truck, lost in thought, Donnie didn't realize Karla had come out until she tapped on the window. "Hello, earth to Dr. Thompson."

Caught off guard, Donnie tried to play it off while opening the door. "I was wondering when you'd get here."

"Nice try, but it looked like you were in another world."

"You're right, I was."

"What's going on?"

"I've been thinking about our meetings and the things Marc told me yesterday. You know, the stuff about listening to God and doing things His way, instead of ours."

"Yeah, I've been thinking about that, too."

Donnie told her about Cassidy, and about wanting God to take over his life. "The only thing is, I'm not sure I'm strong enough to do it," he said. "It's so hard for me to give up control."

"I know what you mean." Karla hugged him tightly.

Donnie pulled back and looked into her eyes. "Do you think maybe it would be okay if I kissed you?"

"I think I would really like that," she answered softly.

She leaned forward, and their lips met for the first time.

Standing at her duty post outside Unit 3, Sarah wondered if Lieutenant Alexander remembered what happened at Dillon's. Earlier, at roll call, he seemed hung over, so she guessed he probably didn't. Still, she knew she had to be careful when talking to Malique, because if she was seen, someone might link her to whatever was going to happen.

She waited for Malique to return from setting up chairs in the visitation area so she could speak with him as he passed by.

"Hey, I found out something last night you should know," she whispered, turning the key in the bar door to let him in the unit.

"When can we talk?" he asked, bending over to tie his shoe.

"Come back in fifteen minutes when I open up the yard," she answered without looking down. "We can talk then."

"Yes ma'am, Ms. Hunter." Malique winked at her.

On Highway 64, Karla sat close to Donnie on the bench seat. Holding hands, they sang along with the radio and enjoyed how right it felt to be together, both sensing something special was happening between them.

"Dr. Thompson," Karla said, looking out the window as they rode along the four-lane highway bordered on both sides by acres of pine trees, "what do you have planned for us today?"

"Well, I thought after lunch, we could go to Pullen Park and just goof around. The park used to be really pretty this time of year with all of the flowers blooming."

"That sounds like fun. Do you think instead of going out to eat we could have a picnic?"

"I guess that could be arranged, Dr. Lynch. It'll cost you though."

"Really? How much?"

"Either a million dollars or a kiss."

"Hmm . . . tough choice. I don't have a million dollars, so I guess it'll have to be a kiss."

Donnie shrugged. "They're worth about the same thing."

Walking toward the end of the cell block where Officer Hunter was standing, Malique wondered what she needed to tell him. He'd been playing her for a few months and hoped she didn't want to tell him something crazy like she loved him. It had happened before, and that situation had ended with him telling the superintendent that the officer was putting pressure on him to have a relationship with her. Sure, it was a lie, but there was no way he was going to get involved with a woman that was not only of no use to him but also dumb enough to fall in love with an inmate who would never leave prison.

"Whatta you gotta tell me baby?" Malique asked after she shut the bar door behind them.

"You ain't gonna believe this," she said excitedly.

Whew . . . At least it don't sound like the "I love you" talk . . .

"Whatever it is, it must be good," Malique observed. "You seem like you're 'bout to bust open."

"Well, I figured you and Lord Abdullah would like to know 'bout the sting operation bein' set up against you."

That changes everything . . .

"Whatta you know?" he asked, trying to decide how much to pay her without appearing to want the information too badly.

"Let's just say I can tell you the man's name and when it's supposed to go down."

This is almost too good to be true . . . It's amazin' what these women will do to hear some compliments and make a few bucks . . .

"That's some serious information, Officer Hunter, 'cause you know neither me or Lord Abdullah can afford this kind of undeserved trouble while our cases are on appeal." He knew she had no idea he'd never leave prison.

"I know what you mean," Sarah said. "I feel terrible askin' for anything, but you know 'bout my daughter and all."

"Sure I do."

"Well," she said, unable to finish.

"Would five hundred dollars help out?" he asked, knowing it would and that the information was worth a lot more.

"Yes, sir," Sarah answered, imaging the things she could buy with all that money.

Malique reached into his gray pants for the cash, and Sarah told him everything without checking her notepad once.

"I can't believe how much things have changed since I was a kid," Donnie observed as they approached Raleigh. "When I was little, the beltline ended here." They crossed over I-440, passing Wake Medical Center on the hill to their left.

"Wow, you're getting old," Karla joked and squeezed his arm.

"I remember going to the hospital behind there," he said, pointing behind Wake Med. "It's a psychiatric hospital my mom used to go to."

As Donnie recalled the difficult times his mom experienced while he was growing up, Karla quietly held his hand. Donnie smiled. "It's been a while since I've thought about that place."

"I bet there's a lot of things you haven't thought about that being back home will bring up," Karla empathized.

"I'm sure you're right," Donnie said. "You know what, though? I'm happy you're here with me."

"Are you?"

"Yeah, a little bit," Donnie answered nonchalantly.

"Just a little bit?"

"Yeah." Donnie grinned. "Just a little bit more than you can imagine."

"This is almost too good to be true," Malique exclaimed. "Officer Hunter said James Ellis is gonna try to set us up."

"You mean that old, skinny white dude that transferred back to Unit 2 a month ago?" Lord Abdullah asked.

"Yeah, that's him. She said he's been makin' small purchases from Dashon in order to gain our trust and that he's gonna make a big buy next week. He's gonna tell Dashon he has to order it from you and he's gonna be wearin' a wire."

"I see." Lord Abdullah tried with difficulty to control his escalating rage. "Whatta you know 'bout Ellis?"

"Not much 'cept he's in for assault and has 'bout fifteen years to do. I don't think he's got any family or nothin' 'cause he never gets mail or visits. Dashon and the other boys on two-side ain't never had no problems wit' him."

"What makes Officer Hunter so sure it's him?"

Malique told Lord Abdullah about the conversation she'd overheard in the bar and how she'd gotten the lieutenant to tell her more.

Like all intelligent men Lord Abdullah knew or had seen on television, he quietly reflected on the situation before ruthlessly deciding what to do.

"Malique," he said cheerfully, "get Roger Spivey and bring him to me. Tell him I'm gonna give him a chance to pay off his debt."

This might only be business, but I sure do enjoy my work . . .

Karla gazed around as they crossed the wooden bridge to the island in the middle of Pullen Park Lake.

"This is beautiful, Donnie." She spread the blanket they'd found in his toolbox on the ground. "Can we rent a paddle boat and ride around the lake after we eat?"

"I don't think that'll be a problem, but it's gonna cost you."

She rolled her eyes. "Seems like you charge for everything. How much this time?"

"Well, everything has its price, especially if you're going to pay," he said, and she laughed. "You know something? The park seems a lot prettier than I remember it."

"Really?"

"It sure does." He looked around like he was trying to figure out why. "Maybe it has something to do with you being here with me now."

Roger Spivey had been at Caledonia off and on since his second drug conviction eleven years ago. While doing his time, he'd received another sentence for selling marijuana in prison, and until a few years ago, he'd been the primary dealer on the farm. Since then, Roger had gone from being a big-time pusher to an ordinary user who was now deeply in debt.

Lord Abdullah looked at him without respect. "Roger, I got a little job for ya."

"How can I help?" Roger answered, as if he had a choice.

"I got a situation with James Ellis."

"I know that dude." Roger didn't ask what James had done. It was none of his business, and Lord Abdullah would tell him whatever he wanted him to know.

"He's been dis'in' me and needs to be taught a lesson. I want you to handle that for me this afternoon."

"Yes sir," Roger replied, knowing what needed to be done.

Officer Hunter's duty post changed when inmate visitation began, and she reported to the recreation yard to supervise inmates who didn't have visitors. It was her job to open the gate to let inmates on and off the yard after frisking them for contraband. She also walked around to check in on groups that formed to make sure they were obeying the prison's rules.

She approached Lord Abdullah and the Five Percenters standing on the field ciphering. She made eye contact with Lord Abdullah but didn't speak. He nodded and the men turned to look at her.

"How are you today, Officer Hunter?" Malique commented. "You sure do look nice. You've done somethin' different wit' your hair. It looks real good."

"Thank you." Sarah blushed.

Lord Abdullah made an unnecessary show of sniffing the air. Even a dead man could have smelled the cheap perfume she'd more than generously applied. "And you're smellin' good, too."

"Look, you better stop now," Sarah said, not meaning it.

"Sorry, I just can't help it." Lord Abdullah smiled sheepishly. "I'll try to control myself in the future."

Okay then," she said, disappointed. "Well, the reason I'm over here is to make sure y'all ain't doin' anything you ain't supposed to be. You ain't, are you?" she asked, as if they'd tell her.

"No, ma'am," Malique said respectfully. "We're just standin' 'round talkin' about people."

"Anyone in particular?"

"Well, we're tryin' to decide who the hottest officer is. And you won." Malique was laying it on thick, trying not to laugh.

"You're just sayin' that."

"No, ma'am," Dashon joined in. "That's exactly what we was just talkin' about."

Sarah's cheeks turned red. Not only had she made five hundred dollars, but men were telling her things she'd always wanted to hear. It couldn't get much better than this. She walked away with a smile so bright it totally blinded her judgment.

Donnie couldn't remember the last time he had so much fun doing something as simple as paddling a boat around a lake. The sunny spring day added to the experience, but he knew the biggest part of it was Karla. Not only was she beautiful, she was incredibly insightful. Listening to her talk made him feel alive, and seeing her smile made him feel like a flower touched by the first ray of sunshine on a bright, spring morning. It gave him hope, and for the first time in quite a while, it allowed him to dream of a future with someone else in it.

At five feet five inches tall and one hundred and forty-three pounds, Roger Spivey was lucky if he could even move the steel bar used to hold the weights, much less lift the rusted plates attached to the ends. Years of smoking dope and any other drug he could find had taken its toll on his strength and left him with little desire to physically exert himself. He was a burnout who had fried his brain a long time ago, and now he settled on getting his exercise rolling cigarettes and watching TV. Nevertheless, he stood at the weight pile and pretended to be interested in lifting so he could watch James Ellis in the exercise yard and surprise him when he returned to the unit.

James Ellis was no stranger to the Department of Correction. He had been incarcerated four times before his most recent conviction of assaulting a government official. He had been on parole after his third DWI when his parole officer decided to pay him an unexpected visit at his run-down shack in rural Leland, North Carolina. He was intoxicated and in violation of his parole, and he knew he would have to go back to prison and serve out the rest of his sentence. Scared, he'd panicked and ran out the door, knocking the officer off balance in the process. She quickly regained her footing and apprehended James without incident, but charged him with assault anyway. He was given an additional ten-year sentence on top of finishing the remaining time on his DWI conviction.

Karla felt like she'd found the answer to her prayers. Donnie was the most attractive man she'd ever met, not just because he was handsome but because she admired his faith. He was shy, but he seemed to be attracted to her, too, and much more importantly, he valued her opinions. He listened to what she said and felt what she described. She had never dated someone who wasn't afraid to admit he wasn't the smartest person in the world and was comfortable with who he was. Sure, she knew that Donnie, like her, had skeletons in the closet. But she felt they could work through them. God had brought them together. Too many things had happened for it to be by chance.

James knew that if everything went the way it was planned, he would be home in less than a month, enjoying the bright sunshine in his front yard instead of a prison yard. He thought about these things as he walked around the Five Percenters who were ciphering at the entrance to the yard. When he glanced over at them, he realized he didn't have any feelings about setting them up. And it really didn't matter to him what they believed or did as long as it didn't affect him. His involvement in the sting was simple; the police had something he wanted back . . . his freedom.

He finished his walk and passed by the Five Percenters again on his way back to the unit, looking for any indication that they might know something was going on.

Not perceiving any strange looks, James walked on toward the weight pile. Roger saw him approach and made a big deal out of telling everyone he was going back inside for his cigarettes.

At the gate to the inner yard, Officer Hunter went through the motions of frisking James and Roger before opening it and letting them in. As they walked toward the corner entrance of the building, neither man talked. The ciphering on the yard ceased as the Five Percenters stared intently at the men walking away.

Officer Hunter opened the steel door to let James and Roger into the building and locked it behind them. The two men walked down the narrow hallway toward the door at the other end. Roger, walking slightly behind the much taller James, reached into his baggy gray pants and quietly pulled out a seven-inch, razor sharp steel shank.

James never knew what lit the back of his neck on fire. He crumpled on the concrete floor as his entire body went numb. He desperately tried to stand but couldn't move his arms or legs.

The last thing he remembered before closing his eyes forever was Roger standing over him, grabbing a handful of his hair, and lifting his head off the floor to pull the shank across his throat.

James was dead by the time the officers found him stuffed in the corner of the hallway behind the plastic trashcans, but the medical staff was called nonetheless. The Halifax County Sheriff's Department was brought in, and an investigation was begun. Everyone suspected Lord Abdullah and the Five Percenters were behind the murder, but they also knew no one was going to come forward and talk.

Officer Hunter was interviewed, and said she remembered Roger and James leaving the yard together. Roger was questioned. A search of his property turned up a bloody shank stuffed inside his mattress, and he was formally charged with first-degree murder.

Investigators attempted to interview Lord Abdullah about his involvement, but he refused to cooperate. At several points during the interview, he told investigators he wasn't sorry James was gone and that he supposed his death would probably cause lots of problems, alluding to the sting operation that had been planned. Lord Abdullah was placed on administrative segregation in Unit 1 while the investigation continued, but everyone knew they couldn't keep him there for long.

Donnie and Karla turned in the paddleboat and had to pay a small fee for keeping it out too long. Neither of them wanted the day to end. On the way to the parking lot, they decided to go to a movie when they got back to Rocky Mount.

Donnie's pager went off during the drive home, and he used his cell phone to call the prison. The switchboard operator told him the lead nurse wanted to speak with him and transferred the call.

"Clinic, this is Nurse Fisher."

"Ms. Fisher, this is Dr. Thompson. You paged?"

"Yes sir," she replied. "We had an inmate get stabbed this afternoon."

"That's terrible. How can I help?"

"Mr. Powell wanted me to page you and get you to come talk with an officer that was involved."

"Sure," Donnie said. "It'll probably take me about two hours to get there, but please tell him that I'm on my way."

ZECHARIAH 8:16 "These are the things you are to do: Speak the truth to each other, and render true and sound judgment in your courts . . . "
(NIV)

Chapter 13

Saturday Evening

Arriving at Caledonia, Donnie parked behind two unmarked cars in front of the main gate and went into the prison lobby, where he saw Mr. Powell talking with two Halifax County detectives in the assistant superintendent's office. Across the hall, two distraught officers were sitting at a desk, writing. In a back room, a heavy-set female officer was talking animatedly with the captain.

"Dr. Thompson," the front lobby officer said from behind a tall wooden desk, "Mr. Powell's expecting you. Go ahead on in." He pointed toward the office on his left.

"Thanks." Donnie opened the door.

"Dr. Thompson," Powell announced without standing, "this is Detective McCoy and Detective Paulson."

Donnie shook each man's hand.

"Doc's our new psychologist," Powell said. "He's actually been here for almost two weeks now."

"That's a record for y'all, isn't it?" McCoy joked.

"Well, we haven't really tested him yet," Powell replied, a bit more seriously than Donnie liked. "I imagine this'll be a good start though." He gave Donnie a summary of what happened. "I want you to talk with Officer Hunter and find out what she knows. She's been very uncooperative so far."

"Is there a place we can talk in private?" Donnie asked.

"Sure, use the office across the hall. I'll have her report to you when she's finished talking with the captain."

"Yes, sir." Donnie headed across the hall.

So much for spending the evening with an angel . . .

While waiting for Officer Hunter, Donnie called Karla to let her know he wouldn't be able to go to the movie.

"I'll call later if it isn't too late," he told her. As they were saying goodbye, Officer Hunter knocked hard on the door.

"Come in," Donnie said, more politely than he felt.

Sarah's obesity made her waddle. She had an extravagant hairdo and wore thick makeup. Her half-inch fingernails were glossy and bright red, and she smelled like she'd used a whole bottle of perfume. It seemed to Donnie that she was trying very hard to impress someone.

"Sir," she hissed, "I don't know why I'm here but I need to go home. I've been here all day now."

"Officer Hunter, I'm Dr. Thompson, the prison psychologist."

"I know who you is, and I don't care. I ain't done nothin' wrong and I sure ain't crazy."

"So why do you think Mr. Powell wants us to talk?"

"I done told you I don't know."

"Do you think we can sit down and try to figure it out?"

She rolled her eyes. "Whatever."

Donnie motioned to a chair across the room and shut the door. He sat across from her instead of behind the desk, demonstrating he wasn't a threat and had nothing to hide. "How long have you worked here, Officer Hunter?"

"I don't know," she answered with an exaggerated sigh. "A few months. What difference do it make?"

"I'm just curious. I've only been here for a few weeks. It seems like a rough place."

"Man, you don't know nothin'. You oughtta try workin' inside eight hours a day. Then you'd know."

"I imagine you've seen a lot," Donnie offered, trying to draw her out.

"Yeah, I have. Stuff you'd never imagine."

"What made you decide to go into corrections?"

"What do you mean? You make it sound like this is my dream job or somethin'. I mean, man, this is the only work I could get."

"It sounds like you don't feel you had much of a choice."

"Nah, I just had to do somethin' besides flippin' burgers."

"Yeah, those jobs don't pay a lot do they?"

She glared at him. "Not when you got a child to support."

"Is the pay for a correctional officer pretty good?"

"It's okay," she answered hesitantly. "Man, why you so interested in how much money I make?"

"You said you had a child to support and needed a job that paid more than flipping burgers. I asked because I'm not sure how much more you make doing this."

"Yeah, whatever," she replied. "I'm pretty sure that's not what Mr. Powell wanted us to talk about anyway."

"Well, what do you think was his reason?"

Putting her guard back up, she answered harshly. "I done told you I don't know. How many times do I gotta keep tellin' you?"

Realizing he was getting nowhere, Donnie turned up the heat. "Why do you think that man was stabbed today?"

"Look, I don't know," she responded, a bit too quickly. "Why should I know? I ain't no mind reader."

"Well, you're sure upset that I asked," Donnie pointed out, forcing her hand.

"Yeah, I sure am," she responded, staring intensely.

Comfortable with silence, Donnie didn't respond. Instead, he looked back without emotion. Sarah soon began looking around the room, unable to maintain her stare. Her leg started trembling. She put her hands over her face and began to cry.

Donnie had learned not to be unnerved by tears. He waited without saying anything that would let her off the hook. After a minute, Sarah wiped her eyes and shifted in her seat. "Look, Dr. Thompson," she said between sniffles, "I can't take this no more. I gotta tell you somethin'."

Donnie leaned back to grab a box of tissues and placed them on the table beside her.

"I know who killed James," she began. Then she told Donnie everything she could remember except for Lord Abdullah's role. She figured she already had enough trouble. She'd just found out firsthand what happened to people who crossed Lord Abdullah.

Lord Abdullah was in Unit 1 on administrative segregation while staff went through the motions of investigating his involvement in James' death, so Malique got the opportunity to be in charge. The other Five Percenters were coming to him for advice on how to move the drugs that were brought in during visitation. Of course, the big decisions still had to be approved by Lord Abdullah, but nevertheless, Malique was getting high on the feelings that went along with being a leader. It also gave him a better understanding of Lord Abdullah's importance and how the power he wielded had life and death consequences for anyone he judged unfavorably.

When, Sarah went back to sit with the captain, Donnie called Karla to let her know he was going to be at the prison late. She told him she understood and that she appreciated his calling to let her know.

"Can I take you to church tomorrow?" he asked.

"I'd be disappointed if you didn't."

"I can't wait to see you. Good night, Karla."

"I'll be thinking of you," she said. "Good night."

They hung up. With a grin on his face, Donnie went to see Powell.

Powell was still in with the detectives. While Donnie waited for them to finish, he thought about Karla. In the midst of the ugliness around him, he didn't feel negatively affected. Instead, it felt like the stranger things became, the closer he grew to Karla.

It's amazing how God takes care of us and uses the things He puts in our world to build a fortress around our heart . . .

Detective McCoy opened the door and motioned for Donnie to come in.

"What do you think, Doc?" Powell asked, still seated behind the desk.

"Officer Hunter certainly provided some scary information," Donnie said. "Well, at least to someone who's not used to this kind of thing yet."

"I guess you got her to talk, then," Detective Paulson observed. "That's something right there."

"Yes sir, but it wasn't easy. She's very defensive and feels pretty guilty about her role in what happened. That's probably why she's acting so hostile."

"That's kind of what we thought, too," Paulson said.

Donnie told them what Sarah had said about her involvement with Malique and the Five Percenters. "I had no idea there was a gang problem here at Caledonia," he commented.

"What do you mean? We don't have a gang problem at Caledonia," Mr. Powell said forcefully. "I'm the only gang here."

"Well, sir," Donnie replied, as respectfully as possible, "from what Officer Hunter told me about the Five Percenters, it sounds like they're involved in a lot of things around here."

Powell shifted slightly in his high-backed chair and spoke directly to Donnie. "Doc, what I'm about to tell you stays here. You're not to discuss it with anyone else. If you do, it could mean people might get seriously hurt or worse. Do you understand?"

"Yes, sir," Donnie answered hesitantly.

"We know about the Five Percenters, and so does the Halifax County Drug Task Force. That's why these men are here." He nodded toward the detectives. "But make sure that you understand, I'm still the one that runs this place."

"Yes, sir."

McCoy propped his foot on the desk. "You see, Doc, we've got reason to believe that a big portion of the drugs coming into Halifax County have a connection to gang members here at Caledonia."

"Are you saying Malique Mohammed and the Five Percenters are controlling drugs not only in here, but also in Roanoke Rapids?" Donnie asked.

"Yes and no," Paulson answered, glancing at Powell. "Yes, they're involved in the flow of drugs, but no, it's not Malique Mohammed who's running it. Members of the Five Percent Nation of Islam are spread out up and down the East Coast, and one of the leaders is here at Caledonia." He looked at Powell again, who nodded for him to continue.

"Tony Jackson, who likes to be called Lord Abdullah, is the gang leader here at Caledonia, and we believe he's pretty high up in the overall organization. Malique is second in command around here and is really just a minor player."

"He might be a minor player, but I think he had a big part in the stabbing that happened this afternoon," Donnie replied, and told them how he was involved.

"Hmmm . . . that's very interesting." Powell picked up the phone to call the captain and tell him to come to the office. While they waited, he turned back to Donnie. "Doc, do you have any idea how Ms. Hunter became involved with the Five Percenters?"

"Well, I don't think it happened all at once," Donnie answered. "It was a process she was probably unaware of."

The captain knocked and entered the office.

"Captain, I need you to do a couple of things," Powell said. "I need you to put Malique Mohammed in handcuffs and leg irons and bring him up front. These men need to speak with him, and then he'll be going to Unit 1. I also want you to get Ms. Hunter's ID card and anything else she has that belongs to us. A female deputy is coming to take her into custody. Finally, I want everything from Lieutenant Alexander's desk and personnel file brought to me. When is he scheduled to work again?"

"I'm not sure," the captain said, "but I'll find out."

"Good, I need to know that."

"Yes, sir. Is there anything else?" The captain still stood at attention.

"No, that's it for now," Powell said.

The captain left.

Powell smoothly shifted his attention. "Now, Doc, tell us about how Ms. Hunter got involved with the Five Percenters."

Donnie recognized he was being tested. "I think she was skillfully manipulated," he answered carefully. "I bet when she first started working here, she didn't have a fancy hairdo or wear lots of makeup."

"No, she didn't," Powell agreed.

"Well, I imagine that Malique identified her as someone he could manipulate because of her size and low self-esteem. Once he identified her, he probably made it his mission to be in close physical proximity to her so they could talk and he could learn things he could use. Things like whether she had children, was married, or had financial problems."

"Pretty good so far, Doc," Smith offered.

"After that, I imagine he started giving her compliments she'd probably never heard. It boosted her self-esteem. He may have told her she looked nice, or 'when I get out of here, we're going to be together.' In her case, he probably even gave her money. Then, once she was hooked, she couldn't get away, even if she wanted to."

"How long did you say Doc's been working here?" Paulson asked Powell. "He might even be around for another two weeks if you're lucky."

The others laughed. Donnie could only smile and wonder.

1 CORINTHIANS 15:28 "Then, when he has conquered all things, the Son will present himself to God, so that God who gave his Son authority over all things, will be utterly supreme over everything everywhere." (NLT)

Chapter 14

Sunday

Malique was arrested and charged with conspiracy to commit murder. It was a tough break, but Lord Abdullah was only concerned about what it meant for his business. With both of them locked up in Unit 1, Pete Holloway, a.k.a. Al-Shirazi Khomeini, was now in charge, making Lord Abdullah uneasy. Pete was completely loyal, but he was inexperienced and could make many mistakes, costing large sums of money. This would cause trouble for Lord Abdullah's superiors out on the street and bring him problems he didn't need. Lord Abdullah had to find a way to get back to regular population quickly so he could take care of business and keep from having that stress-related dream again.

Abdurahman felt like he'd let a man down. He'd been working with James Ellis for several months and had thought the man was starting to have a true appreciation for Islam. James attended daily prayer services and had even begun talking about making a formal commitment to Allah. He'd missed his chance. Now he was gone and lost forever.

The only good thing that could come from it, Abdurahman thought, was that it might be a lesson for others.

See what can happen if you wait . . .

Donnie turned off the alarm without opening his eyes. He lay in bed, slowly gathering his thoughts. Yesterday had begun as one of the best days he'd experienced in years. Then, with a beep of his pager, it had been filled with an evil he had known existed but had never seen.

It was hard for Donnie to imagine a man as evil as Tony Jackson. He couldn't believe the guy had ordered one of his flunkies to beat the eight-year-old child of an officer because she'd disrespected him by making fun of his name. Of course, none of it was proven because no one talked, and Jackson had walked away. *Is this what evil looks like?* Donnie wondered.

The telephone jarred him back to reality.

"Hello," he answered groggily.

"You must be on vacation or something, sleeping so late like this," Karla teased.

Fully alert at the sound of her voice, he replied, "You sure seem cheery this morning."

"Maybe because I didn't stay out until all hours of the night," she said, laughing.

"Ha ha, very funny."

"Well, I was just calling to tell you Mrs. Wilson has called twice this morning to find out if *we* were coming to church."

"Really? What did you tell her?"

"I told her *we* were."

"You know what? I like being a *we* with you."

"Me too. I'll see you in a little while."

For days, men in F block had quietly been passing notes to Marc, wanting to know more about God. Although none of them had told anyone about the dreams they were having, Marc knew, and he had used the opportunity to teach about Jesus. Inmates and staff members who found reasons to be on the block when he was talking had started calling him Preacher Man.

This morning, Preacher Man woke up early and spent time reading the Bible, thinking about the man officers had locked up a few cells down from him last night.

He was concerned about the intense evil that dwelt within that man and the battle to be fought against Satan to save his soul.

I beg you, Father God, please give us both the strength and courage to do Your will . . .

Holding hands, Donnie and Karla found Mrs. Wilson sitting on her usual pew near the front of Hillside Church. She motioned for them to sit.

"I'm so happy to see you," she said, squeezing Karla's hand.

Karla grinned as they sat. "How have you been?"

"I'm great." Mrs. Wilson winked. "But probably not as good as you."

Karla blushed. "It's that obvious?"

"A little." Mrs. Wilson turned to Donnie. "Aren't you glad you listened?"

The organist began playing, and Reverend Hurley and the choir walked down the aisle. After two hymns, a passage of scripture, and taking up the offering, Charles took the pulpit to begin his sermon.

"Ladies and gentlemen, I want to discuss what it means to be a Christian."

Karla and Donnie glanced at each other, recognizing where the topic came from.

Charles continued. "If we look back across history, the problem hasn't been that people didn't believe in God, because most people did. The problem was, and continues to be, what people do. The people of Jeremiah's time are an example of what I mean. Most certainly, they believed in God, and because of that, they went to the Temple that bore His name and presented Him with offerings. Yet, things didn't work out too well for them. Why?" He paused and looked around the church. "Well, the reason was that going to His temple and making offerings were the only things they did. They just believed in God and went through the motions of worshipping Him. They'd forgotten their dependence on Him, and so He destroyed their land and exiled the few survivors to Babylon.

"After that, people tried fixing the problem by making rules for *true believers* to follow so they would be pleasing to God. Well, needless to say, this didn't work, either. I mean, come on, how many of you really think God cares if people walk eleven steps instead of ten steps on the Sabbath? Do you really think God's concerned if a woman looks in a mirror or a man pulls an animal from a ditch on the Sabbath?"

Laughter rippled through the congregation.

The reverend continued. "To their credit, though, they did recognize the previous generations' lack of focus on God and tried to restore it. The problem was, they missed, because the rules they made were placed above human need. So what they got was a focus on deeds, instead of a focus on God.

"The people of Jeremiah's time weren't the only ones unsuccessful at telling others how to be a follower of God. Two thousand years ago, the Pharisees also were unsuccessful, and maybe even more so. They were so busy making rules and judging others, they didn't even recognize God's Son when he stood in front of them or hung from their cross! In fact, not only didn't they recognize him, they refused to listen to him despite overwhelming proof when, on the third day, he arose from the grave."

"Psst . . . Preacher Man," Harold Evans said from his cell next to Marc's. "I need to talk."

"Yes, Harold," Marc said, moving closer to the door. "And I need to speak with you also."

"What about?" Harold asked suspiciously, caught off guard.

"I want to tell you about God and Jesus Christ."

It spooked Harold that Marc already knew what he wanted to discuss, but he didn't let on. "I'm listenin'."

"God is the all-knowing Creator and Sustainer of the Universe," Marc said. "In the beginning, He spoke and the universe was formed. The planets began spinning around and time began clicking off. He spoke again and the land, sea, and sky separated and were filled with plants and animals. Again he spoke, and man and woman were made and given the ability to think, speak, love, and choose.

"It didn't take long, though, for man to choose wrongly and disobey God, causing sin to become a part of human existence. Later, God came among us in human form in order to save us from sin. He did this as a man named Jesus, who took on the limitations that go along with being a human."

Marc paused, listening to Harold's ragged breathing.

"Jesus was thirty-three years old when he was crucified along with two others," he went on. "Unlike those men, he'd committed no crime, but instead, gave His life because his Father, God, wanted Him to. After He died, He was buried, and as predicted by Him and prophesied by others, He arose from the grave three days later. It's because of His death and resurrection, Harold, that we can be forgiven for our sins. All we have to do is believe this and accept His gift of love."

"How do I know God did all of that?" Harold asked. Never had he been as afraid as he was now, after having the dream.

"The reason I know these things is that they are written down."

"I wanna see it for myself. Where can I read it?" Harold asked.

Marc called an officer to his cell.

"Can you give my Bible to Harold, my soon-to-be brother in Christ?"

"Today, we don't really measure ourselves by the number of petty rules we follow," Reverend Hurley preached. "Instead, we spend our time counting how often someone goes to church, or how much money they give, or how many church committees they're on. Others are concerned about how many times a person reads the Bible and the number of things they can recite. Somehow, people believe that the more they can do, the more Christian it'll make them."

Several listeners nodded.

"Well, I suppose that if we could do all of the things Jesus did, then we'd be like Him, only I don't think we can. You see, we aren't perfect like Him, and for this reason, no matter how much we try, we aren't going to be able to do it. But just suppose that we could do all of the things He did. Would that really make us like Him? I still don't think so, because then we'd be trying to follow rules and examples and miss perhaps the biggest, most important guiding principle of His life . . . His dependence on God.

"In this regard, I think God had two primary purposes for sending His only Son to Earth. The first was to have Him pay our sin debt by dying on the cross. The second was that people had the perfect example of how someone who is totally dependent on God lives. You see, Jesus completely turned His life over to the total control of God and sought out His guidance in everything He did. Look at the last hours of His life and you'll see what I mean.

"In those last hours, Jesus went to Gethsemane and prayed, 'O my Father, if it be possible, let this cup pass from me: nevertheless not as I will, but as thou wilt.' I want you to imagine this for a moment. This was a man that raised people from the dead, walked on water, healed the sick, gave the blind sight, and made the crippled walk. Obviously, He was no ordinary man. This was a man with power and strength that had never before been seen and hasn't been seen since. He could have easily walked away from Gethsemane and the cross . . . but He didn't! He could have spoken a word, and the men beating and mocking Him would have disappeared . . . but He didn't! He could have called down an army of angels and fire from heaven to destroy the men nailing Him to the cross . . . but He didn't! Instead, He totally submitted to God's perfect will and died a horrible death."

Nick Caraman wasn't a particularly big man, but he was scary nonetheless. His face was severely pock marked, and his large, crooked nose provided evidence of being in a fight he didn't win. He had an explosive personality, and his behavior was only predictable in that everyone knew he would go to any extreme to prove a point. He was in prison for the rest of his life because of it.

A few years earlier, Nick had been paroled after serving four years for assaulting a man at a bar. When he left prison, he went to see a woman he'd been writing to while doing his time and found her with another man. He left without saying a word and stopped at a nearby convenience store to buy three five-gallon containers of gasoline before going back. He parked his borrowed pickup truck down the street and quietly poured all fifteen gallons of gas around the woman's trailer. The couple inside never had a chance. They died while Nick sat in the truck with the stereo playing, watching the trailer burn to the ground.

Now serving a life sentence, Nick had spent time in just about every facility in the DOC. He usually stayed at each one for only a few months before being transferred because of his hostile, arrogant attitude and impulsive behavior. He finally made it to Caledonia after he angered the wrong prison official, and he would probably never again be moved.

One day, during work call, he told a sergeant he wasn't going out to the fields because he wasn't a slave. This was a frequently heard excuse from inmates who didn't want to work, and the sergeant had been told to expect to hear it since the weather was getting warmer. As a result, Nick was locked up in Unit 1 on disciplinary segregation for work refusal.

He didn't care about being locked up, though, since he wasn't ever going to leave prison anyway. *Besides,* he thought, *at least it's air conditioned.*

Hillside was silent except for the sniffles of people who felt what Charles was saying deep in their hearts.

"The field of psychology has said being dependent is unhealthy and leads to psychological problems. While I believe this is probably true if you're dependent on manmade things or people, I'm telling you now that if you're not dependent on God, then you're even more unhealthy and will never be well."

With passion in his voice, the reverend tried to explain. "The most awesome, mighty, and powerful person that's ever walked the Earth, Jesus Christ, was dependent on God. He prayed for His guidance, He prayed for His wisdom, and He listened for His answers. He told Him His problems and asked for His solutions. He was and is the perfect example of how to live a life that's totally dependent on God, and because of this, my message to you is simple. Believers everywhere need to not only accept Jesus Christ as their personal savior; they also need to learn to become like him . . . dependent on His Father, God! Only then can you be a true Christian."

When Charles finished, he asked anyone wanting to recommit their lives to Jesus and become dependent on God to come to the altar. Everyone in the church stood and quietly walked forward. Donnie and Karla, holding hands, knelt side by side at the altar. Everyone repeated after the reverend, and in a loud, unified voice, the congregation admitted helplessness without God.

Some people cried tears of joy. Others knelt before the presence of the Holy Spirit that had filled the sanctuary. Some sat or stood with loved ones and hugged as they professed their love for Christ and each other. Donnie and Karla continued to kneel with their heads resting against each other, tears streaming down their faces.

After several minutes, Reverend Hurley stood and said, "These things we ask in Jesus Christ's name."

Everyone roared, "Amen!"

"Many people think what they do and how much they do it are a measure of what kind of person they are and will allow them to get into heaven," Marc said as everyone on the block listened intently. "The way you get into heaven, though, is by the grace of God and by having a relationship with Him through His Son, Jesus Christ."

"So it don't matter what we do," asked the man across the hall in cell number eight, "as long as we believe in Jesus?"

"No, that's not exactly true. It does matter what you do, because you can tell a great deal about a person by the way they act. However, make no mistake, we aren't qualified to judge a person because of what they've done. No one is, except God, and He promises us that He will. Instead, what we should do is be true to ourselves and look at the type of fruit we produce with the Holy Spirit as our guide. In that way, it allows us to tell if the fruit we're producing is good, bad, or nonexistent, and then we can determine if our relationship with Jesus is right."

"All right, Preacher Man," said the inmate two cells up. "What if I have produced all of this good fruit and people still dis' me. What then?"

"I say if your relationship with Christ is right, then you'll continue to treat that person with respect."

"Man, you're crazy, Preacher Man," said a voice from the far end of the block. "I'm gonna put some steel in that dude."

"Yeah, that's right," someone else joined in.

"Man, y'all shut up and show Preacher Man some respect," Nick yelled. The block became quiet. "Go ahead on and finish, Preacher Man."

"I think there's a couple of reasons why you'd continue to treat that person with respect after they wronged you," Marc said. "One reason is that it's the right thing to do in the eyes of the Lord. It's nothing to treat someone respectfully when that person is treating you respectfully. Anyone can do that. It takes a man of purpose, one with courage and faith in the Lord, to continue to treat someone with respect, love, and compassion when they mistreat you."

"You mean it takes a chump," the man at the far end said.

"Anyone can strike out at someone that strikes out at him," Marc said. "That takes nothing and often comes from a fear of being hurt, either physically or emotionally. The man that turns his cheek has no fear. Instead, he's totally confident in the Lord as his protector and trusts Him with his life here and now, as well as for all eternity. That man will be seen as a righteous man and will be rewarded in heaven."

"But that ain't right," said the man two cells up. "I mean, if I treat someone a certain way, 'dey supposed to treat me the same. That's the Golden Rule."

"That's *kind of* the Golden Rule," Marc gently corrected. "The problem most people have is applying it. You see, the Golden Rule is do unto others as you would *have* them do unto you. It isn't do unto others, *so that* they will do unto you. The difference is important, because in the first application, we're actively doing things for others. That is, the things that we do for others are the things we'd like to be done for us, and in that way, we can know that they are the right things to do. In the second application, what we do is done only to the extent that it's done for us. In other words, whatever I do for you, is because of what you'll do for me. By applying the Golden Rule this way, it makes you a slave to the people in your world, because they control you by means of the way they treat you."

"I ain't no slave to nobody," Nick forcefully spoke up.

"You're a slave to evil if you let it determine how you're going to treat someone," Marc said, "because that's what happens when you base your actions on the actions of others."

Considering why he was on Unit 1, this struck a nerve in Nick. Being confronted with his own logic, he was forced to make a decision while F block waited in silence to hear his response.

Preacher Man must have a death wish to call Nick Caraman a slave . . .

Nick broke the deafening silence after what seemed to be an eternity. "You know what, Preacher Man? I guess you're right. I never thought about it like that."

The men on F block were stunned. They waited for the punch line that never came.

Instead, the only sound that could be heard was the gentle voice of the Preacher Man praying for Nick Caraman's soul and thanking God for helping him to hear His words.

After the service, Donnie and Karla decided to meet Reverend Hurley for lunch. Pulling into the restaurant parking lot, Donnie saw Steve getting out of his car. He honked the horn.

Steve came over. He seemed excited. "You're never going to believe what happened at my church this morning. Eleven people stood up and testified that they'd been away from Jesus for too long. They described having dreams about making a choice between becoming dependent on God or spending eternity in hell."

Steve looked from Donnie to Karla, realizing neither of them seemed surprised. "Hold on a second," he said in a hurt voice. "Didn't you hear me? What's going on?"

Shaking his head, Donnie said, "I think we need to go in and sit down."

When they were seated at a table in the back of the restaurant, Donnie told Steve that a similar thing had happened at Hillside.

"I'm not sure how it was at your church," he said, "but the people at Hillside were more than just inspired. It was like they'd been filled with the Holy Spirit, and for the first time, realized that God is real."

"When the service was over, no one wanted to leave," Karla said. "It was incredible."

"What do you think is happening?" Steve asked.

"God," Charles answered. "I don't think there's any other explanation."

"If you're right," Steve said, "why *now*? Why here in Rocky Mount and at Caledonia?"

"I've got the same questions, Steve," Karla said. "If we believe all of this isn't a coincidence, then it also means the reason it's happening here and now is also not a coincidence."

"I haven't thought about it like that, but I guess you're right," Donnie said. "Maybe we need to start trying to figure out the purpose behind what's happening and the parts we're supposed to play."

"Do you remember Marc's advice about looking for and listening to God?" Charles asked. "Well, maybe this is our chance to do it."

It was all Lord Abdullah could do not to correct the ignorant Preacher Man. The only reason he hadn't was because he couldn't afford to get into trouble if he wanted to get back out in population. He'd heard all of the stuff Preacher Man was saying a thousand times before, and it always seemed odd to him that people still believed it. Although some of it sounded good, he knew the white man had been preaching it for a long time so he could control people who were too dumb to know any better.

Of course the white man don't want you to fight back, or stand up for yourself . . . Sure, they want you to turn the other cheek and continue to give when everything is bein' taken away . . . How stupid can you be? . . . Besides, I don't need no spook god you can't see or feel or hear to take care of me . . . I'm a god . . . I can get whatever I want, whenever I want it . . . all by myself . . .

When they finished eating, everyone decided to meet back at Hillside. Charles rode with Steve, and Karla went with Donnie. As soon as they got in Donnie's truck, Karla leaned over and kissed him on the cheek. "I just had to do that. Hope you don't mind."

"Yeah, I really, really mind you doing that. You'd better stop." Donnie grinned. "What was that for? I want to make sure I do it a lot."

"I'm not really sure. I just wanted to. Maybe it's because I feel so happy right now. In my heart, I know that it's going to work out because God's in control."

"Whew. For a minute there, I thought you were going to say it's because I'm so irresistible," Donnie joked.

"Well, that's the real reason," Karla said with a wink. "I just didn't want you to get too conceited."

"I'm really glad we've been brought together." Donnie looked at her. "Remember talking about this being a God thing and believing that He's making it happen?"

"Sure. Why?"

"Well, I just can't help thinking He brought us together too."

JOHN 10:3,4 "He calls his own sheep by name and leads them out. After he has gathered his own flock, he walks ahead of them and they follow him because they recognize his voice." (NLT)

Chapter 15
Monday

The sun hadn't risen yet when Nick began tapping persistently on the cinderblock wall.

"Psst . . . Preacher Man. You up?" Nick spoke loud enough to wake him if he wasn't.

"Yes," Marc answered.

"How do I get 'dem things you was talkin' 'bout?

"Do you want to become a Christian?"

"If that's what I need to do, then yeah, I wanna be a Christian." *Maybe that'll make the dream go away . . .*

"Yeah, man," the inmate at the end of the block shouted. "Show us how."

Several others locked up in F block joined in, and the officer supervising the floor went to Marc's cell to open his trap door. Bending down, he too asked to become a Christian.

"Okay, repeat after me," Marc said, squatting in front of the open trap. "Lord God, I'm a sinner . . . Please forgive me and help me to forgive others . . . I believe Your Son Jesus died on a cross for me . . . and on the third day he arose from the grave . . . Amen."

Marc stood and handed the officer outside his door nine letters he'd written during the night to instruct his Christian brothers in what to do after they accepted the Lord.

"Deliver eight of these to the cells numbered on the outside of each," he told the officer. "Keep the one with your name on it."

God chose us from the beginning, and all things happen just as He decided long ago, Marc thought, climbing back on his bunk.

Exhausted after Sunday, Charles slept uncharacteristically late and woke up feeling rested. After his normal morning routine of Bible study and prayer, he showered and shaved, then went to Hillside. He normally took Mondays off, but the excitement of yesterday's service had motivated him to do more. He called his best friend of many years, John Upchurch, the head minister at Rocky Mount Baptist Church.

He answered on the first ring.

"John, this is Charles. How're you doing this morning?"

"I'm great, but I did sleep a little later than usual," John said. "I had trouble going to sleep last night. I've got a lot on my mind."

"That makes two of us. We had something happen yesterday at Hillside that I've never seen before. That's why I'm calling. Do you have a few minutes to get together?"

John chuckled. "If what you're talking about has anything to do with why forty-eight people came forward during the altar call, then yes, I can be at Hillside in a few minutes."

Lord Abdullah lay staring at the ceiling of his cell.

Can things get any worse? . . . This nightmare is makin' it impossible to sleep . . . The drug business is sufferin' . . . I'm in a cell across from a white devil that's usin' knowledge to keep these men ignorant, and I can't say nothin' unless I want to stay on lockup forever. . . And now, they're sayin' Malique and Roger are gonna face the death penalty . . . Man, this is great . . . Who knows what they might say when they're faced with their own death? . . . I ain't too concerned about Malique, but Roger might talk . . . I can't afford that . . . It's time to do somethin' . . .

Abdurahman had thought a great deal about what happened to James and why. Like everyone else at Caledonia, he knew Lord Abdullah was probably involved in the murder. Nevertheless, in the back of his mind, Abdurahman wondered if Satan was at work. James *had* been considering becoming a Muslim.

Abdurahman decided he should try to prepare the rest of his brothers to defend themselves. Their lives might depend on it, and more importantly, so might their souls.

Charles was on the phone when John Upchurch walked into his office and sat down across from the desk.

"That's amazing. Thanks for telling me, Dr. Olmstead . . . Yes, I will . . . Okay, I'll call you later. . . You too. Bye."

"Let me guess," John said. "Fred had a similar experience at the Methodist church."

"That's right. He said they had fifty-six people come forward. At Hillside, the entire church came to the altar." Charles winked. "I guess the Baptists were a little slow yesterday."

"That, or maybe we just don't have as many people that got it wrong the first time," John shot back.

Turning serious, Charles said, "Something's going on in our community, John. Too much is happening for it to be a coincidence."

John rubbed his chin. "Have you talked with any other ministers besides me and Fred?"

"Not yet, but I plan to. First though, let me tell you everything."

After Charles finished relating the details of what was happening at the prison, the two spent the rest of the morning planning a meeting of area ministers at Hillside Church.

Donnie slept well Sunday night and woke up refreshed. He spent the morning at Caledonia completing progress notes on the patients he'd seen on Friday.

Steve stopped by while Donnie was finishing up.

"Good morning," Donnie said. "What's up?"

"Not too much." Steve sat down. "I just thought I'd run something past you to see if you have any ideas. I've been thinking about getting Marc moved to medium custody."

Donnie put down his pen. "Well, if that's something you believe you're being led to do, then it must be."

"I can't think of any reason why he shouldn't be moved. Can you?"

"I haven't really thought about it, but off the top of my head I can't. In fact, I can think of several reasons it might be good. Do you think we should go talk with Powell?"

"He definitely has to approve it."

Lee Powell had lived in Halifax County all his life and was a well-liked man. In high school, he set numerous football and baseball records, and after playing professional softball for a while, he married his high school sweetheart and took a job at Caledonia as a correctional officer. The leadership skills he used to succeed in sports helped him move rapidly through the ranks, and in a few years, the governor of North Carolina appointed him superintendent. He was a hardworking, old-style administrator who didn't take any lip from anyone, including his superiors in Raleigh.

In Powell's early years as superintendent, the ACLU hadn't actively fought for inmates' rights. For the most part, inmates were treated the way they treated others. Correctional officers used blackjacks and anything else they had to correct problems, and they asked questions later. It was a time when inmates respected authority and lived by an unwritten convict code of respect. Rarely were staff members assaulted, or even disrespected, because inmates knew they'd be dealt with swiftly and severely.

Things had changed over the years, and Powell was fed up with the rights inmates were given. In his opinion, it was these rights that were wrong with society in general and with prisons in particular. A man was in prison for breaking the law, and unless a prison policy or civil right was being trampled on, he deserved whatever hardship he was faced with. It was too bad if he couldn't watch cable TV. Too bad if he didn't have air conditioning and had to work in hot fields.

I primed tobacco when I was eight years old, Powell would say to inmates refusing to work. *The only difference*, he told them, *was I wasn't a criminal. I was just poor.*

Powell was on the phone when Steve and Donnie went to see him. He gestured for them to sit at the conference table next to his desk. Finishing his conversation, he hung up and shook his head.

"Some people just don't get it. That was an inmate's mother. Her son, who's in Unit 1 after assaulting another inmate, is only allowed to shower every other day. She says it's cruel and unusual punishment and she's going to sue me." He laughed. "I guess she'll just have to get in line." He leaned back in his chair, indicating he was ready to listen.

Donnie began. "Sir, we'd like to discuss an inmate named Marc Jones. I've talked to him several times, and I don't believe he's a danger to himself or others."

"I haven't had any problems out of him," Steve added.

Powell sat poker faced.

"I think it'd be in his best interest if we promoted him to medium custody," Donnie said apprehensively.

Powell stared at Donnie. After an uncomfortable silence, he began asking questions. "How much time does Jones have left to serve?

"He was sentenced to forty years," Donnie said. "His projected release date is in January of 2017."

"Has he been in prison before?"

"No, sir," Steve said.

"Doc, why are you so concerned about this particular inmate?"

Donnie was caught off guard. "Well, I feel like he's doing well and deserves to be promoted."

"If this man is doing so well in maximum custody, maybe he should stay there," Powell responded.

Donnie's heart sank to the floor, but before he could respond, Steve spoke up.

"Sir, I recently spoke with an attorney who's going to represent Jones. He feels like the conviction is wrong, and he's planning to appeal it. He said it would help him prepare the appeal if Jones wasn't in max custody."

Powell raised his eyebrows. "Mr. Johnson, I'm a little surprised at you. I understand the doc wanting the man promoted, since he's only been here a few weeks, but what you just told me stinks. We both know an inmate's ability to assist in his defense is the same regardless of his custody level. I think y'all are up to something." He frowned. "Johnson, I need for you to step out and let me talk with the doc."

Steve glanced at Donnie, who felt like a deer caught in the headlights of an eighteen-wheeler, then got up and left quietly, shutting the door behind him.

Powell stood and slowly walked around his desk to sit at the head of the table.

"I'm going to tell you something, Doc, and if you ever repeat it to anyone, I'll make sure you never work anywhere in the state of North Carolina again. What I'm going to tell you is very personal." He stared at Donnie and waited for a reply.

"I completely understand, sir," Donnie said, fidgeting and silently praying for help.

"In the *Holy Qur'an*, chapter eight, verse fifty-nine, it says, 'Let not the unbelievers think that they can get the better (of the godly): they will never frustrate (them).' I believe this is important today because the unbelievers are attacking us." Abdurahman folded his hands in front of him. "Look at what happened to our brother James, who was in the process of becoming a Muslim. Since he hadn't declared his Shahadah, he was vulnerable to the forces of Satan."

Donnie's heart felt like it was going to pound out of his chest.

"I've always thought of myself as a Christian," Powell said. "I have been a deacon at Roanoke Rapids Baptist Church for quite some time. I know I'm a sinner like everyone else, but I've tried to live a good life."

Powell looked down and seemed unsure if he should continue. He sighed. "I've been having a dream for almost two weeks about a man standing beside a blood-stained cross. After the incident at the clinic, I realized the man in my dream looks exactly like inmate Marc Jones."

Donnie was speechless.

"In my dream, I'm standing in a line of people at a cross. Some people walk by it without noticing it, while others kneel in front of it and then go on by. Still others lean against it, and after a few minutes, disappear into it. When I get to the front of the line, I wake up sweating.

"I've thought about having Jones brought to my office so I could talk with him about it, but I haven't because it would make me appear weak. I've tried to just forget about it, but that hasn't worked either. Seems I'm having the dream every night, and I'm beginning to wonder if I'm losing my mind. What do you think it means?"

At first, Donnie couldn't meet Powell's eyes. He said a silent prayer, then answered.

"The cross is associated with Jesus dying for our sins. The people passing by without noticing it may represent people who don't know Jesus or at least don't believe what the Bible says happened there. The people who stop and kneel probably symbolize those who do believe. Of those people, the ones that walk by represent people who only do half of what it takes to be on God's team . . . they just believe. The ones that lean against the cross are the ones that not only accept the message of the cross, but also become dependent on it, and thus, on God."

Powell closed his eyes for a moment. "Okay," he said. "But why do you think I wake up when I get to the front of the line?"

Donnie took a deep breath. His hands were shaking. "Maybe you wake up because that's when you have to decide what the cross means to you."

Powell stared out the window, seeming less powerful and imposing. He sighed. "I think you're right. I've thought the dream seemed like a message."

"I'm pretty sure it is," Donnie offered supportively. "I guess now you've got to make a decision what to do about it."

"You know what the scary part is, Doc? I've known for a while, but just haven't seemed to be able to do it."

"It's easy to believe in something," Donnie said. "But it's hard to be dependent on it."

Powell nodded slowly. "Thanks for talking with me."

He called his secretary to send Steve back to the room.

"Mr. Johnson, do you have a vacant cell in your unit?"

"No sir, I don't."

"Well, I need a maximum custody cell for an inmate that's being demoted from ICON."

Steve quickly caught on. "Well, sir, I recommend we promote Marc Jones to medium custody and put this inmate in his cell."

"Good idea, Johnson. Why don't you take care of that for me."

"Yes, sir."

Donnie stood and started toward the door.

"You know, Doc," Powell said, "I think if I'd learned to lean a few years ago, maybe I wouldn't be so tired all of the time."

Donnie smiled and pulled the door shut behind him.

Lord Abdullah spent most of the day thinking about how to get rid of Roger before he made a deal that would ruin him. It wasn't until the early evening, when officers came to escort him to the shower, that he formulated his plan. All he needed to do was get a Unit 1 officer to get him a joint laced with crystal meth. He figured he could slip the joint to Roger tomorrow morning when he passed his cell on the way out to the recreation cages. Roger would greedily smoke it up, and before he knew what hit him, he'd have a massive heart attack and die.

All right, one problem solved. What's next?

Charles began the ministers' meeting by introducing himself and thanking everyone for coming on short notice. He told the twenty-two ministers why Marc Jones was in prison. He described Donnie's meetings with Marc and told them about the situation that occurred in the clinic. He explained how Marc had known what Donnie was thinking, and he told them about the dreams inmates were having.

Two pastors Charles didn't know got up and quietly left as he talked, and a few others shook their heads. Danny Franks, the minister at Goldrock Road Church of Christ, was the first to speak.

"Charles, I've been having a dream every night since last Wednesday. In my dream, I'm with a group of people walking toward a light, and the more we walk toward it, the further away it gets. Eventually, we come to a cross with a man leaning against it, and I ask him if he knows how to get to the light. He tells us to follow a path that appears to have been made a long time ago. The path looks difficult to navigate, and several people say they'll find another way.

"What's left of the group follows the path until it reaches a ledge overlooking a deep, rocky gorge. The light's on the other side, and we know all we have to do is cross the gorge to get to it. We try everything we can to get there, but we can't figure out how. Some of the people, feeling helpless, say that we must not have followed the path correctly and turn around to find out where we erred.

"It's then that a young girl walks to the ledge, and without showing any sign of fear, steps off the edge. Several people try to grab her, but she's out of their reach. But instead of falling, the light seems to grab her and take her across. Then I always wake up."

"Have you thought about what your dream means?" asked Stephen Edwards from Rocky Mount Faith Church.

"I've spent a lot of time thinking about it, and it seems symbolic in several ways," said Danny. "I think the light represents heaven, and the path represents how Jesus lived and the things he did on Earth."

"Then the reason the path looks so difficult could be because it's difficult to do the things Jesus did," reasoned Dr. Samuels, a religion professor at North Carolina Wesleyan College.

"That's what I've thought, too, which fits in with the next part," Danny continued. "The people who turned around could represent how many people react to Jesus' message, meaning they're told about Him and shown how He lived, but they can't, or won't, accept it, and they try to get to heaven their way."

"That's good. I like that," said Harvey Ramone, who had come with Samuels. "I think the people that turned back represent people who obsess about following rules and trying to figure out what they, and others, are doing wrong."

Ray Winston, the minister at Rocky Mount Evangelical Assembly of God Church, didn't accept the interpretations being offered.

"Are you saying it isn't right to follow the behaviors and examples of Jesus? That if we try to be like Him, we aren't going to get to heaven?"

Ray was known for his quick temper. Before he could work himself into an uproar, Samuels interrupted.

"That's not at all what I believe the dream means. I think it means that you have to try and be like Jesus by following *all* of His examples and teachings, not just some of them."

"That's right," Danny agreed. "Remember the little girl that stepped off the edge of the gorge? I think she represents the children Jesus spoke about when He said, 'Anyone who will not receive the kingdom of God like a little child will never enter it.' I think her walking off the edge represented not only her total faith in God, but also, more specifically, her dependence on Him. Unlike the others that thought they could get to heaven their own way or by doing it right, the little girl trusted that only God could take her there and acted on her faith."

Several ministers said, "Amen." Others closed their eyes and prayed.

Ray Winston protested loudly. "Are you saying it doesn't matter what we do as long as we trust God and are dependent on Him? In James 2:17 it says that faith without deeds is dead!"

Samuels looked at Danny and tried to explain. "I think you're misunderstanding me, Pastor Winston. I think the dream *is* saying we have to follow Jesus, because the trail He made is what gets us to the gorge. To cross the gorge, though, we have to trust Jesus' example and become dependent on God. I guess what I'm saying is that Jesus is the way to heaven, but without receiving the Kingdom like a child, we can't cross the gorge and get in."

"I think you're exactly right, and I have another question," Harvey Ramone said. "Who do you think the man is who's leaning on the cross?"

Charles had been waiting for someone to ask the question, and was quick to respond. "Danny, was the man in your dream wearing faded jeans and a white T-shirt, by chance?"

Shocked, Danny stammered, "Yes, he was. How'd you know?"

"Marc Jones, the man I told you about earlier, was dressed like that when he was arrested." Charles paused. "I believe the man in your dream represents Marc Jones, who I think was sent by God to teach us that we need to become dependent on the cross."

Ray Winston couldn't stand it any longer. He got out of his chair to leave. On the way out, he stopped and glared at Charles. "I thought I'd heard just about everything until tonight. Now y'all are tryin' to tell me a convict was sent by God to teach us that it's not enough to follow the path of Jesus. Y'all are insane. Maybe that inmate is the antichrist." Ray stormed out the door, and four other ministers sheepishly slipped out behind him.

The remaining ministers looked at each other until Charles stood up. "I was afraid this might happen," he said, "and I'm sorry. But regardless of why you think things are happening, the fact is, they are. Everyone, including the ministers who left, spoke earlier about the strange but wonderful things that happened at their churches yesterday. I think we need to talk about what roles, if any, we as the clergy are supposed to play."

"Maybe we should talk about the need for dependence on God in our sermons this Sunday," Pastor Edwards suggested.

"It might also be a good idea to contact the clergy in other areas to let them know what's happening," Danny said.

Until then, Eddie Smith from Praise Baptist Church hadn't seemed interested. When he spoke, he surprised everyone. "What about trying to get media coverage? If everyone thinks it's a good idea, I'll talk with a member of my church whose brother is an executive at a television station in Raleigh."

The group talked about the idea for several minutes and everyone agreed he should do it.

As the meeting came to a close, Charles led them in prayer and asked God to guide them. Everyone went home filled with the Holy Spirit.

CHILDREN'S BLESSING: "God is great. God is Good . . ."

Chapter 16
Tuesday

The pager went off at 1:37 a.m., waking Donnie from a deep sleep. It took him a few minutes to collect his thoughts before calling the prison.

"Caledonia Correctional Institution, this is Officer Patterson," the switchboard operator answered. "May I help you?"

"This is Dr. Thompson. I believe you paged me."

"Yeah, Doc, sorry to wake you. Ms. Harris needs to talk with you. Hold on, I'll transfer you to the clinic."

After a short delay, Ms. Harris came on the line.

"Sorry for waking you, Dr. Thompson," she said. "I think one of our inmates is having an acute psychotic episode."

"What's going on?" Donnie asked.

"His name's Paul Watson. He's a twenty-one-year-old black male serving a life sentence for first-degree murder. He's normally cocky and tries to come across as a tough guy in front of other inmates. He's only been here for a few days, but he's already well known to the medical staff, having been seen several times for minor physical complaints. Each time, his requests for pain medication have been denied and he puts on a show, talking loud and making vague threats."

"What's he doing tonight?"

"He doesn't have a psychiatric history and isn't on medication. He's alert and oriented times three and his vitals signs are normal. He denies wanting to harm himself or others."

"I'm confused," Donnie said. "Those things are good."

"Well, the Unit 4 sergeant contacted the clinic half an hour ago and reported Watson was in his cell screaming, 'They're gonna get him, stop 'em!' He was supposedly kicking his cell door, but when I arrived, he was sitting huddled up in the corner repeating what he said earlier. I tried to calm him down to talk with me, but he wouldn't, so I had the officers bring him to the clinic. When we got here, I examined him and again attempted to talk with him. He didn't know who the men were that he saw, or who it was they were trying to get. He said he also heard a voice telling him that it was going to happen. He told me all he wanted to do was warn us in order to prevent it from happening."

Donnie was suspicious. He figured Watson was either doing drugs or trying to manipulate staff. He might be having his first psychotic breakdown, but psychotic individuals weren't typically alert and oriented. Nevertheless, Donnie was concerned for the inmate's safety and placed him on self-harm precautions. He told the nurse he would see the patient first thing in the morning.

"Yes, sir, Dr. Thompson. I'll pass along the order to custody."

"Let me know if anything changes," Donnie said. He hung up and went back to bed.

Officer Fordham had received Lord Abdullah's message. He wanted something to help him do his segregation time. Fordham, who'd been on the payroll for over a year, knew he couldn't refuse. Sure, it was a risk meeting Lord Abdullah's contact in Roanoke Rapids to get it, but that was a lot less risky than saying no. If Fordham did that, he might as well sign his own death certificate. Besides, who really cared if animals like Lord Abdullah fried their brain? Fordham sure didn't.

Donnie thought he was dreaming when he heard the pager again. He rolled over and turned it off. He called Caledonia without getting up.

"Doc," Ms. Harris answered, "I'm sorry to wake you up again, but you aren't going to believe this."

"Probably not," Donnie groaned. "What's going on?"

"We've got another inmate experiencing the same psychotic symptoms as Watson."

"What happened?"

"I received a call from Unit 2 at 3:05 saying Johnny Daniels was, in their words, 'bugging out.' They said he was in the shower area shouting, 'Can't you hear what they're sayin'? You've gotta stop it. Stop it now!' "

"Interesting. How old is Mr. Daniels?

"I believe he's fifty."

"Does he have a psych history?"

"Not that I could tell."

"Put Mr. Daniels on self-harm precautions, too," Donnie said. "I'll be at the prison in about an hour and a half to see them. If either of them gets worse before I get there, page me."

"Yes, sir." Ms. Harris hung up.

Donnie rubbed his eyes while collecting his thoughts. He went to the kitchen to make coffee before taking a shower. Standing under the warm water, he began formulating what could be happening.

The symptoms aren't consistent with a typical psychotic disorder . . . They're experiencing similar symptoms, but not identical . . . A Folie á deux? . . . Nah, these men aren't that close, they're in separate units . . . Plus, even if they are close, they certainly aren't isolated . . . It probably doesn't matter anyway, a shared delusion is very rare and more common among women . . . So what do I do now? . . . Neither of them has a history of psychosis . . . Although Watson is young enough to be having his first psychotic break, Daniels is much too old . . . Both are experiencing perceptual disturbances involving someone about to be harmed . . . Each of them, despite hallucinating, is alert and oriented . . . Drugs? . . . What kind of inmates are these men? . . .

Donnie finished getting ready, grabbed a cup of coffee, and left to go to the prison in the dark. Again.

Abdurahman's eyes snapped open. The dream had terrified him, and for a second, he was paralyzed. Slowly coming to his senses, he remembered what the Ima'am had told him about dreams. If people had a dream they liked, then it came from Allah. If it was the workings of their subconscious, then it probably was something they'd been thinking about when they were awake. If it frightened them, it came from the Shaytaan.

With this in mind, Abdurahman did as he'd been instructed. To annoy the Shaytaan, he vowed not to pay attention to the dream. Instead, he sought refuge with Allah by getting out of his bunk, turning to his left, and spitting dryly three times. He believed that by doing these things, his bad dream wouldn't harm him. The texts, written years ago, indicated the Messenger of Allah had said so.

Donnie went straight to the clinic when he arrived at Caledonia. While waiting for the officers to get Paul Watson, he went through the inmate's chart, but nothing stood out as remarkable. The officers brought Paul to the exam room. His eyes were puffy and swollen as if he hadn't slept in days. His T-shirt was sweat-stained, and his hair looked like he hadn't washed it in a month. Instead of appearing cocky, as Ms. Harris had described him, he seemed frail and quite frightened.

"You've got to keep 'em from gettin' him," he said urgently, still standing.

"Who's going to get you, Mr. Watson?"

"They ain't after me, they're gonna get somebody else," he said, looking at Donnie intensely. "I ain't never seen the dude before."

"Do you know who 'they' are?"

"I ain't never seen them before," he answered in frustration.

Donnie attempted distraction. "How long have you been locked up?"

"What difference do it make? I'm tryin' to tell you a man's gonna be hurt, and you ain't tryin' to do nothin' about it! Come on man!"

Donnie patiently tried another approach. "How do you know someone's going to be assaulted?"

Paul slumped and his breathing slowed. He stopped clenching his fists. "When I first saw it, it felt like I was watchin' TV, 'cept the sound wasn't on. I didn't have no idea what was happenin', but later, I started hearin' the voice."

"What did it say?"

"It told me they was gonna kill the man and make him pay."

"Did they say his name?"

"No."

"What's he going to be paying for?"

"I don't know."

"How many times have you seen or heard it happen?"

Paul paused to think. "I don't know. Look, I know it ain't a dream, like that nurse keeps sayin'. I'm wide awake and what I'm seein' is real."

All psychotic people think what they're experiencing is real . . . That's why they're psychotic . . .

"Do you know where the assault is going to take place or when?" Donnie asked. "Maybe if we knew, we could prevent it."

Paul thought for a second. "I don't know when, but it's light outside. I think it's at a prison 'cause everybody's wearin' gray pants and white T-shirts."

Paul seemed uncomfortable again. He got up and walked to the exam room door before he stopped to look back at Donnie. "Man, I don't know if you believe me or not, but you gotta try to stop it. It's gonna be bad, man." He started to sob.

Thinking Paul might hyperventilate, Donnie motioned for the officers to come in the room. They helped Paul sit back down.

Dr. Redding, the unit physician, had just arrived at the clinic. She overheard Paul's sobs. Donnie left the officers with Paul and consulted with Dr. Redding.

"I'll give him an injection of Haldol to calm him down," she said.

Donnie nodded. "I'll talk to him again later."

Beginning another day, Marc got on his knees and prayed.

Lord God, maker of Heaven and Earth, please be with me today and help me to know Your will . . . Help me to have the strength and wisdom to fulfill Your every command and desire . . . Please lead me and show me how to guide those that You have chosen . . . Give me the words and courage to teach them about You . . . Show me how to help them understand they can't earn their way into heaven . . . Help me to show them the only way is to learn to trust You and become dependent on You like Jesus Christ . . . Lord, I ask You to open people's hearts so they may feel and see and hear the message that you've given me to deliver . . . All of this I ask in Your Son's name . . . Amen.

When Johnny Daniels entered the exam room, he appeared suspicious. He looked at the walls, behind the door, and under the table. He suddenly stopped. "Do you hear that?" he asked, not looking at Donnie.

"Hear what, Mr. Daniels?"

Ignoring the question, Johnny continued to look around. "I can't figure out where it's comin' from. I know it ain't real, but I ain't makin' it up, either. You gotta believe me, Doc."

"Believe what?"

"That there are some people who are gonna hurt a man," Johnny said.

"Do you know who they are or who's in danger?"

"No, sir, I don't. But you've gotta believe me 'cause I ain't making it up. A voice really is tellin' me some men are gonna hurt a man."

He's alert and oriented to person, place, and time, Donnie thought. *He's able to express himself reasonably well relative to his peers . . . He's a little old to be having his first psychotic break . . . He knows the voices aren't real but he believes what they're telling him . . . There doesn't appear to be any secondary gain from claiming to hear voices, since he's scheduled to be released from prison in three months . . . The more he talks about his experience, the more he calms down . . . Is he just delivering a message? . . . Now who's crazy, Donnie? . . .*

Since Johnny didn't appear to be a danger to himself or others, there was little reason to keep him on self-harm precautions. Donnie sent him back to Unit 2.

After making an entry in Johnny's medical jacket, Donnie went back to his office to check in with Amber. She told him he had several calls and teased him about getting one from Karla. Embarrassed, he shut his door and called Karla at home.

"Hey, it's Donnie. How're you this morning?"

"I'm even better now," Karla said in her usual cheery voice. "I hope you're having a good day."

"My day's been pretty long already. I got paged twice last night and I've been here since five o'clock." Donnie explained what had happened with Paul and Johnny.

"It sounds like you've tried to rule out the possible causes accounting for the symptoms."

"The only thing I'm not sure about are the tox screens," he said. "The results won't be in until tomorrow, but both men denied using drugs and neither has a history of drug infractions or convictions."

"So what do you plan to do?"

"The first thing is talk with Steve and get his read on it. He knows a lot about how inmates think and act. He'll probably be able to give me a better feel for these guys."

They talked for a few more minutes and decided they should get together later at Hillside.

As soon as Donnie hung up, the phone rang again.

Steve was already talking before Donnie could say hello. "What happened with the inmates who were placed on self-harm precautions last night?" he blurted. "Do you think it has anything to do with what's been going on?"

Donnie gave Steve a brief summary of what happened with the inmates. "I'm not sure if their experiences are connected to the other things going on," he said. "Can you ask around and find out what those men are like?"

"Sure, it'll give me something to do."

"By the way, have you heard anything from Kenny?

"No, but I have a call in to him. He's in court today, but his secretary told me he'd call when he got back to the office. I'll let you know when I hear something."

"Sounds good."

"Hey, before you go, how are things with you and Karla?"

Donnie wasn't sure how to respond. He knew things were getting serious with Karla, but he hadn't considered that other people had picked up on it. He tried to downplay it. "I guess things are going pretty good. I mean, I enjoy her company and all."

Steve wasn't fooled. "Pretty good? Enjoy her company? Come on, Doc, you sound like an old man talking about a lady he sees at church. I've seen the way you two look at each other. If it's not the look of love, what is it?"

It was useless to protest. Steve was right.

"I think I'm falling for her," Donnie said. "And honestly, I'm a little scared. It's been a long time since I've trusted someone enough to let them inside my world."

"Well, with all that you've been through, it's understandable," Steve said. "I guess you have to trust God to direct you. Anyway, I'm really happy for you, Doc. She's an awesome lady."

"Thanks." For the first time, Donnie realized he and Steve had become friends.

Lord Abdullah was as skilled as a professional magician when it came to performing the sleight-of-hand maneuvers required to pass contraband. He was sure neither of the officers at the end of the cell block noticed when he dropped the laced joint on the floor and kicked it under the opening below Roger's cell door. The only thing he wasn't sure of was how long Roger could wait before he lit up.

If I had to bet, I'd say probably before rec time is over . . .

Donnie felt energized after talking with Steve. He went to the upstairs multipurpose room used by Units 2 and 3 in the old section of the prison to see patients.

The first patient on his list was Abe Tyson, who was twenty-eight years old and serving a life sentence for the brutal rape of an elderly lady. He had committed his crime while out on parole for a previous sex offense involving a young boy.

Abe entered the room wearing dark sunglasses and pants low on his hips with the legs rolled up. When Donnie invited him to sit at the table, he acted like he didn't hear. He stared around the room. After a minute, he turned the plastic chair around so the back was toward the table. He sat down heavily.

"How are you doing today, Mr. Tyson?"

Abe ignored the question. Instead, he began describing his crime to Donnie in vivid detail. He seemed to enjoy bragging about it. He even made a few obscene jokes about his victim.

This was too much for Donnie. Whether it was a lack of sleep or having the right buttons pushed, he felt confrontational.

"Why do you enjoy talking about what you did so much?" There was an unintentional edge to his voice.

"You don't know who I am, dude," Abe said. "I'll hurt you and won't think twice about it."

Donnie gritted his teeth. "There's no need . . ."

"Shut up and let me talk," Abe said. "Your job's to listen to me talk about whatever I wanna talk about."

Things were quickly getting out of control.

"Mr. Tyson, I think it's time for you to leave," Donnie said.

Abe cursed and jumped to his feet.

Donnie stood in reaction to the threat. "There's no need for this to get ugly. Don't do something you're going to regret."

Abe would have nothing to do with reason. "I ain't never regretted anything I've done." He reached in his pants and pulled out a shank.

Acting on instinct, Donnie carefully backed away but kept his focus on Abe, who slowly walked around the table toward him. Donnie's heart raced. He soon found himself backed into a corner of the small room with nowhere to go.

Smiling cruelly, Abe made slashing motions with the shank. Then, in an instant, he took two quick steps and lunged forward.

Donnie sidestepped to the left. Using Abe's momentum against him, he pushed away the hand holding the shank. He pinpointed a kick to Abe's solar plexus and knocked the breath out of him.

Bent over, gasping for breath, Abe gripped the shank. Donnie went on the attack with a right upper cut, breaking Abe's nose. The shank slid across the concrete floor. Donnie connected with a roundhouse kick to the side of Abe's head. The inmate crumbled to the floor, on the verge of losing consciousness.

Officer Warren was closest to the multipurpose room. He threw the door open, almost running into Donnie, who was trying to get out.

"He almost stabbed me!" Donnie said between breaths, pointing to the corner where the shank lay on the floor.

Officer Warren handcuffed Abe and used his radio to call for assistance. Within seconds, several officers with riot batons converged on the room.

For some reason, I knew today was gonna be great, Roger thought, looking at the thick joint Lord Abdullah had kicked under his cell door. It didn't matter what other people said about the man, Lord Abdullah took care of people. Roger was holding the proof in his hand. He pulled out the match he had borrowed from the new correctional officer working on the block.

I bet this is some good stuff, Roger thought as he lit up and inhaled deeply, for the last time ever.

Donnie sat in Powell's office, waiting to talk with him about the incident with Abe. He was mentally exhausted and decided to go outside for some fresh air. He'd had little choice but to defend himself, yet he still felt guilty for breaking Abe's nose and thought he could have handled the situation differently.

Maybe I shouldn't have confronted him . . . Maybe I prejudged Abe and because I couldn't forgive him, ended up in a fight . . .

Powell walked out the door and sat down beside Donnie on the old wooden picnic table used by the honor-grade inmates who cleaned his office.

Donnie stared across the back yard of the prison. "Do you think I did the right thing?"

"As far as prison policy goes, it looks like you did everything you could to keep from getting hurt," Powell said. "As far as personally, it looks like you're being pretty hard on yourself."

"Maybe I shouldn't have confronted him when he started telling me about what he did."

Powell shrugged. "I'm not a psychologist. I do know this, though. There's no way that I'm going to sit and listen to some young punk brag about raping and assaulting anyone, much less an elderly lady. It's hard for me to imagine how that could be very therapeutic. Do you remember what I said about how working in a prison means being faced with evil in its purest form every day?"

"Yes, sir."

"Well, I think the best you can do is try to be nonjudgmental and treat people with respect. I believe you did that and Abe put you in a position where your choices were to fight back or die."

Donnie sat down and leaned his elbows on his knees. "I'm just upset because I feel like I let him sucker me into it. He was trying to get a reaction from me right from the start. Maybe I should have just sat there and listened."

"I know you don't believe that, Doc," Powell said. "It just sounds like you want to feel sorry for yourself."

Donnie looked up. "It kind of felt good to hurt Abe."

"I bet it did, son. I bet it did."

"It makes me question my abilities and my character. Maybe I'm not the Christian I think I am. Maybe I'm not even worthy to be a Christian if I can't do any better than to get in a fight with an inmate."

"You know, Doc, I told you when you started working here that this place is different from anything you've ever experienced. It works on you in a lot of ways, some of which you don't even notice until it's too late." He paused. "I know you're a Christian and that you try to act like one, but today you came face to face with evil and had to make a split-second decision. Had you not made the one you did, it might be you instead of Abe that was taken out of here on a stretcher."

Donnie sighed. "I know what you're telling me is true, but it's just going to take me a while to make sense of it. Anyway, thanks for taking the time to talk to me. It really does mean a lot."

"Any time, Doc," Powell said. Then he grinned. "How long have you been into martial arts?"

"Since I was in fourth grade. My dad signed me up because I got in a fight at school and got beat up."

Powell put his hand on Donnie's shoulder. "Well, for what it's worth, the word's going to get around about this. I don't think any more inmates are going to try you."

Walking back to his office, Donnie heard an approaching siren. It wasn't long before a Halifax EMS ambulance sped by. He assumed they'd been called to transport Abe to the hospital. He continued across the yard to his office.

Amber came running out of the back room, frantically asking questions. "What happened? Are you okay? Is the inmate really in a coma? How long have you known karate?"

Donnie raised an eyebrow. "Where'd you hear all this?"

"Steve called about fifteen minutes ago, and when I told him you weren't here, he said you were probably talking with Mr. Powell. I was curious, so I called Mr. Powell's secretary and she told me what had happened. Is it true?"

"Yeah," Donnie said. "I got in a fight with an inmate."

"She said you beat him up pretty bad," Amber said excitedly. "Have you known karate for a long time?"

"Have a seat," Donnie said, gesturing at the couch across the room. He sat down in the matching chair. "Amber, I'm not proud of beating up that man. I only did it to defend myself and to keep from getting hurt. So please don't make a big deal out of this. Okay?"

"I'm sorry. I didn't mean anything by it." She folded her hands around one knee. "You know, my husband worked here for a while and had to fight inmates several times. If you wouldn't have fought back, you'd probably be dead right now."

"You're right. But I still wish I could've avoided it."

"I'm sure you do." She pointed out the window toward the back of the prison. "But some of the men living behind those fences are very mean and will do anything to get what they want. You, a psychologist of all people, should understand that. Something else my husband says is that those guys do bad things not because they have a reason, but because they like to see people suffer."

"He's right about that." Donnie stood. "I'm going to get my things, and I'm leaving for the day."

"Before you do that, Steve wanted me to tell you that they had an inmate die over there a little while ago. He said his name was Roger Spivey. The siren we just heard was probably the ambulance coming to get him."

"What happened?"

"I'm not sure. Steve wants you to call him."

Steve answered Donnie's call on the first ring. When he heard Donnie's voice, he chuckled. "How long have you known martial arts?"

"I can't believe you're laughing." Donnie could hear the fatigue in his own voice. "I called to find out about Roger Spivey. What happened?"

"No one's sure," Steve said. "They're saying he probably died from smoking a joint laced with something. Dr. Redding said he had a massive heart attack. The officers who found him found a partially smoked joint on the floor of his cell. The ambulance just came to take him to the hospital for an autopsy. But I want to know about the fight you were in. What happened?"

Donnie quickly told him the details, then changed the subject. "Have you talked with Kenny?"

"I spoke to him this morning. He said he thought it was a great idea to get the media involved. It could help to speed up the process of getting Marc a new trial. He said we probably shouldn't get too involved in it, though. The judge and the D.A. that tried the case have very powerful political connections throughout the state. Kenny thinks it could get sticky if it goes the way he thinks it will."

"I'm glad he thinks the media's a good idea. I'm sure Charles will too. By the way, have you found out anything about the men I placed on self-harm precautions?"

Donnie could hear Steve shuffling papers.

"Here it is. I spoke with several inmates, and neither Johnny or Paul had any gambling debts. It seems most guys considered Johnny to be a religious man. He was active in the prison ministry. They described him as the type of inmate that others seek out for advice." Steve rustled more papers. "It sounds like Paul has been trying to change his life and has been asking around about becoming a Christian. One inmate I talked with said he was just a messed up kid looking for something to hold on to that would help him do his time easier."

Donnie connected what Steve told him with his thoughts after he talked with the men.

"I wondered if they were trying to tell me something," he said. "You know, like a message. At the time, I dismissed it as me being too caught up in Marc Jones' case. But I'm beginning to think maybe they're trying to warn me about something that's going to happen to Marc. I'll tell you what," he said with a burst of energy. "Meet me in the Unit 2 multipurpose room in about twenty-five minutes."

Okay, one problem taken care of. Lord Abdullah watched the stretcher with the black bag on it being loaded into the back of the ambulance. Now I just got to be patient until I can get out of here . . . Since they don't have any evidence against me, it shouldn't be long . . . As far as they can prove, I ain't done nothin' . . . It sure is great bein' me . . . I really am a god . . .

Donnie left his office to meet Steve. Two inmates were cutting grass just inside the main gate. They stopped working as he approached.

"Doc, is you really a karate expert?" the older man asked.

Donnie slowed down. "I don't know what you're talking about."

The older man nodded. "Yes, sir, that's what I thought."

Donnie grinned and continued toward the main entrance.

Word sure travels fast in prison . . . I wonder if there's anyone who doesn't know what happened . . .

It didn't take him long to find out. In the main office, several officers were standing just inside the door throwing punches. They fell silent when Donnie neared. The sergeant studied him for several seconds before offering his hand. Not knowing why it was being offered, Donnie grasped the large, callused palm.

"Beatin' up Abe was probably the best therapy he's ever had," the sergeant said. "I bet he don't cause no more problems for ya."

The officers laughed.

Steve walked up and rescued Donnie by announcing that his patient was upstairs waiting.

Inmates had cleaned the blood up from the floor of the multipurpose room, and Marc was sitting at the table. No longer wearing an orange jumpsuit and matching flip-flops, he was dressed in gray pants, black boots, and a white T-shirt. He stood as Steve and Donnie entered, and he shook their hands.

"How are you doing since they moved you?" Donnie asked as they sat down.

"I'm fine. Thanks for getting me moved. It's nice being able to walk around and go outside on the yard."

"Mr. Jones," Donnie said, getting straight to the point, "we have reason to believe that you're in danger. Two inmates told me they've been hearing and seeing things about an inmate being attacked. They don't know who it is, but they said he's wearing gray prison pants and a white T-shirt."

Marc smiled first at Donnie, then at Steve. "You're right to think those men are talking about me. It's part of the reason I've been sent. Through it, God will be glorified and many will learn about having a relationship with Him."

Steve shook his head. "Hold on a second. This is too much. If you know about all this, then how does it happen? What are we supposed to do?"

"Mr. Johnson, I can't answer those questions, only the Father can. All I can tell you is that I've come to teach people about how to have a deep, personal relationship with God." Marc's eyes shifted between Donnie and Steve. "The events that are unfolding are all according to His plan. Let Him guide you, and pray for the strength and wisdom to follow His direction."

He stood and left them sitting in the room.

Abdurahman had tried his best to seek refuge with Allah all day, but he was unable to stop thinking about his dream. He'd tried everything he could remember that had been prescribed to do for bad dreams, but for some reason, the more he tried, the more he thought about it.

Have I forgotten something? . . . Did I perform one of the salats wrong? . . . Maybe I prayed the wrong one or at the wrong time . . . Why am I having such a hard time remembering the rules? . . . Please help me, Allah!

He closed his eyes, trying to find the sleep that refused to come.

Donnie sat at Hillside with Karla and Charles. While they waited for Steve to arrive, he filled them in about the meeting with Marc.

"After thinking about what Marc said, I have questions," he told them.

"What kind of questions?" Charles asked.

"Well, how do you suppose we let God guide us? I mean, are we supposed to sit around and wait for a sign, or do we actively do something to find out? If that's the case, what do we do?"

The reverend crossed his arms. "I think we let God guide us by praying and listening not only with our eyes and ears, but also with our hearts."

"That sounds good, Charles," Donnie said, "but do you think the sign will be that obvious? What if we don't recognize it? I mean, do you really think God still talks to people? We aren't Biblical heroes or anything."

"Donnie," Karla said, sternly enough to get his attention. "Hold on a second."

"I'm sorry." Donnie realized he was venting his frustrations. "I guess I'm just tired and confused. It's been quite a day."

"It sure has," Steve said, walking into Charles' study. "Sorry I'm late. I went by my house to change before I came over."

"You haven't missed too much," Charles said. "Donnie was just telling us about what happened today."

"Did he tell you about his martial arts training and that an inmate tried to stab him?"

"What?" Karla cried out.

"Yeah. An inmate pulled a shank on Doc, and, well, let's just say he probably won't do it again for a while. He's still in the hospital after having surgery to reconstruct his nose."

Karla turned to stare at Donnie.

"I wasn't trying to hide it." Donnie held up his hands. "I just didn't think it was that big of a deal."

"Nah, it's not a big deal when a man tries to stab you. No, that's not a big deal at all." Karla narrowed her eyes at him.

"You're right, it could've been a big deal," he conceded. "But it wasn't, and everything turned out okay."

"Except for Abe," Steve said. "I bet his take on it is quite a bit different."

Everyone chuckled.

"Well, we're certainly thankful you didn't get hurt," Charles said. "But I think there's something else we need to talk about. Right before you came in, Steve, Donnie was telling us Marc said all of this was part of God's plan and that you needed to let Him guide you."

"Like I was saying earlier," Donnie said, "since we talked with Marc this afternoon, I've been thinking about what he said and what he didn't say."

Karla frowned. "What do you mean?"

"I definitely think it's important that he confirmed what we've suspected; that he was sent by God. I think it's also important that he said all of this is part of God's plan." Donnie talked faster. "What concerns me is when he said, 'all of this.' Does he mean starting with what happened to him in Mount Olive, or being sent to Caledonia? Is he referring to the things happening to inmates, or is he saying that those things are warnings about what will happen in the future? Does 'all of this' include the four of us being brought together to figure out what's happened?"

Karla reached over to touch his arm. "Hold on. You're doing it again."

"You're right," he sighed. "I'm getting ahead of myself."

"I like the way you're thinking about this, Doc," Steve said. "I mean, what he didn't say was how he was going to fulfill his purpose. Maybe that's a place for us to begin."

"When you told him about the inmates' dreams and warned him of possibly being harmed, did he seem to be afraid?" Charles asked.

"No, he didn't," Steve answered. "In fact, he seemed calm. That's when he told us about his purpose and God's plan."

"Then I think his calm reaction's important, too," Charles said.

"How do you mean?" Donnie asked.

"We're pretty sure that Marc's purpose is to teach, and when you told him he may be in danger, he didn't deny it. In fact, he actually confirmed it. It seems that it doesn't matter to Marc what happens to him, as long as through it, the people he comes in contact with hear his message."

"Are you talking about learning ways that we know we're doing God's will?" Donnie asked.

"Exactly," Charles replied. "You see, we already know we need to be dependent on God. That's not our problem. Our problem, which is what Donnie was saying earlier, is how do we do it?"

Charles told them about Danny Franks' dream and the little girl stepping off the edge of the cliff. He quoted Mark 10:15 and explained how the ministers had used the verse to interpret the dream.

"Okay, so how do we act childlike?" Donnie asked.

"Several things come to mind," Karla answered, calling on her knowledge as a pediatrician and a Christian. "Children don't have to understand the mysteries of the world around them in order to live in it and grow. They don't look for or need complex explanations, but instead, they operate in simple terms and see things as either black or white. They have an incredible ability to forgive even the worst of behaviors without passing judgment. They believe in things even when they can't touch them, and they don't try to prove why things are the way they are. Instead, they trust that's the way it is without question. They believe without doubt and accept without seeing. They don't try to make the world fit the way they think it should be, but rather, they accept it for how it is." She paused to reflect. "And you know what the best part is? Children really do believe that God is great and can do anything He wants."

Donnie picked his words carefully before responding. "I understand what you're saying, Karla. I know how children are and how they think. But my problem is, how do I become like them?"

Charles offered an answer. "It's actually quite simple. We've got to stop trying so hard to understand everything and demanding more proof. Instead, we need to accept what's in front of us. We've seen it with our own eyes and heard it with our own ears. In our hearts, we know it's true.

In essence, we have to believe and trust that what's happening around us can only be from God and stop trying to find other explanations."

"I want to do it," Donnie said. "I'm just not sure I can."

"I think we all have those kinds of doubts," Karla replied, "but I think those kinds of doubts are different because we're questioning ourselves, not God. I also believe that's where prayer comes in."

"It seems like the world we live in trains us to doubt things and trust only what we can touch and measure," Donnie said. "When we're children, we don't operate that way. Instead, it's the exact opposite. Maybe what we have to do is unlearn our old habits."

Charles smiled. "Exactly, Donnie."

"We have to search for what God is trying to tell us and believe it when we see it," Steve said.

"You're right," Charles said with a nod. "The most important thing we need to do is pray and listen. In the book of John, Jesus tells us that His sheep will recognize His voice and follow it and they will run from a stranger's voice." He turned to Donnie. "Let me answer the question you asked a while ago. Yes, I do believe that God still speaks to us today and that we even recognize His voice. The problem is, I'm not sure we do a very good job of trusting that it's Him when He does."

Sergeant Williams had worked for the Department of Corrections for almost seven years and knew that things often happened that made no sense. He had learned to do them without asking, trusting that the higher-ups knew why. So when the captain called and told him to get Tony Jackson and Harold Evans ready to move to Unit 2, he didn't question it. He just did what he was told.

PROVERBS 3:5,6 "Trust in the Lord with all of your heart and lean not on your own understanding; in all of your ways acknowledge him, and he will make your paths straight."
(NIV)

Chapter 17
Wednesday

"Doc, I'm sure glad to see you this mornin'," Johnny Daniels said. "Somethin's goin' on I think you oughtta know about."

"Are you still hearing the voices?" Donnie asked, leaning back in his chair.

"No, sir, not since the last time I talked to you. This is about a dude called Preacher Man that just transferred to our block from Unit 1. Somethin' about him ain't right."

"How do you mean?" Donnie asked, his interest heightened.

"He don't say much, but looks like he knows all there is to know about ya."

"Have you talked to him?"

"Nah, I ain't tryin' to get in nobody's business. I ain't even sure why I'm tellin' you this 'cept I just had a feelin' you needed to know."

"His name's Marc Jones, and I really think you should try to get to know him," Donnie said. "You might be surprised at what kind of guy he is."

Johnny eyed Donnie suspiciously. "Sounds like you know 'im. What's the deal?"

"Mr. Daniels, I can't discuss that. But I think that if you talk with him, you'll find out for yourself."

"He ain't no psycho or po-lice is he?"

"I can definitely tell you he isn't either of those things."

"So you just want me to talk with him? Is that all?"

"Not exactly," Donnie responded. "I also want you to do me a favor."

"Man," Johnny sighed. "This is crazy. All I wanted was to tell you about this dude."

"I understand, but I just want to know if you hear anything about people wanting to harm him. I don't even want to know who, just when, so I can prevent it."

"You're askin' a lot, man," Johnny stated. "What's in it for me?"

"Depends," Donnie said cautiously. "What do you want?"

"Well, I'd like to go home," Johnny answered, grinning.

Without stating the obvious, Donnie replied, "I might be able to get you promoted to minimum custody so you'd be able to get additional gain time and move your release date up a few weeks."

"I don't know, man," Johnny said hesitantly, waiting to see if Donnie might add something else.

"Well, it's up to you."

"All you want me to do is let you know if people are out to get him?"

"That and talk with him."

Figuring he was getting a good deal, Johnny agreed.

Even though he continued to have nightmares, Lord Abdullah was happy to be back in Unit 2 so he could manage his business. Pete had tried his best to run things in Lord Abdullah's absence, but the thugs at Caledonia had taken advantage of the situation and cost him several hundred dollars. This didn't surprise him too much, but the number of officers Pete said refused to perform the jobs they were paid to do did.

Well, I'm back now, and not only is it time to pay the piper, it's also time to show who really *runs this place . . .*

Recognizing the number on his pager, Donnie turned it off and quickly packed up his things so he could go to the front lobby to call Charles. The reverend answered on the first ring.

"Charles, this is Donnie. I got your page. What's up?"

"I just got off the phone with Eddie Smith, from Praise Baptist Church. He called to tell me he talked with Barbara Pierce, the investigative reporter from WLHR. The owner of her station wants her to do a story about Marc Jones. She wants to interview Eddie to get a minister's perspective on the case."

"When's the interview?"

"They're meeting at Eddie's church this afternoon. He asked me to be there so I can fill in any details he doesn't know about."

"That's great, Charles," Donnie said.

"You sure don't seem very excited. Everything okay?"

"I've just got a lot on my mind." Donnie told him about the conversation with Johnny Daniels. "I feel like I'm missing something."

Until that morning, Abdurahman had been having trouble deciding what to teach at the Ta'alim. Then, for some reason, he began thinking about good deeds. Suddenly, he put things together.

I'm having bad dreams because I'm not pleasing Allah . . . He's trying to get my attention by not rewarding me with a peaceful heart so I can rest . . .

Abdurahman spent the day researching the rewards Allah promised to give men for performing good deeds. He would talk about it that afternoon.

After hanging up with Charles, Donnie went to Unit 1 to see Paul Watson, who was still on self-harm precautions. Paul entered the multipurpose room and took a seat. The officers escorting him remained outside.

"How have you been since yesterday?" Donnie asked. *He seems more relaxed than last time . . . He hasn't been allowed to shave, but at least he's taken the time to comb his hair . . .*

"I'm doin' a lot better. I actually got some sleep last night. I guess that shot calmed me down." Paul spoke cheerfully. Almost too cheerfully, in Donnie's opinion. "Since I been over here, I ain't been hearin' voices or seein' things."

Not quite buying the dramatic change, Donnie probed for more information. "What do you remember about the things you were experiencing?"

"Doc, I 'member everything. I 'member hearin' the voices and seein' 'dem men hurt somebody too."

"I believe you, Paul," Donnie said. "I'm just trying to understand, that's all."

As soon as the words came out of his mouth, Donnie remembered the discussion at Hillside.

Here I am doing it again . . . I'm still trying to understand why . . . Try to be supportive . . . Listen with your heart . . .

Donnie went with what he felt he was being led to do. "Paul, are you a Christian?"

Stammering, Paul replied, "I am . . . but I wasn't. Well, not until yesterday. After y'all gave me that shot and put me over here, I slept for a long time. When I woke up, they moved me across from this dude called Preacher Man. He asked me the same question you just did."

Donnie tried not to show his surprise. "What did you say?"

"I told him I used to believe in God, but it was a long time ago. I said I hadn't really thought much about it in a while, and we just talked after that. He asked me if I wanted to be happy for the rest of my life even though I'm locked up. I told him yeah, just to shut him up."

"Then what?" Donnie asked nonchalantly.

"He told me to repeat a prayer after him." Paul paused to remember. "It was sort of wild. After I did it, I started feelin' different. It was like I had hope. It felt good."

Feeling goose bumps on his arms, Donnie nodded. "It's truly amazing, isn't it?"

"I only wish I'd met Preacher Man a long time ago," Paul said sadly. "Maybe things woulda been different."

"Who knows, Paul."

"Hey, I think they moved that dude to Unit 2. I'd really like to be in his unit when I get off self-harm. Think you could help me with that?"

Paul's transformation was dramatic. He didn't appear to be anxious or scared. Instead, he seemed to be quite reasonable in his presentation.

"Look, I can't promise anything," Donnie offered, listening to his instincts, "but I'll talk with Mr. Johnson and make a recommendation to have you transferred to Unit 2. It'll then be up to the custody staff to approve it."

Rising from his seat, Paul raised his handcuffed wrists and shook Donnie's hand. As he walked toward the door, he stopped and turned.

"Doc, I know I can't undo all of them things I did, but for the first time, Preacher Man helped me to see I don't have to. He said that no matter how good I am or what I do, I can never be good enough to make up for it, so it don't matter. What matters is that this Jesus dude died for my sins and took care of it. Pretty cool ain't it?"

He walked away with his head held high.

Donnie went to Steve's office and sat in the chair opposite his desk.

"I've got some good news," Steve said. "I went by Kenny's office and he told me Marc agreed to let him represent him. He said he's already filed a motion for an appeal and thinks there's a great chance of getting a retrial."

"Wow! That's awesome news. How long does he think it'll take?"

"He told me it would be a while because these things move slowly. Once they find you guilty, the courts aren't in a big hurry to change their minds. He did tell me, though, that if the appellate court decides Marc should receive a retrial, he'll try to get him released from prison on bail."

"This is amazing." Donnie told Steve about Eddie's interview. Things were unfolding very quickly.

If I stop trying to understand things, how will I do my job? . . . I'm a psychologist and my job is to help people . . . To do that, I have to understand what they're doing and why . . . If I stop trying to understand things, won't I be naïve? . . . Surely, God doesn't want me to just accept everything someone tells me . . . How do I know when to try to understand and when to accept things? . . .

With these thoughts running through his mind, Donnie left the prison and went to his office to call Karla. He knew she wasn't working and felt the need to talk with her. Her phone rang several times. Just before he was about to hang up, she answered groggily.

"Hello?"

"Hey, Karla. How are you doing this morning? You sound tired."

"Well, I'm better now that I'm talking with you," she said. "I had a long night. After you brought me home, I went to take care of a little boy with appendicitis. His parents were pretty upset and didn't know the surgeon. So after I checked him out, I went to the ER with them to introduce them to Dr. Horton. I just woke up a few minutes ago."

"How's the little boy?"

"He's doing fine. No complications at all," she answered. "What have you been doing today, Dr. Thompson?"

Donnie told her what had been happening.

"Do you want to meet for lunch?" he said.

Karla accepted, and he told her he would get her in an hour.

"No, sir," Officer Hunt lied. "I didn't do that. I swear. I'd never dis' you like that."

"I don't believe you," Lord Abdullah replied harshly. "I think you knew Billy was tryin' to cut into my business. I'm gonna take care of him later, but that won't get back my money or excuse you for not doin' what you're paid to do. Whatta you think I should do about that?" Lord Abdullah asked, enjoying her discomfort.

"I don't know," Hunt answered, afraid. "The only reason I let him sell the dope in the first place is 'cause they said you was gonna be locked up for a long time."

"Oh," Lord Abdullah said sarcastically. "So if I leave, that means you ain't gotta do what I say?"

"Sir . . . "

"Shut up." He held up his hand. "I'm tired of hearin' excuses. What I want is my money and for you to work for nothin'."

"But . . . "

"And another thing. From now on, you'll call me Lord Abdullah."

"Yes, sir," she answered, relieved he'd decided not to rat her out.

Praise Baptist Church was located off Highway 43 on five acres of once-profitable farmland between Rocky Mount and Gold Rock. With a large, conservative membership, it professed to be a strictly Bible-based, traditional church that interpreted and applied Biblical principles quite literally. Services had always been at eleven on Sunday mornings and seven on Wednesday evenings. When it was suggested that an early Sunday service be held during the summer, the church almost split.

So Charles was surprised to hear Eddie had agreed to be interviewed. The idea that a convict was sent by God to teach Christians that they needed to change was certain to stir more than a few members' tempers.

Charles walked in the main door and found Eddie in his office, sitting at his desk with his head bowed.

"Amen," Eddie said, hearing Charles enter. He stood. "Thanks for coming, Charles. I need to talk with you before the interview."

"What's on your mind?"

"I'm concerned some members of my congregation may reject Marc's message because of his appearance."

"Eddie, I think there's lots of people who'll reject Marc's message for lots of reasons. Whether it's because he's in prison, or looks a certain way, or maybe they don't like that he isn't a Baptist or Methodist or Pentecostal, I don't think it matters. You see, although Marc's presentation of the message may be slightly new, the message itself isn't. It's one that many men of God have tried to teach, and while some people got it, most didn't. In a way, I guess you could say that one of mankind's greatest flaws has been the refusal to pay attention to the thousands of different people and ways that God has used to try and get our attention. It seems we always find ways to reject the messenger along with the message."

"I know you're right, Charles, but I feel responsible for these people, and it hurts me to know most of them aren't even going to hear what Marc says, much less believe it's true. Plus, I think it goes without saying that by consenting to this interview, I'm probably signing my resignation papers as the pastor of this church."

"Do you remember at the ministers' meeting talking about trusting and depending on God?" Charles asked. "Well, I think this is a time to practice it by trusting that the outcome will be the way God wants. I think if we do that, it'll be possible to depend on Him to use us in the way that best suits His purpose."

Eddie sighed. "I know you're right, but I'm still sad. Not because of what this will likely mean for me, but because people I know and love are going to make the worst mistake of their lives and there's nothing I can do to prevent it."

"Some people at my church are probably going to do the same thing." Charles removed his glasses and rubbed his eyes. "Maybe, somehow, it's part of God's plan too." He put a hand on Eddie's shoulder. "For what it's worth, I have a great deal of respect for you to give this interview."

Eddie looked away. "Thanks, Charles. I just feel like it's the right thing to do, but most importantly, I believe it's what He wants me to do."

"That, my friend, is a perfect example of trust and dependence on God."

"I want to teach this afternoon about the importance of doing good deeds," Abdurahman said, beginning Ta'alim. "The *Holy Qur'an* promises us that if a true believer in Allah, all praise and glory be to him, does good deeds, they will be given a good life. They'll be treated with respect and have many possessions. They will also be rewarded in paradise on the day of resurrection in proportion to the best of what they did.

"Because of this, we, as true believers in Allah, need to do more righteous deeds so we can be rewarded not only in the Hereafter, but right now on Earth. You're probably thinking, 'I've wondered how will it be possible for me to be content and have lots of things in prison.' I don't know the answer to that except to say I believe the all-powerful, knowing Allah, praise and glory be to him, can do anything he wants. We just have to do what he says.

"In this regard, I want to talk about a specific reward that's promised for performing a certain good deed. Abu Hurayrah explains that the Messenger of Allah said, 'Whoever's easy-going with a debtor that's facing hardship, Allah will make it easy for him. And Allah will help his slave so long as his slave helps his brother.' It's because of this that I say each of us needs to remember to be easy on those who owe us, because it's a righteous act that'll be rewarded by Allah, all praise and glory be to him!"

Barbara Pierce was a bright, attractive investigative reporter. She began her television career as a summer intern at WLHR while an undergraduate at the University of North Carolina at Chapel Hill. Following graduation with a degree in journalism, she was hired as a reporter and gradually worked her way up within the station. Her work was well respected, and her skills as a reporter, combined with her tough work ethic and stunning good looks, almost ensured she would achieve her goal of becoming an anchor for national news.

Barbara entered Eddie's office and introduced herself. Her handshake was firm but feminine, and she spoke with confidence. Eddie introduced Charles and asked Barbara if she'd like to sit while her cameraman got set up. She explained to Eddie the type of questions she was going to ask. When the cameraman was ready, the taping began.

Barbara started by asking background questions that probably wouldn't be used on the air. When she felt Eddie was relaxed, she began the real interview.

"It seems people have varying opinions about who Marc Jones is. Who do you think he is?"

Feeling a bit more confident than earlier, but still nervous, Eddie answered cautiously. "I honestly don't know, Ms. Pierce. But I'm not sure it really matters."

Barbara nodded.

"I think what's important is his message. He's saying it doesn't matter how often you go to church or how many committees you're on. It isn't important what type of music you listen to. It doesn't matter if you watch *Harry Potter* movies or read the Bible four thousand times. You see, Ms. Pierce, Marc Jones is saying that none of those things should be the focus of Christians. Instead, he's saying people need to trust God like a child and become dependent on Him like His Son, Jesus, was."

"Are you saying it doesn't matter what you do or how you behave?"

"Not at all, Ms. Pierce." Eddie visibly relaxed. "I'm saying it *does* matter what you say and do. In the Bible, it tells us faith without deeds is useless and that you can know a tree by the type of fruit it produces. What I believe Marc is saying is that many people are so focused on what they do that they forget why they should do it. In this way, they're confused and believe they can count someone's good deeds and measure that person's 'Christian-ness.' They think that anyone whose score falls below a number they've decided upon isn't a 'true' Christian. I believe this is wrong. I think what Marc is teaching is that we, as Christians, should be much more concerned with helping people learn how to trust what happened on the cross and have a dependent relationship with God. When we can do that, all of the things people do will take care of themselves because they will be governed by the Holy Spirit."

"You've said Marc's trying to teach a message. Some people think he's a criminal and deserves to be in prison. What do you think?"

Eddie looked directly into the camera. "I certainly believe what he's saying matters, and I'm aware that since he's in prison, many people won't. I find this quite ironic, because many men who challenged the religious thinking of their time were either imprisoned, or worse, killed because people felt threatened by what they said. I wonder Ms. Pierce, is that happening now?"

Barbara fidgeted and deflected the question. "Why are so many people unwilling to listen to what Marc Jones is saying?"

Without pause, Eddie replied, "I think there are two main reasons. First, I think some people judge him as something less than themselves. In their opinion, he has nothing to say that's of interest, much less does he have the right to criticize how they do things. They say to themselves, 'Look at him, he's a bum. *He* doesn't know how to live. How can he tell *me* how to do it?' But you see, Ms. Pierce, they're judging his spiritual life by his outside appearance, and I don't think the two things are equal. In fact, I'm sure they aren't."

"You said there were two reasons. What's the other?"

"The second group of people reject his message because it offends them and implies they're doing something wrong. They hear what he says and immediately know he's wrong because they think they're Christians. They prove it by adding up what they do that fits in with their idea of what a *true* Christian does. They go to church two times a week, they give a certain percentage of their income, they serve on five committees, they don't drink alcohol, and they don't dance or let their children watch MTV. For this group of people, Marc's message hits home directly by telling them that *what* they do doesn't matter nearly as much as *why* they do it."

"So I take it that you personally and professionally believe Marc Jones has an important message that Christians should heed. Do you think he should be in jail?"

"I do personally and professionally believe what he's saying is important. I honestly believe he's been sent by God to teach us." Eddie looked at Charles, who was nodding his support. "I can't say whether he should be in prison or not, because I'm a minister, not a lawyer."

"Reverend Smith, I want to thank you for your time and for allowing me to talk with you," Barbara said. She faced the camera. "Reporting from Praise Baptist Church, this is Barbara Pierce, with WLHR News." She gave the cameraman the sign to stop taping and turned to Eddie. "Do you really believe what Marc Jones is saying?"

"I certainly do, Ms. Pierce. And now I have a question for you. Are you a Christian?"

The question surprised Barbara. *I believe in God . . . I know Jesus is His Son who was sent to die for people's sins . . . I go to church . . . I try to be a good per-*

son and don't intentionally do things to hurt people . . . I give money to different organizations . . . I volunteer my time to help community causes . . .

"Yes, Reverend," Barbara answered confidently. "I am a Christian."

"How do you know?"

Barbara started telling him the reasons and then caught herself. "That's not right, is it?"

Eddie smiled. "Well, Ms. Pierce, I think what you've just done is a perfect example of what I was saying. You measured your Christianity by your deeds, not by your trust and dependence on God. If you listen to Marc's message, you might still be doing the same things, but there would be a difference in the reason why."

Barbara stared at her lap, deep in thought.

"The things people do aren't a measure of their Christianity or a pass to get them into heaven," Eddie said.

The cameraman came back in and told Barbara he was done packing the equipment.

Barbara stood. "Reverend Smith, do you have a business card so I can call you sometime? I really would like to talk more."

He took a business card out of his pocket and wrote a number on the back. "If you can't reach me at the church, please feel free to call my cell phone," he said, handing her the card. "I'd love to talk any time."

The last time Lord Abdullah felt disrespected, he sent Willie Harrison to kill Jamal Richardson as a lesson for anyone else that *played* him. Obviously, Abdurahman hadn't been paying attention, or else he'd forgotten. Those were the only two explanations Lord Abdullah could come up with for why the prayer leader directed his Ta'alim topic at him personally.

Doin' good deeds . . . Ha, he means bein' a sucker . . . I don't need some invisible spook takin' care of me, I'm a god . . . I come from the Original Man . . . What I get is what I earn, and I ain't givin' it to no one . . . Hold on. Maybe the reason he's sayin' this stuff is because he wants to get in on the action . . . Yeah, that's it. He's tryin' to take over and is tryin' to make me out to be the bad guy . . . Just 'cause I won't let these ignorant officers and thugs who owe me money slide by . . . I'll take care of this and get my respect . . .

Charles returned to Hillside and went to his study. The red light blinked on his answering machine. He pressed play, and his heart sank as the condescending voice filled the room.

"This is Pastor Ray Winston from the Rocky Mount Evangelical Assembly of God Church. I was at your meeting the other night and have serious problems with what you're teachin'. I'm having a meeting of concerned ministers to discuss this. We hope you can attend so we can show you the error of your thinking. Contact me if you want to discuss this." He gave his phone number, and the message ended.

Charles stared at the phone. He didn't know Ray personally but had heard of his fiery temper and the ultraconservative church Ray had founded. He wondered who would be at the meeting and what they would discuss.

How many ministers are on his side? . . . I wonder if these are the other pastors that left my meeting early . . . Are we wrong about Marc Jones? . . . Have I made a mistake? . . . I don't understand this. Why's it happening? . . .

As the final thought crept into consciousness, Charles recalled his conversation with Eddie before the interview. He needed to seek God's guidance.

Lord, I want to trust You and become dependent on You but I don't know how . . . It seems I keep being tested and failing . . . Please forgive me and help me . . . Please show me what to do and help me have the strength and courage to do it . . .

Unsure how long he'd been standing there listening for God's answers, Charles jumped when someone in the hallway called out, "Hello. Anyone here?"

"Hello. I'm back here."

Dr. Samuels came down the hall. "Reverend Hurley, good afternoon. Do you have a minute?"

"Of course. Come on in." Charles shook Samuels' outstretched hand. "What brings you by?"

"I'm sorry for barging in on you like this, but I just came from the mall, where I ran into Carl Harris, the pastor at Rocky Mount First Presbyterian Church. He was at our meeting."

"I remember seeing him."

"Well, he told me he received a phone call this morning from Ray Winston."

Charles nodded. "I just listened to a message from Ray Winston right before you came by."

"Interesting." Samuels rubbed his chin. "What did he say?"

Charles told him the message. "What did he say to Carl?"

"He said we had been trying to council people to stop trying to be like Jesus. He told Carl that Marc Jones was a false prophet. Then he invited Carl to meet with his group this evening at his church."

"What did Carl tell him?"

"He said he wouldn't be attending. Pastor Winston hung up."

Charles shook his head in frustration. "I can't believe he thinks we're telling people to stop trying to be like Jesus. We explained this to him at the meeting. Remember?"

"Sure." Samuels took a deep breath. "It sounds like you're trying to understand why Ray is doing what he's doing. I'm not sure that's so important. We need to try to see it as part of God's plan and think of the ways Ray and his group could be a part of that plan."

"What do you mean?"

"Well, I believe God has a purpose for Ray and his group, and that He will use them as part of His plan." He leaned against the door jamb. "I have to be honest. I don't know what that plan is. But I do know this. Whatever it is, He will be victorious over Satan, and all who believe and become dependent on Him will be also."

Charles considered this. "So you're saying that we already know the outcome, that God wins. It necessarily follows that whatever happens between now and then will work out the way He wants."

"Exactly, Charles."

Charles sighed in relief. "It always amazes me when someone helps me understand something I already know, but have either forgotten or simply don't practice. Thanks."

Paul Watson got his wish. He was transferred to Unit 2. Sent to C block, he was given the bunk over Johnny Daniels, near the line of commodes against the wall at the end of the block. Marc was assigned to the bottom bunk beside them.

Paul spent most of the afternoon talking with Johnny. They had quite a bit in common. Both were in prison for murder and had initially been sent to Poke Youth Institution. Neither had graduated from high school.

Paul was in for life and would probably never get out, while Johnny felt like he'd spent the best years of his life behind bars.

Johnny realized this was Paul's first time in an adult prison. He decided to take Paul under his wing and school him in prison ways.

"See 'dem young dudes watchin' TV?" he asked, looking at the floor.

" 'Dem black guys over there?" Paul asked, pointing to the front.

Johnny pushed Paul's hand down. "Man, don't ever point," he whispered. "People will kill you in here for no other reason than they *think* you're talkin' about 'em."

Paul stared at the men anyway, too naïve and stupid to be afraid. "What's their deal?"

"Them men are Five Percenters," Johnny answered quietly. He explained what the gang was about.

Paul laughed nervously. "Man, you just tryin' to scare me. That stuff don't go on 'round here."

"You got lots to learn." Johnny shook his head. "I just hope you don't get killed 'fore you figure it out." He changed the subject. "See 'dem guys over there in the middle of the block?" He referred to a small group of overweight, non-threatening older men.

"Yeah," Paul said, without pointing this time. "What about 'em? You gonna tell me they's a gang too?" He laughed. "Maybe 'dey's called the ole fat man's gang."

Johnny couldn't help but smile. He thought about how he must have seemed to Marvin Evans, the man who'd taken him under his wing when he first went to prison. Like Paul, Johnny had thought he knew all the answers. He realized now that he really hadn't even understood the questions. He'd been afraid but acted cocky. He was too caught up in acting tough to be able to back down. He'd been full of energy and was still holding out hope for the pardon that never came.

Looking at Paul Watson, Johnny felt as if he was staring in a mirror from years ago.

"Well, 'dem men right there might be the only friends you'll ever have in prison," Johnny said. "They're my boys and we're about the only Christians in this block. You'd do well to get to know 'em."

Paul couldn't give up an opportunity to prove he was a big man. "What I gotta do, get fat and lose my hair?"

Johnny answered coldly, "I wouldn't worry about gettin' fat and losin' my hair. As stupid as you are, you probably won't be 'round here more than a few days anyway."

He got up and left Paul sitting speechless.

Everyone gathered in Charles' study again that evening. The reverend told them about Ray's message and what Samuels had said about Ray being a part of God's plan.

"We're going to meet tomorrow to discuss how Ray's group can best be used," he said. "I admit I'm having a hard time *not* trying to understand why Ray is doing this and just trusting that God is in charge."

"I know what you mean," Donnie said. "I think there's another way to look at it, though."

"How's that?"

"We all agree that sometimes we get too caught up in trying to understand why things occur instead of accepting they have and that God's in charge. Well, I'm not so sure it's wrong to try to understand. It may even be one of the ways God communicates with us."

"I'm confused," Steve said. "How do you mean?"

"When we think about why something has occurred and try to understand it, we're searching for answers," Donnie said. "Maybe it's during this search that God talks to us and tells us what He wants us to do and know. The secret is making sure we look and listen the right way."

"How do we do that?" Charles asked.

"I think the first thing is to consider how what's happened could be a benefit to God," Donnie said. "I'm not sure we'll be able to answer that, but we have to keep it in mind while we search. Most importantly, though, I think we have to ask God what He's trying to do and what role He wants us to play."

Karla quickly took up the thought. "Jesus told us to ask God for everything. Remember, 'seek and ye shall find, ask and it will be given to you'? Well, maybe by asking and trying to understand things from God's perspective, we'll be given a *God* answer instead of coming up with a human one. I think it's a way we show our dependence on Him to fulfill our needs."

"I see what you're saying." Charles leaned forward. "It's not trying to understand that's a problem, it's how we do it. Instead of relying on our formulas and abilities, we need to use them to understand God's truths and to look for the answers He shows us."

Dr. Harvey Ramone had been leading the Unit 2 Wednesday night Bible study since retiring as a Baptist minister two years earlier. He was an incredibly intelligent man with perhaps a little closer connection with God than most ministers. His eyes were filled with passion that went far beyond his many years of formal education. He was extremely patient and genuinely cared about the men he fellowshipped with and taught. An analytical man, he tended to look deeply into the meaning of things people said and did. Rarely did he comment on something before he had an opportunity to consider the impact his words would have on the lives of the people he served.

Many inmates had benefited from Harvey's gentle but tough-love approach to spreading God's word. He understood the irony of trying to practice a message based on love in a place filled with hate. More than anything, though, Harvey's life was an example of a man taking to heart the Great Commission and going out into the world to make disciples of men.

Entering the Unit 2 visitation area where the group was held, Harvey saw Johnny Daniels, a longtime member of the group. He was setting out plastic chairs with someone the minister didn't know.

"How are you doing, Johnny?"

"I'm doin' great, Dr. Ramone." Johnny grinned. "I've got someone I'd like for you to meet."

Harvey walked over.

"Dr. Ramone, this is Paul Watson."

Harvey shook the young man's hand. "I hope you're going to be joining us tonight, Paul. Have you been at Caledonia long?"

"Nah," Paul answered cockily. "I ain't been here but a few days. Just transferred to two side 'dis afternoon."

Looking Paul over, Harvey asked, "How long have you been in prison?"

" 'Bout two months." He reverted to his tough-guy act. "I's at the youth spread 'til 'dey couldn't handle me no more. Ya see, I don't play games, so they sent me here."

Johnny winced. "Dr. Ramone, please excuse Paul for his lack of manners. He ain't been down long enough to know his attitude's gonna get 'im hurt." He leaned in and lowered his voice. "That's part of the reason I wanted him to come tonight. I thought while he was here, he could see how real men act."

"Well, if you want to know how the greatest man that ever walked on earth acted, all you have to do is read the Bible," Harvey said to Paul. "His name's Jesus, and the things He did are far more incredible than anything we've ever seen, or will see, until He comes again."

"Amen," Johnny offered.

Ray Winston knew all about sin. He'd spent the first twenty-nine years of his life enjoying it. One night, after spending all day drinking and smoking dope in the back of his run-down, single-wide trailer, he went to the den and passed out in front of the TV. Soon afterwards, he was shocked into a state of semiconsciousness by his family's screams. He had no idea what was happening until it was too late. The trailer was engulfed in flames, and the black smoke was so thick that rescuing anyone was impossible. His wife and two sons never had a chance. They died in each other's arms. Somehow, Ray regained enough consciousness to climb out a window. He escaped with only minor smoke inhalation.

The investigation revealed that the fire was likely caused by a smoldering joint in the back room of the trailer, where Ray and his buddies had been partying. Traumatized, Ray sank into a deep depression, lost his job, and became suicidal. One night, he tried to overdose on Tylenol. He was involuntarily committed to Coastal Plains Psychiatric Hospital. He stayed there for a month and met a pastor from Rocky Mount Assembly of God, who had come to visit another patient. He and the pastor became friends. Ray began attending the pastor's church. He quit using drugs and alcohol, asked God to forgive him for his sins, and accepted Jesus Christ as his personal savior.

After attending church regularly for almost three years, Ray believed he received a call from God to become a minister and start his own church. He enrolled in his church's school of ministry classes. After two years of dedicated home study, he received a diploma in Ministerial Studies and began the Rocky Mount Evangelical Assembly of God Church. Ever since, Ray had been completely intolerant of sin. He was constantly vigilant in the pursuit of his mission to root it out, no matter where it dwelt.

Ray wasn't bothered when he offended people with his in-your-face style of evangelism. The people of Christ's time didn't accept Jesus either when he confronted them with their sins. Ray failed to recognize that his quick temper and aggressive tactics rarely resulted in sinners' being saved. He was relentless in his pursuit to conquer sin.

He believed the evening's meeting of ministers would allow him to continue his battle.

"Thank you for taking time out of your busy schedules to come tonight," he began. "Before we get started, I wanna begin with a word of prayer." Ray took his place at the lectern. "Lord, please watch over us this evenin' and fill this place with your Holy Spirit. Please give us wisdom and strength so we can be your servants. Thank you, Lord, for sendin' your Son, Jesus Christ, to die for our sins. All of this we ask in your Son's name. Amen."

He looked out at the twenty-two men sitting in the pews, mostly members and friends of members from his church. He told them about Marc Jones and the Hillside meeting.

"They're sayin' a person's deeds ain't important, and only faith in God matters." He described the dream they'd discussed at Hillside. "They interpret it to mean men shouldn't try to be like Jesus."

Some of the men shook their heads. Ray shifted into high gear.

"I want you to know I had to leave that meetin' when they said that," he shouted. "In my heart I know it's blasphemy. As a Christian, I study my Bible daily, and can tell you what the Good Book has to say about it." He picked up a worn Bible and quickly flipped pages. "In the second chapter of the book of James, it talks a lot about the importance of a man's deeds."

"Amen brother!"

"Preach it now!"

"Specifically, the seventeenth verse says faith by itself, if not accompanied by action, is dead. In verse twenty-six, it says as the body without the spirit is dead, so faith without deeds is dead." Ray paused for effect and took a sip of water. After making a show of taking his handkerchief from his pocket and wiping perspiration from his brow, he continued. "I don't think it gets any clearer than that, my friends, and that's why I'm tellin' you it only makes sense that our deeds are a measure of how faithful we are to the Lord."

"Amen, Brother Winston," several men called out.

Ray began walking around the rectangular, uninsulated metal building that served as the sanctuary. "In the first book of John, chapter two, verses five and six, it says the way we'll know if someone is in God is if that person walks as Jesus did. To me, that clearly says if we're Christians, we gotta walk like Jesus did. In other words, we have to act like he did."

Bill Sanders, an original member of Ray's church, spoke up. "Pastor Winston, anyone who says different ain't only wrong, but they're sinnin' too." He slapped his hand on his seat emphatically.

Ray stopped in front of Bill and put his hand on his shoulder. "I'm glad to hear you say that, Bill, 'cause you're absolutely right. It is sin." He began walking again and shook his Bible vigorously. "In the book of Matthew, chapter twenty-four, verse eleven, Jesus tells us many false prophets will appear and deceive people. In Matthew, chapter seven, verse fifteen, it says to watch out for false prophets that'll come in sheep's clothin', 'cause inwardly, they're as ferocious as wolves. In verse sixteen, it tells us we'll know 'em by their fruit."

He walked back to the lectern and gently set his Bible down. "Let me ask you somethin', brothers. Where's this Marc Jones right now?" He grimaced as if he'd tasted spoiled milk. "I'll tell ya. He's in prison 'cause he's a criminal. That's the kinda fruit that comes from his tree!"

Ray was on fire for the Lord and earning forgiveness, little by little, for the deaths of his family. His voice began to quiver. "The Lord's prophet, Jeremiah, tells us about a false prophet named Hananiah. Unlike Jeremiah, who told the truth and was hated, Hananiah taught lies and was loved."

The men urged him to continue.

"Go on, Brother Winston."

"Preach to us!"

"Amen!"

"Tonight's Bible passage comes from Hebrews, chapter ten, verses twenty-six through twenty-nine," Harvey began after opening the meeting with a prayer. "Reading from the New Living Translation, it says, 'Dear friends, if we deliberately continue sinning after we have received a full knowledge of the truth, there is no other sacrifice that will cover these sins. There will be nothing to look forward to but the terrible expectation of God's judgment and the raging fire that will consume His enemies. Anyone who refused to obey the Law of Moses was put to death without mercy on the testimony of two or three witnesses. Think how much more terrible the punishment will be for those who have trampled on the Son of God and have treated the blood of the covenant as if it were common and unholy. Such people have insulted and enraged the Holy Spirit who brings God's mercy to His people.' This is the Word of God for the people of God, and everyone says . . ."

"Thanks be to God," the men replied.

"Does anyone have any comments about tonight's passage?"

A new man sitting in the back raised his hand. "Yes, sir, I do." The man rose and began to speak in a voice that was calm but filled with confidence. "In Old Testament times, God used many different ways to communicate with His people. He spoke to Abraham and Moses personally, to Isaiah through visions, and to Jacob in a dream. Despite this, His people continued to worship idols and break the laws He gave to Moses, and as a result, they were put to death. Because of this inability to follow rules in the face of temptation, God revealed Himself by speaking through His only Son, Jesus Christ, during His time on earth. Then He died on a cross according to God's will in order to pay for our sins. After being dead for three days, He arose from the grave and later ascended into heaven. When people reject the salvation offered by His blood, they reject God and His most precious gift. There is no other way for people to be saved. No matter who, or what, they call upon to help them, they will have to spend eternity enduring the fires of hell."

Who is this man? Harvey wondered.

"You see, throughout time, there have been three main types of believers," the man went on. "One group has spent their lives trying to follow rules in order to earn their way into heaven. Another group has failed to completely recognize God, and instead, have relied on themselves and their own abilities to get them to heaven. The members of the final group are the ones that believe, inwardly and outwardly, that Jesus' death on the cross enabled them to receive God's forgiveness. They've accepted that through faith, and they are trying to live a life that gives glory and praise to God for what He's done for them."

I bet this is Marc Jones, Harvey thought. *It's got to be . . . I have to call Reverend Hurley . . .*

The man paused to make eye contact with the five other inmates seated with him in the circle. "In other words, since Adam and Eve were sent out of the Garden of Eden, God gave man the power to rule the earth. It's because of the sin introduced by man and his imperfection that the world is in such bad shape and terrible things exist. Since God is perfect and sinless, He will not, and cannot, tolerate the least amount of sin in His presence and will punish it.

"In Old Testament times, man had to use the blood of animal sacrifices to atone for his sin. Then God sent the perfect sacrifice, His Son, to die on the cross for all sin, and animal blood was no longer necessary or sufficient. What it comes down to is this: God is going to punish every sin that has been, or will be, committed. The only question is whether He will expect you to pay for it with your soul in hell for all eternity, or whether He will accept the blood of His Son as your payment. It's up to you to decide."

After setting the stage, Ray was ready for his climatic ending.

"The Bible tells us two ways to recognize and identify false prophets. The people of the Old Testament looked to see if their prophecies came true. Today, we're advised to check their words against the Bible. If what they say goes against something taught in the Bible, we know they're a false prophet. Because the Lord our God *never* contradicts Himself!" He slammed his fist against the lectern. It crashed to the floor along with his Bible.

The room was silent. No one moved. Ray stared at the ceiling with sweat rolling down his face. Finally, Bill Sanders got out of his metal chair and picked up the lectern.

Ray knelt and collected the material that had fallen out his Bible. He listened to the men whisper among themselves. From what he could hear, they had listened well and were as upset as he was. It was time to present his plan for saving the sinners led astray by Marc Jones and those who sided with him.

"Men," he said softly, "we're in a battle with Satan. The book of Ephesians tells us what we need to fight this battle. We need the belt of truth, the breastplate of righteousness, shoes made from the gospel, the shield of faith, the helmet of salvation, and the sword of the Spirit, which is the word of God. It says we gotta pray in the Spirit on all occasions with all kinds of prayers and requests."

"We're with you, Brother Winston!"

"Hold on a second, Bill," Ray said. "First, we gotta prepare ourselves for battle by practicin' how to use the armor God has provided us. I believe this will be crucial when we're called to take action against Satan and will be the only way we'll be victorious. Second, we need to train our families and our friends how to use the armor so not only will they be protected, but we'll have more Christian warriors. Finally, the fifth chapter of the first of book of Peter, the eighth verse, tells us to watch out for attacks from the Devil, our great enemy. He prowls around like a roarin' lion, lookin' for some victim to devour. I'm tellin' you brothers, the lion is in our midst. The only way we'll be able to withstand his attack is to depend on God's strength. We need to be alert and aware of what's goin' on around us. We need to use every piece of armor He's provided us."

What did you think about the meeting tonight?" Harvey asked as Johnny stacked the last chair.

"That new guy, Preacher Man, is a really smart dude when it comes to talkin' about the Bible."

"Did you learn a lot from him tonight?"

"Well, I don't mean no disrespect to you, but when he was talkin', it seemed like I could understand everything he was sayin'. I mean, it was almost like he was readin' my thoughts and talkin' directly to me. Kinda crazy ain't it?"

"I don't think that's crazy at all, Johnny," Harvey answered. "Maybe he *was* talking to you."

. . . and to me . . . and to Paul . . . and to every other person that's been alive for the last two thousand years . . .

Steve, Donnie, and Karla walked together to the Hillside parking lot, feeling good about trying to understand things from a God perspective and believing that He was definitely in control of what was happening. Steve hugged Karla and shook Donnie's hand, then got in his car and left. Donnie walked Karla to his truck and opened the door for her. She climbed in. As he was shutting the door, he said softly, more to himself than to her, "I love you."

The words surprised him because he hadn't been thinking about saying them; they just seemed to come out. Embarrassed, he walked around the back of the truck and hoped she hadn't heard him.

Where did that come from? . . . What am I thinking about? . . . Have I lost my mind? . . .

He opened his door and got perhaps the biggest surprise of his life.

"I love you too."

Donnie was shocked. For a second it felt like he was dreaming. "What?" he asked, too surprised to be emotional.

"I heard what you said." Karla's sparkling eyes held his. "I just wanted you to know I love you too."

Donnie felt his face turn several shades of red. He was thankful she couldn't see it in the moonlight reflecting off the hood of his truck.

He pulled her close. "I love you, Karla. I really do. More than you'll ever know."

JOHN 6:40 "For it is my Father's will that everyone who looks to the Son and believes in him shall have eternal life, and I will raise him up at the last day." (NIV)

Chapter 18

Thursday Morning

If not for Officer Green, one of the few officers working C block that wasn't on the take, Lord Abdullah could've taken care of his problem the previous night. Instead, he'd laid on his bunk simmering until he drifted off to sleep and was awakened at three in the morning by the terrible dream. Confused and sweating, he realized he had almost two hours to wait before he could confront Abdurahman.

"Psst . . .Pete, wake up." He pushed up on the bunk above him.

"What man?" Pete grumbled after a minute of not so gentle prodding.

"Yo man, get up. Meet me by the sink."

"All right." Pete sighed wearily. He climbed down and went to the back of the block.

"What'cha want?" Pete said, going through the handshake ritual by habit despite the early hour.

"Look dude, I can't sleep 'cause I keep thinkin' 'bout how that prayer leader dissed me. I'm gonna kill 'im."

"Man, that's gonna bring some serious heat down on us."

"Don't you think I know 'dat?" Lord Abdullah snapped. "That dude dissed me in front of all 'dem people. I can't just let that go, man. I gotta do somethin'. If I don't, then every thug at this camp's gonna try and play me."

"Lord," Pete said, "anyone who'd try that would be crazy. Everybody knows what would happen if 'dey did."

"Yeah, I guess you're right." Lord Abdullah liked to have his ego stroked. "Still, I can't let 'im get away with it."

"Maybe you won't have to. We could both go to Fajr and after the prayer, meet him in the dinin' hall. I could talk with him and tell him what'll happen if he does it again."

"I don't know." Lord Abdullah hated backing down.

"Maybe I could tell him he has to apologize and say he didn't mean it towards you or somethin' like that."

"Let me think about it," Lord Abdullah said. "Get me up in time to go, just in case." He strutted back to his bunk, feeling in control of his world again . . . the way a god should.

It wasn't five o'clock yet, but Donnie was wide awake and decided to get out of bed.

Today's going to be great . . . I feel like a new man . . . Thank you, God, for bringing me here and for sending me one of Your angels . . .

Charles' alarm went off at five o'clock, but he didn't need it. He'd been awake all night, thinking about Ray Winston. He wasn't sure why he felt so anxious. He couldn't shake the nagging feeling that something bad was going to happen. He got up and studied what Scripture had to say about recognizing God's spirit.

When Abdurahman approached the octagonal stainless-steel table, Lord Abdullah and Pete said nothing.

"Do you mind if I sit with y'all?"

Pete nodded to the empty seat across from Lord Abdullah.

"Thank you," Abdurahman said. "It's great to see you this morning at Fajr. I believe Allah, all praise and . . ."

"Look man," Lord Abdullah said, loud enough to get the dinning hall officers' attention. "I don't know what's goin' on, but dissin' me in front of all them men was wack. How do *you* know that I need to forgive people? 'Dem sorry people dogged me and owe me money. 'Dey stole from me, man!"

"I'm not sure what you're talking about," Abdurahman said. "I'd never dis' you, man."

"That's a lie," Lord Abdullah spat. He got to his feet.

Sensing that things were about to get out of hand, Pete stood too. "Man," he said to Abdurahman, pointing to the door, "you better get outta here. Now!"

"Sir," Abdurahman said, backing away from the table, "if you're referring to yesterday's Ta'alim, then you're mistaken to believe I was talking about you. For Allah the Most High said, 'You shall not attain piety until you spend out of that which you love. Whatever good you spend, Allah knows well.' I believe it's necessary for true Muslims to be charitable and do good deeds. I'm sorry if you took that to mean I was making a comment about something you've done. Perhaps your conscience is bothering you, and that's why you feel the sting of Allah's words."

Finishing his devotional, Charles felt encouraged and called Ray's church. He didn't expect the pastor to be there and was surprised when he answered.

"Good Morning. Rocky Mount Evangelical Assembly of God, this is Pastor Winston, how may I help you?"

Charles cleared his throat. "Pastor Winston, this is Charles Hurley. I got your message and wanted to talk. Is this a good time?"

Ray's pleasant tone changed dramatically. "Now's fine with me. I think it's horrendous you, a supposed man of God, would try to poison the minds of His flock by teachin' 'em they shouldn't try to be like Jesus."

"I wish you'd let me explain. I think you've gotten the wrong idea."

"No," Ray snapped, "you're the one who's wrong. I'm just sorry you'll have to burn in hell 'cause of it. In Second Peter, the second chapter, it says, 'There were also false prophets in Israel, just as there will be false teachers among you. They'll cleverly teach their destructive heresies about God and even turn against their Master who bought them. Theirs will be a swift and terrible end. Many will follow their evil teachin' and shameful immorality. 'Cause of them, Christ and his true way will be slandered.'"

"Pastor Winston," Charles said, more calmly than he felt, "I certainly think you're correct in testing the information you've heard. In First John, chapter four, it tells us not to believe everyone who claims to speak by the Holy Spirit. It says we must test them to see if the spirit they have comes from God."

"You're exactly right," Ray interrupted. "I've tested them, and I know without a doubt the message you and your so-called minister friends are teachin' goes against the Bible."

Charles managed to keep his cool. "The rest of what I was reading says the way to find out if the person has the Spirit of God is if they acknowledge that Jesus Christ became a human being. If they do, then that person has the Spirit of God, and if not, then they have the spirit of the Antichrist."

"Mr. Hurley," Ray growled, deliberately not addressing him as reverend, "I'm sure you're aware that anyone can say anything, but that don't make it true. What matters is the fruit they produce. Now I ask you, what kind of fruit has this Marc person produced?"

"I think . . . "

"Let me tell you," Ray shouted. "He's produced the type of fruit that's put him in jail. He's produced the type of fruit that's destroyed the house of the Lord. He's produced the type of fruit that's hurt the people of God and made them doubt the Lord." He was almost screaming now. "No sir, this man ain't no Christian. He's the Antichrist and deserves to burn in hell!"

"But Pastor . . ."

"I'll pray for your soul, Mr. Hurley," Ray said. He slammed down the phone.

And I'll do the same for you, Charles thought, staring at the dead receiver.

Donnie heard his cell phone ring even over the loud music. He turned down the stereo and answered without looking at the caller ID.

"Good morning, Sunshine," Karla said brightly. "I just wanted to call you before work to let you know I'm thinking about you."

"That's good," Donnie said, grinning. "I was thinking about you too."

"I guess it works out, then," she said. "Do you have a big day planned?"

"I don't think I have many patients to see, but I do have a lot of paperwork to catch up on. How about you?"

"I don't think my day's going to be too bad, but since I'm on call at Nash, you can never be sure."

"Want to get dinner before we meet Charles and Steve?"

"I was hoping you'd ask."

"Well, I was hoping you'd say yes. Hey, before I forget, I've been thinking about taking you to the beach for a weekend. A buddy of mine has a place at Holden Beach he said we could use sometime."

"Sounds like fun. Let me check my schedule to see when I'm off and I'll let you know."

"Well, then, I'm glad you called this morning. By the way, I meant what I said last night. I do love you."

"I love you too," Karla said. "I really do."

The phone rang as soon as Charles hung up.

Who's calling me this early? . . . Maybe Ray's calling back to apologize . . .

"Hello?" he said. "Pastor Winston?"

"Reverend Hurley? This is Harvey Ramone. I was at your meeting the other evening with Dr. Samuels."

"Yes," Charles replied, trying to remember the man. "I'm sorry. I thought it was someone calling me back."

"That's no problem. Should I call back later?"

"No, no," Charles answered quickly. "What can I help you with?"

"I was calling to talk with you about Marc Jones. I lead a Bible study group at Caledonia, and Mr. Jones was at last night's meeting. I was hoping we could get together and talk about what he said."

The day was gray and dreary, but Donnie was smiling when he got to the farm. Instead of going to his office, he headed to Unit 1. Steve was already in his office.

"What's up?" Donnie said, sitting down in his usual chair.

"Wow," Steve said. "You're sure happy this morning. I bet it has something to do with Karla."

"Good guess, my friend. I can honestly say I've never felt like this before."

Steve rolled his eyes. "It sounds like love to me."

"I do believe it is."

"Well, I'm really happy for you guys." Steve swiveled around in his desk chair. "What do you have on your agenda today? Any patients I need to have brought out for you over here?"

"I don't have any in Unit 1. I just came by to see if you were in before I go see Marc. I'm curious to find out if he went to Bible study last night."

"Let me know what you hear. Hey, are we still meeting at the church tonight?"

"Yeah, around seven o'clock." Donnie headed for the door. "Thanks for being a good friend," he said from the hallway.

"Hey, Doc?" Steve called. "It works both ways."

By the time Lord Abdullah made it back to his bunk, he was furious.

I ain't believin' that so-called prayer leader . . . I don't care what happens, nobody disses Lord Abdullah and lives to tell . . . I'm a god and expect to be treated like one . . .

He felt underneath his thin mattress.

"Come on, man," Pete pleaded. "It ain't worth it. That dude's a nobody. He's talkin' outta his head, man."

Lord Abdullah's nostrils flared and in the next instant, he threw a sucker punch. Pete flopped backward onto the next bunk.

"If you're my boy," Lord Abdullah said, glaring at Pete, "then you'll watch my back. If not, I'll kill you too. It don't matter to me." He turned back to his mattress and found what he was searching for. Sliding the shank into his pants, he threw a towel at Pete so he could stem the flow of blood from his nose.

"Don't ever mess wit' me, boy. I'm a god and I'll destroy you if you get in my way."

"Harvey," Charles said, opening the door. "Come on in. Can I get you some coffee?"

"No thanks. I've been up a while this morning, and I've already had too much." Harvey shut the door behind him. "I guess you could say I'm pretty excited about what's going on."

Charles poured himself a cup. "I've got so many questions, I don't know where to start."

"Well, let me tell you what happened and we can go from there."

Charles gestured toward two chairs. The men sat down, and Charles listened as Harvey related how Marc had explained the passage of scripture like he'd experienced what he was discussing.

"Who do you think he is, Harvey?"

"I'm almost scared to say. It just seems too unbelievable."

"I think we both know it isn't."

Harvey nodded. "I believe you're right."

"Okay then, what do you think is his purpose for coming here, of all places?"

Harvey shook his head. "I don't know. I'd guess it has to do with the people God has brought here. I mean, why do you think He chose for His Son to be born in a stable in Bethlehem two thousand years ago?"

"You've got a point."

"As far as his purpose, I was hoping you might know more about that than me."

"Well, let me tell you what we know," Charles said. He reviewed what they'd uncovered about Marc.

Walking down the hall to Unit 2, Donnie noticed the man lying on his bunk holding a bloody towel over his nose. "Are you okay?" he asked.

Pete didn't hear until Donnie asked him the second time. He struggled to sit up. "Ah, yes, sir. I just got a nose bleed."

Donnie frowned and approached the bars separating the block from the hallway. "Do you get them frequently?"

"Yes, sir." Pete looked at the towel. "I think it's stopped now."

"Have you been checked out by medical?"

"Yes, sir. I've had nose bleeds since I was little."

"All right," Donnie said. "I just wanted to check."

At the end of the hallway, Marc was sitting on his bunk talking with Paul and Johnny. Donnie couldn't hear what was being said, but he guessed Marc was teaching something, because even the dorm janitor, who was wearing a Kuffi prayer cap and cleaning the nearby toilets, seemed to be listening intently.

"Excuse me, Mr. Jones," Donnie said as he approached the bars. "I need to see you upstairs in the multipurpose room, if I may."

"Certainly, Dr. Thompson." Marc excused himself and walked toward Donnie at the front of the block. He stopped and turned back to Paul and Johnny. "Remember, your faith has saved you and your sins are forgiven."

Officer Sawyer was in charge of C block. She was one of the original officers Lord Abdullah had recruited when he arrived at Caledonia, and she knew she didn't have a choice about letting her *real* employer enter when she opened the bar door to let Marc Jones leave. As much money as Lord Abdullah paid her, she really didn't care what he did, as long as the cash kept flowing her way.

Once inside the cell, Lord Abdullah scanned the block for Abdurahman. Seeing him in the back mopping the bathroom floor, Lord Abdullah walked quietly past the row of bunks. He held the shank made from kitchen utensils down by his side.

Abdurahman moved to rinse his mop off in the bucket beside him and caught a reflection of light and sudden movement out of the corner of his eye. He spun around, surprising Lord Abdullah, who slipped on the wet floor and went down hard. The shank skidded across the floor.

Realizing what was happening, Abdurahman tried to run, but Lord Abdullah grabbed his foot and he went down. Lord Abdullah leaped up and went after his shank, which had slid under the wash basin.

Abdurahman scrambled to his feet. Before he could run, Lord Abdullah yelled and lunged for him, stabbing him in the right shoulder. Abdurahman fell heavily to the floor.

Marc sat at the table in the multipurpose room as Donnie placed his book bag in the corner and took a seat.

"Thanks for coming to see me, Mr. Jones. It looked like you were talking with those men when I walked up."

"I was, but I don't think that's why you called me up here."

"You're right," Donnie said. "Last night, a group of people at my church talked about trying to understand things from a God perspective instead of a human one. I think sometimes I rely too much on myself to come up with answers and don't listen to God's answers, even when they are right in front of me."

"Most people aren't even aware they forget to look to God for answers, Dr. Thompson," Marc said warmly. I'm glad to hear you've made the decision to try."

"So, do you think it's possible?"

"Through God, all things are possible. I also know that God has given you many gifts and expects you to use them to the best of your ability to serve His purpose. He knows you'll make mistakes and will sometimes fail. That's why He sent His son. You don't have to worry about being perfect. All you have to do is continue to try and do His will, and I'm sure you'll be rewarded in heaven."

Officer Sawyer couldn't believe what was happening. She hesitated before blowing her whistle to summon other officers for help. She unlocked the bar door and ran to where the men were fighting. Other inmates were gathering to watch. Screaming at Lord Abdullah to stop, Sawyer removed her pepper spray from her utility belt. She raised the canister to administer several short blasts of the chemical.

Unexpectedly, a Five Percenter standing nearby ripped the pepper spray from her hand and turned it on her. The spray stung her face, and her eyes began to water. Gagging and gasping for breath, she collapsed into a fetal position on the floor, rubbing her eyes and moaning in pain.

The man squatted beside her and sprayed her in the face two more times, laughing at her.

Paul and Johnny had jumped off the bunk as soon as they saw Lord Abdullah stab Abdurahman. Johnny grabbed Lord Abdullah in a headlock. A Five Percenter stepped in and grabbed Johnny by the hair, then took a razor blade and slashed his throat. Johnny let go of Lord Abdullah and put his hands to his neck as if to scream, but he was drowning in his own blood. He collapsed to the floor.

Mike Ramsey, a wannabe Five Percenter, decided this was his chance to get Paul. He'd been eyeing him since he first came to C block. Picking up Abdurahman's mop, he struck Paul on the back of the head hard enough to splinter the handle. Paul flew forward, unconscious, and his forehead hit the washbasin. Abdurahman's Muslim brother, Benny Sikes, grabbed a piece of the broken mop handle and hit Ramsey in the upper back. Had it not been for Benny, Ramsey would have continued beating Paul until he was dead.

Officer Sawyer blindly crawled away from the brawl, hoping to avoid further injury. Just then, a man she'd written up two weeks earlier for disobeying her orders grabbed her by the hair and punched her in the face. "I told ya I'd get mine one day." He hauled back his fist to strike her again, but Benny hammered the broken stick he was still holding into the man's neck. Three more blows to the man's face and forehead rendered him unconscious.

Benny bent over to help Officer Sawyer to her feet.

Mike, who'd recovered from the blow, took a shank and stabbed Benny in the back.

Across the cell block, Lord Abdullah picked Abdurahman up by the hair. Holding a razor blade against his neck, Lord Abdullah forced the prayer leader past the rows of bunk beds.

His friend picked up the bloody shank that had killed Benny and held it to Officer Sawyer's neck, forcing her to follow them out of the block.

"Caledonia Correctional Institution, this is Officer Patterson," the switchboard operator said. "How may I direct your call?"

"This is Reverend Charles Hurley. I'd like to speak with Dr. Thompson."

"Sure. Let me transfer you."

After a pause, the phone rang again. Amber answered. "Hello, this is mental health."

"Good morning. This is Charles Hurley. I'm trying to get in touch with Dr. Thompson. Is he in?"

"You must be his minister," Amber said. "I've heard a lot about you."

"I hope it was the good things."

"It definitely was. Dr. Thompson thinks quite a lot of you."

"I'm glad to hear that."

"Well," Amber said, "he isn't in the office right now. I think he went to see one of the unit managers before seeing patients."

"That wouldn't by chance be Steve Johnson, would it?"

"Yes, sir," Amber replied, sounding surprised that Charles knew.

"Would it be possible for you to transfer me to Mr. Johnson's office? I know Steve, and I need to talk with him, too."

"Sure. It was nice talking with you, Reverend." There was a click, and Charles waited for Steve to answer.

"Unit 1, this is Steve Johnson."

"Steve, this is Charles. How are you this morning?"

"Great, and you?"

"I'm doing well. Hey, I spoke with Ray Winston this morning, and then with Harvey Johnson, who leads a Bible study group at Caledonia."

"I've heard he's a good man."

"He is. I was calling to tell you and Donnie about what Harvey said happened last night."

Suddenly, Steve dropped the receiver. The phone line abruptly went dead.

Two other officers besides Sawyer were beaten severely during the brawl. One was handcuffed to a cot and the other was knocked unconscious. A third officer managed to escape and made it to the Unit 2 outer door. "Help! Help!" he desperately screamed into his prison radio. "We've got a riot in Unit 2. Send officers now!"

Lord Abdullah and his friend led their hostages through the Unit 2 inner bar door as inmates from the other blocks screamed their support. They quickly moved down the narrow hallway and turned the corner to climb the steep concrete stairs to the second floor. Lord Abdullah snatched the keys from Officer Sawyer's utility belt and unlocked the bar door, which prevented inmate movement. He then stepped back around the corner.

An officer who had heard the radio call for help turned the corner at the top of the stairs and sprinted down the hall. When he reached the bottom, Lord Abdullah shoved Abdurahman in front of him. Both men fell heavily when they collided. Holding his wounded shoulder, Abdurahman screamed in pain. Lord Abdullah pounced on the downed officer with his razor blade. He grabbed a fistful of Abdurahman's bloody T-shirt and continued up the stairs as an expanding pool of blood covered the concrete floor below.

Lord Abdullah's friend pressed his shank against Officer Sawyer's neck and forced her up the steps. Halfway up, someone screamed at the man to stop climbing. Sensing her opportunity, Officer Sawyer shoved the inmate, and he lost his balance. Tumbling backwards and landing hard at the bottom of the stairs, he let go of the shank.

Her eyes still burning from the pepper spray, Sawyer jumped over him and grabbed the open bar door at the bottom of the stairs for leverage. The door slammed shut behind her, and she tripped over the dead officer. Dazed, she was rescued by other officers, and her captor was taken back into custody.

Lord Abdullah and Abdurahman disappeared around the corner at the top of the stairs.

Steve grabbed two cans of pepper spray and a short baton on the way out of his office. He pointed at Sergeant Houlahan. "I want you to secure this unit and send all available officers to the Unit 2 visitation area."

"Yes, sir." Houlahan ran from the office.

Steve gestured at two other sergeants. "You two, grab your short batons and come with me." He hollered at the control booth officer to open the bar door to the stairs.

The two sergeants followed Steve down. Sergeant Houlahan was in the hallway giving orders to several young, nervous officers. One of them unlocked the bar door, and the officer in the downstairs control booth opened the doors leading into the Unit 2 visitation area. Several more officers were inside waiting for orders.

Steve grabbed a prison radio. "Twenty-two eighty-four to twenty-two twelve. Come in Captain Bradley, this is Steve Johnson. Over."

"Yeah, twenty-two eighty-four, this is twenty-two twelve. Over."

"Captain, I've mustered fifteen officers in the Unit 2 visitation area," Steve said. "I'll await instructions from you before proceeding. Over."

"Right now, I want you to contain the disturbance to Unit 2," Bradley said. "Do not, I repeat, do not allow any inmates to enter Unit 2 by way of the outer bar door."

Charles tried calling back, but no one answered. He tried again and waited. The phone just rang.

At first it seemed like the usual noises around Caledonia: yelling, cussing, and bar doors slamming shut. But when the noises grew louder, Donnie went to find out what was happening. When he opened the door, he came face to face with the man who had been downstairs mopping the bathroom floor. Another inmate was standing behind him holding a razor blade to his neck. For a brief second, no one moved.

Lord Abdullah spoke first. "If you don't get back in there, I'm gonna slit this man's throat from ear to ear."

"Hold on a second." Donnie held up his hands. There was terror in the captive's eyes.

"Doc," Lord Abdullah said without raising his voice, "if you don't move in the next two seconds, you're gonna be wearin' this man's blood. One . . ."

"I'm moving, alright?" Donnie took two slow steps backward.

"Hurry up, get in there." Lord Abdullah followed them in and reached behind him to shut the door. He told Marc to stand and made both men face the wall. Using Officer Sawyer's keys, he locked the door and ordered the men to put their hands behind them.

Donnie and Marc quickly complied.

Lord Abdullah threw Officer Sawyer's handcuffs at Abdurahman. "Put these on them."

When Donnie and Marc were cuffed, Lord Abdullah pushed Abdurahman into a chair. "Sit down."

"What do you want?" Donnie asked.

Lord Abdullah backhanded Donnie across the jaw. """Right now, I want you to shut up and let me think!"

"Mr. Powell, we've contained the situation to Unit 2," Captain Bradley reported. "All of the unit managers are reporting their units are locked down and inmate movement has ceased. Steve Johnson is leading the fifteen officers guarding the Unit 2 outer bar door. The twenty officers manning the inner bar door area are being led by Lieutenant Robbins."

"When you say the situation is contained to Unit 2, does that include the cell blocks upstairs?" Powell asked.

"Sir, it's my understanding the inmates in the two upstairs cell blocks are also involved, and the officers who were assigned to them have been overtaken, as have three of the four downstairs officers."

"Are you saying five officers are being held hostage?"

Captain Bradley hesitated. "Well, sir, I'm saying that of the six officers assigned to Unit 2, only one made it out. I'm not sure what the status is of the other five."

"I understand," Powell said. "Alright, find out about the other officers. Have some men go to the equipment storage sheds and get the riot gear. The PERT team's been alerted and Raleigh's been notified. Keep me apprised of any changes."

He hung up, sensing the situation was going to get uglier.

"Sir," Donnie said respectfully, "that man's shoulder is badly wounded. He needs medical attention or he might die."

Lord Abdullah spun around. "Doc, if you don't stop interruptin' me, you're gonna be needin' some medical attention. Now shut up." He grabbed Donnie's shirt and pressed the razor against his neck. "You understand?"

Donnie's thoughts were racing and he could only nod his head slightly. *This man seems to be easily rattled . . . What's his motivation for doing this? . . . This seems like the result of a situation gone bad, rather than part of a plan . . . I gotta keep my cool and pick my opportunities . . .*

Donnie jumped when his pager began beeping. Everyone in the room turned toward him. He was unable to turn it off because his hands were cuffed behind him. He caught a glance of the flashing number just before Lord Abdullah ripped the pager off his belt and smashed it on the floor.

Pray for us Charles . . . please pray God will protect us . . .

When Donnie didn't return the third page, Charles' concern peaked.

No one answers at the prison . . . Donnie won't return my pages . . . Steve hung up abruptly . . . Something bad's happening . . .

As the feeling of dread grew, Charles paged Karla and began pacing around his study. When the phone rang, he snatched it up on the first ring. "Hello, Karla?"

"Yes, Charles. Did you page me?"

"I sure did. Thanks for calling back so quick." He explained what was happening.

"That's sort of spooky," Karla said, "but I'm sure it's probably nothing. Let me try Donnie's private office number. I'll call you back when I hear something."

Outside the multipurpose room, there were occasional shouts from inmates who were destroying property and trying to open the cell block doors without a key. Donnie knew it was possible, and he thought that when they did, they would take over the entire upstairs portion of Unit 2, which would permit them access to the multipurpose room.

Lord, please protect us. Give us the strength to endure this and help us to come out of it safely . . .

While Donnie prayed, Abdurahman sat nearby in obvious pain, trying to recall what he'd read in the *Holy Qur'an*, Surah 2, verse 214: "Or think you that you will enter Paradise without such (trials) as came to those who passed away before you? They were afflicted with severe poverty and ailments and were so shaken that even the Messenger and those who believed along with him said, 'When (will come) the help of Allah?' Yes! Certainly, the help of Allah is near!"

Is Allah testing me? . . . Am I being punished for a sin I've committed? . . . I've got to be patient and continue to seek the will of Allah . . . No one but Allah fully knows the reason this has happened . . .

"All praise and glory be upon you, Allah," Abdurahman said softly.

Donnie turned toward him. "What did you say?" He mouthed the words without making a sound.

Abdurahman seemed to be in a trance. He appeared to be totally unaware Donnie was trying to communicate with him.

Donnie glanced at Marc, who sat to his right and looked at the ceiling.

Marc lowered his gaze, and his eyes met Donnie's. He smiled. "All of this is the will of my Father in heaven," he said, not trying to hide that he was talking.

Donnie was concerned Lord Abdullah would overhear, but when neither he nor Abdurahman seemed to notice, he turned his attention back to Marc.

"Do not be afraid, Donnie." Marc smiled calmly. Trust in God. He will protect you and will use this to teach many."

"Hello," Amber finally answered. "Mental health."

"Amber, this is Karla Lynch. I'm trying to reach Dr. Thompson. Is he around?"

"Dr. Thompson's here today, but he went over to the prison to see Mr. Johnson. I think he had some patients to see after that," Amber said as a phone started ringing in the background. "Can you hold on a second?"

"Sure, no problem."

A moment later, Amber came back on the line. Her voice was shaky. "Dr. Lynch, I'm sorry but I've got to go. That was the superintendent's secretary. Something's happened inside the prison and all support staff have been ordered to leave. I've got to go."

"What happened, Amber?"

"I don't know. I'm sorry, but I've got to go." She hung up.

A command center was set up across the street from Powell's office in the brick house normally used for staff training. Despite its run-down outward appearance, the house was wired as a communication center and was large enough to accommodate many people. Its primary function was to provide a focal point for analyzing information so decisions could be made about using the Prison Emergency Response Team, or PERT, to resolve situations peacefully.

Powell was in command, and his two assistant superintendents reported directly to him. Jeff Hagerton, the Assistant Superintendent of Programs, also served as the public information officer. Floyd Faulk, a former correctional captain who had recently become the Assistant Superintendent of Custody, was the captain of the PERT team.

Several correctional officers were deployed to secure the perimeter of the prison property in order to prevent people from getting too close once news of the situation leaked out. Members of the PERT team began arriving, and the command center filled up fast with officers ready to fulfill the duties they'd been specially trained to handle.

Although she was a physician used to coping with intense stress without getting rattled, Karla had to admit she was feeling anxious. She tried looking at the situation in a logical manner and began thinking of ways she could find out what was going on. She had an idea and got up from the cubicle in the Nash ER. She walked toward the back where the EMTs gathered after bringing in a patient.

"Excuse me," she said to the tallest of the three men. "You're with the Halifax County Rescue Squad, aren't you?"

"Yes, ma'am."

"Have you had any calls from Caledonia this morning?"

"Funny you should ask," he answered. "On our way here, we heard a call saying that two officers had been injured and required emergency transport to Halifax Regional Hospital."

"Do you know what happened?" Karla asked, her heart racing.

"No, ma'am, I don't. Would you like me to see what I can find out?"

"I would very much appreciate it," she said, turning back toward the cubicle to call Charles.

Sitting at the head of the conference table in the back of the command center with his two assistants, Powell was on the phone talking to the North Carolina Secretary of the Department of Corrections. When he hung up, Captain Bradley came in the room, standing at attention.

"What do you have for me, Captain?" Powell asked.

"Sir, I've interviewed the inmates from Unit 2 that managed to get out and I've talked with Officer Sawyer, who was assigned to C block. A group of the inmates have taken control of the four Unit 2 downstairs cell blocks. They're holding two officers hostage and have the kind of weapons you'd expect—razors, shanks, and two short batons they took from the officers. They also have both officers' pepper spray containers, but used 'em up when this thing started. The bar door leading upstairs to E and F blocks is shut and locked."

"Alright," Powell said, scribbling notes.

"A second group of inmates is upstairs in Unit 2. They have taken one officer hostage. He's been severely beaten and is being held inside of E block. Apparently, he was in the hallway between the two blocks and never had a chance to escape. The other upstairs officer had his throat slit and bled to death when he reached the bottom of the stairs tryin' to respond to the call that went out over the radio. The inmates upstairs can't move between the cell blocks because the murdered officer had the key to F block, and his body was found on the downstairs side of the locked bar door. The inmates in E block have probably taken the keys from the officer they're holdin' and can get outside of their block, but have nowhere to go, since they can't get into F."

"Who was the officer killed?"

"His name's Bernie Wallingham. I've given that information to the assistant superintendent."

"Anything else?" Powell asked.

Bradley nodded. "From what we can tell, Tony Jackson, a.k.a. Lord Abdullah, started this thing after he got in a fight with the Muslim prayer leader in Unit 2, C block. Officer Sawyer went in to break it up, and things jumped off from there."

"Okay, go on."

"According to Officer Sawyer, who's been transported to Halifax Regional, Jackson and another inmate tried to force her and the prayer leader upstairs. That's when the upstairs officer was killed, and Sawyer got away. We've got the inmate that was holdin' her in custody. It's our best guess that Jackson and his hostage are probably locked in the multipurpose room."

"What type of weapon does he have?"

"Sawyer said he had a razor blade and her short baton."

Powell stopped writing and took off his glasses. "I want you to account for every employee that was scheduled to work today. I don't want to be surprised later on."

"Ten-four."

"Also," Powell added, "I want you to interview the inmate who was

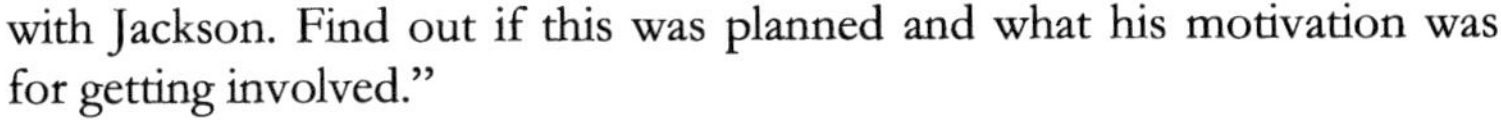

with Jackson. Find out if this was planned and what his motivation was for getting involved."

For four years, Kelvin Oleander had been reporting the news for WHRR, the Roanoke Rapids local television station. Like usual, he'd been monitoring his scanner while at the office, and he heard the call go out for Halifax County EMTs to respond to Caledonia. At first, he hadn't paid it much attention. It was semi-routine for an ambulance to be sent to transport inmates to the hospital for one reason or another. However, after hearing further radio traffic indicating two officers had been severely injured, Kelvin knew something was happening.

He decided to call his cousin, who was a correctional sergeant. The phone rang and rang. He wondered if this was the break he'd been looking for.

Peterson, Dickerson, Bowe, stay here at the outer door," Steve ordered. "Report anything unusual." He walked off to check around the back of Unit 2.

He suddenly remembered that before the alert came over the prison radio, Donnie had gone to talk to Marc in the Unit 2 multipurpose room.

Did he make it out alright? . . . Where is he now? . . .

Steve made an about-face and ran back to the visitation area to use the phone. He dialed Donnie's extension and let it ring several times, then had him paged.

Karla was on the verge of losing control and knew she needed to be somewhere other than the Nash ER. Fortunately, her patient's test results were negative and his symptoms could be treated with antibiotics and a two-week follow-up. She finished documenting her note, and after speaking with the patient's mother, she called Charles. He answered almost before the phone rang.

"Hello, Donnie?" Charles asked hopefully.

"Charles, it's Karla. I just wanted to know if you were still at your office. I need to come over."

"What have you found out?"

"I haven't heard anything else, but I still can't get in touch with Donnie or Steve."

"It's probably nothing," he said, "but why don't you come on over?"

Lord Abdullah was talking to himself and pacing as his anger escalated. "Think man, think." He approached the Muslim prayer leader. "What'cha lookin' at, punk? You know all 'dis is your fault. If you wouldn't of said that stuff last night I wouldn't of had to set you straight." He got in Abdurahman's face. "I'm a god and deserve to be treated like one. That spook god of yours ain't nothin' but just a bunch of wishes."

"Sir," Marc said calmly. "Do you know God?"

Everyone turned.

Lord Abdullah stalked across the room. He leaned over, pressing the razor against the side of Marc's neck. "Do I know what?" He grinned cruelly and waited, thinking intimidation would result in a retraction of the question.

"I asked if you know who God is," Marc said confidently.

Lord Abdullah squinted and carefully considered his next move. If he said yes, this guy would ask him about it. If he said no, the guy was going to try to teach him, and Lord Abdullah would cut his throat.

"Yeah," he finally responded. "I sure do know god. It's me." He laughed, thinking he'd outsmarted Preacher Man.

Abdurahman spoke softly. "Sir, Allah is the one and only . . . "

Before he could finish or turn his face to deflect the blow, Lord Abdullah spun around and punched him in the mouth, breaking his front teeth out and knocking him backwards out of the chair.

Although Kelvin had lived and worked in Raleigh for only a year before being forced to resign and return to Roanoke Rapids, he'd been there long enough to figure out that he wasn't suited for small-city life. He had big dreams of becoming someone famous in the television business and knew he needed a bigger place to make it happen. Sure, he'd failed when he first ventured out in the world, but that had been because he was young and inexperienced. Now that he was older and wiser, he knew all he needed was an opportunity, and he sensed that whatever was happening at Caledonia may be the break he'd prayed for. The prison was one of the largest employers in the area, and if something was going on out there, it would be big, since almost everyone in town either worked there or had a relative that did.

If I can get the scoop on this story, it could be my ticket outta here, he thought as he continued to dial the phone.

After several more minutes of trying, he was convinced he smelled trouble brewing. He climbed in the station's sedan and drove the twenty miles out there to uncover it.

My viewers deserve it, he thought as he sped out of the station's gravel parking lot. *And so do I.*

Hank King and Walter Felton were relatively new to Caledonia and the North Carolina Department of Corrections. They were both in their mid-twenties and had been sentenced to spend the rest of their lives in prison. Hank was convicted of first-degree murder, although he swore he was framed. Walter was convicted of kidnapping, raping, and torturing his next door neighbor over a three-day period of time. Walter never denied what he did. He said the woman deserved it. Both men knew they'd never leave prison alive. They had nothing to lose and everything to gain from participating in the riot, since the most powerful man they'd ever known was leading it.

"Yo, Walter," Hank said to his bunk mate, "let's go try and help Lord Abdullah."

"Help do what?"

"Act as lookouts or somethin', I don't know. I guess I'm just thinkin' we could impress him, and after 'dis is over, he'll ask us to be Five Percenters."

"Yeah." Walter grinned. "We'd be set 'den."

"Let's do it, man."

2 THESSALONIANS 3:3 "But the Lord is faithful;
He will make you strong and guard you from the evil one."
(NLT)

Chapter 19

Thursday Afternoon

After eating a sandwich prepared in the mobile kitchen outside the command post, Powell was ready to meet with Faulk and the PERT team. He was energized, not only because he had a genuine gift as a leader but because he thrived in stressful situations when people's lives hung in the balance. Although he often joked that a lesser man couldn't fill his shoes, the men sitting around the table hoped they'd never have to find out. Not only had they grown accustomed to Powell telling them what, when, and how, but most had a deep respect for him after repeatedly witnessing how he performed under pressure.

"All right, let's settle down," Powell began. The room became quiet. "The situation as it stands is that we have two groups of inmates holding hostages in Unit 2. The downstairs cell blocks have been taken over by inmates and they're holding two officers hostage. Although right now they're being held in cell blocks A and D, the inmates have access to the entire downstairs area, and it's possible their location could quickly change.

"The inmates downstairs are unable to go upstairs, where the second group of inmates is holding one officer hostage in E block. The inmates in E can leave their cell block but can't get into F, which is still locked. This group is also believed to consist of an inmate named Tony Jackson, a.k.a. Lord Abdullah, and an inmate he's holding hostage, possibly in the multipurpose room. Jackson's the leader of the Five Percenters, and his hostage is Abdurahman Abdul-Ahmad, the Muslim prayer leader."

One of the sergeants raised his hand. "Is Jackson the leader of this whole situation?"

Faulk fielded the question. "No, he's not thought to be the leader of both groups. It's believed the current situation began when Jackson got into a fight with Abdurahman, and things fell apart from there."

"So without a central leader," another sergeant said, "would it be correct to assume there's no clear purpose to account for what's happened?"

"That's correct," Faulk said. The room became silent. Everyone knew that without a specific motivation, hostage takers were more likely to act impulsively, making a bad situation worse and greatly increasing the potential for loss of life.

Turning off Highway 561 onto Caledonia road, Kelvin was unable to see the prison behind the freshly tilled, rolling farmland. This didn't deter him, though, because several drivers in uniforms had sped past him in a hurry to get there for something.

Surely they aren't that excited to get to work . . .

He continued three-quarters of a mile, and when he drove over the first hill, he saw evidence that something was happening. A line of about fifteen cars, many he recognized as those that had passed him earlier, were waiting to get through a roadblock manned by correctional officers and a Halifax County Deputy.

Kelvin waited in line. The cars ahead of him approached the roadblock, and after slowing down, were quickly waved through. He knew he had no chance of doing that. He decided he'd try the straightforward approach and ask for permission to drive closer so he could cover the story.

"Whoa, sir," the officer said, bending down to look in the car. "I'm sorry, but I'm going to have to turn you around."

"Officer, what's going on? I'm with WHRR and I've been trying to call the prison for the last two hours. I haven't been able to reach anyone."

"Sir, I can't discuss that," the officer said.

"I know some officers have been hurt pretty seriously," Kelvin replied, sensing the man might talk if he pressed the right button. "It also seems you've got quite a few officers coming in. Let me just tell you what I think and you can let me know if I'm right."

"I'm sorry sir, but . . . "

"I think there's been some kind of inmate uprising, and that's how the officers got hurt. That's also why you're bringing in more officers and won't let anyone on the prison property."

Another car pulled up.

"Sir . . . "

"Please, officer. Just let me know if I'm close to being right." Kelvin discretely pressed a twenty-dollar bill into the man's hand. "I promise not to mention my source."

Without a word, the officer grabbed the money and nodded slightly.

"Thank you very much. I appreciate it." Kelvin smiled as he pulled up to do a three-point turn and head back to the station.

"Hold on, Mr. Johnson, I'll get him," Powell's secretary said, transferring the call.

Powell answered quickly. "Yeah, Steve, what is it?"

"Sir, I believe Dr. Thompson and inmate Marc Jones are being held hostage in the multipurpose room."

"What do you mean?"

"Donnie was in my office before this started. He said he was going to the multipurpose room to see Jones. I've tried contacting him several times, but I haven't been successful and no one's seen him leave the prison."

"You've tried paging him?"

"Yes sir, but he hasn't called me back."

"Okay," Powell replied. "If you hear anything else, let me know."

"Ten-four."

"By the way," Powell added, "the PERT team's here. I'll be sending them out to replace the men you've stationed there so you can take over hostage negotiations."

Lord Abdullah was out of the room talking to Hank and Walter. Donnie used the opportunity. "Are you alright?" he asked Abdurahman.

"No, sir, I'm not. I think my shoulder's broken and maybe a rib too."

"Are you still bleeding?"

"No, but only because of the healing power of Allah."

"Sir, I don't mean any disrespect, but I don't think Allah . . . "

"I don't feel disrespected, sir," Abdurahman interrupted. "I'm sorry you don't know the one true god, Allah, as I do. For if you did, you'd know the one you call God is the one I worship as Allah."

"That's not true, sir," Marc said.

"What do you mean it ain't true?" Abdurahman lost his patience. "I'm the Muslim prayer leader and I've been studyin' the *Holy Qur'an* for years. The God Christians worship is the same as Allah, the one Muslims worship. We just refer to Him by different names."

"The reason that's not so is because the God I worship has a son named Jesus Christ, who was born of the Virgin Mary and lived among us," Marc said. "Through Him, we were given the opportunity to see a glimpse of God, His Father, while He walked among us as a man. In the end, Jesus was crucified, dead and buried, and on the third day arose from the grave so he could be with His Father. So you see, Abdurahman," Marc said gently, "the one you call Allah is not the one I call my Father, God."

"So you, like all Christians I've ever known, put everything on that cross and the things you say happened there," Abdurahman said. His physical pains subsided, and he realized the reason he'd been stabbed and held hostage was so he could teach about Islam. *The only true religion, all praise and glory be upon Allah.* "What if I were to prove to you you're wrong and there was no crucifixion?"

"You can't prove that, because it happened," Marc answered calmly but authoritatively.

Donnie felt like the Kingdom of Heaven was opening before him.

"In the Bible, it says Jesus, peace be upon him, responded to the Jews' requests for a miraculous sign by saying that as the prophet, Jonah was in the whale's belly for three days and nights, so the Son of Man would be three days and nights in the heart of the earth." Abdurahman sat up a little straighter. "We know Jesus was supposed to have died late on a Friday afternoon and was to have risen early on Sunday. If you add that up, he wasn't dead for three days or three nights. Instead, he was dead for only one day, Saturday, and two nights, Friday and Saturday. So you see, Preacher Man, you and the rest of the Christians who hang everything on the cross and the supposed resurrection of Jesus, peace be upon him, are wrong."

"Your use of logic is Satan using man's ability to think to trick him," Marc gently corrected. "It's apparent from your commitment to Islam that you're trying to live a holy life. You spend a great deal of time and energy trying to follow the rules of your religion."

"That's right," Abdurahman said. "Jesus was a prophet that deserves our respect and love, but not the designation as the Son of God. Allah has no son!"

"Jesus was dead for three days," Marc said. "Friday, Saturday, and Sunday. In the twelfth chapter of Matthew, you're referring to when Jesus talks about the sign of Jonah. He doesn't say a specific number of hours, which is what you're trying to assume logically. He says three days and three nights, which is exactly what happened."

Abdurahman sat in silence. Never had anyone refuted the proof he'd offered. *What do I say now? . . . What am I supposed to do? . . .*

"Mr. Ratliff," Marc said, "you have been living a lie for many years."

Abdurahman's mouth dropped open when he heard his name. There was no way Marc could have known it. Abdurahman hadn't spoken that name to anyone for years.

"The crucifixion and the reason for it are real," Marc continued. "The way you're trying to be saved from your sin won't work. You, like the Pharisees of old, use logic to make rules and laws you can follow so you can earn your way into heaven. The Pharisees couldn't do it, and neither can you, because you aren't perfect. God, who is perfect in every way, doesn't tolerate even the least little sin and will punish it severely. No matter how hard you try, you're never, ever, going to keep from sinning. Don't you think you'll be punished for it in the end?"

Abdurahman stubbornly set his jaw. "I respectfully disagree with you. It's not possible to do good, or be good, without rules. Your Bible talks about the commandments and laws God Himself gave Moses. Aren't those the rules that must be obeyed in order to be a Christian?"

"God gave Moses commandments and laws, and it's through them that man was able to identify sin," Marc said. "The problem is, knowing about sin didn't keep people from engaging in it, but rather, it produced in them a desire to do it."

Abdurahman laughed. "So God's commandments caused sin?"

"Not in the least," Marc replied. "Everything that comes from God, including the commandments, is completely pure and holy. It's not the commandments that cause man to sin. It's man's sinful nature. Man becomes aware of what sin is through the commandments, which define it. This, in turn, activates man's sinful nature and leads man to engage in the very sin being defined."

Donnie looked on in disbelief, not only because of what he was hearing but the circumstances in which he was hearing it.

"You make it sound like man doesn't have control over his behavior," Abdurahman replied curtly.

"I'm not saying man doesn't have any control," Marc explained. "I'm saying man has a sinful nature and will always ultimately behave in ways that are a reflection of it."

"That's almost as crazy as thinking Jesus was like God and then allowed himself to be hung on a cross."

"I'm not saying man doesn't have responsibility for his behavior, Mr. Ratliff. On the contrary, man does indeed have responsibility for what he does, says, and thinks. I'm also saying that no matter how hard man tries, or how many rules he makes, he'll never be able to behave in a way that's free from sin. In fact, the more rules he makes, the more he'll be reminded of his sinful nature."

"What about Jesus being a God and a man at the same time?" Abdurahman asked. "What about him letting himself be crucified?"

"It's because Jesus is both God *and* man that we can be saved from our sin. As God, He was, and is, able to be perfect and free of sin. When He allowed himself to be hung on the cross, He was a pure and holy sacrifice that was acceptable to God for everyone's sin. Without that perfect sacrifice and believing in it, you are trusting in yourself and your own ability to live a life free of sin."

"All right," Lord Abdullah said, walking toward the back of the cell block. "Hank, get some men to take the mattresses off the beds and put 'em in front of the windows."

"Yes, sir," Hank said with pride. It couldn't get any better than this.

Just think. A few minutes ago I was a nobody, and now, 'da head of the Five Percenters is givin' me an assignment like I'm one of his boys . . . I knew today was gonna be good . . .

"I want you to watch that po-lice man and make sure he don't try nothin'," Lord Abdullah said to Walter, pointing at the hostage.

"Yes, sir." Walter grinned. *I've been wantin' to take care of one of 'dese guards since 'dey locked me up . . . Somethin' told me today was gonna be a good one . . .*

Hanging up the phone, Powell resumed briefing the PERT team without missing a beat. "Mr. Faulk, when is Dr. Sheffield arriving?"

"She's due in about two hours, sir," Faulk answered, glancing at his watch. "She's coming by helicopter, and there's a line of thunderstorms moving through the state this afternoon."

"Have we made any progress establishing communication with the inmates?"

"No, sir. We've tried, but there doesn't seem be an inmate in charge. I had Sergeant Worthington pull up a list of the men housed in Unit 2, and officers who work that unit are going over it to identify possible leaders."

"They come up with anything yet?"

"The best information we have so far is that it's probably a safe bet that Tony Jackson is the leader of whichever group he's in."

One of the sergeants taking notes spoke up. "Mr. Faulk, do you believe this is a gang situation?"

"At this point, we don't," Faulk said. "It's too disorganized and unplanned. It's more likely Jackson was acting alone when he attacked Abdurahman, and the situation deteriorated into an all out free-for-all."

Powell informed the team about his phone call with Steve and summarized what he knew about the two groups. "Mr. Faulk," he said, pointing to the institution map, "I want you to position your men to gather information about how many inmates are involved, where they are, what types of weapons they have, and the number and status of the hostages."

"Yes, sir."

"For now, unless we observe a hostage in imminent danger, we'll wait it out. It's gonna be dark in a few hours, and they're gonna be getting hungry. Dr. Sheffield should be here by then, and they'll want to talk."

"Ten-four," Faulk replied.

"All right, that'll do it," Powell said.

Everyone stood to go to work.

Charles was staring out the window of his study when Karla sped into the parking lot. He jumped up from his desk to meet her.

"Charles," she said, rounding the corner to his office, "I spoke with some EMTs from Halifax County. They usually take their patients to Halifax Regional but brought a patient to Nash General this morning for specialized care." She was out of breath. "They called and checked in with some EMTs working out of their station and told me an officer at Caledonia had been severely wounded and another was stabbed to death this morning."

"Dear God," Charles exclaimed, moving to hug her.

"That's not all," Karla continued, fighting to control her emotions. "They've taken hostages, and the prison's on lockdown status."

"Where's Donnie? Have you talked to him or Steve?"

"No," Karla replied, bursting into tears.

Speeding back to WHRR, Kelvin was about to explode with excitement. He had to act quickly before another reporter got the scoop. He called the cameraman and told him to meet him at the station. Then he called the station manager and described what had happened.

"That's right, Hal, there's been a riot at the farm," he said excitedly, racing through historic Halifax and past the brick courthouse that seemed out of place next to the old wooden homes nearby.

"Are you sure, Kelvin? I haven't heard anything about it."

"That's just it, Hal, they're trying to keep a lid on it. I found out only because I rode out there and saw the roadblock."

"I tell you what," Hal said. "Get the van and take Sammy back out there. Y'all snoop around, shoot some video, and ask some questions. See what you can find out, and if you get anything, let me know and we'll go to you live."

"Great, Hal." Kelvin's spirits soared even higher.

"Yo," Pete Holloway yelled out the window, "My name's Al-Shirazi Khomeini and I'm in charge. I want a phone or I'm gonna start killin' hostages."

Officer Moody whispered into the microphone clipped to the shoulder of his black jumpsuit. "This is twenty-one forty. Come in, twenty-thirty."

"Go ahead, twenty-one forty," Faulk answered.

"An inmate who says his name's Al-Shirazi Khomeini claims he's in charge and he's demanding a phone. He says he's gonna start killing hostages if the demand isn't met. Over."

"Ten-four. Do you have a visual on the subject? Over."

"Negative. Over."

"Ten-four. Inform the subject you've heard him and that it'll take a few minutes to get it. Let me know if anything changes. Over."

"Ten-four."

Sergeant Worthington overheard the radio transmission between Faulk and Moody. Reasonably sure Al-Shirazi Khomeini was an alias used by Pete Holloway, he double checked with another officer before picking up a secured land line to call the command center.

"This is Faulk."

"Sir, this is Sergeant Worthington. I heard your radio transmission with Moody, and I believe the man he was talking to is Pete Holloway. He's a Unit 2 inmate that's been validated as a Five Percenter. He's one of Tony Jackson's men, and according to the officer I spoke with, they had an altercation before this thing jumped off."

"What happened?" Faulk asked.

"Jackson punched Holloway for some reason and then went after the Muslim prayer leader. We aren't sure what caused it."

"Ten-four. If you hear anything else, let me know."

Dr. Deeann Sheffield had been a hostage negotiator consultant with the North Carolina Department of Corrections for almost eighteen years. Many people owed their lives to her expertise in reading people and life-threatening situations. Most recently, she'd worked with Powell and Steve Johnson at Pasquotank Correctional Institution, where eighteen inmates had taken four correctional officers hostage. During the standoff, Powell had used Dr. Sheffield's advice and Steve's negotiation skills to acquire the intelligence necessary to enable the PERT team to resolve the situation without loss of life.

"Deeann," Powell said, getting out of his chair when she walked through the door. "Please come in. It's good to see you again. I wish it was under better circumstances."

"How are you, Lee?" she asked, setting her briefcase down.

"I was doing pretty good until this happened," he answered, gently shaking her small hand.

"How's the family doing?"

"My wife's keeping me in line, and my son is doing great playing ball," he answered with pride in his voice. "He threw a no-hitter last week, and it looks like he's gonna get a scholarship."

"That's great, Lee. I'm sure you're really proud of him."

"Yeah, we are."

She straightened her jacket. "Well, what have we got so far?"

Everything looked the same as it had before he left, but when Lord Abdullah returned to the multipurpose room, he sensed something was different.

"Sir, this man needs medical attention or he may die," Donnie said, hoping to convince Lord Abdullah to let Abdurahman go.

"Doc," Lord Abdullah said flatly, "I could care less if that idiot dies. He oughtta pray to that spook god of his to come save 'im. Maybe he could get 'im outta prison while he's at it too." Lord Abdullah looked from Abdurahman to Marc. "You know, Doc, you and Preacher Man could have a contest between your god and this man's god." He slapped Abdurahman's injured shoulder. "All of y'all could pray to whoever you pray to, and we'll see whose god rescues 'em. Me, I'm gonna take care of myself. I know I can always depend on me."

Karla was embarrassed that she'd shown Charles her emotions. "I'm so sorry," she apologized, pulling back. "I'm acting like a little girl who's scared of the boogey man."

"Karla, it's okay to be a real person with genuine emotions," Charles said. "Just because you're a doctor doesn't mean you're not human."

"I know, Charles. I'm just scared something's happened to Donnie." She dried her eyes. "This is so unfair. Every time I start to care for someone, something happens and I get hurt."

"Karla, it's . . . "

"I know, I know," she said defensively. "It's childish to feel this way. But I can't help it. I'm just terrified something's happened, and I don't think I can take it. I hate feeling so vulnerable."

"What I was going to say is I think it's time for both of us to start trusting God. It's okay that we want Donnie and Steve to be safe, and it's certainly okay to pray God will make that happen. We just have to know He's in control, and because of that, everything will be right."

"But . . ."

"Karla, I know what happened to your parents hurt a great deal. It was also hard on Donnie when he lost his mother. But think about this. Had it not been for those things, the two of you may have never met or turned out to be the wonderful people you are." He looked into Karla's eyes. "You know, God never gives us more than we can handle. We just have to trust in Him and know this will be okay."

"Will you pray with me for strength?" Karla asked. She knew they would need it.

"You 'member makin' me put out my cigarette the other day?" Walter asked the terrified officer. "Well, let me show ya how I do it."

"Mess 'im up, man," someone encouraged.

"Show 'im who's boss now!"

"You hear that dude?" Walter said. "They want me to finish you off."

"Please . . . " the officer sputtered.

Walter slapped him. "Shut up! I ain't gonna kill ya yet. I'm gonna make ya wonder." He laughed and outted his cigarette on the officer's leg.

"Hey, man," an inmate said as the officer screamed in pain. "Put his belt around his neck like a leash. He could be your pet."

"Yeah," Walter said. "I like that. Get me his belt."

Kelvin and Dennis were in the only car stopped at the roadblock. Kelvin pulled out his wallet to show his press credentials, and while the officer carefully studied the ID, Kelvin told him he wanted access to the prison property. Following orders, the officer politely refused and informed him he could go no further. The sheriff's deputy standing off to the side watched the proceedings with interest, and the other correctional officer, who'd contacted the command center, motioned for the deputy to come over. After talking briefly, the deputy went to the car and instructed Kelvin to pull to the side of the road and wait for Mr. Hagerton to come answer his questions.

Dennis began setting up his video equipment while the curious officers watched.

"Steve," Powell said into the speaker phone, "Dr. Sheffield's here."

"Hi, Steve," Sheffield said. "Mr. Powell's briefed me on what's happened. How're things looking where you are?"

"Things seem to have settled down a bit over the last forty-five minutes," Steve said. "One of my sergeants informed me a hostage taker, Pete Holloway, wants to talk. Sounds like he's got some demands."

"That's why I'm calling. I've talked with Mr. Powell, and we want you to contact Holloway. It'll be a similar setup to what we did at Pasquotank," Deeann said, referring to the use of a special phone that allows the inmate to speak only with the negotiator. "Call me on the land line when you're in place."

"We interrupt the regularly scheduled program to bring you breaking news from Caledonia Correctional Institution. WHRR's Kelvin Oleander is reporting live from the scene." People's television screens went blank for a second. The next image that came into focus was Kelvin standing in front of a large, green metal road sign that read *Caledonia Correctional Institution* in bold white letters.

"Kelvin, what's happening there?" the anchorman asked.

"Casey, I'm standing in a freshly tilled-up field outside of the prison in Tillery, North Carolina. With me is Mr. Jeff Hagerton, the Assistant Superintendent of Programs for Caledonia. Over my shoulder, you can see the notorious maximum security prison in the distance. According to Mr. Hagerton, a riot began early this morning, and several staff members and inmates have been taken hostage. In addition, one officer and two inmates have been killed."

Kelvin turned to the assistant superintendent. "Mr. Hagerton, what can you tell us about the situation as it currently stands?"

After praying passionately for strength to trust in God's plan, Karla went to fix her makeup. Charles sat down at his desk. By habit, he grabbed the television remote control and turned on the set across the room. A reporter was conducting an interview, and the caption *Live: Caledonia Correctional Institution* appeared across the bottom of the screen.

"Karla," Charles yelled, "come quick. You've gotta see this." He turned up the volume. "WHRR is doing a live interview at Caledonia."

"At approximately eight forty-five this morning, an altercation between inmates in one of the medium custody units escalated into a riot," Hagerton said, reading from a prepared statement. "The inmates took three officers, a staff member, and several inmates hostage. It's not known at this point how many inmates are involved. PERT, short for the North Carolina Prison Emergency Response Team, has been activated and is now in charge of the situation under the command of Mr. Lee Powell, Caledonia's superintendent."

"How was the officer killed?" Kelvin asked.

"I'm unable to comment on that at this time."

"What's the officer's name?"

"We can't give out that information until we've contacted the next of kin."

"What's the condition of the hostages?"

"At this point, the hostages are in good condition and have not suffered major injuries," Hagerton answered.

"What's the condition of the officers and inmates who were injured?" Kelvin pressed, searching for information and the promotion he was sure would soon follow a good interview.

"All I can say at this point is that we know two inmates and at least one officer were murdered, and one inmate and one staff member have been seriously wounded. The staff member is currently receiving treatment at Halifax Regional Medical Center for her injuries."

"Why is the seriously wounded inmate not receiving treatment?"

"He's still being held hostage."

"Barbara," the station manager almost screamed into his cell phone, "I'm telling you, something's happening at Caledonia."

"That's where Marc Jones is being held," she thought out loud. "I'm on my way to cover another story. What's going on?"

"A riot started there this morning, and staff have been taken hostage."

"How do you know?"

"We were monitoring news broadcasts around Eastern North Carolina and this just came across from a WHRR reporter interviewing the assistant superintendent at the prison."

"We're turning around to go up there," Barbara said decisively. "This sounds like it could be a major story."

"Thanks, Barbara. Let me know when you're on location."

"I will. By the way, since WHRR is affiliated with us, get me the reporter's name and cell phone number so I can call him before I get there."

Donnie burned with anger as Lord Abdullah made fun of his faith and his God, but this wasn't the time to have a discussion with the man. He doubted he could change the inmate's mind anyway. He'd already seen and felt what would happen if he tried.

Lord, what's happening? . . . Why have you put me in this situation? . . . What do you want from me? . . . Please help me . . . I need you . . .

"How many hostage takers are there?" Kelvin asked Hagerton.

"At this point, we suspect only a small number in one of the four units are actually involved."

"Are they armed?"

"We believe they have knives, razors, and perhaps some homemade weapons, but no firearms."

"What's being done with inmates in the other units?"

"Those men are being maintained in either individual cells or their assigned cell blocks under close supervision. The entire facility is on lockdown status, and inmates are not permitted to move about."

"How many officers are on the PERT team?"

"I'm sorry, but I can't comment on that."

"What's the purpose of taking hostages?" Kelvin asked. "Have the inmates made any demands?"

"Pastor Winston," Bill Sanders said excitedly, barely giving Ray a chance to answer the phone. "You gotta turn on the TV. You ain't gonna believe what's on that Roanoke Rapids station. Hurry."

"Slow down, Bill," Ray responded, recognizing the voice of his largest financial contributor. "What are you talkin' about?" He crossed the room to turn on his television.

"I just got home and was flippin' through channels when I came across a live report from the prison where that man you said was sent by Satan is bein' held."

"Is that so?" Ray said as the picture came into focus. "What's going on?"

"I think what you said was gonna happen is happenin'. The convicts sensed Satan was among 'em and have rioted."

Ever the opportunist, and sensing this was a golden one, Ray didn't miss a beat in deciding how to use the situation to his *and* God's best advantage. "Bill, call as many brothers and sisters as you can, and y'all meet me here at the church as soon as possible."

I oughtta be able to earn quite a few points for this . . . It's amazin' how the Lord always provides a way . . . Glory to God . . .

"At this point," Hagerton said, "we aren't sure why hostages were taken. We're in the process of establishing communication with the men involved and should know more in the near future."

"Are the inmates involved gang members?"

"I can't comment on that at this time."

Kelvin tried to keep the interview going. "Was there any warning that something like this was going to take place?"

"No, sir. We had no warning, but when everything is finished, a full investigation will be conducted to determine if something was missed."

"Are you suggesting something could've been missed?"

"Not at all, Mr. Oleander," Hagerton replied smoothly. "Effective management, as well as prison policy, requires anyone in a position of leadership to always evaluate what's happened and to make changes that could result in a safer, more stable environment. In this regard, I'm sure Mr. Powell and other leaders of the Division of Prisons will want to examine what's happened so that if something could be done in the future to prevent similar situations, it will be."

"Caledonia Correctional Facility houses some of the worst inmates in the state of North Carolina. Do you believe this contributed to the riot?"

"I am not aware of any North Carolina prison facility's being officially designated as the place where the worst inmates are housed. It's true that Caledonia has that reputation, but I believe that's a matter of opinion."

"Is it your opinion?"

"My opinion," Hagerton answered, sidestepping the question, "is every prison houses very dangerous people who've been removed from society for one reason or another. The staff here at Caledonia are some of the best in the state and work very hard to provide a safe, stable, rehabilitative environment. It's because of our staff members' dedication that more situations such as this haven't occurred over the years."

Sensing the interview was over, Kelvin thanked Hagerton and turned to the camera.

"Reporting live from Caledonia, this is Kelvin Oleander."

He gave Dennis the cut signal.

"Thank you, Mr. Oleander," Hagerton said, and left to return to the command center.

No, thank you *for helping me get back to the big city . . .*

"Why are you so bitter towards God?" Donnie said without thinking.

"What?" Lord Abdullah seemed almost as surprised to hear the question as Donnie was for asking it. "Bitter with God? I don't know what you're talkin' 'bout. The only god I know is me, and I'm very happy with me."

This dude thinks 'cause he's a doc he's gonna play mind games . . . So what if he knows that psychology stuff . . . I don't care . . . I'm smarter . . . I'm a god . . .

"Who's 'dis other god? I mean, you act like he's alive and real. How do you know? You ain't never seen 'im or heard 'im."

"You're right," Donnie said. "I haven't seen God. But I know He's real. I know through faith."

Lord Abdullah laughed. "Through faith? You've gotta be kiddin' me. You're a science man, and now you're gonna sit there and tell me somethin's real just 'cause you believe so? Gimme a break, man." He shook his head. "I guess the next thing you're gonna say is that ghosts or somethin' is gonna get me when it gets dark."

"You think the only things that are real are the things you can see or hear?" Donnie asked.

"Nah." Lord Abdullah smiled. "I'm too smart to be trapped off like that. It ain't 'bout havin' to see it or hear it, it's about bein' able to know if it's real or not. You ain't one of 'da five percent smart enough to understand."

"Charles," Karla said nervously, "the staff member that's been taken hostage is Donnie. I just know it." She wrung her hands.

"Me too."

"I don't know what to do," Karla said helplessly and closed her eyes.

"This is giving us an opportunity to grow as Christians," Charles said.

"Are you saying God caused all of this to happen so He could teach us something?" Karla asked with a touch of anger.

"Not at all. I don't think it's possible for God to do anything that's bad or evil. It's inconsistent with who He is."

"Then why does He let things like this happen?"

"I believe bad things happen because of the evil that exists in the world. I believe God will be completely victorious over that evil, but it will be in His time and in His way, not ours."

"Oh, I see," Karla said sarcastically. "God doesn't cause evil. He just doesn't stop it."

"I don't think that's quite right, either." Charles put his hands on her shoulders. "I know when we pray, God hears us and answers. Sometimes this may mean preventing things from happening, and sometimes it may mean letting them happen for the overall benefit of the people involved."

"Now I'm confused."

"I don't know how to explain it except to quote you a line of scripture from the book of Romans: 'And we know that in all things God works for the good of those who love Him.' To me, this means that no matter what's happening, God's ultimately in control of the situation, and whatever happens will be right and perfect for the people that are His."

"I know you're right, Charles, and I believe what you're saying. It's that I just have a hard time living it. I guess when I'm tested, I fall back into doing the thing that's easiest for me to do—hide in my shell and shut everyone out. That way, I'm not hurt."

"I really think we can use what's happening to help us grow more dependent on God," Charles said.

"I'll try," Karla said with a new resolve.

"I think that's exactly what God wants from us," Charles said. "Let's pray." He bowed his head. "Father, please be with us and with Donnie, Steve, and the others who are involved in this situation. Please protect them and keep them safe. Lord, we believe You're in control and we ask You to please help us to continue to trust in You. All of this we ask in Your Son's name. Amen!"

Donnie sensed Lord Abdullah's mounting frustration and decided not to push him further. He began to analyze the man he was dealing with.

His most important values are power, influence, intelligence . . . He believes he's intelligent and deserves power and influence, which he's probably spent his life trying to obtain . . . He feels he's been treated unfairly . . . This makes him angry . . . His ego is fragile and easily threatened . . . He feels justified to use any means necessary to obtain what he believes he rightly deserves . . . He's an extremely dangerous, unpredictable man . . .

Steve stood on the yard in front of the prison with a bullhorn in front of his mouth. "Mr. Holloway, this is Steve Johnson. I'd like to talk with you about that phone."

Inside the prison, Pete crouched behind the mattresses in front of the windows. He knew Steve from his time in maximum custody. He decided to wait before answering. He wanted to show him who was in charge.

After a long moment, he shouted, "All right, I'm listenin'. What's the deal? Where's my phone?"

"I've got it right here," Steve said through the bullhorn. "I just need know how to get it to you." He wanted Pete to feel in control.

"Just give it to me, man," Pete impatiently yelled back.

"Do you want me to have it brought to the window, or would you rather have me give it to you through one of the bar doors?" Steve realized Pete had no idea what kind of situation he was in.

Pete contemplated for a minute. "Just have someone walk up to the windows and toss it inside real easy. Don't try nothin' though, 'cause I'll hurt this po-lice man here if you do."

"We aren't going to try anything, Mr. Holloway," Steve reassured him. "I just want to get you the phone. But I want to get something in return."

"What?" Pete cried, his anger escalating. "No way. You tryin' to trick me, man. I oughtta slice this man's throat right now."

"Hold on a minute, Mr. Holloway." Steve tried redirecting Pete's anger. "I'm sure you know how this works. We both want something, and have to compromise a little. That way we both end up getting what we want. You get the cell phone, and I get a hostage."

There was no response for a long time. Steve could hear men arguing within the building.

"Look man," Pete finally shouted, "you give me the phone and bring us some hamburgers. Not 'dem sorry soy burgers they serve here, real hamburgers. If you do that, I'll give ya a hostage."

"All right, Mr. Holloway," Steve replied quickly. "How do you want the exchange to take place?"

"First, I want the phone," Pete said, feeling in charge and sensing he was beginning to get the respect Lord Abdullah had always said a god deserved. "After that, call me and we'll talk about 'da food."

"This is quite different from Pasquotank, Dr. Sheffield," Powell said.

"You're right, Lee, but I think we can use the lack of cohesion among the hostage takers to our advantage."

"How do you suggest we do that?" Faulk asked.

"We keep the situations separated and treat them that way," Deeann replied. "You know, divide and conquer. Steve should continue to ask for and talk with Pete Holloway. That will validate Pete as the leader of the men downstairs."

"What about the upstairs situation?"

"Assuming Jackson is the leader of that group, Steve should talk with him, but let's wait until he contacts us first. If we're lucky, he'll take his time, and we can use it to work on the men downstairs."

All right, think . . . I've gotta use the men out there to create a diversion. Then I can escape . . . Creatin' a diversion will be easy, but getting' outta here won't . . . Hold on a second. If I can get an officer's uniform, maybe, I can get lost in the confusion and disappear in the crowd . . . Yeah, that might just work.

There was a knock at the door. Lord Abdullah looked up and saw Hank standing there. "Yeah, what'cha want, man?"

"Yo, I don't know if it matters, but the po-lice is talkin' with some dude downstairs 'bout gettin' a phone."

"How long ago?"

"A minute ago, I guess."

"Alright, let me know if you hear somethin' else."

I wonder who's talkin' with the po-lice . . . Pete? . . . Nah, he's a follower, not a true leader . . . It don't matter though, maybe I can use it to my advantage . . . I've just gotta get in the conversation . . .

When Charles and Karla finished praying, Harvey Ramone was standing at the door. Neither of them knew how long he'd been there.

"Sorry to interrupt, Charles," Harvey said. "When I got home, I saw a report about a riot at Caledonia, and I wanted to come back and see if you knew about it."

Charles stood and walked to the door. "Harvey, this is Dr. Karla Lynch. She's a pediatrician at Nash General and a member of Hillside. Karla, this is Harvey Ramone. He's a retired Baptist minister who leads a Bible study group at Caledonia."

"It's nice to meet you, Dr. Ramone," Karla said, putting out her hand and forcing a smile.

"Please call me Harvey. I really hope I'm not interrupting."

"No sir, not at all," Karla said. "We were just praying about the situation at Caledonia."

"Charles and I recently talked about Caledonia and one of the inmates who attended my Bible study group the other night," Harvey said.

"You must mean Marc Jones," Karla replied. "I know about him."

"Have y'all thought about going out there?"

"It's interesting you asked, Harvey," Charles said. "Karla just said she wanted to."

"I think it would be a way for us to be supportive and perhaps be able to witness to others about what we know is happening," Harvey replied.

As Ray finished dressing in his best suit and tie, his thoughts raced ahead to what he'd say. He desperately wanted to make a good impression on the many people who would be watching the news. This was the chance he'd been looking for to use the weapons God made available so he could convince people to turn away from the evil one. Maybe Paul hadn't written that the armor of God could best be used by men that looked a certain way, but to Ray, everyone knew fancy clothes made the Christian Warrior more credible.

. . . and feel more important.

1 CORINTHIANS 16:13,14 "Be on guard. Stand true to what you believe. Be courageous. Be strong. And everything you do must be done with love."
(NLT)

Chapter 20
Thursday Evening

The phone's ring startled Pete. It took him a few seconds to figure out how to answer.

"Hello," he said bluntly.

"Mr. Holloway?"

"Yeah, what'cha want?"

"This is Steve Johnson. I wanted you to know I've talked with Mr. Powell, and he's sent some officers to get your food. How would you like to make the transfer?"

"Look, man, I done said you ain't gettin' nothin' until I get the food. So you just need to wait until those po-lice get back wit' it and I'll let you know 'den."

"I remember, Mr. Holloway," Steve said, carefully picking his words. "I was just hoping we could save some time if we discussed it now. That way you'd get your food sooner."

"Nah, I ain't fallin' for that," Pete responded, growing louder and more irritated. "I'm in charge here. I'm callin' the shots!"

"I'm sorry, Mr. Holloway. I just wanted to help you out," Steve said, trying to defuse the situation. "I'll call back when the officers get here with your food."

"Yeah, you do that," Pete said proudly. He'd shown Steve who was running the show.

I ain't stupid . . . I really am a god! . . .

"Can I have everyone's attention," Ray said, walking to the podium. "I wanna thank you for comin' this evenin'. Most of us are gonna get on the new church van donated by Bill Sanders and go to Caledonia. Bill and Casey are gonna take his truck and meet us there. Before we go and battle Satan, though, let's pray."

"Amen," Bill yelled out, along with the other twenty-three Christian warriors who'd been told to meet at the church.

"Father God, we're thankful for the opportunity to be here and to be Your children," Ray started calmly. "We beg for Your guidance and pray You'll be with us as we battle against the evil that's come against us."

"Amen," Bill said, as was his custom when Ray preached or prayed or talked, or sometimes, even when he just looked at him.

"Yes, Lord, yes," voices echoed.

"We know You're with us, Lord, and that You're the all powerful, mighty Lord of the universe." Ray's passion took over and his voice took on the familiar quiver that let everyone know the fire inside him was lit. "We know Marc Jones, who's here in prison, is from Satan because the Bible You so graciously gave us identifies him. Yes, we know he's from the great deceiver and has tricked many people into thinkin' he's greater than Your Son Jesus Christ, who You sent to die on the cross for our sins!"

"Praise God!" someone shouted. Others mumbled, "Amen."

"We haven't been deceived, Lord," Bill cried, trying to match his pastor's enthusiasm. "Satan can't fool us!"

"We know there's only one God, and we're prepared to do our part to defend Your Holy Name. Oh, Lord," Ray cried out as if he were in terrible pain, "we beg You to fill us with Your Holy Sprit so we'll be victorious tonight and forever over Satan."

"Yes . . . Lord, yes," a woman wailed, as if the pain in her voice validated Ray's words.

"We've heard Your command, mighty God, and we're ready to go out into the world and convert sinners. We're gonna take up the cross and spread the healing power of the word of Christ. Amen and Amen," Ray shouted with an intensity that shook the small room.

"Amen," everyone shouted and released each other's hands, feeling what they'd been taught to recognize as the power of the Holy Spirit flowing through their bodies.

With Karla and Harvey riding along, Charles drove past the post office and turned left on Highway 561. After passing the dark swamp surrounding Tillery and crossing the narrow bridge just before the turn to Caledonia Road, they saw quite a number of vehicles parked along the highway. The rolling farmland hid the roadblock from view, but the white glow on the horizon from the powerful spotlights that had been set up there let them know it was nearby.

"There's already quite a few people here," Karla observed. "Maybe we should park out here."

"Charles, go to the Resettlement Restaurant up there," Harvey said, pointing to the country diner ahead on the left. "It mainly caters to the prison staff, and it shouldn't be too hard to get in."

"Mr. Powell," the young officer at the roadblock said nervously, holding the radio so tightly his fingers were cramping, "I think we need more officers out here to control the number of people showin' up."

"Calm down, son," Powell said. "How many people are out there?"

"I'd guess there's about a hundred now, sir, but more and more keep comin'. They're havin' to park out on 561 'cause there's no more room alongside Caledonia road."

"Okay, son. I'll have Captain Bradley get the sheriff to send more deputies out there to help y'all. Let the captain know if anything changes."

"Yes, sir," the officer replied, sounding relieved, if just for the moment.

As soon as Powell hung up, the phone rang again. "This is Lee," he said, knowing only a few people had his private number.

"Sir, this is Steve. I just talked with Holloway and wanted to let you and Dr. Sheffield know."

"Hold on a second. Let me put you on the speaker phone." Powell clicked a button. "There, can you hear me?"

"Yes, sir."

"All right, what do you have?"

"Well, Holloway is desperately trying to prove he's in control," Steve said. "I think we can use this to manipulate him to some extent. The only problem is, when he feels disrespected, he responds emotionally, and I'm afraid he could act impulsively. It's also pretty clear he doesn't have any idea what he's doing."

"That's very insightful, Steve," Deeann said. "Let us know if you have any more thoughts about the man."

"Where should we park?" Barbara's cameraman asked, turning onto crowded Caledonia Road. "It looks like cars and trucks have taken all the places along the sides."

"Let's drive up to the roadblock," Barbara answered. "I'll ask the officers if we can pull over up there to set up."

When they topped the hill and came to the roadblock, the van crept to a stop and Barbara got out. They'd rehearsed this routine many times before.

"Good evening, officers," Barbara said, turning on the charm. "I'm Barbara Pierce from WLHR in Raleigh, and I've been sent out here to cover the story." She pointed to a grassy area off the side of the road. "After we get set up over there, can I interview you guys?"

"Ma'am," the first officer replied hesitantly, "I'm not supposed to let anyone beyond this point."

"I understand, officer, and I'd never want to do anything to get you into trouble. I just thought that since we're already up here, it might be okay if we just parked right over there and did the interview with you. But since you have orders, I guess we'll just turn around and go farther back." She paused as if thinking about what to do. "By the way, are there any other officers that could come out there to talk with me?"

"You know, Ms. Pierce," the officer said, not wanting to miss his fifteen minutes of fame, "it shouldn't be a problem if you park here. Just let me know when you're ready."

"Thank you so much, officer." Barbara flashed him a flirtatious smile. "I'll be back after we get set up."

"Mr. Holloway, this is Mr. Johnson. I wanted to let you know the officers are back with the food."

"All right," Pete said, loud enough for everyone to hear, "this is what you're gonna do. You're gonna have one of your men bring the burgers 'round to the inner bar door. If I see more than one po-liceman out there, I'm gonna cut this man's throat."

"I understand, Mr. Holloway," Steve answered. "I promise you, there won't be any tricks."

"One of my boys'll be standin' there, and he's gonna open the metal door from our side. When your officer sees that, he needs to open the bar door and put the food inside, then back away."

"All right. Then what?"

"Whatcha mean, 'den what'?"

"How are we going to get the hostage?"

Pete had forgotten about trading a hostage. "I'll have him walk out when I see we've got the food."

"Sounds good, Mr. Holloway," Steve said, knowing it wouldn't happen.

Lord Abdullah walked around the conference table to make sure Marc's handcuffs were still tight. Then he walked over to Abdurahman and uncuffed him. Grabbing him by his collar and jerking him to his feet, he pushed him toward Donnie, who was handcuffed to a steam pipe against the back wall. Lord Abdullah held the razor to Abdurahman's neck and gave him the key.

"Take that cuff off the pipe and put it around your wrist."

When Abdurahman finished, Lord Abdullah checked to make sure the men's cuffs were tightly secured. Then he left the room to give the police *his* demands.

Charles locked the car, and he, Karla, and Harvey started walking away.

A man came out of the restaurant. "Excuse me, sir. Are you plannin' on parkin' there?"

"Umm . . . yes," Charles said.

"Well, this is my family's restaurant," the man said proudly. "We're chargin' five bucks a car."

"You're charging people to park here?" Karla asked in disbelief.

"Yes, ma'am. This is a much safer place to leave your car than out in the road. Plus, I'm gonna be here to make sure nothin' happens to it."

"This is unbelievable," Karla said. "I can't believe you want us to pay to park out here in the middle of nowhere."

Harvey handed the man a five-dollar bill. "Here you go."

"Thank you, sir." Then man stuffed the money in his pocket and went back inside.

"You know, Harvey," Charles said, walking toward the lights, "that man charging us to park makes me wonder what it must have been like in Jerusalem when Jesus was crucified."

"Perhaps things are more similar than we can know," Harvey replied.

When the van was unloaded, Ray gathered everyone in a circle and prayed again. Then he began giving orders like a general in war time.

"We're gonna need several signs with Christian sayings or Bible verses on them. You ladies write the sayings on the cardboard, and you two men staple 'em to the broomsticks. When you're finished, bring 'em up to Bill's pickup. It'll be near the roadblock. Any questions?"

"No, sir, Pastor Winston," everyone said enthusiastically.

Ray and the rest of the group started walking and singing.

"Onward Christian soldiers, we are . . . "

"Lee," Deeann said, "based on what we know, I agree with Steve's observations about Holloway. There's something about the guy that bothers me. I don't like the way he reacted to making the hostage exchange."

"How's that?

"A couple of things. First, he seemed to be trying too hard to make sure everyone knew he was in charge."

"I agree."

"Second, I don't believe he's even thought about giving us a hostage for the phone and food. Mostly though, I'm concerned he's got no idea what he's trying to accomplish, and pretty soon, he's going to start reacting to pressures from the men he's locked up with to do something. He's not really a leader, so I think that's when things will have the highest potential to deteriorate, and he might do something to prove a point."

"Do you see a way for us to prevent that?"

"Maybe we need to stall for a few minutes to give us time to plan. Steve can delay giving them the food by talking more about needing to get a hostage."

With Lord Abdullah gone again, it didn't take long before Abdurahman picked up where he'd left off.

"I've been thinking about what you said, Preacher Man. You Christians are arrogant. You think you don't have to do anything to be saved, just have faith. Come on. The idea of saying you're a Christian and a follower of God without having to do anything is wack. I mean, isn't a sign someone believes in something shown by what they do? If someone says they're on a diet, and they believe being in shape is important, I expect them to do certain things." Abdurahman spoke with increasing intensity. "They should eat healthy food and work out. If they don't do these things, then I've got to question how committed they are to the diet."

"Abdurahman," Donnie said, "I think you're not quite understanding the faith-oriented theology that's central to Christianity. With Islam, you have a works-oriented theology, which has many rules and requires a lot of self-discipline to follow. The problem is that no matter how hard you try, you're never going to be able to do it, and thus, never will you be able to *earn* Allah's favor."

"You're incorrect about that, sir," Abdurahman said. "And even if that were true, it's not a problem if you just ask for Allah's forgiveness the same way Adam did, who, by the way, was not only the first sinner, but also the first prophet. We humans, just like Adam, have the ability to make ourselves right with Allah without having anyone intercede for us. All we've got to do is submit to him and follow the five pillars of Islam."

"It seems to me you're measuring your submission by how closely you follow the rules," Marc said. "So there are degrees of submission."

"That's right," Abdurahman said. "Don't you think some men are better or worse than others?"

"No, sir," Marc replied. "I don't believe there are degrees of sinning, but that all sins are equally bad. You see, the way you know if something is sinful is if God disapproves of it. If you believe that God is perfect, how is it that He could or would ever accept anything less than perfect? If he were to accept even the smallest sin, then it would mean He's accepting imperfection."

"You don't understand what it means to be a devout Muslim," Abdurahman countered. "A true Muslim prays five times a day and asks for forgiveness as well as follows the traditions and behaviors of Mohammad, peace and blessings be upon him. In this way, he's always tryin' to be sinless, just as Mohammad was."

"That's just it," Donnie emphasized. "You'll be *trying* to be sinless, but you'll never, ever get there. Besides, what makes you think that you'd be any different from Mohammad if you could become sinless on your own by what you do?"

"You're disrespecting me and the one true God, Allah," Abdurahman said fiercely. "May he have mercy and pity on your soul."

"Yo, po-lice, get me someone in charge," a voice demanded from behind the mattresses covering the upstairs windows.

"This is Steve Johnson," Steve said through the bullhorn. "Who am I speaking with?"

"I'm Lord Abdullah. I want a phone. We're gonna lower down a sheet and you're gonna have an officer tie it on. After I get the phone, I'll call ya and tell ya the rest. You got thirty minutes or a hostage is gonna die."

"I understand, Mr. Jackson," Steve said, using Lord Abdullah's given name to test how he'd react to being disrespected.

There was a long silence before Lord Abdullah responded. "The next time you refer to me as anything other than Lord Abdullah, I'm gonna kill somebody. I ain't playin' games. You understand?"

"Yes, sir," Steve responded, trying to keep the disgust from his voice. "What are you planning on giving us when you get the phone?"

"I'm gonna give ya my demands," Lord Abdullah yelled out. The other inmates started laughing. "You ain't talkin' to some stupid black man that's gonna fall for 'dem games. Now run get my phone, boy!"

"Did you copy that, Dr. Sheffield?" Steve asked over the secure phone hooked up to the command center. "Jackson, a.k.a. Lord Abdullah, wants a phone."

"Yeah, Steve," Deeann answered. "Mr. Powell and I are discussing it now. What are your thoughts?"

"A couple of things," Steve answered. "Jackson means business, and he's going to be difficult to manipulate. Unlike Holloway, he's very sure of himself."

"I agree," Deeann said. "I also think Jackson's been planning a way out of this, and the reason we're hearing from him now is he has an idea."

Powell grunted. "That convict's been around long enough to know that no matter what, we aren't gonna let him get outside the fences."

"So Dr. Sheffield, it sounds like we should be much more concerned about Jackson than Holloway," Steve said.

"Hold on a minute." Powell turned off the speaker phone and consulted with Deeann in private. Then he came back on the line. "Steve, I want you to delay transferring the food to the men downstairs. We'll get back to you in a few minutes."

"This is a great place to set up," Ray said to Bill, looking across the road at the cameraman connecting satellite cables to the WLHR van.

"What can we do, Pastor Winston?" a woman asked between breaths after the long walk from the van.

"Ms. Capps, I want your group to pair up and walk around. Talk with people and explain how Satan's workin'. Tell 'em to come up here after we get set up and I'm gonna talk to 'em about it."

"Yes sir, Pastor."

"All right, Christian warriors," Ray boomed, raising his hands high into the air. "May the peace of the Lord God Almighty, the love of His son Jesus Christ, and the power of the Holy Spirit be with us all. Amen!"

"Amen!" everyone shouted and went to fulfill their duties.

The phone rang. Steve didn't want to answer because he knew it would be Pete wanting to know where the food was, but he pressed the button anyway. "Hello, this is Johnson."

"Man, where's my food?" Pete sounded angry. "Y'all po-lice is playin' wit' us."

"Mr. Holloway," Steve interrupted, "We've got a problem. The officers bringing the food have been detained. It's going to take a little longer than we thought to get it here."

"What?" Pete screamed. "That's bull man. Now I know y'all's runnin' a game. I guess I'm gonna have to show ya I mean business."

"Mr. Holloway. Sir? *Sir?*" Steve heard the dial tone and immediately hit redial.

Ring . . . ring . . . ring . . .

Walking over the hill, they saw the roadblock for the first time. Charles shook his head in disbelief at the crowd from surrounding communities that had gathered to see what was happening. Some people stood around talking, while others had come better prepared and were sitting in groups off to the side of the road in lawn chairs, drinking soft drinks and beer from coolers sitting beside them. Young children were out in the fields playing tag in the light of the full moon, and an older group was trying to get up a game of football.

"Can you believe this?" Charles said. "It's like a carnival minus the rides."

"How many people would you say are here?" Karla asked.

"I don't know." Charles looked around. "There's probably close to two hundred or so."

"I bet there's going to be even more after that television station starts broadcasting," Harvey said, pointing toward the WLHR news van.

"Hey," Charles said. "Isn't that Ray Winston over there holding up signs?"

"Certainly looks like him," Harvey answered. "I wonder what he's doing here."

"Let's walk that way," Charles said. "Maybe we can find out."

"Twenty-thirty, this is twenty-two twelve, come in," Captain Bradley said, trying to reach the PERT commander.

"This is twenty-thirty," Faulk answered. "Go ahead, twenty-two twelve. What do you have?"

"Sir, the eyes and ears are in place, and you should be receiving info now. Over," Bradley said, referring to the cameras and microphones that were inserted into the cell blocks.

"Roger that, twenty-two twelve. Good work. Out."

Faulk called to tell Powell the intelligence he'd requested was available.

"Sorry I've offended you," Donnie said to Abdurahman. "I was only trying to help you consider the ramifications of what you believe."

"I assure you, I have," Abdurahman said. "You insist man isn't capable of behaving in ways that result in salvation. I'm insisting he can. Maybe you Christians just don't have any discipline. All you have is a person named Jesus, who you say is your savior, and through him, you gain admission to heaven. Seems like you aren't willing to accept responsibility for what you do."

"Christians do accept consequences for their behavior," Donnie said. "But the consequence for either believing or not believing that Jesus Christ is God's Son, who was sent to die on a cross for your sins, is that you get to spend eternity in heaven or hell."

"That makes no sense," Abdurahman said. "How's it that you receive his approval and the approval of God if you don't have to do anything? I mean, how's it that all you've got to do is believe or not believe?"

"That's just the start, Mr. Ratliff," Marc said. "Once you believe, you form a personal relationship with Jesus and become dependent on him."

"A personal relationship?" Abdurahman rolled his eyes. "You're crazy to think a human could have a personal relationship with God."

"That's the beauty of Jesus," Marc said. "Jesus, as God's Son, is both a man and God, and because of this, we can have a relationship with him. It's *only* through Him that we're able to be accepted by God."

"Okay," Abdurahman said reluctantly. "Let's suppose, just suppose, that's true. If it is, then how do we form this relationship with Jesus?"

"There's two things you must do," Marc said. "First, love the Lord God with all of your heart, your soul, your mind, and your energy.

Second, love others as He has loved you. If you do these things, you will keep all of the commands, commissions, and prohibitions of the law *and* form a relationship that no man, power, or spirit can break apart."

Hank pulled up the crude rope made from shredded sheets. Lord Abdullah untied the phone and called Steve.

"Here's the deal. First, I want the followin' men released from the New York Department of Corrections by noon tomorrow." He read off the names. "They're to call me when they get out. I know their voices, and you don't wanna try and play me.

"Second, I want a helicopter wit' a full tank of gas to take me where I wanna go. I'll tell the pilot where after we're in the air. You have until tomorrow noon. Third, I want food and drinks in the next hour."

"Sir . . . ," Steve tried to bargain.

"Failure to comply with these demands will result in the loss of life!"

Lord Abdullah hung up.

Powell sat in front of the monitors in the office next to the conference room. Deeann came in and sat beside him. "Are they up?"

"Yeah, they just came online."

The intel room sergeant pressed buttons on the control panel.

"This looks interesting," Deeann observed, studying the screens. "How long before we have sound?"

"Shouldn't be but just a minute, ma'am," the sergeant replied, pressing more buttons. "Try it now."

"That's it," Powell confirmed, turning up the sound on the monitor in A block, where two blindfolded men sat side by side on a cot with their hands tied behind their backs. A large inmate stood in front of them. He poked them in the stomach with a short baton and threatened them.

"I bet the men on the bed are the officers who've been taken hostage," Deeann said. "Can we get someone out here to identify them?"

"No problem." Powell picked up the phone. "Captain Bradley, send the Unit 2 manager back here ASAP." He hung up. "Show me the other cell blocks."

"Yes, sir." The sergeant pressed more buttons.

"There," Powell said after the screen changed twice. "In cell block C. Those men dressed in CO uniforms aren't restrained in any way. Kind of strange, don't you think?"

Deeann laughed uneasily. "Definitely."

"How long before the unit manager gets here?" Powell asked.

"About a minute, sir."

"Good." Powell studied the screens. "We might have to go in soon."

"Officer," Karla said, approaching the deputy at the roadblock, "have you heard anything about the hostages? My really good friend is a doctor here, and he was taken hostage."

"I'm sorry, ma'am," the young deputy said. "We haven't been given any information."

"Do you know if anyone's going to come out to make a statement?" Harvey asked.

"No sir, I don't. You may wanna ask the reporter over there. She's talked with someone in the command center. Maybe she can help you."

"Thank you," Karla said and headed toward the WLHR van with Charles and Harvey. As they crossed the ditch separating the road from the field where a group was singing hymns, two men approached them.

"Excuse me. My name's Bill Sanders, and this is Harold Fabian. We're from the Rocky Mount Evangelical Assembly of God Church. Do you know what's happening here?"

"What do *you* think's happening?" Karla asked.

"Ma'am," Bill said pleasantly, "would it surprise you to know Satan is responsible for this? He sent a man here named Marc Jones . . ."

"What?" Karla interrupted, trying to maintain her composure. "You've got to be kidding."

"He's not kidding," Charles broke in. "Mr. Sanders is a member of Ray Winston's church."

"Yes sir, we both are," Bill said. "Pastor Winston will be speakin' in a few minutes about what's happenin'. We'd love for you to come hear his message and receive salvation."

"Thank you," Karla said, "but I wouldn't . . . "

" . . . miss it for the world, Mr. Sanders," Harvey finished. "Thanks for inviting us."

"So you're saying all I have to do is love God first and then love others like I love myself?" Abdurahman asked. "If I do those two things, I can be saved?"

"That's right," Donnie answered.

"It just doesn't seem possible."

"Considering the life you've been living's been based on the idea that your works equal your degree of faith, I think I understand how difficult this must be for you," Marc replied. "The difference between being saved by faith or by works is this: works gives you a detailed list of specific things you must, and must not, do. The list may begin with a commandment or a general principle that man reads and interprets. He then uses that to make laws which he in turn judges as being met or unmet. The punishments for violating those laws are then given out by man, and the end result is that God has little, or nothing, to do with the rules and laws you order your life by."

Abdurahman listened intently.

"When you do the two things Jesus commanded, you'll actually be doing quite a bit. The difference is, instead of giving you a detailed list of things to do in specific situations, you're given two commandments to carry out, which, based on your relationship with Jesus, will be acted upon as you're directed by the Holy Spirit. So I'm not saying you don't have to do anything. I'm saying you have to do two things. I'm just not telling you how to do them. That's between you and God."

"Mr. Burton, the Unit 2 manager, just drove up," the sergeant said.

Powell looked up. "Have him come back."

The sergeant left, quickly returning with Burton close behind. "Mr. Powell," Burton said, out of breath, "how can I help?"

"I need you to identify the officers and the inmates."

"Yes, sir." Burton moved closer to the monitors.

"Look right here." Powell pointed to the screen showing A block. "Do these men with their hands tied behind their backs look familiar?"

"Yes, sir. They're two of the officers assigned to the downstairs cell blocks." Burton provided their names.

"Okay." Powell turned to the sergeant. "Bring up C block." He waited for the picture to change. "Who are the men in uniforms?"

Burton pointed to the screen. "That man is Pete Holloway." He leaned in closer. "That's Ryan Wallace. He's serving three consecutive life sentences. And that inmate they're with is Theodore Pendalton."

"Ladies and gentlemen," Bill Sanders said to the sixty or so people gathered around the back of his truck. "It's my pleasure to introduce to you Pastor Ray Winston, a true man of God." He clapped, and others from the church joined in as Ray climbed up on the tailgate.

"Thank you, thank you." Ray nodded his head and smiled like he'd seen actors and politicians do on TV when they were introduced. "Thank you very much. Before I start, I wanna begin with a word of prayer. Dear Lord," he said softly, tightly shutting his eyes, "I wanna thank you for the opportunity to be here."

"Yes Lord," Bill cried out, "thank you, thank you!"

"It's through Your wisdom and power that we've been brought together and it'll be because of Your blessings that we'll learn and grow."

"Amen . . . amen."

"You're the great and mighty One, the Alpha and the Omega," Ray said passionately, his fire igniting. "You're the Great Shepherd and we're Your lost lambs. Protect us, Lord God, and save us from the power of Satan."

"Please, please, please save us," a woman cried out, her tears evident in her voice.

"Amen," Bill shouted.

"Amen and amen." Ray lowered his hands and opened his eyes.

"Where's my food?"

"That's why I'm calling, sir," Steve said into the phone. "We've got it and want to bring it to you."

"All right, here's how it's gonna happen," Lord Abdullah said. "I want a female officer to bring it to the bar door goin' upstairs. She's gonna throw the keys up the stairs and leave."

There was no way Lord Abdullah was going to get the keys to anything. "I'll have an officer put the food on your side of the stairs," Steve said.

"That ain't what I told you, is it?"

"No, sir. But if you want us to cooperate, we're going to have to go slow. Right now, my supervisors aren't going to let me give you the keys. I can talk to them about it, but that's gonna take a while."

"Nah," Lord Abdullah said after a tense moment. "Just bring the food and set it on our side of the bar door. In the future, you better do things exactly the way I say or I'll hurt somebody just to prove I'm serious."

"Lee," Deeann called. "You've got to hear this."

Powell quickly returned to the intel room. "What is it?"

She nodded toward the screen. Pete was speaking angrily to the inmates standing with him. "Listen."

". . . Don't you think I hear 'da phone ringin'?" Pete said. "I ain't ready to talk, so I ain't gonna answer. I'm runnin' this, not the po-lice."

"That's cool." Ryan held up his hands but glanced at Theodore.

"What's the plan?" Theodore asked.

"First, we gotta prove we mean business," Pete answered. "They don't believe we're gonna do nothin', and we ain't gettin' no respect. I think we gotta hurt one of 'dem po-lice tied up over there. If we start cuttin' one of 'em, I bet they'll get us what we want 'den."

Ryan grinned.

"That's all I need to hear." Powell picked up the phone. "Floyd, get your men ready. The situation's deteriorated and I may need to send you in downstairs."

"Yes, sir." Faulk passed the order along to his PERT team positioned outside each cell block.

"Many of you've come tonight 'cause you've got family or friends workin' behind those fences." Ray pointed toward the prison lit up in the distance. "Others of you came just 'cause you're curious. Whatever the reason, all of us know somethin' is goin' on. This is the worst prison in the United States. The men who're sent here are terrible, evil men, and their lives are filled with Satan. That's why I'm standin' before you this evenin'. My name's Pastor Ray Winston, and I started the Rocky Mount Evangelical Assembly of God Church." He waited out the applause from his congregation. "For those of you who haven't heard or don't know, there's an inmate in this prison named Marc Jones." He raised his voice. "This man's not just evil. He's totally controlled by Satan."

"Yes he is, Lord," Bill Sanders shouted.

"How do I know this?" Ray asked. "Well, let me tell you why he's here and what he's done. You see, ladies and gentlemen, Marc Jones is in prison 'cause he started a riot at a church. Some of you may even remember readin' about it in the newspapers a few months ago. For those of you that don't, let me tell you so you'll know who we're dealin' with."

He gave his own interpretation of the events that had led to Marc's arrest and incarceration.

After cutting the power supply to the downstairs cell blocks, the PERT groups crept into place near strategic doors and windows. Each team knew what to expect and was clear about each officer's specific duties for extracting hostages and taking control of a situation. Nevertheless, despite the many hours of training, they all felt adrenaline pumping through their veins.

They knew things rarely went as planned.

The phone was ringing.

Pete finally answered it. "What?"

"Sir," Steve started.

"Shut up," Pete snarled. "I only got one thing you need to know. I want my food, and I'm givin' you five minutes to get it or I'm gonna give the order for my man to begin cuttin'. You understand?"

"So you see, ladies and gentlemen," Ray said, "Marc Jones has seriously violated the laws of the state of North Carolina. If that isn't bad enough, the effect he's had on members of the clergy is even worse."

"Oh my," a woman gasped.

"That's right, ladies and gentlemen." Ray twisted his mouth in disgust. "Marc Jones has convinced supposed men of God that he was sent here to teach us that we don't have to be like Jesus."

"Have mercy on their souls, Lord!" yelled a lady standing nearby.

"So convinced are these so-called men of God that they tried to tell me Jones was sent by God Himself," Ray screamed. He dropped to his knees in the bed of the truck. Several his warriors followed his lead, and others began speaking in tongues. Still others pleaded for the Holy Spirit to intervene.

Powell overheard Pete's threat and snatched up a phone. "Floyd," he said calmly, "we have five minutes."

"Yes, sir," Faulk responded. He already knew what was coming next.

"Give the order to go in as soon as your teams are ready," Powell said. "You know where the hostage takers are located and where the officers are being held. Concentrate on those areas first. Advise me when you're in place. We'll monitor things and will advise if the situation changes."

"Ten-four." Faulk picked up his walkie-talkie.

Ray stood up slowly, assessing the impact his words had on the crowd. He pulled a handkerchief out of his pocket and took his time wiping the perspiration from his forehead.

No one said the work of the Lord was accomplished without sweat . . .

"Ladies and gentlemen," he said softly, in stark contrast to his prayer tone, "I'm standin' before you this evenin' pleadin' with you to turn from Satan and away from the sin that comes from him."

"Amen, Pastor Winston," Bill yelled. "Preach it, brother, preach it!"

"In here," Ray said, holding up his well-worn Bible, "it tells us we must carefully test a man's words to determine if they're with Christ or from somewhere else. It says that when we do this, we'll know a man's character by lookin' at the fruits he produces."

"That's right," called a man standing off to the side. More and more people were caught up in the contagious emotion of the moment.

"Well, I've done that," Ray's voice rang out with authority. "It's obvious the fruit Marc Jones has produced is from a tree that was planted in Hell."

"Glory be to you, Pastor." Bill fell to his knees and raised his hands. "Save us, Lord, save us!"

"Praise to You, Merciful, Mighty, Wonderful, Father God," wailed a lady standing nearby.

The team leaders reported their status.

"Team three is ready, sir."

"Team two is ready, sir."

"Team four is ready, sir."

"Twenty-two twelve, this is twenty-one forty, over," the lead PERT team officer said softly into the microphone on his shoulder as he crouched below the emergency door to cell block A.

"Go ahead, twenty-one forty," Captain Bradley replied.

"All units are in place. Over."

"Get up," Ryan shouted, tugging on the officer's T-shirt. "Now!"

The blindfolded officer, dressed as an inmate, stumbled to his feet. Ryan pressed the razor to the officer's throat and led him to the middle of the block. He wanted to make sure everyone could see what he was going to do. "Don't move a muscle or I'll kill you right now," he ordered.

"Be cool," Pete ordered. "Wait 'til I tell ya."

Ryan pressed the razor even harder into the officer's neck.

"An examination of this man's fruit tells us he was sent from the bowels of hell itself," Ray screamed in a barely controlled rage. "And it's our duty as the Lord's Christian Warriors to defeat him."

"Amen and amen." People fell to their knees. Others lay on the soft ground around the edges of the newly planted field.

"What do we do, Pastor?" someone shouted from the back of the crowd. "How do we defeat the evil Satan has brought against us?"

"Son," Ray shouted back, even though the gentleman was at least his own age, "in the book of Ephesians, Paul tells us to stand our ground by puttin' on the belt of truth and the body armor of God's righteousness."

"Glory to God, brother," the man yelled back.

"He tells us to wear shoes that come from the peace of the Good News."

"We're prepared, Pastor. We're prepared!"

"We're to use faith as shields to stop the fiery arrows Satan shoots at us. Our salvation will be our helmet and the word of God will be the sword of the Spirit."

"Yes, Lord, yes." Bill fell back to the ground in apparent exhaustion.

"Lastly, we're to pray at all times and on every occasion in the power of the Holy Spirit."

"Amen," the crowd shouted in unison.

"Amen, and amen," Ray shouted back, his fists raised high in the air.

"All teams go!" Captain Bradley said. "I repeat, go!"

"I feel like I'm at an old-time tent revival without a tent," Charles observed as he walked with Karla and Harvey away from the growing crowd.

"Me too," Karla said, "and it bothers me the context it's occurring in. We're outside a maximum custody prison attempting to put down a riot, and this man's trying to convince people one of the men inside is Satan."

"What Ray is doing is perhaps well intentioned," Harvey said, "but it's grossly out of place."

"Well intentioned?" Karla shook her head. "His intentions are to use the situation to promote his own agenda. I wonder when he's going to pass collection plates."

Officer Peterson waited for the flash bangs and tear gas to detonate. Then, as had been scripted, he threw open the fire escape and entered cell block A. Officers Dikerson and Bowe followed, covering his silent movement through the darkness and tear gas fog toward the back of the block where the hostages were being held. Most inmates put up no resistance and were lying on the concrete floor coughing, with tears running down their faces. But Ryan had anticipated that this would happen. He held his hostage with one hand and had a wet washcloth pressed over his face with the other. He spotted Peterson out of the corner of his eye.

"Throw down your weapon and get on the floor!" Peterson yelled.

"You're crazy," Ryan yelled between coughs. "Back off or I'm gonna kill this man!"

"Take it easy," Peterson called. "Don't do anything stupid. I'm sure we can work this out." He assessed the scene through the night sight on his assault rifle.

"Put your gun down," Ryan yelled, "or this man's gonna die."

"No way, sir," Peterson countered, activating the laser sight and putting the red dot in the middle of Ryan's forehead. "I want you to slowly drop the razor and lay face down on the floor. Do it now!"

"That ain't gonna happen," Ryan said, moving backwards with his hostage. "I ain't gonna go by myself."

"Sir, don't do it. There's nowhere to go." Peterson focused on the hand holding the razor.

This feels weird putting a laser beam on a man dressed in a CO's uniform . . .

Cornered, Ryan sensed he had to act. But like most decisions he'd made throughout his life, his next one was poorly thought out and had little chance of success.

"Don't do it," Peterson screamed, seeing the muscles in Ryan's right hand flex slightly.

Bam!

It was the last thing Ryan heard before he dropped to the floor.

Lord Abdullah was walking back to the multipurpose room when he heard the gunshot ring out. Recognizing what was happening, he ran to E block and grabbed the officer Walter was holding. Other inmates ran to the mattress-covered windows.

"Get up. Now." Lord Abdullah yanked the officer to his feet. "If you try somethin', I'll cut your throat so fast you won't know it happened."

"Yes, sir," the officer said, knowing this wasn't the time to be a hero.

"Move!" Lord Abdullah ordered, pushing him toward the front of the block. "Hank," he yelled without turning, "let me know if the po-lice are comin' up the stairs."

"Yes, sir!"

"Walter, help Hank guard the bar door!"

"Did you hear that?" Karla said, clutching Charles' sleeve. "It sounded like a gunshot."

"Something's happening." Charles turned in the direction of the muffled sounds.

"Oh no," Karla said.

"Don't panic." Charles tried to sound calm. "I doubt the inmates have guns, so I imagine we're hearing officers firing at something or someone."

"But why?" Karla asked in desperation.

"I don't know." Charles turned to Harvey for support.

"Dear God," Karla said, with tears forming in her eyes, "please don't let anything happen to Donnie. Please Lord."

As one PERT team moved into cell block A, the team covering the back of the prison moved into cell block C. They knew Pete Holloway was in C block and dressed like an officer. When the smoke cleared, they saw him backed against the gray cinderblock wall, holding a razor to a man's neck.

"I got 'im," Pete yelled, walking forward. "This is one of the inmates!"

"Don't move any closer, sir," the PERT team leader ordered. "Drop your weapon. Now!"

"You don't understand," Pete said. "'Dis is an inmate. I can't let 'im go." He continued forward despite the three red laser dots centered on his forehead.

"Sir," the PERT officer ordered loudly, "for the last time, stop and drop your weapon! Do it now!"

"No way!" Pete yelled, moving the razor slightly.

Bam! Bam! Bam!

No one moved.

Suddenly, a man leaped out from behind a mattress leaning against a wall. Screaming he was a god, he ran toward the officers, holding a short baton in one hand and a metal shank in the other.

Bam! Bam!

Donnie flinched as each shot rang out. The echoes off the concrete walls made it impossible to determine how many shots were fired, but it seemed an entire army was shooting, and he sensed it was only a matter of time before Lord Abdullah came in and killed them. Handcuffed with no weapon and nowhere to hide, he felt more helpless than he ever had. He truly knew only God could protect him.

With fear in his voice, Donnie prayed out loud. "Lord, please protect us and give us strength. Raise us up on eagle's wings and hold us in the palm of your hand. Give us courage and show us Your mercy. We don't know why this is happening, Lord, but we believe and trust with our hearts that You're in control. Yes Lord, we're scared and afraid, but in our hearts, we know that You'll be victorious. Help us to take comfort in knowing that no matter what happens, we will always be safe with You. In Your Son's name . . . Amen!"

"Amen," Marc said.

"Amen," Abdurahman said softly a moment later. He looked up to see Donnie and Marc smiling, realizing what had just occurred.

ROMANS 8:12,13 "So, dear brothers and sisters, you have no obligation whatsoever to do what your sinful nature urges you to do. For if you keep on following it, you will perish. But if through the power of the Holy Spirit you turn from it and its evil deeds, you will live."
(NLT)

Chapter 21

Friday Morning

Sunrise was an hour away, but the spotlights at the roadblock made it seem as bright as noon when Jeff Hagerton drove up in the muddy prison truck. He had been told the crowd had grown overnight, but he was still surprised to see hundreds of people sitting in lawn chairs and standing around in groups along the edges of the fields.

The media instantly recognized him as the public information officer when he climbed out of the truck, and he was swamped by eager reporters. The major networks and news bureaus, as well as every hometown newspaper within two hundred miles, had sent someone to cover the story. Had it not been for the additional deputies sent to control the crowd, Hagerton was sure he never would have made it to the makeshift podium set up in the back of a flatbed farm truck.

Like everyone else, Karla, Charles, and Harvey were desperate for information. They crowded behind the press to hear the official briefing. Everyone had been on edge since the rifle blasts had rung out around midnight, and many theories circulated among the crowd. People with family and friends working at Caledonia believed officers had been forced to shoot inmates when they went in to rescue hostages. Inmates' relatives said the sounds hadn't come from the prison but were from one of the old trucks they'd heard backfiring around the farm. Ray and his group wanted everyone to believe Marc Jones had convinced other inmates to overpower officers and shoot them. One man, who appeared intoxicated, was yelling that aliens were responsible.

"Good morning. I'm Jeff Hagerton, the Assistant Superintendent of Programs at Caledonia Correctional Institution." Hagerton straightened some papers on the podium. "Since the situation at the prison began yesterday morning, four officers, a staff member, and an unknown number of inmates were taken hostage. One group of hostages was downstairs and one group was upstairs. After prison officials spent most of the afternoon and a better part of the evening negotiating with the downstairs hostage takers, members of the North Carolina Department of Corrections' Prison Emergency Response Team, or PERT for short, were sent in and successfully rescued two officers. The two inmates who were holding these officers attempted to harm them and were fatally wounded. Another inmate, who threatened a member of the PERT team, was also fatally wounded."

The reporters waited for him to pause, then clamored for information.

"Is it true . . . "

"Sir . . . "

"Did you . . . "

"Could . . . "

"Please, ladies and gentlemen, if you'll hold your questions until I finish, I'll give you an opportunity to ask," Hagerton said. He continued to read his statement. "Once the PERT team had the downstairs cell blocks under control, correctional officers entered to secure the situation and move inmates to an area where they could be medically evaluated and receive treatment if necessary. To my knowledge, other than the three inmates who were shot, there were no other serious injuries to either staff or inmates."

"Sir," one reporter tried again.

Hagerton ignored him and continued. "At this time, we're monitoring the situation upstairs, and we will continue to negotiate the release of those hostages. We'll do everything within our power to resolve the situation peacefully, and we are quite confident this will be the case. I'll be happy to answer your questions at this time."

Steve clutched the receiver. *Come on . . . answer the phone . . .*

Lord Abdullah's voice came on the line. "Whatta ya want? I done told ya we ain't got nothin' to talk about. Either I get what I want or I'm gonna hurt 'dis man."

"There's no need to hurt anyone," Steve said calmly. "I'm sure we can work this out. Getting you more food isn't a problem. It'll be here in a minute. It's gonna take time to get the other things because we're having to work with agencies in other states."

"You're tryin' to handle me. I know if y'all really wanted to make 'dem things happen you could."

"Sir," Steve said, not using either of the man's names, "everything I've said has been the truth. I told you I'd get you food last night and I did, didn't I?"

"It took too long. You ain't dealin' with some chump."

"I know, and that's why I'm sure we can work this out," Steve replied. "I know you're way too smart to do anything stupid."

"Yeah, we can work it out," Lord Abdullah said. "Just like you worked it out with 'dem men downstairs."

"It wasn't like that, sir. Those men, unlike you, weren't very smart and were about to hurt their hostages. My bosses couldn't let that happen. That's the only reason the PERT team was sent in."

"Look, man," Lord Abdullah said with frustration in his voice. "I ain't some naïve little officer you can build up with compliments and 'den ambush. I hope you do send in those special po-lice. We're ready for 'em. We got a plan."

Despite the fact that the three men were facing death, the mood in the multipurpose room had changed dramatically. Peacefulness overtook the place. Donnie imagined angels in heaven rejoicing because one of God's lost lambs was found and ready to return.

"God answered our prayers," Abdurahman said. "He saved us."

Marc looked up. "You might be right. But I hope you don't believe in God *only* because you think He answered our prayers."

Abdurahman looked puzzled. "The things y'all said made sense. That's why I prayed with you. And after that, the shooting stopped."

"Abdurahman, I'm happy you've decided to follow the Lord," Marc said. "But it shouldn't be just because we prayed and the fighting stopped. When Jesus lived among us, He criticized people for following Him only because He performed miracles. He said true believers follow Him because they know He's the way to live, and the only way to salvation."

Abdurahman frowned. "What difference does it make why I want to believe, as long as I do?"

"It makes a great deal of difference." Marc smiled patiently. "If you believe only because you think God will give you everything you want, then you're going to be disappointed, because some things you want aren't what He wants you to have."

Faulk sat down next to Powell. "This is going to be very different than the situation downstairs. Jackson is smart, and he really thinks we're going to get him a helicopter so he can fly home."

"You're right, Floyd," Deeann said.

"Maybe instead of the helicopter, we could get him some ruby red slippers he could click together." Faulk chuckled. "He's got about as much chance of getting one as he does the other."

"It's too risky to forcibly enter the multipurpose room, but maybe we could use the helicopter to lure him out," Powell said.

Faulk nodded thoughtfully. "It's going to be tough to fool him."

"Maybe that's where I can help," Deeann replied. "We can start working on him psychologically and use what he believes to our advantage. It'll certainly be risky, since he's so volatile, but Steve's really a good negotiator. Besides, Jackson's so convinced he's special, he may not even realize what's happening."

"How many are being held hostage?" asked the *Daily Herald* reporter.

"At this time, two DOC personnel and an unknown number of inmates," Hagerton said.

"What is the condition of the hostages?"

"As far as we know, the men are doing well."

"Have the hostage takers made demands?" asked a broadcast news reporter. "And if so, what are they?"

"Yes, the hostage takers have made demands, but I can't comment on them at this time."

"Do the demands involve being released from prison?"

"Again, I'm sorry, but I can't comment on that."

"Do you believe you'll be able to meet the demands?" another reporter probed.

Barbara Pierce pushed to the front of the crowd before Hagerton could respond. "I understand an inmate named Marc Jones is housed at Caledonia. Is he involved in this situation? And if so, how?"

Hagerton felt like a cornered animal looking at the teeth of a hungry predator.

Who's this woman? . . . How'd she know about Marc Jones? . . . What do I say? . . . Be calm . . .

"I can't comment on that, ma'am," he stammered.

"Was he involved in starting this riot?" Barbara pressed on.

"I can't comment on that."

"Who's Marc Jones?" another reporter yelled out.

Ray couldn't believe he'd heard the name Marc Jones from the throng of reporters.

No wonder the prison don't wanna talk about his role . . . This must be Your purpose for bringing me here . . . You want me to tell these people and the rest of the world about who Marc Jones is and the evil that follows him . . . You want me to be Your spokesman . . . Then I can save 'em . . . Thank you, Father God, for givin' me this chance . . . I won't let You down this time . . . I promise . . . Glory to You, Father God . . .

Ray walked toward the reporters, hoping to talk with the lady who'd asked about Marc.

"That's the reporter who interviewed Eddie," Charles pointed out. "She suspects Marc's involved."

"He is," Harvey said. "Only I don't think it's the way most people think."

"Pastor Winston's convinced a lot of people that Marc Jones is pure evil," Karla said. "It wouldn't take much to convince them he started the riot."

Harvey looked at the crowd of reporters. "We should talk with Barbara Pierce to give her our perspective."

"Count me in," Karla said, relieved to be doing something to take her thoughts off of Donnie.

"Steve, this is Dr. Sheffield," Deeann said into the phone. "We heard your conversation, and we have a plan."

"Yes, ma'am."

"You're on the three-way hookup with Mr. Powell, Mr. Faulk, and myself," Deeann said. "Okay, here it is. We all agree Jackson's narcissistic and believes he's much more intelligent than he really is."

"Yes, ma'am."

"We want to use his inflated perception of himself to our advantage. It's going to be tricky, but I think it's the best angle we have."

"I would agree," Steve said.

"I think the way to do it is to keep making it seem difficult for you to get him what he wants," Deeann said. "Then, when he pushes it, tell him you've convinced us to give in and give it to him. Make sure you tell him you believe we're finally doing whatever it is because we know we can't trick him. Make him think you're on his side and you believe he's as smart as he thinks."

"I'll do my best." Steve knew it was going to be extremely difficult to read Jackson and not push him too far.

Lord, please help . . .

"Can you give us *any* information about who's responsible for the riot and taking hostages?" asked a reporter from the associated press. "I've heard there's gang connections."

"At this time, I believe it would be inappropriate to draw that conclusion based on what we know," Hagerton said.

"It certainly sounds possible," commented the reporter. "What are the names of the hostages?"

"We're unable to release that information until the families have been contacted."

"Why was the PERT team sent in downstairs but not upstairs?"

"The two situations are being led by different people," Hagerton explained. "The situation downstairs had deteriorated, and the hostages were in imminent danger."

"Does that mean the hostages being held upstairs aren't thought to be in imminent danger at this time?" the reporter followed up.

"That's correct."

"How many hostages are being held upstairs?"

Hagerton held up his hand "I'm sorry, ladies and gentlemen, that's all I have for now. I'll return to brief you when there's more information. Thanks for your understanding." He stepped down quickly. Reporters continued shouting questions at him.

"I think I know how to help you understand," Donnie said. "To believe in God, you must have faith. If you got everything you prayed for, not only would it mean you'd have complete knowledge of what was good for you, it would also mean your motivations for wanting it were righteous."

Abdurahman reflected on that. "It's kind of like what Preacher Man said about man's sinful nature and never being able to get away from it."

"That's correct," Donnie said. "If you got everything you prayed for, people would follow Christ because they got what they wanted, instead of following Him because they believed His way is the only way out of sin."

"Excuse me, ma'am," Ray said, putting out his hand. "My name's Ray Winston. I'm the pastor at Rocky Mount Evangelical Assembly of God Church. I'd like to speak with you about Marc Jones."

"It's nice to meet you, Reverend," Barbara said, shaking his hand. "Let's walk toward my van."

Along the way, Ray told her who he thought Marc was.

"That's very interesting," Barbara said. "Would you mind if I interviewed you in a few minutes about what you've told me?"

"Anything I can do to help, ma'am." Ray smiled as he headed back to the church van to get ready.

Steve waited as the phone rang.

"Whatcha want?" Lord Abdullah spat.

"Your food's here," Steve said. "What you said about not playing games worked. The prison administrators sent officers right out to get it."

"Yeah, well 'dey better respect me, 'cause I'm a god," Lord Abdullah said, loudly enough for the inmates standing near him to hear.

"I *know* what kind of man you are," Steve said. "But the people making the decisions had to see for themselves."

"Whatever, man," Lord Abdullah replied. "Look, I want one of 'dem females to bring the chow up to the backstairs bar door like last night. If anyone tries anything stupid, I'm gonna cut 'dis po-liceman's throat. You understand?"

"Hello, Ms. Pierce," Charles said. "We met a while ago when you interviewed Eddie Smith. Do you recall?"

"Of course I remember you," Barbara said as she unloaded some equipment from the station's van. "How are you, Reverend Hurley?"

"Honestly, I've been better."

"What do you think about what's happening out here?"

"There's a lot going on," Charles said. "I'm very concerned that people close to me are still in harm's way. I'm also concerned about people's perceptions of Marc Jones and what they think his role is in this."

"I see." Barbara turned toward him. "Why does that concern you so much, Reverend Hurley?"

"You know how some of us feel about Mr. Jones and why we believe he's here. It troubles me that people are again going to miss an opportunity God has given them to learn about having a relationship with Him. I'm not sure how many more opportunities He's going to give us."

"But what about people who strongly believe Marc Jones is evil and was sent by Satan?" Barbara pulled a notebook and a pen out of her purse. "How can I be sure you're right and they're wrong?"

"I think if you examine their motivations, you'll see that they have much to lose if people listen to Marc and follow his message," Charles said. "I think that's because his message is similar to the message Jesus tried to teach two thousand years ago. Just like then, people refuse to hear it today."

Barbara jotted down a few words. "Charles, would you mind letting me interview you later?"

"I'd like that. If it's okay, I'll bring a friend of mine, Dr. Harvey Ramone, a retired Baptist minister. He's worked with Marc in a prison Bible study group."

"In the book of Hebrews, it says it's impossible to please God without faith," Marc explained. "It takes faith to believe God exists, and He rewards people who earnestly seek Him."

"Rewards?" Abdurahman asked. "So aren't you saying God's going to give me something only if I do something?"

"What you have to do isn't a matter of performing prescribed rituals or duties," Marc said. "Instead, you must honestly seek to find God in everything you do, see, think, and say, so you can have a personal, dynamic relationship with Him."

"It's going to take me a while to understand how I, a mere mortal, can have a relationship with God."

Marc nodded. "It can only happen through faith. Many times, people hear the Good News and want to be a Christian, but they give up because they don't immediately get what they prayed for."

Powell stared at the screens. "We need to decide where we want the helicopter to land."

"What route do we want the hostages and inmates to take?" Faulk asked.

"I think where the helicopter lands will dictate that." Powell stood energetically, despite not having slept for over twenty-four hours. "All right, start working on it. Talk with your PERT snipers about the best shooting angles and ranges. We'll reevaluate in ten minutes."

Ring . . . ring . . . ring . . .

"What?" Lord Abdullah answered.

"I just wanted to make sure you got the food," Steve said.

"Yeah, but what about 'dem other things?"

"We're doing our best to get them for you. We're in contact with the governor about the helicopter, and we have people talking with New York State Prison administrators about releasing the men you want."

Lord Abdullah responded harshly and without hesitation. "Don't mess with me, Johnson. When twelve o'clock gets here, I want 'dem things. Don't tell me 'den that it's gonna take longer. If the governor's involved and he wants somethin', he's gonna get it. Maybe I need to make 'em want it bad enough."

Steve took a deep breath. "Everyone knows you mean what you say. You've convinced the administrators here to the point they've contacted the governor. You don't think Mr. Powell calls the governor every time an inmate wants him to, do you?"

Lord Abdullah was silent. Steve knew he believed he was receiving special treatment.

Score a point for the good guys . . .

"Good morning, North Carolina," the anchor said to viewers across the Tarheel State as they woke up and began getting ready for the day. "Thanks for tuning in to "NC Overnight" this Friday morning. I want to quickly get you out to Barbara Pierce, who's been covering the hostage situation at our state's most notorious maximum custody prison. Barbara."

"Thank you, Walter." The picture cut to Barbara standing beside a freshly planted field with Halifax County patrol cars blocking the road behind her. "We're at Caledonia Correctional Institution covering the story that began yesterday morning as a riot and has evolved into a hostage standoff."

"What can you tell us about the situation, Barbara?"

"The riot started in one of the four units at the prison." Barbara went on to describe the events that had unfolded.

"It sounds like a volatile situation. Do you have a feel for where it might be headed?"

"The prison has a specially trained team of officers and negotiators who are working diligently to resolve the crisis as peacefully as possible," Barbara said. "Jeff Hagerton, the Assistant Superintendent of Programs for the prison, indicated he's pleased with the progress of negotiations and is confident further loss of life can be avoided."

"Did he say what the inmates are demanding or why the riot began?"

"Walter, there seem to be many theories about what caused the riot, but at this point, they all seem to be speculation. For now, we're going to remain on location, covering the breaking story as it develops."

"Ephesians chapter two, verse eight, tells us we're saved because of God's grace through faith, which is a gift of God."

Donnie leaned back to listen to Marc's gentle teaching voice.

"It's because of this that we must pray for faith, Abdurahman."

"That's it, just pray?"

"That's the starting point, yes." Marc shifted, his handcuffs clinking. "Something else that will help is to begin learning about God's character so you can learn that He is who He says He is. Once you do, you can start knowing and believing that He does the things He says He will do. In this way, you'll come to have the kind of faith the Bible tells us is the confident assurance that what we hope for is going to happen, and that the things we don't see can, and do, exist."

Steve answered the call, knowing only one phone could get through to the special line used in hostage negotiations. "Hello, this is Johnson."

"Look, man," Lord Abdullah said. "Somethin' else. I want Pete Holloway brought up here."

"I'll have to discuss it with the administration," Steve said calmly, but his thoughts raced. *What's going to happen when he finds out Pete's dead?*

"You've got thirty minutes." Lord Abdullah abruptly hung up.

"Pastor Winston, I appreciate your allowing me to interview you," Barbara said while her cameraman set up to tape.

"I'm just happy to be able to help, Ms. Pierce." A*nd even happier* you're *gonna help* me . . .

She told him the types of questions to expect. "Are we ready?"

"Yes, ma'am."

"Okay, let's start filming then." Barbara picked up her microphone. "I'm with Pastor Ray Winston from the Rocky Mount Evangelical Assembly of God Church. Pastor Winston and several members of his church have been outside Caledonia since yesterday afternoon. Reverend, can you tell us why you felt it necessary to come and bring members of your congregation?

"Yes, ma'am," Ray answered, sounding calmer than he felt. "A few weeks ago it was brought to my attention by several clergy members in Rocky Mount that a man named Marc Jones was incarcerated here. They said he was sent by God to teach people that they didn't need to be like Jesus Christ."

"How did you respond to that?" Barbara asked.

"I immediately knew somethin' was wrong," he said passionately. "In my many years of service and devotion to the Lord, I've learned one of the biggest jobs a Christian has is to try and be like His Son, Jesus."

"Did you discuss this with the clergy members who were telling you this?"

"I certainly did." Ray smiled at the camera. "I tried reasonin' with 'em, but they couldn't hear me. It was like they were under some power or somethin'. It wasn't until later I figured out what was goin' on."

"Amen, Brother Winston," screamed someone in the crowd.

"What did you figure out?" Barbara asked.

"When I left that meetin', I went and did some research about Marc Jones and reviewed it in light of what Scripture has to say."

"What conclusions were you able to draw?"

"The most obvious thing was that Marc Jones wasn't sent by God. He was sent by Satan!"

"Tell 'em preacher," someone yelled.

"God save us," a woman cried.

"How did you determine that, Pastor Winston?" Barbara asked over the vocal crowd.

"He's in prison for startin' a riot at a church durin' the Sunday Service," Ray said. "The people at the church testified he was on drugs. Obviously, he's got special powers, since he's able to convince supposedly well-educated ministers that Jesus ain't important anymore. I guess what I'm sayin' is this: the Bible tells us to look at the fruits a person produces to measure their character."

"Yes it does, Pastor," a voice rang out. "You tell 'em."

"I've been tellin' you about the fruits of Marc Jones' life. Now he's at this outstandin' correctional facility, and we're seein' yet more of his fruit." Ray smashed his fist into his other hand. "He's gotta be stopped at all costs."

"Mr. Powell," Steve said, "did you hear that conversation with Jackson?"

"Yeah. I'm talking with Dr. Sheffield about it now. Any ideas?"

"I don't really see any other way besides telling him the truth."

"I agree, but Dr. Sheffield says we need to decide how."

"I'm not sure I understand."

"We could tell him straight out that Pete was shot," Powell said. "We probably wouldn't get much out of it except an angry response."

"Okay." Steve considered his options. "What's another way?"

"Well, the officers assigned to the downstairs cell blocks said Jackson got mad and punched Pete before attacking the prayer leader. I assume Pete offended him in some way. We can use that to our advantage."

"I see where you're going with this," Steve said. "I tell Jackson about Pete's apparent plan. Play up the idea he was only thinking about himself, planning to create a diversion so he could get lost in the confusion."

Dr. Sheffield came on the line. "Steve, after you've created the stage, I want you to say that if Pete would've been a little smarter and not tried to harm the officer he was holding, his plan might have worked. You and I know he didn't have a chance of escaping, but Jackson doesn't. Tell him that instead of getting out, Pete got shot between the eyes."

"Yes, ma'am."

"This is going to be delicate, Steve," Powell said, coming back on the line. "We just want to try and get Jackson to doubt himself a little bit so we can use it later."

"Don't believe in God just because you prayed for protection and got it," Marc said. "In the future, He will give you victories, but they'll probably be in different forms. They'll probably be related more to the role He wants you to play in His Kingdom."

"What do you mean?" Abdurahman asked.

"Well," Donnie said, "if you look at the lives of men and women of faith, you'll see that most of them were treated very poorly by society. Some were tortured and some were even killed. But the Lord never deserted them. He always gave them the strength to endure their treatment and used their situation for the glory of His Kingdom."

"That's right," Marc said. "Many people believe that when they become a Christian, it means they'll be free from pain and won't suffer. When their troubles don't disappear, they think God deserted them, and they try to figure out why. Instead, Christians should remember that Jesus suffered on the cross, and he promised to never leave us and to always intercede on our behalf."

"You see, Ms. Pierce," Ray said, his excitement growing, "the Apostle Paul wrote in the Good Book that we ain't just fightin' against people. We're fightin' against powers of the unseen world."

"Amen, amen, amen," Bill Sanders screamed. "Save us, Lord, save us!"

"These wicked spirits and mighty powers of darkness can only be overthrown by Jesus Christ," Ray continued, getting his rhythm. "Jesus commands an army of angels, and only He can defeat the powers of Satan."

"It sounds like you're saying Marc Jones is being led by Satan, and all of this happened because of it," Barbara shouted over the noisy crowd.

"Yes ma'am, that's exactly what I'm sayin'." Ray pushed his windblown hair back into place.

"How do you propose authorities can take care of this problem?"

"They can't," Ray answered quickly. "The only way this problem can be solved is for people to turn to the Lord. To fall down on their knees and beg for His forgiveness. To turn away from messages and messengers like Marc Jones that use fancy talk to convince people to stop followin' Christ and stop tryin' to be like him." Beads of sweat rolled down his cheeks. "Ms. Pierce, if society don't change, many people will burn in the pits of hell. Now is the time to save yourself and to save our world."

"It's incredible that he can pass judgment on someone he's never met," Karla whispered, watching Ray Winston from the back of the crowd.

"He knows the right words," Harvey said. "But he says them at the wrong time and for perhaps the wrong reasons."

"It's like his whole purpose is battling evil," Charles observed. "So much so that he's incapable of seeing the goodness that exists right in front of him."

"It's almost like he's figured out what goodness is supposed to look like," Harvey said. "Anything that doesn't meet his criteria is bad."

Karla folded her arms. "Well, one thing's for sure. If you look hard enough for something, you're bound to find it, whether it's there or not."

"That's true," Harvey said, "but even if we don't agree with his opinion, we need to remember something Paul wrote in his letter to the Philippians."

Charles nodded. "Paul knew that since he was in prison, some of the men preaching at that time were doing so out of selfish ambition in order to build their own reputations in his absence."

"He said God wouldn't excuse their motives and neither would he," Harvey said. "But he wasn't upset with them. Instead, he rejoiced that the Gospel was being taught and God was using their message, regardless of why they were giving it."

God, please give me the words to say . . . Steve thought as the phone rang. *Help me and please be with Donnie and the others being held . . .*

"You better be callin' to tell me Al-Shirazi Khomeini's comin' up here," Lord Abdullah mumbled around a mouthful of food.

"Sir, I was calling to talk with you about that."

"That don't sound like he's on the way up here," Lord Abdullah snapped.

"Let me explain what happened," Steve said. He presented the edited version of events just as Deeann had instructed. The only sound Steve could hear was food being chewed. "Sir," he said, "I'm sorry, but there was nothing that could be done. Pete just wasn't as smart as he thought."

"I'll be in touch," Lord Abdullah said, emotionless, and hung up.

"Something you should always remember, Abdurahman, is salvation by faith in Christ may sound too easy," Marc said. "Because of that, people think they've got to do something else to *really* save themselves. When this happens, religion becomes a reflection of self-effort, which ultimately leads to pride or disappointment, based on how a person's actions are measured. In salvation by faith in Christ, Christians don't measure success. They know the ultimate victory will only come when Christ Jesus returns."

"I'm beginning to understand, Preacher Man," Abdurahman said. "Can you show me how to get to know God?"

Lord Abdullah had never considered dying. Even when he'd been on death row, the idea never seemed real or possible, and when his sentence was commuted to life in prison, it merely reinforced his belief. To him, death was something that happened to others, the weak and the unprepared. Pete was one of those people, but not Lord Abdullah. He was always strong and always ready, and he'd always survived. Now, for the first time in his life, he wasn't sure.

Pete's plan was pretty close to my original plan . . . Could I be that dumb? . . . Maybe bein' in here's changed me . . . Am I doin' the right thing? . . . How will I know? Man, what's wrong with me . . .

He unlocked the door and headed into the multipurpose room.

"What do you suppose he's thinking, Dr. Sheffield?" Powell asked when the conversation between Steve and Lord Abdullah was over.

"My best guess is that he's contemplating what it all means. Given his personality style, I'd have to say he's probably trying to assign some type of meaning to the fact that someone he considered less intelligent than him was killed doing something he was going to try."

"Any guesses what he'll do?"

Deeann leaned back in her chair. "Well, Lee, at first, I guess he'll question himself, but for only a short time, since intelligence is so central to who he thinks he is."

"Hi, Charles," Barbara said as he walked up with Karla and Harvey. "I saw you standing there during the last interview. What do you think?"

"Well, I guess the best way to look at it is that Pastor Winston is doing what he thinks is right, and he's telling people about Jesus Christ," he answered, remembering the apostle Paul's letter.

"That's a nice way to put it."

Charles smiled. "Let me introduce you to my friends. Barbara Pierce, meet Dr. Karla Lynch, and this is Dr. Harvey Ramone, a retired Baptist minister."

Karla shook the reporter's hand. "It's nice to meet you, Ms. Pierce."

"Are you also a minister?" Barbara asked her.

"No," Karla said, smiling slightly. "I'm a pediatrician and a member of Reverend Hurley's church. We're friends with the psychologist here at the prison who's being held hostage." She held her emotions beneath the surface, but barely.

"I'm sorry to hear that."

"You haven't heard anything, have you?" Karla asked, already knowing the answer.

"Nothing you probably don't already know." Barbara smiled sympathetically. "They're not giving out a great deal of information, for security reasons. But if I hear anything, I'll let you know." She turned to Harvey. "Dr. Ramone, I understand you've worked with Marc Jones in a Bible study group."

"Yes, ma'am. He came to the group and had some very interesting things to say."

Barbara gave her cameraman the signal to start taping.

"Who do you think Marc Jones is, Dr. Ramone?" Barbara asked pointedly.

Harvey chose his words carefully.

"Ms. Pierce, I'm not really sure that what *I* believe about Marc is nearly as important as what people come away with when they hear what he has to say."

" . . . Amen," Abdurahman said with a smile, after repeating the sinners' prayer and accepting Jesus Christ as his savior.

"What are you doin'?" Lord Abdullah demanded, slamming the door shut behind him.

The smile vanished from Abdurahman's bearded face.

"I just heard you say 'Amen,' " Lord Abdullah said. "You ain't done let 'dese hillbillies get to ya, have ya?"

"I, umm . . . ," Abdurahman stuttered, unsure of what to say.

"We didn't get to him." Donnie spoke up without lying. He believed it was the Holy Spirit, not them, who'd touched the man's heart. "We were just talking about faith."

"About what?" Lord Abdullah turned toward Marc. "Preacher Man, you think you're smart, don't ya?" He leaned in, inches from Marc's face. "Well, let me tell ya somethin'. You ain't nothin', and it don't make me no difference whether I kill you now or later. So you better stop dissin' me!" He sucker punched Marc in the stomach.

"Hey!" Donnie yelled and received a backhand across his jaw.

Lord Abdullah rubbed his knuckles. "Now, I don't know what y'all idiots think y'all is gonna do, but let me tell ya, I'm in charge and that's it. Maybe y'all need to have some faith in 'dat."

"What is it that Marc Jones has to say?" Barbara asked Harvey.

"It seems his message challenges the basics of most Christians' faith," Harvey responded. "By that, I mean his message causes most people to examine their motivations for the way they live and the way they insist others should live. His message pushes people to rethink how they see their salvation and challenges them to stop judging others. In my opinion, I don't believe he's adding anything to or taking anything away from the message that Jesus delivered two thousand years ago. But I think some people are offended by it because it reminds them what Jesus died for on the cross, and they realize that what they've based their salvation on isn't the same. In essence, I guess in some ways, just as Jesus offended the powers of His time, so has Marc Jones."

"It sounds to me like you're saying Marc Jones is a modern-day version of Jesus," Barbara observed.

"That's not my intention," Harvey responded pleasantly.

"What do you think is Jones' intention?"

"I think he intends to remind us of Jesus' message. He points out that by adding to and taking away from that message, we've put it to use in ways that benefit us, not the Kingdom of God."

Barbara nodded thoughtfully. "How do you think Jesus' message has been changed?"

"In much the same way God's commandments were altered by man."

"How's that?"

"People in the Old Testament spent a great deal of time telling society what they could and couldn't do. They made laws, interpreted the application of them, and created rules that had to be followed if people wanted to be righteous. Then they judged people accordingly. As for Jesus' message, I believe it was dedicated to his dependence on God, His Father. I think he expressed that in many ways, not only verbally but in the ways he lived, which ultimately meant dying for our sins. In changing his message, I think many modern-day Christians, with perhaps good intentions, spend their energy trying to define what people have to do and not do in order to be a Christian. We use the things that Jesus did without considering His motivation. His dependence on God was evidence for including and excluding certain behaviors. We spend a good bit of time measuring how well someone does these things in order to assess that person's degree of 'Christian-ness.' "

No one spoke, and the only sounds were Marc's gasping and Abdurahman's occasional coughing. The left side of Donnie's face stung, and blood trickled from the corner of his mouth. Lord Abdullah sat at the conference table with his face in his hands, thinking.

For the first time in my life, I don't know what to do . . . Well, I always thought I knew, even if it was wrong . . . Now, I can't think straight . . . Man, you gotta get it together . . . All it is, is you ain't gettin' no rest . . . Well, 'dat and the hassle of havin' to deal with all of these idiots . . . It ain't your fault . . .

"Sir," Marc said, catching his breath, "I'm going to pray for you."

At first, Lord Abdullah sat in silence. A minute passed before he turned to glare at Marc. "Whatta you think prayin' is gonna do for me, man? I ain't ever seen that spook god of yours do nothin' for nobody, and I done seen lots of weak fools in here ask him for lots of stuff."

"Maybe you haven't been looking for His answers. Or maybe you were expecting the wrong ones. I'm not sure, but this I do know: God definitely hears and answers prayers."

"All right, 'den. Show me." Lord Abdullah narrowed his eyes. "Pray for somethin' and tell me what to look for and where. 'Den we'll see."

"God doesn't work that way," Donnie said. "He . . . "

"He what?" Lord Abdullah jumped out of his chair. Donnie braced himself for the punch he feared was about to follow. "He don't really answer prayers, 'dat's what, man. I mean come on, if he did, everybody would be rich, white, and beautiful. But since they ain't, I guess God's a spook that don't exist. You know, just like ghosts and goblins."

"Sir, God doesn't respond to challenges to prove His existence," Marc said patiently. And, Donnie noticed, fearlessly. "You're probably right that God isn't going to answer the types of prayers you're talking about, but it's not because He can't. It's because He chooses not to."

"So it sounds like Marc Jones is saying people need to be more concerned about the reasons they do things rather than about the things they do," Barbara summarized with more than just professional interest.

"Let me see if I can make it clearer." Harvey rubbed his hands together thoughtfully. "I think that having an attitude of dependence on God *and* trying to do the things Christ did are both important and interconnected. Without a dependence on God, I don't think Christ would've been able to do the wonderful things He did. I believe what He did was an outward expression of His inner dependence on God, not an attempt to give us a list of things to do in order to be considered Holy."

"How *does* someone become dependent on God?"

"The short answer is, they don't," Harvey said easily. "No one can, or ever will, be totally dependent on God like Jesus was, because none of us are perfect. The best we can do is try."

"How do we do that?"

"Well, I believe that in order to be dependent on something, we first have to know about it. I believe that with God, this involves getting to know Him by studying His word and having a relationship with Him through prayer. In that way, we can experience His love and learn that everything He promises has and will continue to come true."

"Then what?" Barbara asked, hanging on every word.

"Then I think that over time, we come to trust Him and have faith that He will lead us to living better, happier, more fulfilling lives."

"It sounds like you're saying that to be dependent, we just have to trust God and have faith in Him to give us what we want."

"In a way, I think that's close to being correct, as long as the things you want are consistent with God's will."

"All right," Barbara said. "So assuming what we want is consistent with God's will, *then* all we have to do is to trust and have faith that God will provide it to us?"

"Sort of," Harvey said, pausing to think. "Let me try to explain it. I believe trust and faith are important components of dependence, but I think there's more to it than just believing God will provide us with the things we need."

"What do you mean?"

"I think by being dependent on God, we not only trust Him and have faith in Him, we also look to Him for direction in every situation we're in and at all times. This way, instead of making decisions or doing things based on our needs and desires, we look for and follow His will, which is based on a perfect understanding and knowledge of all things."

Barbara gave the cut signal to her cameraman. "Thank you so much for letting me interview you, Dr. Ramone."

"You're welcome, Ms. Pierce," Harvey said. "If you have any more questions, I'll be happy to try and answer them."

"I'd really like to talk with you more," she said. "I feel like there's something missing when it comes to my faith, and I think you can help me find out what it is."

"You know, Preacher Man, I think I'm beginnin' to understand your deal," Lord Abdullah said, becoming more interested in the debate. "First, you say God answers prayers, and 'den when I say prove it, you say he don't do it like that. It's like a convict tryin' to sell magic beans. They tell you if you plant 'em right and make a wish, you'll get whatever you ask for. Then when you do it, do you think you'll be gettin' anything?" He laughed to himself. "And 'den when you ask why it didn't work, 'dey say you didn't wish for the right things or you wished the wrong way. I don't know 'bout you, but if some convict tried sellin' me somethin' like that, I'd kill 'im." He was beginning to feel like himself again,

Marc waited patiently for Lord Abdullah to finish. Then he said, "In a way, your analogy is exactly correct."

Donnie's mouth dropped open.

Marc continued. "You're correct in recognizing that in order to use something, you have to follow the directions you're given for using it. It's the same way with believing in God. There are directions for how to do it. And you know what the best part is? When you do follow the instructions, it's guaranteed to work."

"Man, you better shut up, 'cause you're 'bout to get on my last nerve," Lord Abdullah said. But it was with much less intensity than the previous times he'd lost his temper.

Has something changed? . . . Donnie wondered as Lord Abdullah walked out of the room.

JOHN 10:11 "I am the good shepherd.
The good shepherd lays down his life for the sheep."
(NIV)

Chapter 22
Friday Noon

How can somethin' I can't see or hear give me somethin'? . . . That's crazy . . . Can't they see that? . . . Only stupid people believe in somethin' 'dey can't see . . . I'm one of the five percent who knows the truth. That's why I'm a god . . .

So what's happenin' now? . . . How come you're trapped off with nowhere to run?

You gotta stop thinkin' like 'dat . . . Be strong . . . Take care of yourself . . . You'll figure it out . . . You always have . . . You been goin' too easy on 'em and 'dey think you're weak . . . You gotta show 'em who's in charge and who they're dealin' with . . .

Lord Abdullah briefly studied Hank and Walter, who were obviously trying hard to impress him. They *knew* he was better than they were. He sensed it.

They ain't doin' nothin' but waitin' for me to tell 'em what to do next . . . That's power . . . and authority . . . That's real 'cause I can see it and feel it . . . That's how people treat a real god...

What time is it? . . .

Glancing at his plastic watch, Lord Abdullah remembered what was supposed to happen by noon and quickly regained his composure.

My brothers in New York better be by 'da phone . . .

"Mrs. Wilson," Karla called out, seeing the older woman standing with a group from Hillside. "When did you get here?"

"Karla! I wondered where you were." Mrs. Wilson walked over and hugged her. "We arrived a little while ago. Where's Charles?"

"He's over where the media set up." Karla pointed across the field at the numerous news vans.

"Have you heard anything from Donnie?"

"No, ma'am," Karla answered, her exhaustion apparent. "It's been a while since a prison official's updated us."

"Are you okay?"

"Not really," Karla responded softly, lowering her defenses.

Please help Donnie, Lord . . . Take care of him and the others . . . Protect them, Lord . . . I don't know what I'd . . .

"Karla?"

"What? Oh." She sighed. "I'm sorry, Mrs. Wilson. I was thinking about something else."

"Want to talk about it?"

"Yes, I think I do."

Ring . . .

Steve answered reluctantly, sensing what the call was going to be about. "Yes, sir?"

"Why ain't I heard from my boys in New York?"

"Sir," Steve answered, as smoothly as possible, "we've been working on getting the helicopter you requested."

"I done told you what I was gonna do if you tried to handle me."

"Sir? . . . Sir?" Steve said to the dial tone.

"Keep trying him, Steve," Deeann instructed. She turned to Powell. "Lee, we've got a problem."

"Yeah, we do," he said calmly, taking control. "Floyd, make sure your men are in position in case we gotta go in. What's the status of the damaged microphone?"

"It should be up anytime, sir," Faulk said. "One of my men has been on the roof working on it for almost forty-five minutes."

"All right, let me know when he gets it going."

"Ten-four." Faulk left to go check in with his PERT officers.

Powell paced while reviewing his options. *I don't want to send in PERT . . . If I do, it's likely the hostages will be injured or worse before we can get to them . . . We don't have the element of surprise, since there's only one way in, up the stairs . . .*

He stopped pacing and stared blankly out the window at the prison across the recreation yard. Then he started pacing again.

Deeann, who'd seen his routine before, watched silently.

When would I send in PERT? . . . Powell thought. *At this point, only as a last resort . . . if the hostages' lives were in imminent danger . . . What if Jackson only threatens one of them? . . . If I send in PERT, the rest will probably be killed before we can get there . . . How will I face the families if I don't send in PERT and someone dies? . . . Dear God, please help me make the right choices . . .*

The phone rang.

"Get up. Now!" Lord Abdullah yelled at the semi-conscious officer still suffering from Walter's last beating.

Ring . . . ring . . . ring . . .

"Move!" Lord Abdullah shoved the officer toward the multipurpose room. "Stop!" He grabbed the back of the man's dirty, blood-stained shirt. "Don't move." He let go of the shirt and pressed the tip of the razor into the officer's back, using it to push him against the locked door.

Fishing the key out of his gray pants, Lord Abdullah tried to unlock the door, but his hand was shaking too violently from rage to force the key into the lock.

Ring . . . ring . . . ring . . .

"Something's about to happen," Abdurahman said, hearing the key rubbing against the metal door. "God, help us."

The door flew open, and the handcuffed officer stumbled in and fell with a grunt.

"I want y'all to watch this," Lord Abdullah said. Evil burned so brightly in his eyes, it threatened to singe his soul.

"Thank you for tuning in to WLHR for the midday report," Walter said. "We're continuing to cover the standoff at Caledonia, and our own Barbara Pierce has a report for us. Barbara?"

"Thank you, Walter. The hostage standoff, which began yesterday morning, is continuing." Barbara summarized what had occurred since her earlier report.

"It sounds like things are quite hectic."

"They sure are, Walter. The tension continues to mount."

"Barbara, how many people would you estimate are there?"

"I'd say approximately four hundred people. Most have family or friends either working or incarcerated here. The rest seem to be connected with area churches and believe it's necessary to be here to express their opinions about what they feel caused the situation."

"I'd assume we're seeing an example of that now," Walter commented as Barbara's cameraman panned around the area behind her, focusing on sign-carrying members of Ray's church.

"That's correct, Walter. The people you're seeing are from the Rocky Mount Evangelical Assembly of God Church. I interviewed the pastor of that church, Ray Winston, earlier this morning. Here's what the pastor had to say."

The picture cut to Ray's interview.

"Sir," Donnie said, with more courage than he felt, "isn't there some way we can work this out?"

"Shut up, Doc!" Lord Abdullah screamed. "I done told you I didn't wanna hear you no more." He yanked the officer up and pushed him toward a chair against the wall where Donnie and Abdurahman were cuffed together. He shoved the officer into the chair and put his face in front of Donnie's. "Before I cut your throat, I just wanna know what we gotta talk about."

Ring . . . ring . . . ring . . .

Donnie was paralyzed and could only look back at the hate-filled man threatening to kill him.

Lord, open this man's eyes . . . Please give me the words to say . . . Please Lord, please help me . . .

"Come on, Doc," Lord Abdullah challenged, pressing the razor against his throat. "Whatcha got to say now, big man? Maybe you oughtta ask God to help ya, 'cause it don't look like nobody else is."

Donnie squeezed his eyes shut. "Merciful, mighty God," he began softly, "please protect us and give us strength. Help us to see and feel Your presence. Most of all, Lord, please help us know that through all things, You work for the good of those who believe in You."

"Twenty-thirty, this is twenty-one forty," the PERT leader whispered into his shoulder mic. "Come in, Captain Faulk. Over."

"Go ahead, twenty-one forty. What do you have for me? Over."

"Sir, the new mic's in place, and should be transmitting. Over."

"Ten-four, twenty-one forty. Let's make sure there's no problems before you move. Over."

"Roger that, twenty-thirty. Twenty-one forty standing by."

"Barbara," Walter said, "it certainly seems Pastor Winston is quite sure of who caused the situation. Do you have a feel for how people are receiving his message?"

"Walter, it seems people's reactions fall into one of three categories. One group agrees, supporting him totally, without question. Another group doesn't seem to care about what he's saying and perceives him as a religious fanatic. The last group disagrees with him and believes Marc Jones is far from evil. They suggest Pastor Winston and his supporters are making the same mistake people have made for over two thousand years."

"What mistake is that?" Walter asked.

"They say they believe people aren't listening to Jones' message because he doesn't fit their definition of what a Christian is supposed to be. Here's what another minister had to say."

The picture cut to the interview with Harvey Ramone.

"You look tired, Karla," Mrs. Wilson said. "Maybe we should walk to the church van so you can lie down and close your eyes for a minute."

"I don't think I can sleep. I'm too scared." Karla's eyes filled with tears.

"I know you are." Mrs. Wilson reached out and took her hand.

The tears streamed down Karla's cheeks. "Everything's happened so fast, Mrs. Wilson," she sniffled. "I feel like I have no control."

"Do you mean this situation, or your relationship with Donnie?"

Karla was caught off guard.

"That's what I thought," Mrs. Wilson replied knowingly. "And you know what? You aren't in control, just like anyone else who's in love. Because when it happens, you give up control and become completely vulnerable."

"We're listening now," Powell radioed to Floyd. "Tell your men good work."

"I can't believe you're prayin'," Lord Abdullah said. "I got a razor to your neck, and you start prayin'. You really believe that stuff, don't you?" He unconsciously relaxed the pressure he was applying with the razor.

"I believe in God with all of my heart and soul." Donnie kept his voice steady despite his terror. "What makes that so hard to believe?"

"I guess it ain't so crazy someone would start prayin' when their life was about to end," Lord Abdullah admitted. "But it's crazy you'd pray about havin' strength to endure what's happenin'. How come you didn't pray to have that God of yours end what's happenin'? You know, ask him to kill *me* or somethin'. I woulda."

Donnie had no idea how to answer. Then, like when he'd started praying, the words just came out. "As a Christian, I don't believe someone has to be harmed for me to prosper. Yeah, I'm angry with you. But that's because I'm human. In my heart, I know everything happening is controlled by God and will ultimately be used by Him for the glory of His Kingdom."

"So you think God makes bad things happen to get what He wants?"

"Not at all. I believe Satan makes evil things happen so he can win souls."

Lord Abdullah grinned cruelly. "All right 'den, if that God of yours is so powerful, why don't he just take care of Satan once and for all? He could just kill 'im and 'den there'd be no more problems." *Any real god knows that . . .*

"One thing I do know," Donnie said, "is that in the end, God will win."

"Karla, if you think about it, we really are helpless."

"That's just it, Mrs. Wilson." Karla sighed. "I know I'm powerless to control things, and that's bad enough. Why do I want to make it more difficult and worry about somebody else's problems hurting me, too?"

"I don't know." Mrs. Wilson shrugged. "Why *would* anyone want to do that?"

"I guess that did sound selfish," Karla said. "But as bad as it sounds, that's how I've learned to think when it comes to relationships."

"Is that why you're so distraught when it comes to the way you feel about Donnie?"

"Maybe," Karla said, "but I think it's something else, too. For a long time, I've kept people at a distance. Now, all of a sudden, I've let down my guard and started trusting a man I've only known for a few weeks. The obvious thing would have been to go slow, but it seemed like I couldn't."

Mrs. Wilson gave a smile that would have warmed the most hardened of hearts. "You know, Karla, I think your perspective is wrong. You'll never be one hundred percent sure someone isn't going to hurt you."

"So what do I do?"

"It sounds like there's quite a difference of opinions out there, Barbara," Walter said after Harvey's interview.

"That's correct, Walter. One group believes Marc Jones represents evil and the other feels he was sent by God. Both groups provide numerous reasons to support their positions and to refute the other's claims."

"Given the close proximity of the groups and the obvious differences of opinions, are authorities concerned about crowd safety?

Lord Abdullah finally answered the phone. "Whatta you want, man? What lies you gonna tell me now?"

"I wanted to let you know the helicopter is en route, sir," Steve said.

"And? What about my boys in New York?"

"We're waiting to hear from the New York State prison system." Steve prepared himself for the tirade.

Instead, there was a long silence.

What's happening? . . . Should I say something? . . . What? . . . Is he hurting someone? . . . God, please help . . .

"When's the 'copter gonna get here?"

Steve quickly recovered. "We just received the info from Raleigh. If you'll give me a minute, I'll check and call right back."

"Yeah, you do that."

"This is almost unbelievable," Deeann said. "It seemed like he couldn't help being drawn into the conversation with Dr. Thompson."

"I've got my own opinion about that," Powell interjected, "but I think what's important now is that Jackson seems to have changed his attitude. How long it's going to last, I don't know. He's got a long history of extremely volatile, aggressive behavior. Things could deteriorate quickly."

"The best way to know about love is to look at Jesus' life," Mrs. Wilson said. "He gave us the perfect example of what it means to truly love."

"Are you saying I have to give up my life and die?" Karla asked.

"In a way, that's exactly what I mean." Mrs. Wilson smiled. "You see, when we truly love someone, we do give up our life for them. Maybe not by dying on a cross, but more symbolically. Things that are important to us change or die in order to give rise to the new. Our priorities change from focusing only on our needs to helping the person we love get what they need. We give to them without expecting them to reciprocate. We rejoice in their successes and cry at their disappointments. We're honest and true to them and trust them with our life and well-being. We become completely vulnerable to them and trust them to respect the power we give them."

"You're right," Karla said, on the verge of breaking down again. "But I just don't think I'm strong enough to do it."

"You aren't, darling." Mrs. Wilson put her arm around her. "Only Jesus is capable of that kind of love. The best we can ever do is try to be like Him, and the only way we do that is to first believe in God's amazing love for us."

"How do you mean?" Karla asked through her tears.

"If we think how much God must have loved us to send His Son to die for us, I think we can begin to trust that no matter what, He's going to protect us. Once we believe that, then loving others is simple, because our faith is in God's promise to keep us in the palm of His hand and to protect our soul for eternity."

"That's what you meant about changing my perspective," Karla said, smiling for the first time in almost two days.

"Exactly," Mrs. Wilson replied. "You see, by learning to love like that, you have something you can trust not only with your heart, but more importantly, with your soul."

Doc don't know why God don't kill Satan . . . I know . . . It's 'cause He don't exist . . . I mean, come on man, anybody knows if someone's causin' you problems, you make 'em go away . . .

Lord Abdullah made sure his hostages were secure and stepped outside the room to think.

I gotta make my problem go away . . . I gotta figure it out . . . Man, I just need a plan . . . I'm a Five Percenter, a real god . . . I can figure this out . . . Think! . . . All right, first thing is . . .

"What's going on?" Abdurahman asked when Lord Abdullah left and shut the door. "That ain't the same Five Percenter. Something's up."

"You're right, something's different," Donnie said. "He seems confused about who he is."

"It's more than that," Marc said. "There are times in peoples' lives when they're given a chance to see themselves as God sees them. It's these times when they see themselves as they really are, not as they *think* they are, or the way they *want* to be seen."

"Why don't people change when they're given that opportunity?" Abdurahman asked, even though it had happened to him only a few hours earlier.

"Some people don't know Jesus and don't understand what they're seeing," Marc explained. "They aren't aware anything's wrong, and nothing changes. Others know Jesus and some even understand what they're seeing, but make excuses for why they're that way or try to change how God sees them by changing how they look."

Abdurahman looked confused. "Shouldn't we try to change the way God sees us?"

"Yes, we should," Marc said. "The question is how. People must realize they can't do it by just *acting* like Christians. The only way possible is to accept the free gift of Jesus' blood, which He shed for us on the cross. When we do this, we stand in front of the perfect, flawless Mirror of Christ, and God sees us not as the sinners we really are but as a flawless reflection of His perfect, sinless Son."

Ring . . .

"Yes?" Steve answered.

"All right, 'dese are my demands, and we ain't gonna negotiate. You understand?"

"I'll do everything I can, sir," Steve replied, as Dr. Sheffield had told him to do.

"First, if I don't get a call within the next hour from my boys in New York, I'm gonna slit the po-liceman's throat. Second, you've got 'til five 'dis afternoon to have the chopper sittin' on the ball field ready to fly. If you're late, I'm gonna kill a hostage every thirty minutes until it arrives. Finally, I want a briefcase filled with a hundred thousand dollars in unmarked bills waitin' for me. If I get out there and it ain't there, I'll push a hostage out 'da door when we get airborne."

"Sir, I'm not sure . . . "

"Look, man," Lord Abdullah said, his frustration mounting. "I know what you're gonna say, and I don't wanna hear it. We both know you can make 'dem things happen if you want to bad enough. Maybe I just need to make you want to bad enough."

"Hold tight," Powell said, listening to the implied threat. "Let's see what he's gonna do."

"Listen to 'dis," Lord Abdullah hissed. He held the phone close to the officer's mouth and pressed the razor to the man's throat. "Tell 'im I mean business!"

"Please, do . . . what he says," the officer moaned. "He's . . . got . . . a razor. He's . . . he's . . . he's gonna kill . . . "

"Don't play wit' me anymore," Lord Abdullah said, yanking the phone away from the officer. "No excuses. Just do it."

He hung up.

If people just understood me, then I wouldn't have to hurt 'em to get what I want . . . what I deserve . . . what's supposed to be mine . . . I never wanted my life to be like this . . . The world's made me 'dis way . . . It's always testin' me . . . tryin' to see how far I'll bend before I break . . . I ain't bad, it's the only way I can get what I should have . . . If only people would listen to me in the first place, then they'd give me what's mine . . . what I deserve . . . People just won't listen . . . that's all it is . . . I just gotta make 'em hear me louder and clearer . . . Bet they'll show me respect 'den . . .

"I think this round's over." Powell radioed Faulk. "Have your team stand down and get ready to take up new positions. I believe he's posturing to try and force us to take him seriously."

"Ten-four," Faulk responded.

"Jeff, make sure the governor's office knows how badly I need the helicopter. Tell them I want it as soon as possible. If they have any questions, they can talk directly to me."

"Yes, sir," Hagerton answered.

"Also, find out how far he can fly if he leaves here. I don't intend to let him go, but I need to keep my options open."

"What about the money?" Deeann asked.

"Jeff, send a lieutenant to get a briefcase and fill it with paper. Put some real money on top." Powell didn't intend to let the situation get that far, but he wanted to be ready. "The pilot's supposed to be a Special Forces Marine aviator. Make sure that's been cleared and let me know when you have an ETA."

"Yes, sir," Hagerton replied, going next door to make phone calls.

Feeling someone's eyes on him, Lord Abdullah turned suddenly to glare at Marc. "What are you starin' at, Preacher Man?"

"It seems you're troubled."

"I ain't got nearly 'da troubles you're 'bout to have."

"You believe your unhappiness is because of other people's actions. When people don't do what you want, you try to force them."

"That's pretty good, Preacher Man. Now you're gonna find out how well it works."

Marc didn't flinch. "There's no doubt that threatening people with physical pain can make them do things. But I wonder if you've ever thought about how that works when it comes to getting people to make real changes. I'm talking about the kind of changes that come about because someone wants to change, as opposed to someone doing something because they're scared about what'll happen if they don't."

"What difference does it make?" Lord Abdullah asked, reaching his boiling point. "As long 'dey do what I want, I don't care!"

"So you're saying your happiness is the result of the degree that you can make someone fear you. Have you ever wondered if that's why you're so unhappy?"

How does 'dis man know what I'm thinkin'? . . . How does he know I'm unhappy? . . . I'll listen for a little while . . . Then I'll cut his throat . . .

"I tell ya what, Preacher Man," Lord Abdullah finally replied. "Given the circumstances I'm in, I'm as happy as I can be. Ya see, I'm the kinda man who gets what I'm supposed to have. Other people are either too stupid or too weak to do that. But I ain't. I'm a god. So when people get in my way," he said with a wink, "I take care of 'em."

Harvey and Charles walked close enough to hear as Ray started talking.

"Ladies and gentlemen," he began, "in First Peter, chapter two, the apostle who dropped everything he had to follow Jesus Christ tells us how to conduct ourselves when we're confronted with unbelievin' people. He says when we're accused of doin' wrong and people make false accusations against us, we should silence 'em by the way we live."

"Amen, brother," Bill yelled. "Preach it!"

"Hallelujah!" a lady exclaimed.

"That means you gotta go to church and pray every day!"

"That's right, Pastor!"

"You can't drink alcohol or be a homosexual."

"Tell 'em preacher!" yelled a man up front. "God don't like queers."

"You can't lie, cheat, or steal," Ray said, burning with conviction. "You can't commit adultery. In everything you do, you gotta stay away from sin."

"Yes, Lord yes!"

"Now hold on a second, 'cause I've gotta warn you." Ray raised his hands like he was parting the Red Sea. "I wanna make sure you know that livin' honorable lives apart from sin ain't enough."

"That's right preacher," Bill shouted. "It ain't!"

"You also gotta love other people." Ray wiped sweat from his forehead. "And most of all, you gotta fear God and show respect for the King!"

"Mr. Powell, I just talked with the Governor's office," Hagerton reported. "Everything's go for the helicopter."

"When's the ETA?"

"Sixteen hundred hours."

"All right. That only gives us a short time to get PERT into place."

"The men inside that prison," Ray said, pointing at Caledonia, "have no respect for themselves, much less for the King of kings. They only love Satan and the pain and fear he causes in people's lives."

"Glory only to You, Lord," an elderly woman wailed.

"Praise God!"

"Protect us, Lord," Bill screamed, falling to his knees and stretching out his arms.

"That's right, ladies and gentlemen. The only one who can protect you is the Almighty Lord." Ray was working the crowd into a frenzy. "Satan, the great deceiver, is among those convicts behind those fences, and he's affected not only their lives but the others he's come in contact with, too. Those people aren't protected by the Almighty. Satan's caused them to doubt. He's confused them with false teachin' and deceived them with lies in order to convince 'em he's righteous. Yes folks, the evil one's in our midst. And we, the slaves of God, must rise up and challenge him!"

"Amen, Brother Winston! Amen!"

"Let us pray," Ray cried out, bowing his head and raising his trembling hands. "Our Father, who art in heaven . . . "

This man is unbelievable, Barbara thought.

"Are you getting this?" she asked her cameraman.

"Yes, ma'am," he answered, continuing to film.

"You talk a great deal about how important it is for people to respect you," Marc said. "But I think you know most people don't. They fear you. Respect is earned because what you do makes people admire you. Fear comes from people being scared of you and not wanting to anger you."

"That's right," Lord Abdullah said. "They better not anger me."

"Or else what? You're going to hurt them?"

"If I gotta."

"If people really respected you, they'd do what you wanted, not out of fear but because they admired you and cared about you."

"Man, it don't make me no difference if people like me or not as long as they do what I want 'em to."

"What happens when you aren't there to make sure they do it?"

"That's when I show 'em how many people I control and how powerful I am," Lord Abdullah answered with pride.

"That's not power," Marc said. "That's just another way of inflicting fear. Power, real power, is being able to crush someone and choosing not to."

"Say what?"

"Jesus Christ is the most powerful man that ever walked on Earth. He surely could have *made* men follow Him, but He didn't, He let them choose. He could've *made* men bow at His feet, and could've lived like a king, but instead, He let them choose whether or not to worship Him. He could've impressed mankind with His strength by calling down flames from heaven against those who didn't listen to Him, but He didn't. Jesus was, and is, interested in the true power and strength that only comes from following God. He died on the cross because God promised Him that through His death, all men could be saved. He trusted God's promise enough to give His life. That's true strength and power, Mr. Jackson. *Forcing* people to give you things is not."

"Dr. Ramone, Reverend Hurley," Barbara called out, walking toward the two men as they left Ray's impromptu sermon. "Can I speak with you?"

"What can we do for you?" Charles asked.

"I saw you listening to Pastor Winston. What do you think?"

"That's a good question." Charles cut his eyes toward Harvey.

"I think his approach is in some respects confusing, but in other ways very interesting," Harvey answered.

"How so?"

"Well, he starts off with what he believes is right, and then finds Scripture to support his position. He does this by taking verses out of context or interpreting them incorrectly. When he finishes, he always seems to connect whatever he's been talking about back to the *fact* that sin can only be made right by Jesus."

"Isn't that true?"

"We as Christians certainly believe it is," Charles said. "But Pastor Winston adds to it by telling people how they have to act *in order* for Jesus to make them right. In essence, he tells people they can only be saved if they do or don't do whatever it is he's talking about."

"Faulk, what's the status of PERT?" Powell asked over the radio.

"Everyone's in place, standing by, sir."

"Good. We're getting close. The helicopter will be calling in for landing instructions soon. Stand by."

Ring . . . Ring . . . Ring . . .

Lord Abdullah grabbed the phone. "What?" he snapped.

"This is Mr. Johnson. I'm calling to let you know the helicopter should be here about four o'clock."

"Good. Now what about my boys in New York?"

See, you just gotta make 'em understand you're for real and mean business . . .

"Sir, we've been trying . . ."

"That's what I thought," Lord Abdullah interrupted. His pulse quickened and his palms grew sweaty. "I knew y'all was gonna play me for a chump. Just remember, I made a promise to you too. The only difference is, I'm gonna keep mine!"

I just gotta go take care of business . . . that's all 'dis is, business . . . I bet they listen 'den . . .

"So Pastor Winston's message is wrong?" Barbara asked. "I thought helping people accept Christ was what preachers did."

"The problem isn't his message of accepting Christ, it's the way he says it has to happen," Harvey said. "What he's saying is just a modern-day version of what Judaizers did when the church first began. He's telling people what they have to do in order to be a Christian or to be saved. He's defining it on the basis of what someone does. Just as Paul told the early church, the *only* way you can be saved is by trusting Christ and giving Him your life."

"But in Pastor Winston's defense, aren't the things he said people needed to do good things? I mean, if you follow them, won't you be a Christian? You'd be doing all of the right things."

"Barbara," Harvey said, "that's the mistake Pastor Winston, as well as many, many others, have made over time. Just because people do good things doesn't make them Christians. Being a Christian, or becoming a Christian, has nothing to do with the things you do or have done. It doesn't matter if you've been the most moral person or the worst criminal, because in God's eyes, we're all sinners. Being a Christian involves having a relationship with God that can only be obtained through the blood of His Son, Jesus Christ. Nothing we can do, other than trust in him, will save us."

"Guess what, Preacher Man? Let's see how much power you got." Lord Abdullah leaped toward Marc and shoved him to the floor.

"Don't hurt him!" Donnie shouted.

"Shut up, Doc, or you'll be next." Lord Abdullah pulled Marc to his feet and pushed him toward the door. "Those po-lice shoulda listened. I ain't playin' 'dis time!"

"Please don't hurt him," Abdurahman said.

Lord Abdullah backhanded Abdurahman. "I done told y'all to shut up!" He screamed. "This man's gonna die!"

"Lee," Deeann shouted, running next door. "You gotta hear this! Jackson's gonna kill Jones."

Powell ran to the intel room.

" . . . Get ready for 'dis, po-lice," Lord Abdullah screamed, forcing Marc to his knees between the cell blocks. "Y'all wanna see what it looks like when I cut this man's throat and he chokes on his own blood?"

"Kill 'im, man," Hank and Walter hollered. "Cut 'im up!"

"Powell, you readin' this?" Floyd urgently asked over the radio.

"Ten-four."

"Sounds like he's serious. You want us to go?"

"Mess 'im up, Lord Abdullah," inmates shouted as the gang leader stood over the helpless, handcuffed man. "Show 'dem po-lice you ain't playin', man!"

Ring . . . ring . . . ring . . .

"Y'all ready?" Lord Abdullah shouted as he grabbed a handful of hair and pulled Marc's head backward to expose his throat.

"Lee," Deeann said anxiously, "this is out of control. You've got to send in the PERT team. That man is . . . "

"Hold on," Powell said firmly. "I don't think he's going to do it."

"Good afternoon," Walter said. "We interrupt the regularly scheduled program to bring you this important news update. We're going to take you live to Barbara Pierce for special news coverage of the hostage standoff at Caledonia Correctional Institution. What do you have for us, Barbara?"

"Who's got power now, Preacher Man?" Lord Abdullah hissed, meeting Marc's eyes as he stared up at him.

See, I'm a powerful god . . . Preacher man's totally at my mercy . . . I can kill 'im with just a flick of my wrist . . .

"Show 'em who's in charge," Walter cheered.

Why ain't he scared? . . .

"Come on, man," someone yelled. "Do it!"

Ring . . . ring . . .

"Slice his throat," Hank hollered.

Jesus is the most powerful man who's ever walked the earth . . .

Preacher Man's words crept into Lord Abdullah's consciousness.

Why's this man kneelin' here unafraid? . . . He ain't tryin' to resist . . . He ain't beggin' for his life. . . Is this what he meant? . . .

"Kill 'im . . . kill 'im . . . " inmates chanted.

Ring . . .

"Kill 'im . . . "

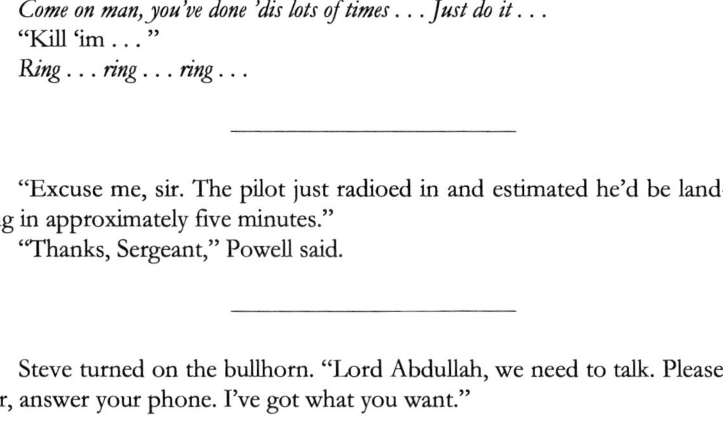

Come on man, you've done 'dis lots of times . . . Just do it . . .

"Kill 'im . . . "

Ring . . . ring . . . ring . . .

"Excuse me, sir. The pilot just radioed in and estimated he'd be landing in approximately five minutes."

"Thanks, Sergeant," Powell said.

Steve turned on the bullhorn. "Lord Abdullah, we need to talk. Please, sir, answer your phone. I've got what you want."

Lord Abdullah was going to show the idiots in his world his power by snuffing out Preacher Man's life. Now, he couldn't make himself do it, and he didn't understand why.

Have I gotten weak? . . . Am I losing it? . . . Why can't I do it? . . . He released Marc's hair and grabbed the phone from his pocket. "Man, you better have what I want."

"I've just received word the helicopter is about to land on the rec yard," Steve said urgently.

"Yeah, that's what I thought would happen. I told you I meant business." Lord Abdullah said it loud enough for everyone to hear. The last thing he wanted was to appear weak for sparing Preacher Man's life.

"We need to talk about how to get you and the hostages out to the yard and on the helicopter. It might be easier to talk if you go back in the multipurpose room," Steve suggested. "That way, nobody will interfere with your plan."

Or persuade you to hurt the hostages . . .

"Just know 'dat I'm callin' the shots."

Inmates clapped and cheered.

See, they're worshippin' their god . . .

"Barbara, it sounds like things remain quite tense," Walter observed. "Do you have a feel for how long this situation will last?"

"Walter, I'm sorry, but a helicopter has just flown over us," Barbara reported as her cameraman focused on the helicopter flying low toward the prison. "It appears it's landing in the prison yard."

"This is it," a man told his wife. "The big boys are here now. Them convicts ain't got a chance."

"Somebody made a deal with Satan and is lettin' 'em get away," a man in Ray's group shouted.

"Dear God, protect them," someone else pleaded.

"Preacher Man and me are gonna go in the multipurpose room. Keep 'dem others on the floor against the wall," Lord Abdullah ordered.

"Yes, sir," Walter replied.

"Charles," Mrs. Wilson said, "I'm worried something bad is about to happen."

"Me too, Mrs. Wilson. Me too."

"Dear God, please protect Donnie," Karla prayed out loud. "I'm begging you, Lord, please keep him safe."

"Amen," Harvey responded, watching the helicopter disappear below the horizon. "Amen."

Lord Abdullah sat on the conference table. Hank pushed Marc, still handcuffed, into a chair and then left.

"Who are you, man?" Lord Abdullah demanded.

Marc held Lord Abdullah's gaze and waited.

" 'Dis is what I mean, man." Lord Abdullah slammed his hand against the table. "I ask you a question and you don't say nothin'. You just stand there and look stupid. Do you know who you're messin' wit'? What's your deal, man?"

I oughtta just kill you . . .

Marc finally spoke. "Mr. Jackson, your life's been spent battling your anger at not getting the things you believe you deserve. You've convinced yourself, and anyone who'd listen, that life hasn't been fair and you've used that to rationalize how you've lived. You've spent your time measuring yourself by how much you think people respect you and how many possessions you have."

Lord Abdullah was a killer. He had never let anyone talk to him the way Marc was. But in his heart, he knew the words were right. For this reason, he could only sit in silence and listen, not only with his ears, but perhaps more importantly, with his heart.

"Mr. Jackson, in your world, the only thing that's mattered for many years is you. You've found ways to manipulate others into sharing your beliefs so you could feel important and special. Now, you're seeing how little all of what you think you have is really worth. You're seeing that people don't respect you, they fear you. Most of all, though, I think you're seeing you're not a god, but a sad man with many problems."

"I oughtta kill you."

"It isn't too late to make yourself right with God. All you have to do is admit that you're a sinner. You are not the god you've spent years trying to convince everyone, including yourself, that you are. Accept that there's only one God and that He sent His Son, Jesus Christ, to die on a cross for your sins. Accept that only He is truly powerful and mighty. Then, and only then, you'll be saved from destroying yourself and spending eternity in the fires of hell you've been dreaming about."

Lord Abdullah dropped his gaze.

How does he know about my dream? . . . I ain't told nobody about that . . . Maybe I really have been foolin' myself all this time . . . I ain't no god . . . I'm a convict, a liar, a thug . . . That's why I've spent most of my life behind bars . . .

"What do you mean, it ain't too late?" Lord Abdullah asked softly without looking up. "Do you have any idea what I've done?"

"I do know the type of life you've lived. It's true you're a sinner, but you aren't any different or any worse than anyone else. Everyone's a sinner. In God's eyes, it's impossible for humans not to sin. He's totally perfect in every way, and this means that all sins are equally bad to Him. The belief that some are worse than others is one men created to measure themselves against each other. It's wrong."

"So you're sayin' 'dat no matter what I've done, it ain't too bad for God to forgive?"

Marc smiled. "That's right. All you have to do is ask Him for forgiveness and accept Jesus as your Savior."

"You make it sound like anyone can do it."

"You're right again. Salvation is available to all, but only a few will accept it. Some people, like you right now, are reluctant because they can't comprehend it. Others refuse to believe it. Then, there are some people who believe it but don't want it, because they enjoy what they think they have too much to give it up."

For a long moment, no one moved or said anything. Lord Abdullah continued staring at the floor as images from his past raced across his mind. When he looked up, he spoke in a voice barely above a whisper. "A few minutes ago, you said it wasn't too late for me. What do I gotta do?"

"Bow your head and pray after me." Marc closed his eyes. "God, I admit I'm a sinner and need your forgiveness. I believe in Your Son, Jesus Christ, and I know He was crucified so that You would forgive me. I know I don't deserve it, but nevertheless, I know You give it freely. Father God, I want to accept Your gift and walk in Your light."

Tony sat unmoving with his head bowed for several minutes as the years of hate that had pressed down on him relentlessly were released. It had been longer than he could remember since he last cried, but now, his tears were the only way he could express himself and extinguish the flames of evil that had been lit inside of him years and years ago.

"This is unbelievable. It sounds like Jackson just became a Christian," Deeann said.

"In all the years I've been working with PERT, I've never witnessed anything like this," Powell admitted.

"So what do we do now?"

"Well, I've never heard a hostage taker accept Christ in the middle of a situation, but I've seen lots of inmates accept Christ one minute and give Him up the next. We've still got a very serious situation that could quickly get ugly. We've got to get the hostages out of there. Dr. Sheffield, call Steve, tell him what's happened, and tell him to call Jackson and request the release of the hostages."

Walter pounded on the door to the multipurpose room. "Yo, man!" he yelled. "What's goin' on?"

After several seconds of silence, he pounded again. "Hey man, what'cha want us to do?"

"Now what I gotta do, Preacher Man?" Tony asked.

"I think you need to ask God what He wants you to do," Marc said.

The phone was ringing again. Tony bowed his head and then quickly looked up. "How do I pray?"

"Just talk to God. Tell him what you want, how you feel, and ask for His guidance."

"That's all?"

"Then listen with your heart instead of your ears."

Tony bowed his head again.

After a long moment, he rose and picked up the phone. "Hello?"

"Sir, this is Mr. Johnson. I want to talk about releasing the hostages."

"What do you want me to do?" Tony asked without hesitating.

Steve paused. "I think we should keep it simple. Come down the stairs in a group and let them go when you get to the bottom."

"I don't know. What about the other po-lice? They might try to get even for what's happened. I need protection."

"I'll be there to make sure nothing happens."

"I was thinkin' we'd take the hostages out the Unit 2 outer door to the rec yard where that chopper is. Get one of 'dem TV stations to film it so 'da po-lice can't try nothin'. I'll turn 'em over 'den."

"Let me run it by Mr. Powell," Steve said. "I'll call you right back."

"Mr. Powell, how do you want to handle this?" Steve asked, knowing the superintendent and Dr. Sheffield were listening.

"Give us ten minutes to get set up."

"Yes, sir." Steve hung up.

"Floyd," Powell said into his radio, "clear the pathway out of Unit 2 to the rec yard. I don't want anything to spook Jackson on the way out."

"Ten-four."

"Have a lieutenant go to the roadblock and get Barbara Pierce from WLHR and her crew. Set them up a safe distance outside the fence so they can film what happens. And place EMS on their highest state of alert."

"Ten-four."

"Let me know when everything's in place."

"Ma'am, I'm sorry to interrupt," said an officer in a white shirt, "but I need for you and your cameraman to come with me immediately. I'll explain when we get in the car."

Barbara turned to him, surprised. Her cameraman stopped taping.

"I know this seems strange," the officer said, "but I promise you won't be disappointed, ma'am. Please, we need to hurry."

"You don't know how hard 'dis is, man," Tony said, walking toward the door.

"I'm sure it is, Mr. Jackson," Marc replied.

"When 'dis is over, I wanna talk to ya. Maybe we can write or somethin'."

"The first thing you need to do is get a Bible and start reading it. It'll tell you everything you need to know. I promise."

"Thanks." Tony looked at Marc. "I mean it, man. Thanks." He opened the door and faced Hank and Walter.

"All right, here's the deal. We're gonna be leavin' to go to the chopper in a sec'. Bring 'dem in here now," he said pointing to the men sitting against the wall.

"That's right!" Hank said, high-fiving Walter. "We're goin' home."

"I knew it, man," Walter almost screamed, thinking about the freedom he thought he'd lost forever.

"Here's how it's gonna go down," Tony said. "I want Preacher Man up front with me. Hank, you take Doc and Abdurahman. Walter, you stay with the po-liceman."

"Yes, sir," Walter said, slapping the battered officer across the back of the head.

There was something different about the man who'd taken them hostage and terrorized them for more than a day.

Where's his anger? Donnie thought. *He isn't making threats . . . Am I imagining it, or is there actually a lightness about his demeanor? . . .*

Donnie finally began to understand who Marc was and why he was there.

"Twenty-two forty-nine, this is twenty thirty-two," Floyd said. "What's your status, Lieutenant? Over."

"We're in place, standing by sir. Over."

"Ten-four. Twenty-two eighty-four, what's your status? Over."

Steve answered from the bottom of the stairs. "I'm in place and standing by, sir. Over."

"Ten-four. Twenty-one forty, what's the status outside? Over."

"Ground team and snipers are in place, sir. Over."

"Ten-four. We're goin' live shortly."

"All right. Stand by, Floyd." Powell turned to Deeann. "Tell Steve to call Jackson. Everything's in place. Let's do it."

Ring . . . ring . . .

"Yeah," Tony answered, almost politely.

"Everything's ready, sir."

"All right, that's what I wanted to hear."

"Yeah, it's about time, man," Hank said in the background. "I knew you'd come through!"

"That's right," Walter chimed in.

"Okay, just go slow," Steve said. "And whatever you do, don't make any threatening moves. I'll be at the bottom of the stairs, and we'll walk out together."

"All right, boys," Tony said to Hank and Walter. "Let's roll." He let

Marc stand up and motioned for him to walk out the door in front of him. Donnie and Abdurahman didn't wait to be told. They stood as Hank neared them, and they went out next.

"Get up, man," Walter said to the correctional officer, grabbing his shirt and pulling him to his feet. "If you even breathe wrong, I'm gonna put this piece of steel in your back." He reached around to make sure the officer's hands were still securely cuffed. "You understand?"

"Yes," the officer replied before Walter slapped him on the head and pushed him through the door.

"Stay close," Tony ordered as the group turned in the small hallway and headed for the stairs.

"Yo, man," someone in F block yelled. "What's up?"

"Hold up," someone else shouted. "Y'all's dissin' us, man!"

"Hey, don't do this."

"Come on Hank, you can't 'dis me, man. I thought you was my boy!"

"Don't stop," Tony ordered. "Keep walkin'!"

When they reached the top of the stairs, someone from F block threw a book through the bars, narrowly missing Hank. The group walked faster. Tony slammed the bar door behind them, and they headed down.

Since the helicopter landed, Ray Winston hadn't stopped moving. In his heart, he knew God Almighty Himself was there watching, and he wanted to be sure he didn't miss his opportunity for redemption. He jumped up and down, spoke in tongues, and laid hands on anyone he felt needed to have Satan purged from the depths of their soul.

Here I am, Lord . . . I know You're here and can see I'm on fire for You . . . Thank You for giving me this chance . . . Thank You, thank You, thank You . . .

At the bottom of the stairs, Steve heard the inmates shouting. He quickly unlocked the bar door. He exchanged glances with Donnie as he passed by, then locked the door after the group and quickly moved to the front to lead them down the hallway.

The officer winked at him.

What's that about? . . .

Reaching the entrance to the downstairs hallway, Steve turned right and walked between the empty Unit 2 cell blocks. They were eerily quiet. Hank and Walter looked around suspiciously, jumping at the noises coming from inmates upstairs, who were banging on the floor and walls. Proceeding toward the exit door leading to the inner rec yard, Steve opened the bar door that led outside.

"Be careful, Lord Abdullah," Walter cautioned. "Make sure it ain't a trap!"

"Yeah, watch out, man," Hank echoed.

The group stopped abruptly.

Tony made a show of surveying the scene ahead of him. "I don't see nothin', man," he said over his shoulder. "Let's go."

"What's happening?" Karla asked, loud enough for the group of Hillside Church members standing nearby to hear. "The helicopter's been down for a long time."

"I don't know, Karla," Charles said.

"I'm really scared something bad's about to happen."

Harvey bowed his head. "Let's pray for the safety of all the people involved." He led them in prayer.

The group walked quickly between the buildings to the inner rec yard. Walter got distracted by the helicopter and the hope of freedom he'd believed he would never again see. He didn't notice that the officer he was escorting had finally managed to get his hidden cuff key and release his right hand. With the cuffs dangling from his left wrist and Walter's attention elsewhere, the officer took advantage of the opportunity. Walter never saw what hit him. The steel dug into his eye, crushing his left orbit and fracturing the bridge of his nose.

Hank heard the crack. He spun around as Walter crumbled to the dirty concrete. From the corner of his eye, he saw the officer closing the distance between them, but was too slow to avoid a crushing blow to the right temple by the dangling cuffs. He was unconscious before he hit the ground. He never felt the first of several hollow-point bullets explode in his back.

Bam, bam . . . bam, bam . . . bam, bam . . .

Three bullets struck Walter as he clumsily tried to get up. More bullets whizzed by, narrowly missing the officer, who was on his knees and advancing forward.

Bam, bam . . . bam, bam . . . bam, bam . . .

The first shots ricocheted off the brick walls. One hit Donnie in the side as he lay on the ground with Abdurahman, taking cover.

The handcuffed officer stood to go after Tony. Tony raised his arm to deflect the blow, forgetting he was holding a shank. A PERT team sniper immediately took aim.

Bam . . .

The bullet flew by Tony's head. Marc ran toward him, knocking him off balance. They fell in a pile.

Six more shots followed. The officer was hit in the chest and the shoulder.

Bam, bam . . . bam, bam . . . bam, bam . . .

As the final shot rang out, a white bolt of lightning flashed across the sky, which had suddenly grown ominously dark, and a heavy downpour erupted. The crowd at the roadblock who'd been listening to the gunshots echoing in the distance flinched at the brilliant light display. Then there was silence.

"Hold your fire! Hold your fire!" Steve screamed into his radio. He jumped up and ran to Donnie, whose shirt was covered in blood.

"Doc! Are you okay?"

"Get these handcuffs off me," Donnie gasped. "Marc's been shot."

"Get an ambulance in here, now!" Steve shouted, taking charge.

"Marc! Can you hear me?" Donnie struggled to crawl toward him.

Steve reached him first, rolling him off of a severely shaken but uninjured Tony Jackson. He felt for Marc's pulse. Seeing the massive gunshot wounds, Steve looked at Donnie and closed his eyes.

"Please . . . no," Donnie gasped and passed out on Marc's chest.

JOHN 1:1–5 "In the beginning was the Word, and the Word was with God, and the Word was God. He was with God in the beginning. Through him all things were made; without him nothing was made that has been made. In him was life, and that life was the light of men. The light shines in the darkness, but the darkness has not understood it."
(NIV)

Chapter 23
Friday Night

Within seconds of Steve's order, the wide chain-link gates topped with razor wire were unlocked by heavily armed officers, and ambulances were quickly escorted onto the yard by a prison truck. EMTs immediately went to work, triaging the extent of the men's injuries and administering first-aid. Despite CPR and the use of a defibrillator, the officer, still with blood-stained handcuffs dangling from his left wrist, died on the scene.

Hank, Walter, and Marc were beyond resuscitation, and no attempts were made to revive them.

Abdurahman and Tony received only minor scrapes, which were treated at the scene. They were taken back into custody by members of the PERT team.

Donnie was bleeding profusely from his side, and the EMTs worked feverishly to stop the bleeding and get an IV line inserted. They knew he had extensive internal injuries and bleeding. He was transported to Nash General. Steve used his cell phone to call Karla. The ambulance picked her up to ride with them to the hospital.

By nine o'clock, flashing blue lights from law enforcement vehicles could still be seen in the distance. Most of the curious onlookers had left hours before, seeking shelter from the unrelenting downpour and the brilliant lightning that continued to scorch the sky. Barbara and her cameraman had sought out the shelter of their cramped news van. They were the only members of the media that remained on location. Barbara was preparing her final live report, to be aired in an hour, and was on her cell phone with Charles and Harvey, who were waiting outside the operating room with Karla.

"How can I go on live television and tell the world God sent a man to Caledonia to give his life for a gang leader?" Barbara asked.

"Is that what happened?" Charles said into the phone.

"I think so. I don't know." Barbara stared at some papers on her lap. "Maybe I want that to be true so badly that I'm missing the obvious. I mean, when you really look at the facts, a gang leader caused a riot and took hostages, and a brave officer managed to spoil the escape before being killed by stray bullets. That's all."

"How do you account for what Steve said Marc did when the officers began shooting?" Charles asked.

"Maybe he jumped *on* Tony instead of in front of him, and got shot because he got in the way," she countered wearily.

"Maybe. But I don't think you believe that, Barbara. In your heart, you know he gave his life to save a man who didn't deserve it."

"I think most people would agree with that," Barbara said, knowing what she would say in her final report.

Kelvin returned to the WHRR newsroom. The outside line rang as he unlocked the door. Exhausted, he headed for the first desk that had a phone on it and picked up the receiver, pressing the blinking red button. "Kelvin Oleander, WHRR."

"Kelvin, this is Tim Shockley, the station manager at WLHR in Raleigh."

"Yes, sir," Kelvin responded, instantly straightening up. "You were the assistant manager a few years back when I worked there."

"That's right. I wanted to catch you this evening to tell you what a great job you did uncovering the situation at the prison. It says a great deal about how much you've matured as an investigative journalist."

Kelvin beamed. "Thank you so much, sir. I really appreciate the compliment."

"Call my secretary Monday and set up a time for us to meet. I think we could put your talents to good use up here in the capitol if you came back to work for us in Raleigh."

"I'll call first thing Monday morning, sir. Thanks for the opportunity." Kelvin hung up with a smile brighter than the sun.

Ray Winston gathered together his faithful warriors and returned to the metal-framed Rocky Mount Evangelical Assembly of God Church. He was on fire for the Lord, even more so than usual. To him, the violent deaths were a sign from God that he'd been right about Marc Jones. The louder he raged on about the evil that was crushed, the more his status as a *True Man of God* increased . . . at least in his eyes.

MATTHEW 6:22 "Your eye is a lamp for your body.
A pure eye lets sunshine into your soul."
(NLT)

Epilogue

Six Months Later

In the months following the standoff, Karla spent many hours with Donnie while he recovered from his gunshot wounds. They talked a lot about Marc Jones. The things that happened seemed to change everyone who'd been involved. Donnie no longer just believed in God, but trusted that He really loved him. He gave up his need to be in control and started living without fear of rejection. He realized he'd never really been in control. More importantly, he discovered firsthand that nothing could separate him from God's unconditional forgiveness.

For the first time, Donnie had seen himself in the Mirror of Christ and felt God's amazing love.

The experience changed Karla, too. She no longer used the past as an excuse for shutting out the people in her world. She was no longer afraid of love. She didn't need to look for guarantees that she wouldn't be hurt. She learned that true love sometimes involves being hurt, and often reminded herself that even Jesus wept. She realized that only when a person opened up and became vulnerable could they care deeply enough to enjoy the heights and depths of true living. When Karla saw herself in the Mirror of Christ, she learned that Jesus' love for His Father involved not only unimaginable joy but inconceivable sadness when he bore the sins of mankind and was nailed to the cross.

It was the cross, and Jesus' reasons for allowing himself to be nailed to it, that continued to be missing from Ray Winston's ministry. Still too busy battling sin and saving the world his way, he was unable to see the hypocrisy he was living. He continued to use the *Jesus* he created to further his personal agenda in hopes of earning his salvation. He taught others to see themselves in front of *his* mirror instead of the Mirror of Christ and never realized that without love, a man could speak in tongues, prophesy, and use faith to move mountains, yet gain nothing. Ray never learned to see himself as God saw him. He continued to see himself as he wanted to be seen. This would never be enough to redeem him. The fire that he proclaimed came from the anointing of the Holy Spirit might instead have been preparation for the time he would spend in hell.

Steve was named superintendent of a minimum custody prison in Rocky Mount. He became one of Donnie's best friends. They spent a great deal of time talking about Marc Jones. They came to believe he was a Christ-like figure sent by God to remind men of what it takes to enter the gates of heaven. In their opinion, his message of love was similar to Jesus' in that they both forgave the sins of a criminal and then gave their lives to save him. The difference was that Marc's blood was shed for Tony Jackson to remind us of Christ, who shed His blood so the forgiving love of God could be available to all.

Listening to Marc teach about Jesus and then seeing him give his life to save Tony changed Abdurahman, too. Unlike Ray, who believed it was the sin, not the sinner, that needed to be fixed, Abdurahman changed because he didn't like the person he'd become. Not knowing Jesus, he'd never understood what was truly wrong, and he thought he could be different by just *acting* differently. Islam, with its many rules for how to act, had appealed to him. But when he was willing to look into the Mirror of Christ, he discovered he could never be good enough on his own. After his ordeal as a hostage, he changed his name back to Chris Ratliff and became an active member in the Caledonia Bible study group. He brought many former Muslims with him to teach them about the one true God and His Son, Jesus Christ.

Charles and Harvey became co-leaders of the Caledonia Bible study group and spent many hours with Donnie, Karla, and Steve. The five became very close friends. They met at Hillside regularly and produced a Christian video with Barbara Pierce, who recommitted her life to Christ and joined Hillside Church. The major focus of the project was teaching about God's forgiveness. It featured interviews with Tony Jackson.

Barbara interviewed Tony, who was handcuffed, shackled, and dressed in a red prison jumpsuit, outside of his cell block on death row at Central Prison. The change in Tony was obvious. Despite his situation, the light glowing in his eyes clearly showed what Jesus had done in his life. Tony finally realized that the life he'd been living was really a façade he'd created in an attempt to earn people's love and respect. It was only when he figured out he didn't know what love was that he was able to see himself in the Mirror of Christ and receive the most perfect, forgiving love of all. He learned to respect himself for the person he was and forever said goodbye to the criminal he had been.

Tony, along with a Chaplain at Central Prison, started a Bible study group for death row inmates. Several of the men who attended the first meeting went because they were curious to hear more about what happened at Caledonia. Tony witnessed to them about how it felt to have met a man he was sure had been sent by God. He told them about being forgiven for his sins and how Marc had given his own life to save him. Every inmate at the meeting, facing execution for the crimes of his past, broke down in tears and asked Christ to be his Savior.

Donnie and Karla walked hand in hand along the ocean's edge in the fading September sunlight, happy to be able to finally take the beach trip they'd been planning since the morning the standoff began. They both knew God was holding them in the palm of His hand, and this comforted them in ways they couldn't put into words. Neither knew what the future held, but they weren't concerned. They knew that as long as they listened, He would guide them to where He wanted them to be . . . in His time.

They finished walking and arrived back at the cottage where they were staying. They sat on the wooden stairs leading up to the beach house and enjoyed the serenity of the ocean scene as the sun set behind them. Karla snuggled close to Donnie.

"I sure am happy to be here with you," she said, looking deeply into Donnie's eyes.

"I'm pretty happy to be here, too. Of all the sunsets I've seen, I've never noticed the purple and pink colors in the sky look as beautiful as they do today. Maybe it's because now that I've stood in front of the Mirror of Christ, God not only sees me differently, but I see things differently, too."

About the Author

Dorsey Edmundson has practiced forensic psychology with the state of North Carolina for over ten years. He obtained an MA and PhD in clinical psychology from the University of Mississippi and serves as the hostage negotiator consultant for the North Carolina Department of Corrections. He has worked as an advisor on gangs in the prison system and has received national awards for his work on preventing unduly familiar relationships among prison staff and inmates. In addition to his work in forensics, he worked as a Sport Psychology Assistant for the U.S. Olympic Team during the 1994 Olympics and has provided sport psychology services to NASCAR, NFL, and PGA professionals.